A

NINE SAILED STAR

Nine Sailed Star © 2023 Glynn Stewart

All rights reserved. For information about permission to reproduce selections from this book, contact the publisher at info@faolanspen.com or Faolan's Pen Publishing Inc., 22 King St. S, Suite 300, Waterloo, Ontario N2J 1N8, Canada.

This is a work of fiction. All the characters and events portrayed in this book are fictional, and any resemblance to any persons living or dead is purely coincidental.

This edition published in 2023 by:
Faolan's Pen Publishing Inc.
22 King St. S, Suite 300
Waterloo, Ontario
N2J 1N8 Canada

ISBN-13: 978-1-989674-32-1 (print)

A record of this book is available from Library and Archives Canada.

1 2 3 4 5 6 7 8 9 10
First edition
First printing: March 2023

Cover art by Elias Stern
Faolan's Pen Publishing logo is a registered trademark of Faolan's Pen Publishing Inc.
Read more books from Glynn Stewart at faolanspen.com

AETHER SPHERES
BOOK ONE

NINE SAILED STAR

GLYNN STEWART

FAOLAN'S PEN
PUBLISHING

CHAPTER

1

THERE ARE FIVE THINGS that define the spheres: aether and air, dirt and stone, and lastly, the light that illuminates it all. Where all five are present, life is born and the var thrive. The var can leave their lodestone-cored worldlets and travel the spheres where only some of those five things are present, but the absences are always felt.

At that particular moment, Cat was feeling the lack of *light* most of all. The sphere of Shadowcastle was a "dark sphere," one with aether but no light. Even in the tall blond elvar's quarters, the gloom outside his ship seemed to press inward.

Crystal lamps illuminated the captain's quarters of the ninesail warship of the Elvar High Court, though, and he drew strength from their arcane light as he dressed carefully in the blue-and-gold uniform of the High Court Navy.

With each layer of clothing, Cat assembled one more piece of the mask he wore in public. Face and status were critical to his var—if not always in ways other var would see—and there were only elvar aboard the ninesail.

Only the elvar and their ancient gobvar foes could survive in the aether without air, after all. Cat commanded the warship *Running Fox*, but how his crew and officers saw him was critical to his status among the High Court Navy—and his status among the Navy affected his House's status amongst the High Court.

So, Captain Cat Greentrees of the House of Forests finished assembling the physical and mental aspects of his uniform, belting his sword on his right hip and his blackwood-wand focus on his left.

Taking in one last moment of full light, he then waved the lamps to darkness and stepped out onto the top deck of his ship.

His quarters were in the aftercastle of the top deck, allowing him to walk out and look up at the three masts on that deck. The sails were furled, but large crystal lamps had been mounted at intervals up the masts and across the spars, bringing light to a sphere that had none.

To his left and right, Cat could see the glow of the same lights on the masts of the port and starboard sail decks beneath him. The three sail decks were separated from each other by smaller weapons decks, openable to the galleries beneath that carried *Running Fox*'s storm staves.

"Sir!" The dark-skinned elvar who'd spoken had clearly been waiting for Cat, standing just far enough away from the aftercastle to not crowd the doors into the captain's quarters.

Cat held up a hand for the Master of Sails to wait a moment, closing his eyes and laying his other hand on his focus as he reached out with his magic. With the sails furled, *Running Fox* wasn't going anywhere, but he still needed to know the shape of the aether currents around his command.

Today, the currents were away from the strait they guarded, back toward home. There were other currents nearby he could use if he needed to maneuver, but the main motion of the aether around them was toward High Court territory.

Woven through the currents of the aether, he could sense the presence of the other three ninesails of the squadron led by Lord Commander Ashfall Bronzemelter of the House of Forges. Four of the most powerful warships available to the Elvar High Court formed a line in the aether and, if Cat's senses were right, none were more than a yard off from perfect alignment.

Certainly *Running Fox* was perfectly aligned with Bronzemelter's *Oath of Flames*, with her top deck—defined as "the deck with the captain's cabin," given the lack of real distinction between the three sail decks—aligned at both the same elevation and angle as the other ninesail.

With his sense of the surrounding aether locked in, Cat opened his eyes again and turned to face Grass Cooper, his Master of Sails. Cooper was one of the ship's three Masters, the highest-ranked non-officers aboard the ninesail—and the Master of Sails was traditionally first among equals amidst the Masters of Sails, Deck and Staves.

"Report, Cooper," Cat ordered.

Cooper had no House and could never be an officer of the High Court Navy. She'd worked her way up from a sailor recruit to Master of Sails, which deserved respect even from the noble-born mages who commanded the ships she served on.

Her pointed ears flicked forward in acknowledgment of his command, and she took in a long, slow breath of aether.

"No new orders from the Lord Commander while you were sleeping," she began. "No trouble with the crew. Stonesliver reports that his inspection of the stave galleries turned up a problem. One of the low-deck storm staves appears to have acquired a fracture. He recommends against discharging it until he's gone over it with one of the officers."

"Understood," Cat said. "I'll have Bronzepillar speak with him shortly."

Fox Bronzepillar of the House of Forges was *Running Fox*'s fourth officer, the most junior of the five mages who commanded the warship. Unlike many new-minted officers, though, they were wise enough to listen to the Masters' century-plus of experience when it came to their areas of expertise.

Patient Stonesliver might not have enough magical power to fix the damaged storm stave himself, but he'd watched hundreds, if not more, such repairs over his career. So long as Bronzepillar listened to the Master of Staves, the repair would go smoothly.

"Any other news?" he asked, turning past Cooper to look at the reason they were all there. Four ninesails mustered over thirty-five hundred elvar, and it was rare indeed for that many ships to be sent *this* far from the High Court itself.

But there was a source of light in Shadowcastle that *wasn't* the crystal lamps positioned on the railings and rigging of the elvar warships. Brilliantly purple and orange, heavy with magic and void and aether alike, the strait was easily visible off *Running Fox*'s port side.

The streak of color marked where the boundary of the sphere opened, creating a passageway of aether less than a dozen cables across that linked to another sphere. The strait was a bottleneck, where four ninesails could potentially hold off a hostile fleet.

And that was important there. Because Shadowcastle *wasn't* High Court territory. It wasn't even part of the Kingdoms, the vaguely defined group of spheres loosely allied with the Court. It was the true border, and that strait led directly to the Clan Spheres of the gobvar.

"Nothing else to report, Captain," Cooper confirmed. "The crew is getting a bit bored and the dark is wearing on them."

"But that hasn't changed since yesterday," Cat noted. He considered something *else* from yesterday. "Where's Crystal Voice?"

"The seer is on the main mast of port deck," the Master of Sails said slowly. "I don't know what they see from there."

"What neither of us sees," Cat replied. He wasn't much fonder of Fallen Crystal Voice of the House of Fires than Grass Cooper was. Even among mages, seers were an odd bunch, with peculiarities and attitudes that rarely fit smoothly with the rest of the Houses.

But while he respected Cooper, he couldn't let the Houseless Master even imply derision toward another member of the Houses.

Plus, his statement was literally true.

"Of course, sir."

Cat looked up at the mainmast of the top deck, towering almost eighty yards above the deck, and wished for a fraction of a moment that the seer had picked somewhere *normal* to do their work. *Fox*'s lodestone keel kept his feet on the decks, pulling him toward the center of the aether ship...but that same pull could easily injure him if he misstepped on the top of the mast.

"I will go speak to them," he said calmly. "And, Cooper?"

"Captain?"

"Arm the crew," Cat ordered. "Have Master Stonesliver clear the staves and Master Carpenter rig up the surgery."

There was a long silence.

"Crystal Voice saw something yesterday, didn't they?" the older elvar woman said.

"They did," Cat confirmed. "I hope a clock-day has given them more certainty, but we expect a danger of some kind in the next clock-day or two. We shall all be ready for what comes."

"Does the Lord Commander know? We have no orders to clear for battle," Cooper warned.

"We're not clearing for battle," Cat said. "We're just drilling the crew."

Even the captain of a ninesail could not clear for battle without orders, not when the squadron commander was *right there*.

It was even worse than Cat had anticipated from Cooper's description. He had expected that Crystal Voice would be on the watch platform near the top of the mast. Or, at least, balanced on one of the cross-spars.

Instead, the seer was balanced on the very tip of the mast. Cross-legged, with only one foot even touching the cloudwood of the mast. Wrapped in a gray cloak interwoven with blue feathers, Crystal Voice was barely distinguishable from the aether beyond them—except for the pulsing nexus of *power* that Cat could feel the moment he was within a dozen yards of the seer.

Cat was a powerful mage, he knew that without false modesty, but he was no seer. Even among seers, Fallen Crystal Voice of the House of Fires was a strange and powerful creature. Cat had only felt a stronger nexus of power a handful of times in his life—usually when meeting one of the archmagi who'd run his training.

"Have your runes told you more of what is coming, seer?" he called up from the watch platform.

Crystal Voice didn't reply, and Cat turned a sharp look on the watchvar as that worthy clearly tried to conceal their amusement.

"Leave us, sailor," he ordered.

"At your command, Captain!" the var said crisply. They wrapped a chunk of heavy rope around the rigging and half-stepped, half-jumped off the platform to begin their descent to the port sail deck.

"Can you hear me, Crystal Voice?" Cat called up again.

The seer was muttering something, but it didn't appear to be addressed at the ninesail's captain.

Alone with the seer at the top of the mast, Cat allowed himself a grimace of frustration before drawing his focus. The darkwood was always warm against his skin, prickling slightly like it wasn't quite smooth.

The wand was a House focus, one that would work for any mage of the House of Forests. That made it more powerful than the general focuses which the Navy issued mages who didn't warrant that kind of support from their House.

Not as powerful, of course, as a true focus—but any focus required an archmage to craft, and those powers had better things to do than make personalized focuses for every mage in the High Court Navy.

As always, Cat pushed past the initial prickling discomfort. The magic of the focus met his own magic, and the two interwove with a warm purring sensation. He took a moment to delight in the power, the one thing in the spheres that was truly only his to command.

Then he lifted himself up with his power, levitating to rise in front of Crystal Voice and draw the unkempt seer's attention.

"Fallen Crystal Voice," he said sharply. "Can you hear me now?"

"I could always hear you, my captain," the seer replied, their voice vague and distant. "But the time was not right."

"Not right for what?" Cat asked. He managed to keep his frustration from his voice. Seers required long practice and patience to survive.

"For you to have the answers," Crystal Voice told him, their voice still softly distracted. "My runes have woven a tale of the future, Captain, and not all of it is for mortal var to be told."

"You told me yesterday that there was a danger coming," Cat said patiently. "Do you know more?"

"Yes, I have completed my augury," the seer replied. "But you were coming here, so I did not need to leave."

Cat waited for the seer to explain.

"You will need to warn the Lord Commander," Crystal Voice finally continued. "Ironsworn looks to the steel, not the rune, and has missed the sphere for the aether."

The only part of that Car followed was that Strongheart Ironsworn of the House of Forges was the seer aboard Lord Commander Bronzemelter's flagship.

"What is coming, Crystal Voice?"

"Doom. Yours. The Lord Commander's. Everyone's?" The seer shook their head. "Not everyone's," they corrected themselves. "Not...yet?"

Cat swallowed his irritation, focusing on the magic keeping him suspended near the seer's perch on top of the mast.

"I need more detail than that, Crystal Voice, if I am to advise the Lord Commander," he told the seer.

The cloaked figure sighed, ruffling their cloak and finally fully looking at Cat.

"There are things that are foreseen and things that are foretold," they told him. "I can *foresee* that an enemy is coming. Their decisions are made and unchanging. Something is coming that defies divination as to its nature, casting a cloak that my magic cannot pierce.

"I can *foretell* that they bring doom and that your choice will decide many fates," Crystal Voice continued. "But those choices are not made, so I cannot foresee. Do you understand?"

"No," Cat admitted. "What's coming, seer?"

"Gobvar, I think," the other mage told him. "But it's shrouded in a way that is strange for foresight and decisions made.

"Most of the decisions of what happens today are set, already made," they said slowly. "There is a decision of yours that will be made before the clock turns, that will shape your doom."

"Most of today's decisions are the Lord Commander's," Cat pointed out. Even a captain was subject to orders, after all.

"Not this one. And the Lord Commander's decisions are made and his doom set," Crystal Voice replied, their gaze flickering past Cat. "Only you, my captain, can choose. All others are set already."

"I don't understand," Cat said.

"What in all spheres gives you the impression I do?" Crystal Voice asked sharply, a sudden clarity to their tone. "This is not an exact magic, my captain. Some things I see and pass on in my own words. Some words are given to me.

"By the time the clock turns, the enemy will have arrived. I cannot see more and that scares me, my captain. All I can say for certain is that an enemy *is* coming and that your decision *matters*."

They shook themselves, the feathers rustling.

"Tell the Lord Commander it is gobvar," they concluded. "There is… something else, but I can *foresee* that sharing that will only cause difficulties."

Seers, Cat reflected, were not subject to the strictures of rank and face. Not least, he suspected, because most of them were only questionably sane.

CHAPTER

2

Bells tolled through the aether, starting on Lord Commander Bronzemelter's flagship, *Oath of Flames*, then echoed on *Running Fox* and carried back through the line of four ships.

"Clear for action!"

Cat had returned to the top sail deck and stood in the forecastle, staring out over the central bowsprit and its triple bronze figureheads. He didn't need to confirm or even repeat the order given by Listener Waterfall of the House of Rivers, his first officer. She'd heard the bells the same moment he had and interpreted them correctly.

His message to Lord Commander Bronzemelter had been sent by flags and simple enough: *Divination reveals gobvar strike by clock-turn*.

The Lord Commander's response was the bells—the call to bring the squadron to battle stations. *Running Fox*'s crew was already halfway there, thanks to Master Cooper's early instructions.

"Keep most of the riggers on the deck," Cat ordered. "We don't need to lose anyone to unneeded risks."

The farther his crew moved away from the lodestone keel, the less pull it had. He was more concerned about them falling to the deck, but it was entirely possible for a rigger to jump wrong and float off endlessly into the aether.

While Cat spoke softly enough, there were half a dozen runners waiting to carry his orders to the ship's three Masters and four officers. A shuffling sound and a sudden sense of power behind him told him that Crystal Voice had joined him on the forecastle.

The seer said nothing, but their presence was reassuring in some ways. Fallen Crystal Voice saw things no one else did, which had its value.

"Stave galleries are clear," Bronzepillar reported swiftly, the young officer audibly snapping to attention behind Cat. "All stavemasters are in position."

"The fractured stave in the low gallery?" Cat asked.

"Master Stonesliver and I were assessing it when the bells rang," they admitted. "I did not have time to complete my inspection, but the Master of Staves says the stave cannot be used safely."

There was a long pause. Cat knew the order that needed to be given—an order neither Stonesliver nor Bronzepillar had the authority to give—but he wanted Bronzepillar to make a suggestion.

A heartbeat passed. Then two. Then ten.

"Your recommendation, Fourth Officer Bronzepillar?" Cat finally asked, his gaze turning from the bronze foxes at the foremast to the orange and purple strait in the sky.

"Master Stonesliver has been working on storm staves for longer than I've been alive, Captain," Bronzepillar noted. "If he says the stave cannot be used safely, then we should disarm it for the safety of the crew and ship."

"Indeed," Cat confirmed. "See to it personally, Fourth Officer. I will not risk this ship to a damaged stave when we fight a real battle."

That would reduce his lower armament by a twelfth, but he didn't expect to *use* the lower stave gallery. The port and starboard galleries were easiest for a var navigating from the top forecastle to line up on the enemy.

And if twenty-four storm staves weren't enough to handle the enemy Crystal Voice couldn't foresee, the difference between thirty-five and thirty-six wasn't going to change much.

Bronzepillar saluted, fist to chest, and the sound of his footsteps retreating faded from Cat's awareness.

His attention remained focused on the aether straight above and to starboard of his ship. That was where the enemy would emerge when they arrived. Regardless of the vagueness of the seer's predictions, there were only two ways into Shadowcastle. There was the aether strait from the Clan Spheres, and there was an aether strait to Bluelight, a sparsely inhabited sphere claimed by no one in particular.

From Bluelight, there were multiple courses to other spheres. One strait led in the direction of the halvar Kingdom of Stonewill. Others led, by various roundabout routes, to other halvar and darvar kingdoms and principalities.

The only one that truly mattered to the High Court Navy, however, was the strait that led to the Navy base at Forgedcrystal. Forgedcrystal wasn't, technically, a High Court sphere—it was ruled by a darvar principality—but with a major anchorage for the Navy there, it served as the base for patrols and blockades like *Running Fox*'s current duties.

It was also on the shortest and most direct route to the High Court itself, the collection of lodeplates orbiting an immense life crystal that anchored the entire elvar civilization.

"How long?" Cat asked aloud. He could *feel* Crystal Voice's presence.

"The doom grows stronger with each swing of the clock," the seer told him. "Before the turning."

The clocks would turn to a new day in about twelve hours, Cat judged. But Crystal Voice had already *said* that the attack would come in that clock-day and not the next.

"Not within the hour, but before the turning," the seer continued after a moment. "There is no light here to judge by."

The frustration in the seer's tone forced Cat to conceal a smile. Even the somewhat off-kilter diviner was affected by the shadowy nothingness of the dark sphere.

"Officer Waterfall, to me," he ordered.

A moment later, the willowy redheaded form of his first officer appeared next to him, the var leaning on the railing of the ship and studying the aether strait.

"Seer Crystal Voice…has warned us," she finally said, carefully.

"And even if they are wrong, it is an excellent exercise for the crew," Cat noted. His gaze turned to *Oath of Flames*. The Lord Commander's flagship was nearly identical to *Running Fox*, an uneven hexagon most of a cable long. Three sets of masts rose from each of the ninesail's three sail decks, giving her the titular nine sails.

Or, more accurately, nine *masts* and closer to thirty sails—but the name was old and Cat wasn't going to argue about it.

"Can we keep the crew on alert till the clock turns?" he asked her.

"They know as much as we do. They'll keep watch that long."

They studied the strait in silent companionship for a moment.

"How long has it been since the gobvar last breached the border?" Waterfall finally asked.

"Six dances," Cat told her. That meant that the lodeplates of the High Court had gone through the complex interwoven movements of their orbits six times—a maneuver that took just over three hundred and sixty clock-days.

"I was first officer on *Shining Blade*," he continued. "We were sent forward as support to reinforce the blockade at Flamebreach. The initial line held, though, and we didn't see any combat."

The aether currents shifted slightly and a tingle ran down the back of Cat's neck.

"It's been thirty-six dances since I fought them at Hideshield," he murmured, searching the strait for what he suspected. "I was third officer on *Blade* then."

"Sir?" Waterfall said. She'd caught the change in his body language.

"I believe someone has entered the strait," he told her. "We are ready… and it seems we are on the earlier side of the seer's predictions."

After hundreds of dances of on-and-off war along the border, the High Court Navy knew their opponents' moves. The first ships out of the strait were always the fireships: massive constructs assembled from the wreckage of old ships stripped of their lodestone keels.

"Fireships breaching the strait," the watchvar above Cat shouted. The captain saw them a moment later, five of the ugly aggregate structures drifting almost lazily into Shadowcastle. Each was at least a full cable across and high, propelled by sails and guided by a handful of brave souls.

Cat's gaze turned to the flagship ahead of *Running Fox*, watching for the flags. There were a few variations on what the Lord Commander could order, but the sequence of large colored flags hung over *Oath of Flames*' stern were about what Cat would have ordered himself.

One-third sail.

Circle to alternate galleries.

Hold the blockade.

Engage at will.

"Master of Sails!" Cat bellowed, trusting in his voice to reach Cooper and the runners to reach the other two sail decks. "Unfurl the topsails. Prepare for maneuver."

"Aye!"

It was less than five steps to the main wheel from where Cat had stood watching the aether strait. Locks held it in place, preventing the magical device from moving in any of its three dimensions—the wheel could turn or pitch, but any movement of the wheel would be reflected in the positions of all nine masts.

"Master of Staves," Cat continued, laying his hands on the wheel and waiting for the topsails to unfurl. "Do you have eyes on the fireships?"

"Port gallery is ready to release, but we do not have a line," Patient Stonesliver replied. Cat couldn't *see* the Master of Staves, but the elvar's battle station was at the fore of the port gallery—barely a dozen yards away through the ship's decks. They barely needed to shout to hear each other.

Cat watched as *Oath of Flames'* sails unfurled and the flagship lunged forward, her captain adjusting the sails to bring the ninesail into a long turn that would present first her port and then her starboard stave galleries as she carved a circle through the aether that would keep her either above or below her compatriots' line of discharge.

So long, of course, as the other three ninesails followed *Oath*'s course with enough precision—but Cat Greentrees could do that in his sleep. He had faith in the other captains as his magic flickered down the wheel and released the locks holding it in place.

"Topsails unfurled, Captain!" Cooper barked up to the forecastle.

Cat could tell. *Running Fox* was moving with the aether currents now, picking up speed in the wake of *Oath of Flames*. The fireships continued to loom closer, but they were still a dozen cables, almost half a league, away.

Without lodestone keels, they moved *far* more freely with the aether currents than any ship Cat had ever served aboard. But without a sense of *down* to keep the crew aboard and the ship together, the fireships were doomed from the moment they were unleashed.

But loaded with combustibles and explosives as they were, there was no way that the elvar ships could let them get close.

"Master Stonesliver," Cat called, his voice lower than before but still clear and projected. "You may discharge staves when you have a line."

Thunder rolled in the deep aether as *Oath of Flames* moved far enough through her turn to draw the line to the lead fireship. Storm staves discharged in brilliant flashes of light, arcing beams of lightning that hammered into Lord Commander Bronzemelter's target.

Cat couldn't see the crew abandoning the fireship, but he *could* see the moment the fuses ignited. The storm stave strikes started some of the fires, but most were far enough along to be clearly intended.

A moment later, explosions tore the ship apart, scattering flaming debris across several cables of empty aether and covering the approach of the other fireships from the stave discharges of the elvar warships.

It wasn't perfect, and thunder crashed underneath Cat's feet as his own stavemasters drew their lines through the debris field. The next few lightning strikes from the ninesails flickered ineffectually in the chaos, but the second fireship swiftly lit up from the successful discharges.

"Port gallery is clear," Waterfall reported, the first officer watching as Cat turned his ship in *Oath*'s trail. "Two fireships down."

"Five fireships aren't a threat to the blockade," Cat replied. "Watch for—"

"Cutters!" one of the watchvar bellowed. "At least two dozen!"

"Watch for the real fleet," Cat finished drily. "They know we can't ignore the fireships, but it's the cutters and galleons we need to watch."

He studied the strait carefully as *Running Fox* swung through her turn to present the starboard gallery. The cutters were far smaller than the fireships, harder to pick out at a distance, but their sails were more even, more geometric, than the rough assemblies of the fireships.

There. The watchvar was right. He could pick out at least a dozen sets of sails, and his view was more constrained than that of the var on top of *Running Fox*'s masts.

The cutters were sharp triangular ships, lacking the stave galleries of a ninesail and only carrying a single mast on each deck. Cruder and less elegant than a ninesail, a gobvar cutter used ropes not just for management of the rigging but even for controlling the masts and steering.

They had a single storm stave mounted in the prow, but the magical weapon wasn't the purpose of a cutter. Its task was to deliver its crew of gobvar to a target and storm a ninesail's decks with warriors hardened by dozens of dances of inter-Clan warfare.

"Starboard gallery lining on the fireships," Waterfall told him—and thunder announced that *Oath of Flames*' stave gallery had already lined up.

The two trailing ninesails had already hammered the fireships with their own second galleries. Two of the fireships were still intact, but they were still five cables—a thousand yards—distant and weren't going to get much closer.

As Cat watched, *Oath*'s staves lit the second-to-last fireship ablaze and his own ship's weapons thundered at the last ship. Explosions tore the two gobvar vessels apart simultaneously.

The fireships had served their purpose, though. Aether didn't sustain fire for long, but there were enough incendiaries and chemicals and magic woven through the fireships' hulls to keep the debris burning as it spread toward the elvar blockade squadron.

They could aim at the fireships through the debris, but the cutters were smaller, faster and more maneuverable. The blockade was a full league from the strait, a position intended to force the gobvar to close through the full range of the elvar's staves.

The gobvar warlord on the other side would have been pleased if a fireship had collided with one of the ninesails, but their *purpose* was to allow the cutters to close to within five cables of the elvar before coming under heavy fire.

A purpose they had fulfilled admirably, to Cat's frustration.

"Starboard gallery clear," Waterfall reported, warning him that he had no weapons pointed at the oncoming flotilla.

"Get me a count on those cutters," Cat replied, projecting his voice so the watchvar would hear him.

"Twenty-eight," that worthy shouted back down. "Still ships in the strait!"

The second division of the blockade squadron was discharging at the cutters, but Cat had no faith in their success. No matter how good their stavemasters, they couldn't *see* the enemy ships with any certainty.

"One hit," Waterfall told him. "*Oath* will range with her port gallery in a moment."

The spiraling formation Lord Commander Bronzemelter had ordered meant that at least one ship was discharging staves at the oncoming flotilla at any moment—and given that it took *time* to recharge a storm stave, it was faster to turn the ships to alternate the stave galleries than wait.

"*Now,*" Fallen Crystal suddenly snapped. There was no explanation for their words...but Cat knew what they meant.

He pushed the wheel forward and spun it sideways, lurching *Running Fox* temporarily out of formation as the cutters discharged their own storm staves. Lightning flashed through where the ship would have been, stray energy sparking from metal parts across *Fox* as the enemy's power lashed emptiness instead of Cat's ship...this time.

CHAPTER

3

"Thank you, seer," Cat told Crystal Voice as he twisted the wheel once more, pulling *Running Fox* back into her position in *Oath*'s wake.

"*Crystalhammer* is hit," the watchvar shouted.

"Waterfall, get eyes on *Hammer* and tell me how bad it is," Cat ordered. His own gaze was focused on the incoming gobvar. They'd missed his ship, thanks to Fallen Crystal's warning—but that was *why* the seer was on the forecastle.

His port stave gallery was about to have clear lines, which meant the cutters were going to have a bad time. The flags on *Oath of Flames*' stern hadn't changed, either. *Hold the blockade.*

The flagship's staves thundered again, and the lead cutter simply ceased to exist as a dozen storm staves hit her in a perfectly coordinated blow. A skilled strike...but overkill, Cat judged. He trusted Stonesliver to do better.

The lack of thunder as he brought *Running Fox* through her turn spoke to the weakness of that coordinated strike. There was no follow-up, nothing to keep the rest of the cutters from continuing to carve across the empty aether.

Until, that is, he brought *Fox* far enough around and his own staves started to thunder under his feet. Stonesliver's stavemasters discharged in pairs. Two lightning bolts smashed into the lead cutter, then another two into the cutter next to her. Both ships were damaged but still coming—and then four more lightning strikes hammered into them.

One ship disintegrated entirely. The other lost two of its three masts and much of its decking, spinning off into the aether with little or no control.

More cutters were still coming, though—and the last four storm staves in Cat's port gallery thundered as one, hammering a third ship into a similarly crippled state.

"*Hammer* is in rough shape," Waterfall reported, reappearing at his elbow. "Top forecastle was hit. Captain Stormvoice is dead. Flag says third officer Blackwood is in command."

Cat grunted. He didn't know Blackwood at all—he wouldn't even have been able to name *Crystalhammer*'s third officer, though Waterfall clearly could. All the flags would tell her was that the third officer was in command, after all.

"So long as they follow formation, they'll be fine," he said.

"Agreed. Port gallery clear," she reported. "Their staves will be ready again soon."

The cutters were barely three hundred yards away and closing *far* too quickly for Cat's peace of mind. The lead ships were suffering as *Crystalhammer*'s stave galleries began to discharge. The ninesail might have lost her captain, but her Master of Staves and their stavemasters knew their jobs well enough, Cat judged.

"Galleons!" the watchvar shouted. "I make it ten." A beat passed. "No Clan banners."

"No Clan banners?" Cat repeated. "That makes no sense. No one would muster this kind of attack without proclaiming their Clan everywhere they could!"

There wouldn't be Clan insignia on the fireships, and the cutters would be drawn from every Clan that could be bribed or bullied to join an attack, but gobvar galleons were the pride of the Clans that built them. They might not be the true equal of a ninesail—but they were built to fight them.

Ten galleons were a problem. From what Cat knew, that had to be a *multi*-Clan fleet—but that would only make the gobvar even more inclined to declare their Clans.

So, if the galleons' sails had no banners, something strange was going on.

"Watch them," Cat ordered. "We need to know their arms and courses."

The cutters were close enough and numerous enough that the elvar squadron was in danger—but only of damage like *Crystalhammer*'s. The fourth ship in line was unleashing her storm staves as the warning about the galleons came down, and the lightning bolts tore apart another cutter.

The gobvar ships were closing the range, but they were dying to do it.

"*Now*," Crystal Voice barked again, only the second time they'd spoken.

This time, Cat pulled his ship up and to starboard, and didn't quite make it fast enough. He felt *Running Fox* lurch underneath him as a storm-stave bolt struck home.

"Runners, find the damage, get me a report from the Master of Decks," Cat ordered as he pulled the ship back into formation. She didn't respond. "The control crystals are damaged," he continued. "Master Carpenter needs to replace them *now*."

He considered for a moment, swallowing a curse.

"Master Cooper," he barked. "I need riggers up. We're going to have to guide her back into formation manually."

"Flagship has dropped a *hold formation* flag, sir," Waterfall warned him.

"Of course they have," Cat muttered before he could stop himself. *Running Fox* was already visibly out of formation, and his failure to turn meant that he was now heading *away* from the battle.

"Riggers are going up," Master Cooper announced, the Master of Sails stepping onto the forecastle for the first time since the battle began. "We can steer to your command in a moment."

"Thank you, Master Cooper," Cat said. "Officer Waterfall, throw up a battle damage flag to warn the Lord Commander.

"We will return to formation momentarily and both our galleries will be charged," he reflected aloud. "Those gobvar will regret this attack."

Cat didn't even know *why* the gobvar would have attacked. What limited contact there was between the High Court and the Clans' Quadrumvirate was far above the head of the commander of a single aether ship.

CHAPTER 4

Even with the riggers up the masts, it took longer to turn *Running Fox* back toward the battle than Cat liked—especially since Lord Commander Bronzemelter's flagship *still* hung the *hold formation* flag, ordering his ship back in like a wayward puppy.

"Cutters closing on the flagship," the watchvar shouted down.

Cat nodded grimly. Most of the cutters were wrecked or destroyed now, at least a dozen of them spinning off into the deep aether, propelled by only a single sail. Half a dozen of them were now making the final plunge toward *Oath of Flames*, storm staves ignored as the crews turned out on the decks with grappling hooks and swords.

"Stonesliver is wounded," Waterfall told him grimly after the runners reported. "The port forecastle is wrecked, so it'll take Carpenter a while to restore control. We've lost the forward staves in the port and lower galleries!"

"Then it's a good thing we're showing them our starboard side," Cat replied. "Stavemasters!"

His hand was on his focus and his magic wove around his voice, projected his words along the length of the starboard stave gallery. A dozen storm staves were serviced by sixty elvar there, and the fate of *Oath of Flames* rode on those stavemasters' skill.

"Target the cutters on the flagship," he ordered. "Discharge as you bear!"

With the riggers following his commands, *Running Fox* turned far enough just in time. The first pair of storm staves discharged in the same moment as the grappling hooks from the lead cutter touched onto *Oath*'s decks.

Momentarily paused by catching on to the ninesail, the cutter was vulnerable, and *Fox*'s lightning came in from "above," descending directly into her decks and her gathered boarders.

The paired lightning bolts tore through the cloudwood decking and hit the lodestone keel. For a moment, the entire ship was illuminated as electricity arced to the prow and stern simultaneously…and then the cutter simply came apart.

Three storm staves unleashed on the next cutter as it lunged for *Oath of Flames*. Only two struck, but those bolts were enough to destroy the ship's sails and send it spinning away below the elvar flagship.

Four more spoke in pairs, hammering into two cutters simultaneously. One remained intact enough to complete her charge, slamming her half-wrecked decks into *Oath*'s starboard stave gallery. The survivors swarmed onto the flagship's deck, but elvar marines were there to meet them. Single-purpose battlewands sparked in the darkness, and swords flashed in the light from the flagship's lamps.

The last three storm staves discharged as one again. Only one bolt connected, but it was enough to send one of the last cutters spinning away—and then *Oath*'s own staves finished recharging.

The handful of remaining cutters vanished like leaves in the wind as the flagship's weapons discharged at point-blank range.

"Signal to the flagship," Cat ordered. "We're returning to formation. Damage remains; control is impaired."

He couldn't see the state of the battle on *Oath*'s decks clearly, but he suspected that Bronzemelter was a bit distracted. The sparks of battlewands were fewer now, at least, which suggested that the situation was under control.

"Galleons are clearing the fireship field," the watchvar shouted.

Cat looked across the aether, judging distances with a practiced eye. They'd fallen almost three cables away from the squadron, but they could close that distance as easily as they'd lost it. With the cutters gone and the fireships expended, the galleons were the last remnant of the enemy attack.

Unfortunately, the galleons had always been the real attack. The cutters had crews of fifty to sixty. The galleons had crews of five to six *hundred*, over half as many as the ninesails they were built to fight.

They had maybe a dozen storm staves apiece, but the gobvar had their own kinds of arcane weaponry as well. Shorter-ranged but in some ways more powerful, their flamethrowers were a real danger to the blockade squadron.

"We can engage past the rest of the squadron, thankfully," Cat murmured to Waterfall. "We can support, but they'll carry the weight of it."

Ten galleons versus four ninesails was a fair fight. Ten galleons versus *three* ninesails was a disaster in the making. *Running Fox*'s support could make all the difference, even if Cat couldn't get his ship properly back into the line.

"Is the port gallery intact enough to replace the lost staves with two from the lower deck?" he asked.

"No," Waterfall admitted. "We got hit hard. It'll be clock-days of repairs in a proper yard before we can mount thirty-six staves again."

"Then we use what we've got," Cat said. He closed his eyes as the ship headed back toward the line. His starboard staves were depleted; he could feel their magic drawing in energy from the aether around him. His port and lower staves hummed with full energy, but he could feel the missing weapons.

He hadn't been so lucky that one of the lost lower staves had been the damaged one, either. He only had nine staves left on that deck.

His focus was on the currents around his ship, trying to find the slight edge that could bring him back to the battle faster. He couldn't risk unfurling full sail. That would take him from a few cables every minute to two-thirds of a league or more in the same time.

Control was critical. He couldn't raise sail, close the distance and lower the sails in time to engage safely. But if he found the right current, he could increase *Fox*'s speed without losing control.

Except there was something wrong in the currents. Something *pulsed* with power in a way he'd never felt before, and he opened his eyes as fear prickled down his spine.

"Sir?" Waterfall asked.

"Nothing," he said sharply. He wasn't afraid of the gobvar. The blockade squadron was battered, but he had confidence in his own ship and in Lord Commander Bronzemelter. He couldn't see *anything* to match that pulse of power he'd felt rippling through the aether.

"Watchvar," Cat called up. "Spread your eyes. Anything beyond the galleons?"

Heartbeats passed, and thunder rolled as the galleons finally broached the debris field. Lightning from the ninesails and galleons flickered across the dark aether. In a moment, *Fox*'s discharges would join them, but the turn was slower with the control crystals broken.

"Nothing!" the watcher shouted down. "We have them, sir!"

For the first time since the battle had joined, Cat turned back to look at his own ship. Little of the damage was visible on the main deck—the bolt that had hit *Running Fox* had struck beneath his feet, on the port deck.

The masts and sails were tilted, angling to bring his port gallery into play. They'd join the hail of lightning that was meeting the galleons' emergence as the elvar attempted to destroy their enemy before they closed to the range of their deadly but short ranged arsenal.

Even with limited control, his ninesail was a powerful ship. As was the rest of the squadron. The blockade squadron was four ninesails because nothing more was needed.

And yet fear was rippling down his spine and he found himself meeting Crystal Voice's gaze. The seer's eyes were unfocused, a gray haze settling over them in a way that even Cat found uncomfortable to see.

"Doom, my captain," Crystal Voice whispered softly. "Yours approaches. The Lord Commander's...is here."

The scream that tore through the aether as the seer finished was impossible. *Nothing* living had the lungs to project that much noise through the thin medium of the aether between worlds—and it drew every eye, every ear, toward Lord Bronzemelter's flagship as the ninesail's doom appeared.

Magic had concealed its approach, but magic couldn't conceal its passage through the strait, so it had expended an entire fleet of gobvar to clear its way. Now the dragon released its illusion and landed on *Oath of Flames*' deck with a scream that echoed across half the dark sphere.

Power rippled through the aether, and a single beat of the beast's wing flung the elvar marines to the deck. Cat couldn't see many details of the immense beast, only that it was easily a third of the length of the ninesail itself—and he saw the fire it unleashed as it burned through the back half of Bronzemelter's ship.

Fire and magic blazed around the ninesail as the dragon tore into its prey, consuming crew and wood alike as it pursued its true meal: the arcane artifices that powered and controlled the aether ship.

"Spheres preserve us," Waterfall whispered. "*Crystalhammer!*"

Cat had been focused on the flagship's death—and the death of the one var who could order him to run—and had missed the *second* dragon. The already battered ninesail *Crystalhammer*, commanded by one of its most junior officers, never stood a chance. The dragon tore the prow off the ship, driving claws and magic alike into the forward sections where the control crystals lay.

"The galleons are falling back!" the watchvar shouted. It wasn't a steady report, but it told Cat what he needed to know.

The dragons and the gobvar were working together. He'd never heard of such a thing…which meant that the High Court had to be warned.

But another ninesail remained in the fight, and his orders were specific and clear: hold the blockade. Hold the formation.

Lord Commander Bronzemelter was dead, and the laws of the High Court Navy said that Captain Cat Greentrees was bound by the Lord Commander's orders until a new Lord Commander was appointed.

"What do we do?" Waterfall whispered. "Our orders…"

"Our *duty*," Cat cut her off. "We do our duty."

"Our doom," he heard Crystal Voice mutter. "They're slow, my captain; they cannot pursue at full sail."

The galleons could, Cat knew.

"We have to warn the base at Forgedcrystal," Cat snapped. "Riggers, turn us full to port and unfurl all sail!"

"My captain, we can't…"

"We do our duty," Cat ground out at his first officer. Disobedience to orders was dangerous. Potentially even lethal. But if he didn't turn, if he didn't take his ship back toward the High Court spheres, no one would ever know what had happened here.

"One dragon is going after *Bladefall*," Waterfall told him. "The other…"

"Is coming for us," Cat finished. "Get those sails unfurled and this ship turned!" he bellowed up to the riggers.

He could see the dragon, winging its way toward them. He could hurt it; he knew that. Unlike *Crystalhammer* and *Oath of Flames*, he could see it approach, and Crystal Voice was correct: the beast was slow, compared to a ninesail.

But not slow enough, not with the level of magic the creature commanded. Tradition said it took a *dozen* ninesails to fight a dragon…and

Bladefall was already doomed. *Running Fox* was all Cat could rely on, and *someone* had to warn the Court.

"Sir," Waterfall said softly. "I would like to note in the ship's log that I ag—"

"You will do no such thing, First Officer," Cat told her calmly. A new fear locked his spine in cold iron now. Not even fear, truly. *Knowledge.*

"It is my duty to make this choice," he continued. "And it is my duty to bear the consequences of it. Our course is for Forgedcrystal, as fast as we can travel."

He looked back to where the galleons were beginning to shake themselves out.

"Our enemies will follow, but I think we can evade battle until we clear Shadowcastle. We must reach Forgedcrystal and warn the Navy."

If nothing else, Forgedcrystal had a reserve squadron of another half dozen ninesails, plus fortified worldlets with storm staves built into stone bastions. Let the dragons follow Running Fox to the fleet base.

That would give Cat Greentrees his revenge.

CHAPTER 5

"You have made your choice, my captain."

Cat wasn't even sure how Crystal Voice had even got *into* his quarters. He was reasonably sure the door hadn't opened, though his own focus had been outside the ship. He'd been trying to find an even-faster current, one that could carry his ship and people to safety before the galleons caught them.

They'd left the dragon behind swiftly enough once they'd unfurled full sails, but the gobvar warships were chasing them now. A ninesail didn't have much of a speed edge over a galleon normally, but Cat had already found a path that was carving a dozen leagues from their course to the aether strait.

"Doom, you said," Cat told the seer as he opened his eyes and studied the feather-cloaked figure in front of him. "Did you know what kind?"

He knew the punishment his choice had earned. It was his duty *anyway*, and that was the part that stung.

"No," Crystal Voice said. "I rarely know more than I see, my captain, not with certainty. It doesn't work like that. I can…see more now, if you want to know."

"What is there to see, seer?" Cat asked. "My choice is made; my fate is set. I know what the law calls for."

"Shadows and darkness lie before you, my captain," the elvar said, leaning on his table. "I can neither foresee nor foretell all that will come to pass. I *know* that I live because of your choice, so my…leaning is clear."

Cat shook his head at the seer.

"Tell me," he finally said.

"All that will come to pass is shadow for some time now," Fallen Crystal Voice told him. "You must understand that. You are one of three parts. Until they come together, you must endure."

"I'm not sure what there is to understand of that," Cat replied.

"Captain and Shaman; Shaman and Archmage," the seer said, intoning capitals like tombstones. "Your doom is to be one of them. All that passes until you meet the Archmage is nothing but shadow."

"I don't understand," Cat admitted. "And I'm not sure it matters."

Not many archmagi were going to spend time with condemned criminals, after all, and Cat well knew the consequences for disobedience to orders in the face of the enemy. Only one of that exalted number would visit *him*…and there was nothing *she* could do.

Crystal Voice pulled their feathered hood back. Their gaze was surprisingly alert as they focused on Cat.

"It's important, Captain," they told him. "*Everything is shadow.* Understand that and you will find it easier to endure what comes."

"I know what comes," Cat said quietly. "I will endure. That, too, is my duty."

Forgedcrystal was an outerlit sphere. There was no central point in the sphere emitting light and energy to fuel life on its worldlets and ships. Instead, the entire outer barrier between aether and void glowed with a diffuse illumination that provided light everywhere at all times.

It was, at least, gentler on the eyes than most light crystals or embers, but the lack of shadows or any darkness at all was an ironic counterpoint to the dark sphere that Cat and his people had just abandoned.

He stood on a tower on the edge of the High Court Navy base, a lodestone-based defensive position linked to the sprawling construct of lodestone and cloudwood that served as the heart of the Navy's position here, at the edge of their power.

Five storm staves were positioned in the tower beneath him, but this *particular* tower also served as the headquarters of Lord Commander Hunter Diamond of the House of Fires. Cat had been sent up to the roof after giving his report, and he waited patiently, watching the ninesails of the Forgedcrystal squadron.

Only one of the big ships was currently in the aether, sweeping a long and patient patrol around the artificial worldlet of the Navy base. Nine more were docked with the base—but three of those, including *Running Fox*, were there for repairs.

Six capital ships were permanently assigned to Lord Commander Diamond's authority. It was a powerful fleet...but not strong enough to fight a dragon. Let alone two. To challenge the enemy that had emerged in Shadowcastle would require even Diamond to send for reinforcements.

When the door to the inner tower finally opened, Cat wasn't surprised to hear multiple sets of boots on the stairs. He remained where he was, looking out into the aether as he picked out the sound of at least four sets of marine boots as well as two sets of Navy dress-uniform boots.

"Captain Greentrees," Lord Commander Hunter Diamond said quietly. "I have reviewed your report and the reports of your officers."

Cat remained silent with his gaze focused on *Running Fox*. He knew what the codes of the High Court Navy demanded for what he had done.

"You're under arrest," Diamond told him. "Are you going to cause me difficulties?"

Cat smirked into the outerlight of Forgedcrystal. Hunter Diamond *knew* how powerful Cat was. With a House focus instead of the Navy focus held by the Lord Commander, Cat could easily defeat the other mage. Depending on who the marines and the other officer were, he could probably defeat them all without even particularly *injuring* them.

He couldn't, however, fight his way through an entire fleet base, steal a ship and flee into the aether. If nothing else, he had nowhere to flee *to*.

He turned to face the var who had been forced to decide his doom and spread his hands wide.

"I will not," he promised. He almost reconsidered, though, when he saw who the second officer with her was.

Fox Bronzepillar had the skin tones of his name, with a metallic shimmer to his long ears in the scattered light of Forgedcrystal's outer barriers. His hand was on his own focus—and like Cat, his focus was from his House, a mark of favor and power.

Cat knew he could take the younger mage, but he'd probably be forced to kill Hunter Diamond to level the field. And while the Lord Commander's words condemned him, he knew Diamond had no choice.

"I need you to surrender your blade and focus," Diamond told him, holding out a delicately fingered hand.

Cat stared at her hand for several heartbeats, then exhaled a long sigh. That was the line he knew he had to cross, the one that officially surrendered his command and his freedom.

"Captain," she said sharply.

"My focus belongs to the House of Forests," he said softly, reaching down to unhook the belt that held both weapons. "It is not the property of the High Court Navy."

"And your focus and blade will both be held in safe trust for you until the Navy has concluded your fate," the Lord Commander promised. "If the Navy's judgment turns against you, your focus will be returned to your House in the hopes they find a worthier scion to carry it.

"If the Navy's judgment favors you, your blade and focus will be returned to you with honor. But for now, you must surrender them both."

It took real physical effort for Cat to wrap the leather belt around the twin scabbards and offer the weapons to the nearest marine. Bronzepillar had stepped forward to take the weapons belt, but Cat refused to hand it to the young mage.

He knew it was petty. He *knew* he'd left his officers no choice. *Someone* had had to tell the Lord Commander that the last orders Bronzemelter had given were to rejoin the formation and hold the blockade.

"The charges?" he asked as the marine stepped away. The elvar was at least treating the weapons belt with the respect it deserved.

"Disobedience to orders and cowardice in the face of the enemy," Lord Commander Hunter Diamond said flatly. "You will be held until I can spare a ship to carry you to the High Court itself, where you will face the judgment of the Lords of the Navy in the light of the Prime Crystal."

Cat winced. Disobedience he knew and had accepted, but *cowardice*?

Shadows, he told himself. He didn't know what Crystal Voice's words meant, but…it was a mantra he could cling to.

All of this is but shadows.

"I am your prisoner, Lord Commander," he conceded. "As you command."

CHAPTER

6

THE INCENSE SMOLDERING in the corners of the cave could not cover the scent of burning horn. Brushfire Hammerhead held *very* still as the shaman worked, the superheated knife in their hand radiating enough heat to burn the hair around her horns as they worked the pattern into her.

The horns themselves couldn't feel the work, but the heat was enough to send shivers of not-quite-pain through her scalp. Still, the gobvar woman remained utterly still as the shaman laid aside their knife with a satisfied grunt and lifted a crucible from the same fire they'd heated the knife in.

This wasn't the first time Brushfire had been through this ritual, and she braced herself for what came next. There were scars, concealed under her hair, where the liquid silver had spilled and not been cleared away fast enough before.

This time, though, *this* shaman made no mistakes. The silver poured perfectly into the grooves carved into her horns, and the scent of burning horn grew even stronger.

The crucible went back into the fire, and the shaman grunted with satisfaction again.

"Who marked your first circles?" they finally asked. "Scorched fools. Never spill the silver, child. It is bad luck."

"It wasn't here," Brushfire told the old gobvar. The shaman had never even given her a name, though they'd trained her for almost two dances now. A few clock-days here and there, as her journeys had allowed.

"I knew *that*," they told her. "Which leads me to our choices, I suppose."

Brushfire's horns were still smoking slightly as the shaman gestured her to a cushion and offered her a flagon of water. The cave had been natural once, but magic had shaped it to be both concealed and comfortable for the shaman.

So far as she knew, the old gobvar never left their hidey-hole. They were brought food and water by the various members of the gobvar community on the worldlet of Blueswallow, both a sign of respect and a petition for aid, usually.

"Choices?" she asked after taking a long swallow of water. It had been a full clock-day since she'd eaten or drunk anything. She'd spent that time in fasting meditation there in the cave, the last task necessary to earn the third circle on her horns.

She was still, at best, a senior apprentice. The gobvar shaman sitting with her didn't *have* countable rings on their horns—the two spurs that protruded from their temples and swept back were entirely coated in silver.

"Your ship has been visiting Blueswallow on and off for two flarings of the Great Fire," the shaman reminded her. "In seven hundred clock-days, you have received the training an older child or young adult of your talents should have received in *seventy*."

"I have responsibilities and employment," Brushfire replied. "I recognize the difficulties it causes me, but…my duty is to my family and my tribe first."

"And such is why you will make an excellent shaman," the older var told her with a sigh. "But this third circle, little sister…it is as far as you can get like this. You must dedicate time. *Real* time, uninterrupted.

"If you cannot dedicate at least a quarter-flaring at a time, you will never earn the rest of the circles." They shrugged. "Some shamans might be willing to try, perhaps even to inlay the markings on your horns, but you will never master what you should master to become a true shaman of our people."

"We are a long way from our people," Brushfire said quietly. "These are not the Spheres of Our Clans."

"And perhaps we may be better off for that," the shaman reminded her. "One of your gifts would not be given a choice in the Spheres of Our Clans. Her Sisters would have found you by now. You would wear the crimson or die."

Brushfire had been born in exile, in a gobvar ghetto on a halvar worldlet like Blueswallow. She knew *of* Her Crimson Sisters…but she knew very little of them.

And none of it was pleasant.

"What would you have of me?" she asked softly, looking around the dark cave. After over a clock-day in the enclosed space, she could see relatively well by the light from the incense braziers. There wasn't much in the underground dwelling. A dozen cushions, a handful of cupboards, a thin-looking mattress.

The shaman was perfectly capable of maintaining the darvar-made crystal lamps found in every market if they wanted. Or even of building their own magical lights. The dim light was as much a choice as their isolation.

"A quarter of a flaring of the Great Fire," the old gobvar reiterated. "It will take more than one to finish your training, but I need you to give me those five and eighty clock-days at a time, Brushfire. Or there is no purpose to continuing your training."

"Four and a hundred gobvar look to me," Brushfire told them. "My family, my tribe, my crew. They have no control over where our ship carries us or when. If I leave them, I cannot even guarantee that *Skyfish* will return here.

"My first duty is to my family, Elder. All other duties, even this, must fall."

"Bound to elvar ships and tasks," the shaman spat, but they shook their horns as they did. "Unfair, unfair. I ask your charity."

"Granted and more than earned," Brushfire said. "We *are* bound to elvar. By contract and gold alike. *Skyfish*'s captain is better than many, but if there are any gobvar captains in these spheres, I do not know them."

"Even I know none that have not covered their hands in innocent blood." The shaman considered her for several heartbeats, then rose again. "You will eat before you return to your tribe," they instructed. "You have grown, and you learn quickly. But there is no growth in my training you now. Not unless you can give me what your duty to your tribe commands.

"That duty is a worthy one, Brushfire Hammerhead, but it will cost you the full use of the power you command." They chuckled. "Unless, I guess, your elvar captain will teach you *their* ways of power."

"Crystals will shatter and speak the secrets of the spheres first, I fear," Brushfire conceded. "I have heard of elvar training halvar and darvar—and receiving training likewise—but never gobvar.

"No one trains our people but our people."

"Such is my knowledge as well," the shaman agreed. They were filling a pot with various ingredients from the cupboards as they spoke. "I cannot teach you any more. But I will feed you before I send you on.

"A final duty, I think."

Leaving the cave, Brushfire had to blink against the crystallight as her eyes adjusted. Blueswallow was the outermost of half a dozen worldlets orbiting the large light crystal at the heart of the sphere of Birdsbreath.

One of the birds the worldlet was named for dove at her a moment later, followed by several of its friends. They hadn't bothered her the previous clock-day—which told her that *someone's* eggs had started hatching.

"Peace, little sisters," she murmured. They were only trying to drive her off…and she was quite willing to *be* driven off. The shaman's cave was hidden away in a chunk of wilderness on the edge of the port city of Rising Swallow.

Or at the *base* of the city, to be more accurate. Rising Swallow was built onto a pair of mountains that emerged from the spin-line of Blueswallow, rocky natural structures that rose almost a league high from the worldlet's surface.

The line between air and aether grew…*fuzzy* at the peaks of such mountains, but they also made for easier spaces to dock aether ships without needing to risk bringing them close to the ground and the lodestone core of the worldlet.

It spoke deeply of the status of Brushfire's people that most employment for gobvar would be found at the peaks of the mountains, where their ability to breathe and work in aether was absolutely critical, but the battered and cheap neighborhoods her people had to live in were at the very bottom of the mountains.

Every clock-day, those workers made the long trek up the mountains, ascending staircases and switchbacking roads to reach workplaces no one else could breathe in. There were gondolas that made the same journey in half the time…but from what Brushfire knew of the wages paid to the dockworkers, few if any of them could afford to pay those prices regularly.

After a clock-day of fasting and magical workings, Brushfire was prepared to make that sacrifice for herself. The guards at the gondola station looked at her askance as she entered, and she made herself feel and look as small and inoffensive as possible.

That was hard, not least because the darvar guards were half a yard shorter than she was and narrower across the shoulders. They had granite-gray skin that blended into undyed wool overcoats and steel chain mail armor—but the battlewands and blades on their harnesses gleamed with fresh oil.

Brushfire could take the four guards with ease, but that would do neither herself nor those of her people who had to live there any favors.

"Gondola's closed," the ticket seller grunted as she stepped up to the kiosk. "You're out of luck for the day."

Brushfire could *see* half a dozen halvar walking through the gateway toward the vehicle. The gondola itself was completely empty, and the passengers she could see wouldn't even half-fill it.

"Are you serious?" she asked, gesturing at the open gate.

"Gondola's closed for *you*," the halvar said with a brilliant white smile. "Takes half a clock-day to clean the stink out after your horns wander through."

It would take almost no power for Brushfire to walk through the pathetic barrier between her and the ticket seller. Breaking the halvar wouldn't take any magic at all.

And it would doom her, her family and her people on the planet.

She inhaled heavily and stepped back.

"I'll be writing a complaint," she warned the seller.

"Don't care. Get out of my station," the other var snapped. A small gesture summoned one of the darvar guards.

The small warrior did his best to loom at Brushfire. In another circumstance, it might have been funny. As it was, he was more threatening than his size implied…and the whole situation just stank.

Swallowing her complaints, Brushfire turned and stalked from the gondola station.

It seemed that, willing to pay or not, she was walking up the mountain.

CHAPTER

7

There were just over forty docks across the two mountain peaks. The largest, easiest to access and thus most prestigious docks were at the top. The smallest, hardest to access and cheapest docks were at the bottom—far enough into air instead of aether to be able to hire darvar and halvar workers instead of elvar and gobvar ones.

Skyfish was about halfway up the docks, which meant that Brushfire's long walk became more difficult toward the end as she reached the transition line between air and aether. It was easy, at least, to tell when she was approaching it.

Suddenly, the security guards who were keeping a wary eye on her were no longer squat darvar or thick-built halvar. Instead, the soldiers were now elvar—still shorter than Brushfire but slimmer and more delicately built than either of the non-aether-breathing var.

Brushfire knew from personal experience not to underestimate the strength or speed of an elvar. Few gobvar in these spheres made it to adulthood without seeing the wrong side of an elvar, even if many spheres—like Birdsbreath itself—were ruled by halvar kings or darvar princes.

The air grew thinner, began to change composition as Brushfire walked higher, approaching the dock where her ship waited. She could breathe aether as easily as air, but the transition was always hard.

"Eldest sister!" a voice called as she passed the last set of signs warning of the transition to aether. Any halvar who'd made it this far without magic or a litter with an air envelope was blind *and* stupid.

That meant the speaker was elvar or gobvar—and no elvar would give a gobvar that title.

Brushfire turned to see an even-larger gobvar striding toward her and swallowed a sigh. Fistfall Hammerhead was *actually* her younger brother, though the title he'd called her was due to her position with their tribe.

Fistfall's growth to adolescence had been painful to watch. The biggest and strongest of the tribe, he was also possessed of one of the kindest and warmest hearts his sister had ever seen. His size drew attention that his kindness couldn't disarm, and the big gobvar was actually *missing* a horn where it had been torn off by an angry elvar.

He'd learned even more tricks now, and she wasn't aware of him getting into fights for a *long* time…but she knew that took her brother far more effort than it took the rest of the gobvar, and a heart that had been as large as his muscles was all the more twisted and torn for how warm it had been.

And yet…somehow, Fistfall was *still* more of an optimist than she was.

"Brother," she greeted him, wrapping him in a tight hug. "All is well?"

He returned her embrace in silence.

"Brother?" she asked.

"All is not well," he admitted. "Windheart and I were able to keep the tribe working and occupied while you were gone… but it wasn't enough."

"What is it?"

Windheart was the eldest member of the tribe, older than even the elvar members of *Skyfish*'s crew. He didn't move as quickly as the younger gobvar anymore, but his hands had a precision unmarred by his fading vision or limping legs. Brushfire had never met a better sailmaker or tailor—or a wiser soul, though the old gobvar's scars spoke to the price of that wisdom.

"Axhand and Sparrowcall had apparently found a pub in the upper districts, close enough to stumble back to the ship from," Fistfall told her as he released her and turned to look up the mountain toward their ship.

"In the elvar districts," Brushfire presumed. She could *hope* her tribe's young troublemakers hadn't gone looking for drinks in halvar or darvar bars—not that an elvar bar was *better*. There just would be fewer people to beat on them in an elvar bar.

"Yeah," her brother confirmed. "Bartender seemed willing to serve anyone who was ship's crew—many are. We've more in common with elvar crew than they do with their captains."

Fistfall wasn't wrong there, but it wasn't *that* helpful, in Brushfire's experience.

"How bad was the fight?" she whispered.

"Squad of elvar in service to the King of Birdsbreath apparently heard there were gobvar drinking in the place."

Brushfire couldn't say anything to that. She could just about envisage how it would go. The soldiers objecting to the presence of gobvar, the traditional enemy of *any* military outside the Clan Spheres. The bartender, just wanting money, trying to make peace.

Her young fools would have tried to talk their way out of a fight, too. They'd definitely been fools to drink *anywhere* that didn't serve just gobvar, but they weren't fools enough to want a fight with *anyone*—let alone royal soldiers.

"Anyone killed?"

"No. Sparrowcall broke an arm, though," Fistfall said grimly. "Blackvoice and Firehand went with them last night, too. All four ended up in the district cage."

"Burn all spheres," Brushfire cursed. "I need to go get them, do I?"

"No, eldest sister. Captain Spherefox already did. Paid the bail and everything." Fistfall stared ahead, away from Brushfire. "You were with the shaman and we didn't know what to do. She bailed them out, brought them back to the ship.

"Windheart and I told everyone to stay aboard until you were back. I knew you should be done, so I came looking for you."

There was a long silence.

"What do we do, sis?"

That wasn't a tribesvar asking his—however undertrained—shaman for advice. That was a little brother who was worried he'd screwed everything up, asking his big sister to fix things.

Brushfire *always* fixed things. This one definitely wasn't Fistfall's fault—very few of the problems the big var was involved with were, as a rule—but it was definitely Brushfire's responsibility.

"I'll talk to the captain," she told her brother. "We'll get it sorted, pay her back the coin for the bail."

She exhaled, wincing at a spike of pain from her newly inlaid horns.

"We'll get it fixed," she repeated.

Somehow.

Skyfish was a triangular cargo schooner, with three sail decks merging to a point at the bow and a flared stern. Docked on the lower edge of the middle-quality docks, she was one of a dozen visible ships of her size and build.

She was in better repair than most of those others, a fact that Brushfire took a certain degree of justified pride in. Her tribe made up just over half of the cargo ship's crew and handled basically all of the maintenance. Some of that, she knew, was the inevitable flow of unwanted tasks to the gobvar…and some of it was that her people were cursed *good* at the work.

Fistfall followed behind her as she walked out the gangplank to the ship. Flimsy as the dock *looked*, it was solid underfoot, supported by well-forged iron trusses and reinforced with magic. The influence of Blueswallow's lodestone core was lighter up there but not light enough to allow the aether ship to float without assistance—and the gangplank provided that assistance.

The weight of two gobvar was nothing to the magically enhanced structure they crossed.

Skyfish's elvar Master of Sails was waiting for them. Brushfire knew Songvoice Tailor well, and something in her eyes warned Brushfire that trouble was coming.

"Cap'n's waiting for you, Master o' Sails," Tailor told her softly. "Fistfall, this ain't your talk to sit in on."

"Wasn't thinking it was," Fistfall said cheerily. "I'll head below deck, check in on the family."

The big gobvar swept past Tailor and headed toward the ladder into the ship, leaving the two Masters of the ships to share a long glance.

"He told me what happened," Brushfire said. "How pissed is the cap'n?"

Her voice shifted inflections somewhat as she spoke to Tailor. Language wasn't a barrier between the var, but dialect could be. She was readily capable of switching between the shortened cadence of lower-class elvar and the simple but extended diction of her own tribe.

"She isn't pissed," Tailor said. "I've seen the cap'n pissed. This is weird. I don' like and I don' think it's good for your fam."

"The fam will hold together," Brushfire replied. "We owe the cap'n a lot. I'll make this right."

"You'll try. Cap'n's on the foredeck. Luck to you."
"Thanks."

Captain Adamant Spherefox of the House of Wilds was extremely tall for an elvar, nearly reaching Brushfire's own height. She was still less than half of the gobvar shaman's bulk, a frail-seeming creature of skin, bone, and power.

"Brushfire," she greeted her Master of Sails as the gobvar stepped onto the deck.

Brushfire inclined her head, looking past her captain at the vast gap between the two mountains that hosted Rising Swallow's docks. There were a number of bridges, based on the same artifice and arcana as the docks themselves, that crossed that gap—but it was still a long way down.

And it *felt* like down, in a way that the vast emptiness of the aether did not. An aether ship in the deep drew the crew's feet toward the lodestone keel. Here, though, Blueswallow's core overwhelmed the relatively small effect of the keel.

"Captain," Brushfire finally said after a few breaths of silence. "I heard about what happened."

"Of course. I presume Fistfall found you," Spherefox said drily.

"He's a clever lad," the shaman confirmed.

"Let's go to my cabin, Brushfire," Spherefox said after another long silence. "This is not a conversation to be had where anyone can wander in."

The main deck of the schooner was utterly empty, in a way that was unusual even in dock. Tailor had vanished down the dock to provide security at the far end of the accessway. *No one* wanted to "wander in" on this conversation, but Brushfire nodded and followed her captain down the steps and into the cabin inside the main aftercastle.

Brushfire had never spent much time in Spherefox's cabin. The entire purpose of the captain having her own cabin was to give her somewhere quiet and private, away from the rest of the crew no matter what.

The handful of actual officers on the ship—the navigators and mages, elvar to a one—had spent more time in the cabin than Brushfire or Tailor would have, but even they were only allowed in when invited.

The cabin was the captain's sanctuary. There was a muffled feeling to it, the effects of an envelope of magic that contained sound and maintained the captain's secrets.

Otherwise, though, it was simply a larger version of the small cabins in the other aftercastles the officers and Masters shared. A table and chairs occupied most of the extra space, used for the very occasional dinners Spherefox hosted.

Now the captain gestured Brushfire to one of the chairs and grabbed a flask and two small wooden cups from a cupboard. Pouring a thin green liquid into the cups, she put the flask away and offered a cup to Brushfire.

"I am not certain I should be drinking," Brushfire said softly.

"It's firevine spirit. Take the damn drink, Brushfire," Spherefox replied, with no real heat to her words. Just…an underlying, overwhelming sense of fatigue.

Brushfire obeyed, accepting the cup and taking a careful sip of the liquor. Firevine was an elvar spirit, distilled from a plant native to the lodestone plates of the High Court itself.

The elvar had brought firevine plants with them to most worldlets they'd colonized, but the strongest liquor still came from the High Court…and from the darkness of the green liquid and the burn as Brushfire swallowed it, this was the good stuff.

On the other hand, firevine was what the elvar planted around their vineyards to keep pests and vermin out of the grapevines. It was *poisonous* in its undistilled state…which meant that "good" was always a matter of perspective.

"I'll make sure that my var repay the bail money you put up for them," Brushfire promised after swallowing away the burn.

"You and I both know that you and the other elders keep a third of their coin anyway," Spherefox pointed out, looking down at her own cup. "But I won't need that. Not this time."

"Captain?"

Spherefox sighed.

"Our var didn't start this fight," she conceded. "But they didn't start the last fight. Or the fight before that—or the fight before that or the one before *that*. Seven of our last nine ports of call have seen crew caged by local watchvar."

She shook her head.

"We are growing a reputation as a ship that brings trouble, and it's starting to impact my ability to find work, Brushfire," Spherefox said grimly. "Merchants don't want to send trouble to their partners, as a rule, and we are now known as trouble."

"Our *gobvar* are known as trouble."

"You know we don't start fights," Brushfire protested.

"I *know*," the captain agreed. "But carrots to worldlets, your 'little brothers' *end* them. The reputation has swirled around us for a few dances now, but it has grown hard to ignore.

"And the cost to this ship has grown impossible to accept."

That hung in the cabin and Brushfire swallowed.

"What...do we do now?"

"I have to look out for the good of the ship, Brushfire," Spherefox told her. "For the whole crew. For my investors, my family. My own reputation, even, I suppose. And while my *honor* demands that I return faith with faith...the spheres are not always as we wish them to be."

Now Brushfire was silent. There was no answer she could give that would change the decision Spherefox had already made.

"I hate this," the captain said softly. "I know that lacks meaning to you, but it's true. Here on Blueswallow, I can find new crew. And you... Your tribe can find new work. There are gobvar neighborhoods here."

Ghettos. The term, Brushfire knew, for the kind of run-down and segregated communities that her var lived in on Blueswallow was *ghetto*.

"You're putting us aground." It wasn't a question. It couldn't be one, but she needed to make the captain say it.

"You will be paid out in full, shares and wages, every last one of you," Spherefox promised. "That's what's owed, even if we both know some would find a reason to dock you."

Brushfire wanted to rage. To scream and yell at Spherefox—even attack her. The elvar was a mage, yes, but so was Brushfire. She couldn't match the power of an elvar captain with a focus, but surprise alone would carry her far enough to kill the other var.

But that would be a poor recompense for years of fair treatment.

"This is how you repay faith and good service, is it?" Brushfire finally whispered. "We were cheap, I suppose, but now we're *inconvenient*."

"Your tribe was *inconvenient* dances ago," Spherefox snapped. "My fellow elvar be cursed. I *know* I am breaking faith, Brushfire. But I can't find a merchant in Rising Swallow who'll hire me with a 'notoriously troublesome' gobvar crew.

"So, it's my gobvar or all my var. I won't say it isn't a choice, but I don't see a way out. I'm sorry."

"So am I," Brushfire said, still whispering as if speaking softly would contain her rage. "And you've left it to me to tell them, haven't you?"

"I'm sorry," the elvar captain repeated helplessly.

Like her apologies could somehow make any of this better.

CHAPTER 8

THE TOWERS OF THE Great Red Forest glittered in the night as Armand Bluestaves looked out. Eighteen of the stone buildings rose out of the mighty red-leaved trees around their roots, soaring high enough that the highest levels only held air thanks to continually renewed magic.

The trees of the Great Red Forest rose high enough that an entire city was built under their canopy, shielded from the bright light of the Shining Eye, a powerful light crystal, even during the day. The Shining Eye's light fed the forest and the rest of the…enthusiastic plant life of First Eye but was often hard for the people living there to bear.

Armand Bluestaves had been born on the worldlet and was used to it. He was still grateful for the night when it came. The sandy-haired halvar archmage could feel the magic of the Towers thrumming around him and smiled as he mentally touched it.

Each tower belonged to an archmage and their students. The reality, of course, was that Armand suspected there weren't eighteen halvar archmagi in the entire sphere, and only seven of the towers were claimed.

All eighteen combined to serve as the premier training institute for halvar magi across the spheres—and if only seven archmagi lived in the Towers of the Great Red Forest, that was still the largest concentration of halvar archmagi Armand knew of.

He was the youngest and newest of those archmagi, only having proven his position half a dance before, but his gifts were acknowledged by his peers…*almost* as often as his relatively limited knowledge base was pointed out.

Still, this was *his* tower. Bluestaves' tower. With a smile, the chubby small var bowed slightly to the other Towers that made up the academy and stepped back inside.

Armand was still in the process of rearranging the interior of the tower, but he'd done very little with the top level. No one had lived in this tower for over a hundred dances, and most of the top floors had been in disrepair.

Somehow, though, the observatory was intact. Given that it was woven of artifice and magic that was still beyond his knowledge, Armand had dedicated countless hours to its study—as had the previous two owners of the tower.

Their notes had been magically protected, carefully sealed away in a corner of the tower. Armand had read them all, which had taken dozens of clock-days on its own.

The centerpiece of the observatory was a large crystal the height of a halvar. From the notes and his own examination, it was a solid diamond, enhanced and aligned to an unnatural perfection with powerful magic.

It hung in the air, supported by a careful lattice of lodestone installations around the room. The inner half of the room was entirely focused on that diamond, with artifice and arcana alike focused on it to let it do...*something*.

Even the previous archmage residents of the tower had been circumspect about what the diamond observer did in their notes. Armand was *reasonably* sure he'd put it together, but it was still... risky.

This was old magic. The diamond had been aligned into its near-transparent perfection before the towers had been built. Potentially before First Eye had been settled at all...assuming there *was* a time when First Eye had been unsettled, something neither myth nor history were clear on.

Stepping past the crystal, Armand stopped at the other key part of the observatory—the one he'd already spent the time and resources to restore. The orrery of the Shining Eye Sphere was running again, once more magically linked to the crystal and its orbiting worldlets.

Eleven of those worldlets were populated, almost entirely by halvar. The Shining Kingdom was anchored there, and it was among the most powerful of the halvar realms. The Golden King was still an ally of the elvar High Court, but he could truly say he was an *ally* instead of a supplicant.

Between magic and artifice, every major lodestone core in the sphere was represented in the orrery. Only eleven of the worldlets had enough dirt and light to hold life, but the orrery marked over a hundred with enough lodestone to anchor the artifact's magic.

Several of those dead rocks were being mined for that very lodestone, the gravitational rock providing the keels for aether ships by the dozen—and *that*, as much as the population and armies he could command, explained the Golden King's position with the High Court.

The mines of the Shining Eye provided over half of the keels for the elvar's ninesails. The High Court's greatest weapon was dependent on the resources that flowed from Armand's home sphere.

But all of the resources and artifice and magic of the Golden King's realm had not yet solved the oldest of problems for the halvar and darvar realms: they could not breathe aether. Two of the four var thrived only on worlds with enough light and life to hold air.

Magic could create sealed spaces to carry darvar and halvar between spheres, but it took elvar or gobvar to crew the ships that contained those envelopes—and Armand knew of few gobvar crews outside the Clan Spheres.

A flicker of magic charged the orrery and activated its other function in a spray of light. Half a thousand motes of light steadied in the air, marking the position of smaller amounts of lodestone... *Refined* lodestone.

Each mote of light around the mechanism marked the location of an aether ship.

Another wave of magic set the artifact back into its quiet mode, and Armand turned back to the diamond observer.

He considered sleep once more, but it had already eluded him once tonight. He wasn't sure if insomnia was a normal side effect of being an archmage, but he knew at least a few of his fellows shared the suffering.

Something in the diamond glittered at him, drawing his eye. He stepped closer, letting impulse guide him as he studied the floating crystal once more.

Sleep wasn't coming, and he *knew* what the next step was. He could study the crystal for a thousand lifetimes without being certain—and he was halvar, not elvar. He only had one lifetime.

Inhaling deeply, Armand centered himself as if he was making a focus. The beat of his heart echoed through his body. The beat of the spheres followed. Both echoed through his power, flowing his magic out in front of him.

He drew his palms apart, bringing his power with him and opening two separate channels of his magic. The gold-anchored lodestone lattice started to *sing* as it felt his power, and he flung his hands wide, feeding his power into the golden sconces awaiting it.

The singing intensified, audible to both his magical senses *and* to his ears as the artifact around him woke to his power. The diamond began to glow with an inner light, the sparkle he'd seen expanding rapidly until the entire crystal glittered with power.

Somehow, it not only wasn't too bright to look at, but it was impossible to look away. Armand's power flowed through the device, filling the ageless diamond with magic and linking his mind and will to the observatory.

And then he fell. The lodestones flared in power and he was falling forward, sideways, upward…falling in every direction, in a way that was absolutely impossible.

The glittering light flashed, and for a moment, Armand could see nothing. He blinked and there were stars in the darkness. Blinking again, he realized he was floating in the aether—but also still in the observatory in his tower.

He was *safe*, but he was somewhere he'd never been…somewhere even an archmage halvar would have trouble surviving. He had no idea what was going on—until a brilliant flash of light drew his eyes.

A squadron of elvar ninesails in a broken line was battling a swarm of gobvar ships. Armand didn't know enough about ships to pick out the attacking ships beyond "those are gobvar," but they were big ships, large enough to challenge the ninesails he'd thought were the most powerful aether ships in existence.

Given practice and time, he knew he could control what the diamond showed him—but he needed to *get* that practice, which meant he was along for the ride this time. He wasn't certain how the diamond would decide what he was shown, but he doubted another skirmish along the border spheres was relevant to him.

And then the dragons appeared. A hundred yards from nose to tail tip, their bodies alone were a third of the length of the two ships they descended on.

Tails and wings and claws tore through the crews of the elvar ships, and fire ripped off chunks of the ships to allow the thaumovores to dig into the magical hearts of the ships. Ninesails were powerful warships, but against even immature dragons, they were outmatched.

Armand had enough detachment from what he was watching to judge the age of the aether beasts. Creatures *of* magic as much as creatures that *ate* magic, dragons were rarely seen. One was a member of the Quadrumvirate that ruled the gobvar Clans, but that was the only dragon he knew any details about.

Still, he'd studied them in books and he could see the signs. The frills around the two attacking dragons' jaws were too short and too flexible for them to even be adults. As they aged, the bottoms of the frills would merge into a bony fringe that protected their vulnerable lower jaws.

Their scales were similarly small and soft. Those would merge and grow over each other, going from a mesh of nigh-impenetrable natural armor to an overlapping layer of completely unbreachable defenses.

None of that was enough to save the elvar ships. One survived because they fled—but what were dragons even *doing*, attacking an elvar fleet in company with gobvar?

Armand had barely finished thinking the question when he found himself falling again. Spheres and worldlets and lodeplates spun around him, none pausing long enough for him to identify any of them.

He finally careened to a stop in the aether once more. He could see a worldlet beneath him, larger than most he'd seen in his books—maybe as much as three thousand leagues across. Water swirled across its surface—but he didn't recognize it.

He *did* recognize the defenders. Sealed fortresses, anchored on artificial lodestone plates, towed into place by elvar-crewed aether ships. Even Shining Eye didn't have many of the aether forts, but Armand had at least seen them.

Dozens of them filled the skies above this worldlet, with an entire fleet of the High Court Navy gathered around them. Armand didn't know the place, but he knew that he was looking at something that had rarely happened in history.

The High Court rarely gathered more than perhaps a score of ninesails in one spot. They intentionally made it difficult for anyone to count how many of the big warships the elvar even *had*.

But Armand's quick count suggested there were at least eighty nine-sailed warships in the skies above the unfamiliar world, supporting at least twice that many aether forts. It was a force unlike anything he'd ever expected to see in his life…and he wasn't sure why the diamond was showing it to him.

And then the gobvar arrived. There were no waves, no staged attacks. The Clans had clearly been mustering their forces in the sphere for some time, unchallenged by the elvar…and the reason why was swiftly clear.

His first vision had shown ten galleons and a pair of young dragons devastating an elvar squadron. *Now* a dozen dragons led the way, at least four of them full adults able to shrug aside even the storm staves of the forts and ships opposing them, and hundreds of gobvar ships of every size followed them.

There were even *ninesails* in the fleet following the dragons—and if Armand was inclined to assume those had been captured and crewed by gobvar, the diamond didn't show him enough detail to be certain.

What he knew, even before the battle was joined, was that the defenders of the planet he was watching were the most powerful forces the elvar and their protectorates had ever mustered—and that they were outmatched.

The dragons waited until the storm staves on both sides began to fill the skies with lightning, and then they moved. Magic swept them across the aether far faster than their wings could, and suddenly the dozen great creatures were amidst the defenders.

Chaos followed. With the most-dangerous enemies amidst the defending fleet, they tried to turn their weapons on the dragons…and only succeeded in hitting each other as the dragons tore ship after ship apart, consuming the arcane devices that propelled them.

The fleet of aether ships the dragons had brought could likely have carried the battle on their own. With a dozen of the great beasts in the middle of the defenders, there was no hope. Armand could see that the battle would take some time but the fate of the defenders was already set.

As he thought that, the spheres fell away underneath him again. He had no sense of *what* he was standing on—part of him knew he was standing on the solid floor of his tower observatory, but in the visions, he was standing on a piece of aether.

His fall was shorter this time, though the chaotic grandeur of the swirl of worldlets and spheres was much the same. He didn't emerge into the aether this time, either.

He recognized where he was, too. His viewpoint was from the top of his own tower in the Great Red Forest, watching as power flickered into the air from the towers. Ancient artifice merged with modern arcana as the archmagi of the forest summoned their power to some unknown cause.

With the content of the first two visions, Armand could guess that cause, and he looked up. A glittering shield of magic covered the sky, diffusing the light of the Shining Eye…but he could see the lights of the gathered fleet beyond the shield.

Cloudwood skiffs, made lighter than air by magic, floated beneath the shield. Armand couldn't see them well, but he could *feel* the storm staves mounted on their decks, pointing upward for when the shield finally failed.

Even as the thought crossed his mind, the light of the crystal was suddenly eclipsed. A trio of dragons slammed into the magical barrier, directly above the towers. They began to walk around on top of the shield, examining the towers through it like it was a glass wall at an aquarium.

It was then and only then that Armand caught the taste of the power holding up the shield. He knew the archmagi who had woven their power into First Eye's defense, but it took him longer than it should have to recognize the central figure. The central mage, whose will and life force were the focus of the spell, was *him*.

A dragon's laughter echoed across an entire world, and the three great creatures gathered above the center point of the spell, looking down on the archmagi with…*amusement.*

Then all three dragons drove var-high talons into the shield, power pulsing through their bodies as they focused the natural might of the beasts into their motions.

The archmagi focused more power into the shield, and for a few moments, the balance of power and will between seven halvar and three dragons swung back and forth.

And then Armand Bluestaves felt himself die. The dragons had *lured* the archmagi into that duel of wills, and now their power flared along the balance, following the link between magic and mage to pour raw, unfiltered power into the archmagi's bodies.

They died as one…and the barrier shielding First Eye from the attackers fell. Lightning descended from the sky a moment later, shattering the defensive skiffs before many even realized the shield had failed.

And as the skiffs fell, so did Armand.

There was no blurring between spheres and worlds this time. He fell through air and time and emerged above another worldlet of the Shining Eye's sphere. He'd seen this place before, and it was difficult to forget. The Golden King had spared no expense on the marble expanses of his court, though those with the eyes to see had known the great court of the Shining Kingdom had been surrounded by defenses both magical and mundane in equal measure.

Those defenses were gone now, melted to wreckage by impossible temperatures that had turned the perimeter of the great court into slag heaps. Enough of the court remained to make it unmistakable—and in the middle of it, flanked by conspicuously disarmed guards, the Golden King himself knelt as one of the dragons oh-so-delicately traipsed across the ruins.

Time flickered. The court was partially rebuilt—but only partially. Where the Golden King had once sat, a massive couch, easily a full cable wide, drew every eye.

The occupant of that couch was an immensely fat dragon. It was hard to tell the difference, but Armand could see some of his own softness in the way the dragon carried its bulk and weight. Still an adult dragon, with a closed fringe and overlapping scales, but he wasn't sure the creature could take flight under its own power.

Not that it would matter. A dragon was quite capable of mustering enough magic to lift itself into the air regardless of whether its wings worked. And if that wasn't enough, a much younger and fitter dragon was curled up at one end of the divan—and a thousand warriors clad in black iron, a mix of all four var, stood guard in perfect lines around the divan.

All of those guards' attentions were on something Armand had missed so far, and he followed their gazes to the party of raggedly dressed elvar being escorted onto the plains by more black-armored warriors.

Their clothing battered from clock-days in chains, it took the archmage a full minute to recognize the formal colors and robes of the House

Heads of the elvar, the First Council of the High Court. Several of those House Heads were archmagi in their own right, and *all* of them were powerful mages.

Strange manacles—they appeared to have been formed from *teeth*? Perhaps dragon teeth?—bound all of the elvar's wrists, preventing them from using magic as their captors herded them before the draconic governor of Shining Eye.

If the leaders of the High Court were *there*, prisoners of the dragon's servants…this was not a future where the elvar saved Court and Kingdoms as they always had.

And nothing in the body language of the legions of black-armored var suggested that the gobvar were any more highly valued than the rest. The soldiers around the dragon weren't valued friends.

They were slaves to a var.

CHAPTER

9

ARMAND BLUESTAVES fell backward and landed on his ass with enough of an impact to hurt. Shaking his head, he blinked up at the suddenly dark diamond and swallowed his shock and discomfort.

"Why show me *that*?" he asked it.

He didn't really expect the crystal to answer and was unsurprised when it didn't.

A flicker of magic around his fingers confirmed that the observatory was still functional. He hadn't broken anything in his visions or in his fall—and he had plenty of padding to make sure the fall didn't hurt him.

Staring at the crystal for several more moments, Armand could *vividly* remember every part of the vision. That was unusual for scrying in his experience. Most visions of the future were hazy, wrapped in fog or even just dumped into the scryer's head in gibberish verse.

Still...

"Well, I'm *not* dead," he observed softly.

Still. He rose to his feet and crossed back to the orrery of the Shining Eye. A touch of magic woke the device again, and he examined the orbs of the worldlets as he considered. Goldeneye was the capital of the Shining Kingdom and the location of the court he'd watched the dragons take over.

Armand reached out to touch the model of Goldeneye and closed his eyes, funneling magic into the mechanism to allow him to *see*.

It was day at the great court, and the Golden King appeared to be on his throne, seeing petitioners. Armand knew enough to know that nothing he saw of the court would be reliable in the details—if nothing else, one of his tasks when he'd first graduated from the Towers on First Eye had been helping reinforce the anti-scrying wards on the court!

But the court was intact and the Golden King was alive. He'd *figured* most of the visions were of the future.

"Only most?" he said aloud, turning back to look at the crystal. "You can show me the past? But why…"

The notes he'd retrieved had been intentionally vague on just what the diamond observer could do. He was certain that, like the orrery of the Shining Eye's sphere, it could be used to see what was going on *now*—except that where the orrery would let him view most places in the sphere he was in and the mechanism was tied to, the diamond observer should let him see *anywhere* in the spheres.

If he could learn how, at least. Right now, all he could do was link in to the diamond and let it show him what it showed him. Armand wasn't sure *how* those visions were…selected, for lack of a better term.

He suspected it was at least partially because he'd *died* in one of them. Without any clear guidance, the diamond had shown him his death and the key points leading to his death and following on from it.

"So." He considered the observatory, then gestured.

A desk and chair flew out of a corner, settling around him as he considered his next steps. The diamond observer wasn't reliable enough for him to use it for details. That meant he was going to have to fall back on older tools.

But his instinct was that the first vision had already passed—and that meant that he needed to learn what had happened to that one ninesail that had fled.

Because even if Armand Bluestaves, Archmage of the Towers of the Great Red Forest, hadn't been sworn to the defense of the halvar and the Shining Kingdom—which he was—he did not want to die.

CHAPTER

10

THE COURTHOUSE WAS a simple stone building, only angled where it would help the structure withstand the currents of the dances. Elvar could build ornately, but the var that lived the longest thought in terms of endurance in their structures.

Shutters could cover the skylights in the ceilings to block the ever-present light of the Prime Crystal. The lodeplates of the High Court never turned away from the Crystal, which meant they never saw the night of a regular worldlet.

The shutters were open as Cat Greentrees stood in front of the bench holding his judges. The light of the Prime Crystal filled the room, but the skylights were designed to focus it where he stood.

The Hierophant was one of the farthest-out of the sixteen lodeplates that formed the High Court. Each of them was a flat world roughly a thousand leagues across, oriented toward the Prime Crystal to allow its light to fuel the life on their surfaces. The sixteen lodeplates forever carried out a strange interwoven dance around their crystal, trading places and orbits as they carried the heart of elvar civilization around.

That dance took three hundred and sixty clock-days and was the primary marker of time for the elvar and most of the associated halvar and darvar kingdoms.

Despite the Hierophant's distance from the Prime Crystal, the light focused in on Cat made it difficult for him to see anything, let alone identify the five senior Navy Lord Commanders who sat in judgment of his choices.

There was no audience. That wasn't how the High Court Navy did business. Each witness had been interviewed alone with the court. A single aide transcribed everything said, but the records were often sealed.

The Navy did not air its dirty laundry in public.

"Captain Cat Greentrees of the House of Forests," the central judge greeted him. "We have read your report, interviewed your officers and, indeed, interviewed you. We prepare to make our decision, but our questions until now have been around *what* happened."

Cat nodded calmly, reminding himself of Crystal Voice's words. *All this is shadow.*

"We recognize and appreciate your forthrightness and openness in explaining *what* you did," the shadow-enshrined Lord Commander told him. "Therefore, the court has decided to allow you the grace of explaining your thoughts and your intent.

"We know what happened," a second judge noted. "We know the orders you gave."

"We even know that several of your officers attempted to conceal the final orders Lord Commander Bronzemelter gave you from the record," another judge noted. "While this speaks poorly of *their* judgment, it speaks to their belief in your decisions."

"So, we of this court feel we must understand *why* you disobeyed orders and retreated in the face of the enemy," the central judge concluded. "Speak, Captain Greentrees. You will not have this opportunity again."

Cat hadn't expected to have the opportunity at all. It was not the nature of the laws of the Navy to take *intent* into account.

He took a steadying breath, blinking against the light shining down on him, and tried to meet the gazes of the shadowed judges as best as he could.

"It is…the duty of a captain of one of the Court's aether ships to obey the legal and legitimate orders of the Lord Commander assigned over them," he said slowly. "This is the fundamental principle of our chain of command.

"It is also, however, the duty of any officer of the High Court Navy to place the Court and the elvar above any interest of their own. It is the duty of an officer—of a captain—to look to the safety of our people.

"Dragons have never before led a gobvar fleet in battle. When the High Court Navy has fought dragons, we have done so in isolation, dealing with single aether beasts by deploying multiple squadrons of ninesails."

Cat shook his head slowly.

"The nature of the attack at Shadowcastle was new," he told them. "The danger to the elvar and our protectorates if that offensive continued was…immense. A warning had to be given. My orders were to return to formation and hold the barricade.

"But if I followed those orders, the base at Forgedcrystal would never have known what happened to Lord Commander Bronzemelter's squadron. The High Court would never have known that dragons were working with the gobvar."

Cat considered his next words very carefully.

"It was my duty to obey Lord Commander Bronzemelter's orders," he told the court. "It was *also* my duty to warn the High Court of what we had seen. Left to choose between two duties, it becomes my duty to… face this court and accept your judgment of my actions."

The penalty for disobedience to orders in the face of the enemy was death. Only Crystal Voice's predictions gave Cat any hope of a different result…but he'd made that choice and he'd make it again.

"You understand, Captain, that the gobvar squadron engaged in minor raiding in several halvar spheres and then withdrew to Shadowcastle, yes?" one of the judges asked. "While we have chosen not to challenge them for a dark sphere, no dragons were seen in those raids."

"We do not doubt the reports," another judge countered. "But it seems that the dragons worked with the gobvar on a one-off basis, potentially as mercenaries. There was no grand threat."

Cat said nothing. He'd been allowed to review those reports as a prisoner. He had sacrificed his career—potentially even his life—to stand off a threat that did not appear to have existed in the end.

Of course, if he'd rejoined the squadron, he would have died anyway—and the thousand var under his command would have died too.

Cat was escorted to his waiting area, a glorified cell with a single skylight in the roof to let light in. Thankfully, he had a cord to close the shutters, blocking away the Prime Crystal's light for at least a few moments.

He didn't have a clock in the cell, and the Prime Crystal didn't visibly move from any of its attendant lodeplates. There was no way for him to know how long the court deliberated while he waited.

Eventually, the door to the cell opened and a pair of marines in dark blue uniforms collected him, delivering him back to the pillar of light at the center of the court hall.

"Are you prepared to hear the judgment of the court of the High Court Navy?" the central judge asked him.

Cat could tell it was the same Lord Commander as had led the court all along. He didn't know any of their names or duties—that was tradition. Anyone who'd served with him or was related to him would have been removed from the court, but he was not permitted to know who sat in judgment of him.

Whether or not he was ready was utterly irrelevant, he knew, so he simply nodded.

"Very well."

The courthouse was silent for several moments, long enough for Cat to wonder what was going on, before the judge continued.

"It is the opinion of this court that the facts of the events in the Shadowcastle sphere cannot be disputed, nor can your actions, Captain Cat Greentrees of the House of Forests. That you disobeyed orders from your Lord Commander and took it upon yourself to retreat in the face of the enemy is without question or challenge.

"On the charge of disobedience to orders in the face of the enemy, this court finds you guilty without question."

Only years of training kept Cat straight-spined and facing ahead. He hadn't expected anything else, but...that was enough. That was enough for them to take everything he was and execute him in the light of the Prime Crystal.

"On the charge of *cowardice* in the face of the enemy, this court judges that charge a crime of character...and finds you not guilty. Your disobedience is without question. So is your courage."

Cat remained frozen in the witness box. Whatever had been decided had been decided, after all.

"This court can neither permit nor tolerate breaches of the hierarchy, laws and traditions that maintain the strength and integrity of the Navy of the Elvar High Court," the judge continued.

"Nor, however, can this court stand to discourage future officers from choosing the service of race and Court over their careers," another judge declared.

Another long silence hung in the courthouse and Cat found a shadow of hope in those last words.

"You will be taken from this court to the Heartfall Prison," the central judge told him. "There, you will be formally stripped of all ranks, rights and privileges as an officer of the High Court Navy and as a mage of the elvar.

"You will be branded against focus use for thirty dances and you will be exiled from the High Court for the same thirty dances," the Lord Commander continued.

Cat was familiar, at least in theory, with the kind of brand they meant. It would disrupt any attempt he made to form a link with a focus. It wouldn't completely remove his magic, but without a focus, he was restricted to only the smallest magic.

And he was a child of the Houses of the High Court. He'd been born in the eternal light of the Prime Crystal, raised on the dancing lodeplates that held the beating heart of elvar culture. He'd *only* ever left the High Court aboard a ninesail of the High Court Navy.

But exile was not death.

He said nothing. He wasn't expected to say anything. He simply bowed his head as the marines returned to take him away for the last time.

CHAPTER

11

FOR ALL OF THE FORMALITY and ritual involved, Cat's visit to Heartfall Prison lasted only a few hours. His right hand still hurt from the brand burned into his flesh as dress-uniformed marines escorted him back out the front gates.

There was a carriage waiting there, but it wasn't the one he'd been expecting. His transport *to* Heartfall had been a black-painted enclosed vehicle pulled by a single draft horse. The carriage waiting now was also black, but that was where the resemblance ended.

Two elegantly groomed ebony horses pulled the carriage, clearly chosen to match the color of the vehicle. Delicate silver trimming covered the handful of metallic components, and the entire carriage thrummed with the power of defensive magics.

Enough so that it took Cat half a minute to realize *who* was in the carriage. By the time he did, one of his escorts had already stepped up to the carriage.

"Um, we're supposed to be meeting a transport?" the var asked.

The driver appeared from behind the vehicle with an unnatural suddenness, in the marine's face before they could react.

"We're the transport. We will carry Greentrees to the dock."

"We're to see him all the way to a ship," the marine said grimly. "Can't hand him off; those're the orders."

The driver met the marine's gaze silently, shifting slightly so the focus on his hip was clearly visible. The dark-haired elvar matched the coloring of the carriage, but he was clearly a full-trained mage.

"Orders are orders," the marine said. They were clearly intimidated, but they also stood in front of the Navy's premier prison. A single shout could bring a hundred more marines to deal with the problem.

"Fine," the driver finally said. "You and your friend ride on the back. Greentrees, get inside."

Cat considered holding out for an official transport—there presumably *was* one, somewhere—but there was no point.

"You have my word, marines, that I will not participate in any scheme to escape my exile," he promised his escorts. "My word as...as a scion of the House of Forests."

He was no longer an officer of the High Court Navy. His House was the one thing the court *couldn't* strip from him.

"We'll take the back seat, but we'll be watching for trouble," the marine told the driver with a firm nod to Cat. "We're tasked to make sure he arrives at the dock. *Whatever* form that making-sure takes, am I clear?"

Not every marine would have taken that order to mean they had to protect Cat. The ex-captain was touched and returned the nod as formally as he could.

Then he sighed and opened the carriage door, stepping through the defensive magics into the protection of his House's power.

"Hey, little brother."

Cat sighed as he took a seat across from the elvar in the carriage. She wore the blue-and-black formal tunic of her position as an Archmage of the Academies, though she'd left the formal hat on the seat next to her.

Hearth Greentrees of the House of Forests was a golden-haired elvar with deep emerald eyes, who'd been swarmed with suitors even before she'd forged her first focus and been acclaimed as an archmage.

She was also, despite being sixty dances older than him, Cat Greentrees' half-sister.

"Honored Archmage," Cat told her, with a small bow. "Is it appropriate for one of your stature to be seen with a lowly criminal?"

"The advantage, little brother, to being an *archmage* is that my stature is beyond the reproach and power of petty rumor and bullshit rules of face," she told him. "And if you call me 'Honored Archmage' one more time, I *won't* heal your hand so that brand doesn't hurt."

"Fine. *Fireplace.*"

Hearth laughed and reached over to grab his branded hand. Pain tore through him from the fresh wound and he hissed—but there was a focus in her other hand, and soothing magic wove over the brand.

"I can't remove it," she warned. "This whole mess makes me wish I'd got around to making you a personal focus."

"*Face*," Cat reminded her quietly, looking down at his healed but still branded palm. "In that case, *mine*. Carrying a House focus was a sign of respect from the House of Forests. Carrying a personal focus made by my *sister*, well. That would have been…weak."

"I'd say it wouldn't matter now, but you can't use one, anyway." She was examining the rune. "I'm hardly surprised that it's well forged. It would *take* an archmage to remove it."

"Don't risk anything on my behalf," Cat said. "I don't want to drag the House down with me."

"This is an interesting mess," Hearth said. "On the one hand, yes, one of our rising scions, a var we expected to be a Lord Commander of the Navy and perhaps even a hero, has been discharged, branded and exiled. We lose face for that, yes.

"On the other, the Houses know what you did," she continued. "We *gain* face for having raised a var willing to *be* discharged, branded and exiled to better protect the High Court."

"I doubt we come out ahead," Cat murmured.

"No. We don't," Hearth admitted. "But your honored father gave me a message for you."

Cat shivered. He hadn't seen Lord Commander Adamantine Bladehand of the House of Forges since the Lord Commander and his mother had parted ways, shortly after Cat had entered the Navy.

"He made me repeat it a few times to be sure I got it right," the archmage noted. "He said, 'It is in the battle between duty and honor that the worth of a captain is truly known.'"

She shrugged.

"I'm not one of your Navy types and I don't understand Navy honor," she warned. "Mages and Archmagi have their own…grazer nightsoil. But by my read, you have sacrificed your honor on the altar of your duty."

"That…was not the response I expected from my honored father," Cat murmured.

"Our honored mother, on the other hand, was much blunter," Hearth said. "There were others to hear what the Lord Commander said. None to hear what Mother said."

Cat waited.

"She said you made the right choice and she's proud of you," his sister told him. "Face and politics mean that she can't tell you that herself, but I can tell you that for her. She'll show the Houses the image expected, but know that your family understands why you did it and believes you did the right thing."

"But the Navy must enforce obedience," Cat reminded her. "And that is the fate I knew I would face. But the High Court needed to know."

"Indeed. Our mother is concerned about the dragons and is pushing the House Council to investigate." Hearth shook her head. "I'm not certain if she will convince Head Rainfall, but she is trying."

Rainfall Cloudwood was the House Head of the House of Forests, the elder var whose word was final for House members and who spoke for the House among the First Council of the High Court.

Ascension Greentrees, for all her relative youth at a mere three hundred dances, sat on the House Council by virtue of her skill and knowledge—and *also* served as Rainfall Cloudwood's personal doctor.

"I hope someone investigates," Cat said quietly. "I fear the next step of what we saw in Shadowcastle. Other than Old Bloodscale, I've never heard of dragons working with gobvar."

"And Old Bloodscale *rules* gobvar; he doesn't *work* with gobvar," his sister agreed.

Old Bloodscale was the ancient—potentially immortal; he'd been around as long as the elvar had useful histories—dragon that served as the oldest and most powerful member of the Quadrumvirate of the gobvar.

So far as anyone outside the Clans could tell, though, Old Bloodscale's rule was more on the order of "provide me tribute and service so I don't eat you" rather than more-active participation in gobvar affairs.

They were silent for a few minutes and Cat looked out the carriage's window. Magically blacked out from the outside, it allowed him to trace their route. The road from Heartfall Prison to the nearest port—on the edge of the lodeplate—covered almost thirty leagues. Even with mage-bred horses, they weren't going to cross it quickly.

"Where will you go?" Hearth finally asked. "The House will see a remittance follow you, as best as we can, to make sure you are taken care of. We cannot really employ you, not even outside the High Court spheres, but we can make sure you live an…appropriate lifestyle for a senior member of the House of Forests."

"Blueswallow," Cat said quietly. "I kept up a correspondence with my first Master of Decks, an old aetherhand who took a young noble idiot under her guidance and turned him into an officer I feel was mostly worth the effort.

"She has a bar in the city of Rising Swallow on the worldlet of Blueswallow." Cat shrugged. "I figure spending the next thirty dances being drunk and bored in halvar spheres is the least harm I can do anyone—and if I stay with an old friend, that coin from the family goes to someone I *want* to benefit."

"I see your reasoning," Hearth agreed. "I am not permitted to give you funds until you stand on the deck of the ship," she warned, "but you will not leave the High Court with an empty purse, little brother."

"Thank you," he whispered. "I…admit that I was afraid I would lose the House's support."

"You are stripped of rank and magic, not of bloodline," Hearth told him. "I *have* been told to make an alternative suggestion to your plan of drinking yourself into a thirty-dance stupor, though."

"Which is?" Cat asked carefully.

"Our honored mother wished me to remind you that a full formal pair-bond only lasts twenty-five dances—and a House can always use fresh blood."

He'd expected something of the sort and sighed theatrically—to which his sister giggled.

The elvar would live upwards of five hundred dances. They rarely permanently paired off, mostly relying on formal, term-limited pair-bonding for the purpose of having children.

Any child of Cat's in a formal pair-bond would be part of the mother's House…so long as the mother was part of a House, and roughly three-quarters of elvar weren't. If the mother was Houseless—or if she was of a lesser House and the Houses agreed in advance—the child would be of the House of Forests.

"I have never, in all my dances, been attracted to anyone who could bear the House of Forests a child," he pointed out. "Neither have you."

"To our esteemed mother's disappointed understanding," Hearth agreed. "Of course, since she is a *doctor*, she has all kinds of *suggestions* for solving that problem."

Hearth was attracted to women. Cat was attracted to men. He supposed he could see a solution to his mother's satisfaction in there, but it still didn't appeal.

"Warn our honored mother that I don't plan on siring her grandchildren in the halvar spheres," he said drily. "I have no intention of doing anything to bring honor or dishonor to the House while I wait out my sentence.

"Thirty dances is far from forever. In time, this brand will be removed and I will once more be a mage of the elvar." He shrugged. "I hope that then I can bring honor to our House once more."

"Most likely," his sister agreed, but her voice was sad. "I'm going to miss you, little brother. Write more than you did in the Navy, all right? Birdsbreath sees enough ships to send mail to the Court.

"Keep in touch and stay safe, little brother."

CHAPTER

12

Brushfire's horns hurt, and it wasn't the days-old inlay of her half-complete apprenticeship.

"That's all they paid you?" she asked Fistfall, looking at the tiny handful of silver coins her little brother had poured into her hands.

A moment later, her brain caught up with her mouth, and she sighed.

"I don't mean you're holding back, brother," she told him. "It's just… there were six of you and you were working all day."

Fistfall looked exhausted, new lines carved into the big gobvar's face by light and wind over the last few days.

"We spent the whole time up on the roof," he said grimly. "The new temple is tall enough that the priest was having trouble finding workers to work at the top. Heights don't bother us, so…"

Axhand, Blackvoice and Firehand were out with Fistfall every clockday. Brushfire was trying to rotate the groups who went out into town to find work, to keep too much of the burden from falling on any one of her people…but those four, each for their own reasons, felt at fault for what had happened.

They were also all riggers and had spent dance after dance hanging out in the aether on tiny chunks of wood and rope. The upper rafters of the new Temple of the First Sphere were nothing compared to that.

But even unskilled labor usually paid five or six silver pennies a clockday in Rising Swallow, from what the better listeners in the tribe had gathered. The least Fistfall and his companions should have brought back was thirty silver pence.

Even having stepped up to do work the Temple couldn't get others to do, Brushfire's little brother had brought her eighteen silver coins. They'd been paid *half* of what their time alone was worth, nevermind the skills that highly trained and experienced aether-ship riggers had brought to the construction site.

"You did what you could," she assured her brother. "Here."

She split the coin into two piles, twelve pennies for the tribe and six for the gobvar who'd done the work. "Make sure Axhand and the others get a coin each," she told him. "It's poor recompense for the work you're all putting in."

"They don't want it," Fistfall said levelly, not touching the money. "We all contribute to the family, eldest sister. We need to make sure everyone eats."

Brushfire wanted to argue with him, to insist that a single penny for their clock-day's work was already too little for them to keep...but she also knew how hard it was getting to feed a hundred and four mouths camped in a field on the edge of the gobvar ghetto.

"You know none of you did anything wrong, right?" she asked gently.

"There's knowing and there's *knowing*, eldest sister," he told her. "Until we're shipboard again and leave this muddy field behind...the var who got in that fight are going to feel it was them. And I should have kept them home, regardless."

Brushfire sighed and pulled her brother into a tight hug.

"You did nothing wrong," she whispered in his ear. "Just the way of the spheres, sometimes."

She let him lean into her for a long moment, pretending that *she* needed the support, then released him.

"Go get some food, Fistfall," she ordered. "And let Petal give you seconds, brother. You're no good to anyone if you waste away. Let her fuss over you."

Petal wasn't *officially* her brother's partner and he flushed at Brushfire's instruction. Sooner or later, the pair would sort things out, she figured, but until then...she'd lean on her status as the tribe's shaman to help her brother see the obvious.

Brushfire remained on the perimeter of their crude camp as Fistfall headed inward, keeping a careful eye on the surroundings. The field wasn't officially part of a park or anything of the sort, so far as she could tell. Just an open camping ground, likely used by other tribes for similar purposes in the past.

They'd spent a good chunk of their existing coin just purchasing the tents and pots and such to be able to set up camp at all, and Brushfire worried about how long their remaining funds would last.

"Eldest sister," a voice murmured. She looked up to see Sparrowcall approaching. The gobvar carpenter's arm was still in a sling—Spherefox had been kind enough to heal the break, but the arm still needed to finish healing, and Brushfire wasn't letting him work yet.

"We have a guest," the injured carpenter told her—and his tone set Brushfire's horns on edge before she even saw the var following her tribesvar.

Regardless of race, there was a certain type of var that Brushfire could recognize anywhere in the spheres. In this case, the individual was darvar and barely came up to Sparrowcall's chest. They were almost as broad as the carpenter, though, and far better dressed.

The darvar didn't seem concerned about traipsing through mud in their silver-buckled black leather shoes, walking with the kind of disregard that spoke of a var whose shoes were cleaned by someone *else*.

"You are the leader of this...assemblage?" the darvar asked, gesturing around at the tribe.

"I am the shaman of the Hammerhead tribe, yes," Brushfire confirmed. "Sparrowcall, return to your watch, please."

"Of course, eldest sister."

Her tribesvar had the same sense of something very wrong as she did. Well dressed and soft-spoken or not, something about this darvar made Brushfire's horns crawl.

The stranger waited for Sparrowcall to move far enough away to at least pretend he couldn't hear, then smiled emptily at Brushfire.

"I am Virtuous Axhead," he introduced himself with a small bow. "I speak for certain...commercial interests in the city of Rising Swallow. Those interests, among others, include the legal ownership of this parcel of land your tribe has set up on."

"There was no one here when we arrived," Brushfire said, very carefully.

"The land was not in use, no, but that doesn't change ownership," Axhead told her. "Since it was not in use, though, my employers believe we can come to a reasonable compromise. Don't you, Shaman Hammerhead?"

Brushfire wasn't entirely sure she believed the darvar's claims of ownership. She *was* sure, however, that the darvar's employers could make her tribe's existence extraordinarily unpleasant.

"A compromise sounds promising," she told him. "Several of my people are finding work around the city with their skills, but we hope to keep our presence here temporary. We are trained as aether-ship crew and hope to sign on with a new ship soon."

"A positive hope, I agree," Axhead said. "I'm sure you agree, then, that it is reasonable for us to ask for a small token to cover some of the rent we would normally expect to collect for these grounds."

He waved a hand to generously encompass the park.

"Say, a mere two golden sparrows a clock-day."

Brushfire managed not to clench her fists visibly. The spike of anger she swallowed down was dangerous. Axhead was almost certainly speaking for the local crime guilds, after all.

But the entire amount that Fistfall had handed her, the wages for six skilled gobvar for a clock-day, barely translated to a *single* golden sparrow.

If her people were making the wages they should have been or if she could somehow find work for them all, Axhead's demand was entirely doable. As the last few clock-days had gone, however, they couldn't afford that.

And she suspected that the guild representative *knew* that.

"We can cover that for a few days," she said, as levelly as she could, "but it does seem a rich price for a patch of bare mud."

"Were it *your* mud, that would be your call to make," Axhead replied. "But since it is *our* mud and you have occupied it without permission…"

He spread his hands.

"It is not the place of the thief to place a price on what they have stolen, is it?" he asked bluntly. "Two gold sparrows a day, Shaman. Or you will find this patch of mud much less pleasant than it already is."

Axhead's smiles never reached his eyes. He was trying to appear kindly and supportive, even as his words were an ultimatum, but his eyes were flat throughout.

"Very well," she told him. "Come back tomorrow and I'll have your two sparrows."

"You've been here for ten clock-days already," he pointed out. "We are owed twenty gold, Shaman. I would be remiss in my duties to my employers were I to leave here without payment for the time already spent."

Twenty gold sparrows were thirty clock-days of wages for a skilled worker—like a senior carpenter or rigger, though the pay rates were somewhat different for aether-ship crew. The exchange between silver and gold varied from sphere to sphere as well, mostly with the weight of the coins.

Weight for weight, a given gold coin was usually worth twenty silver coins. A gold sparrow was smaller than Birdsbreath's silver pennies, though, reducing its relative value slightly.

The tribe had been paid out and had pooled most of their funds together to support the family as a whole. Brushfire *could* pay the darvar's demand. They could pay that rent for a while…but they also needed to *feed* a hundred-odd mouths out of that reserve, a task that was already depleting it faster than the odd jobs they could find were refilling it.

"If, of course, that would be beyond the resources of your tribe…" Axhead said after a few moments of silence.

"It is not," Brushfire said sharply. "I simply feel that it is an unreasonable demand."

"We could always establish a…rent-for-service agreement, I suppose," the darvar told her. "We allow you to stay here unmolested and, in exchange, members of your tribe carry out certain tasks and duties for us."

And there, Brushfire realized, was the real goal. They didn't want her people's *gold*. They wanted to use her people as *thugs*. There were a lot of doors that could be opened—or kept closed, for that matter—by the presence of var who averaged a quarter-yard more height and width than the other races.

The ghetto might be half-filled with gobvar, but Brushfire doubted many of them had weapons or weapon skills. While it wasn't something they thought about much, her people had both. Service on an aether ship was never safe, after all.

"It is possible we may yet become that desperate," she told Axhead quietly. "But we both know what you're looking for, and my people aren't leg-breakers or thugs. They're skilled workers, born to the rigging and the aether."

"If you find a use for those skills, then paying the rent shouldn't be a problem," the darvar told her. "If you do not…we have a use for your other skills. We can reach a reasonable compromise, Shaman Hammerhead."

"Maybe," she conceded. "But today… Today, you can bloody well come back tomorrow," she ordered. "You'll get your twenty sparrows then."

"I said I wasn't leaving without them," Axhead pointed out.

"And I said you'll get them tomorrow," Brushfire repeated. She was large enough, even for a gobvar, that she had spent a great deal of effort training herself into body language that made her less intimidating.

But knowing how to be *less* intimidating also meant she knew what *was* intimidating. She shifted her body language as the darvar opened his mouth to challenge her, straightening her shoulders and lifting her head to make the full extent of her height and breadth clear.

Even without magic, she could break Axhead in half. *With* magic, she'd barely need to break a sweat—and she saw that realization in his eyes as he paused before speaking.

"That will be acceptable," he finally allowed. "I will send someone every five clock-days after that. Keep up the payments, and your tribe will be safe. You have the word of my employers."

"And if we fail to make the payments?" she asked grimly.

"Then I hope some of your brothers are prepared to break legs, 'eldest sister.'"

CHAPTER 13

"SIBLINGS-IN-MAGIC. Thank you for coming."

Armand Bluestaves looked around the gathering in his dining room and felt a small surge of pride. He hadn't *had* a dining room when the diamond observer had decided to show him a possible future.

His magic had allowed him to transform the long-abandoned dining hall back into something entirely passable, even for an Archmage of the Towers of the Great Red Forest. Given the nature of his guests, that was critical—though, of course, the five archmagi attending tonight could guess exactly how much of the place was actually repaired and tell that the decorations were entirely illusory.

Armand was *proud* of his illusions, though. They were and always had been his greatest skill. Any of the six archmagi in the room could carve a focus or fling a fireball. To conjure the illusions of crackling fires and sumptuous tapestries and make them beautiful took proficiency and art.

He suspected that even his companions would take time to realize that the servants were *also* illusions. He'd recruited a chef from the city around the roots of the Great Red Forest and hired a trio of promising students to help her out in the kitchen tonight, but the actual servers were constructs of illusion and force.

They couldn't do much, but they could follow simple instructions and carry platters of food.

"It would be rude of us to decline an invitation from one of our fellow archmagi," the young-looking green-haired elvar across from him said brightly. She smiled brilliantly, eyes that matched her hair flashing in a way that could *almost* make Armand forget that Patience Skyfall was several hundred dances older than he was.

The Houseless elvar archmage would have been gladly adopted or married into any of the elvar Houses. She'd *chosen* to remain Houseless and live among the halvar there. Armand didn't know why…and the youngest of the Towers' archmagi wasn't going to ask the oldest her reasons!

"And I, for one, was curious to see what you'd done with the place," a halvar archmage said. Herald Darkskies was the second-newest archmage and had been the "baby" until Armand had chosen to reside in the towers.

"I'm just happy to drink through someone else's wine budget," Forechosen Axblade told them all, the white-haired and golden-skinned darvar woman gesturing for the constructs to refill her glass.

Again.

"We can conclude from all of these pleasantries that the Blackshield is rude and neither curious nor thirsty," Red Strong Voice told the other archmagi, the black-haired halvar woman chuckling as she considered the empty seat.

From what she'd told Armand at one point, she'd been red-haired when she was born. The color hadn't stuck but the name had.

"The Blackshield is all of these things, yes," Skyfall said cheerily. "He also never leaves his tower. Don't feel offended, Armand. *I* only see him when I go to visit, and even then, sometimes he arbitrarily locks me out."

"Well, I will gladly eat and drink his share," Axblade said with a chuckle. "Assuming you laid on any particularly darvar dishes for him and me?"

"The Blackshield" was Portentous Blackshield, a darvar archmage who had been at the Towers almost as long as Skyfall. He was either nearing the end of a darvar's several-hundred-dance lifespan or had found the oft-sought key to extending life, but either way, Armand had never seen him.

"If we do not expect the Blackshield, then I suppose dinner can be served," Armand said aloud.

"If he is somehow merely late, I will take the blame, Armand," Skyfall promised. "Trust me, he'll believe that!"

Dinner was even better than Armand had planned or hoped. His chef was, he suspected, angling for a permanent job as an archmage's personal chef, and she was making an impressive pitch.

When the food was cleared away and the constructs had refilled everyone's wine, he swirled the liquid in his glass as he considered how to broach the real reason for holding the dinner. The other archmagi were also sipping their drinks and seemed to be waiting for him to speak first.

Finally, Skyfall chuckled.

"You had a reason for calling us here, and it wasn't to feed us," she observed. "If it was a tower-warming party, you'd have more than the kitchen, dining hall and bedroom cleaned up. Half of the apartment up here is still in dustcloths."

"Scrying through someone else's home is a tad rude, isn't it?" Axblade asked. "I figured the same, if only because Armand has *no* taste in wine, so someone else selected the vintages."

"The chef," Armand admitted. His taste in cakes and liqueurs was far more refined than his taste in wine, though *most* people wouldn't find him lacking. "And yes, I did need to talk to you all. Mostly because there is one more space I have restored that the esteemed elder archmage did not mention."

Skyfall straightened, all of her often-coquettish attempt to minimize her age suddenly vanishing into the focused attention of one of the most powerful mages alive.

"There is only one space in this tower warded against even casual observation," she said slowly. "Have you…"

"I have repaired and restored the observatory to full function," Armand confirmed. "Yellowstar's orrery and other tools are complex and powerful, but the concepts are easy enough to follow to undo dances upon dances of neglect."

Yellowstar Shadowwoods had been the first archmage living in the tower Armand now occupied, a near-legendary halvar seer and student of the spheres.

"Yellowstar was before even my time," Skyfall warned. "But I was told that he merely brought the observatory's contents here. Even he was only a student of the power he assembled."

"None of his notes survived," Armand admitted. "But the notes of the archmagi who came after him did. Between their work and my own, I have repaired it all."

None of the other archmagi seemed as taken aback as Skyfall. Something in her sudden focus told him that she knew about the diamond observer—and that she hadn't expected Armand to get it working.

"You play with dangerous toys, Archmage Bluestaves," she murmured.

"So do we all, Skyfall," Strong Voice replied. "I know what was in this tower." She shrugged. "That kind of scrying was always beyond me. If Armand can make it work…"

"The observer does not show perfect truth," Skyfall snapped.

"No scrying does," Armand replied. "The future is forever in motion, shaped by the interlacing tapestry of choices yet to be made. Only the results of choices fully set in stone can be guaranteed. All else is prophecy.

"But prophecy is not without value." He shrugged. "I tested the observatory. To learn to control it, I must accept what it shows me the first few times."

"It shows you death," Skyfall said flatly.

"It did, yes," Armand confirmed. "All of our deaths, in fact, and the events leading to and following on from those deaths."

A new illusion swept over the dining-room table, causing even the archmagi to recoil as their remaining snacks and dishes were subsumed by the image of the Towers of the Great Red Forest—and the magical shield conjured by the archmagi themselves in some unknown future.

With the illusion, as opposed to the vision, Armand had more control. What he was showing was his true memory—at least some of the other archmagi could tell—but he could accelerate and slow the flow of time in the illusion to make his point.

A series of events that likely took a third of a clock-day or more played out in minutes across his table, including the deaths of all six of the room's living occupants.

"Dragons do not lead gobvar," Axblade said as the illusion faded. "This is a strange future you have seen."

"It also showed me part of the past," Armand told them. "A battle between gobvar and elvar along the border spheres, where a pair of dragons turned the tide against our elvar allies. I have confirmed that this did happen, less than sixty clock-days ago.

"The rest of my visions I am certain remain in the future. A risk we know nothing about and a danger that eludes my attempts to scry any source of it."

"There is no reason for dragons to enter the service of gobvar or vice versa," Skyfall said grimly. "If this is a possible future at all and not merely an ancient artifact being misunderstood in its intent, it is an extraordinarily unlikely one."

"Perhaps," Armand agreed. "But I feel that it is something that must be…challenged. Its causes searched out, its course assessed…its creators met and defeated before our spheres burn."

The archmagi around the table traded long looks.

"The future is always in motion," Skyfall repeated back to him. "The present is as well. None of us are idle, my young friend."

"I believe you saw what you saw," Axblade said. "I even believe that this observatory showed you *a* future. But…what would you have us do? Breach the gobvar border and wage war against the Clans with just the six of us?"

"Investigate," Armand said. "Quietly, I suppose."

"Then you don't really need us," Strong Voice pointed out, "beyond our vague words of support and the resources provided to you as an archmage of the Towers. It is not within our remit to wage war against futures that are not fixed."

"This does seem like a task that requires care and requires an archmage," Darkskies told Armand. "But *you* are an archmage, the same as the rest of us."

"Our siblings-in-magic are gentle but correct," Skyfall concluded. "We are not unwilling to help, but we have our own duties and projects. I, for one, do not trust Yellowstar's observatory in the slightest…but I will give what aid I can for your sake, young Bluestaves."

Armand nodded silently.

"I will send letters to friends among the elvar," she promised. "I will learn what I can of this battle against dragons. I doubt it ended well for my var."

"Encounters with dragons rarely end well for anyone," Axblade said grimly. "Watch your step as you meddle in the paths of the great beasts of the aether, Armand. They are not var and they neither think nor believe as we do."

"The spheres shape as they shape," Darkskies concluded. "There is a limit to how much weight we can put on the visions we have of the future. A thousand choices must line up in a thousand specific ways for any vision to come to pass."

"This feels…heavier than that," Armand admitted. "I worry that the course of fate is already being led down this path."

"Then as an archmage of the Towers, you are both able and charged to face it," Skyfall told him. "We will aid as we can, and the resources of the Towers are always yours to command. But this future you have foreseen… If you feel it must be stopped, that task is yours."

CHAPTER

14

Armand wished his guests good night as they left his tower. They hadn't been as much help as he'd hoped, but they'd given him a lot to think about. There were downsides to being an archmage, he was realizing—and the biggest one was the assumption that you didn't *need* help.

With the massive trees overhead, it was dark at the base of the tower. The paths leading away toward the other towers and the rest of the city were gently illuminated by crystal lamps, but he still missed the young var approaching until she appeared out of the night into the courtyard.

She was a shapely young darvar who barely came up to his shoulder, wearing a tightly fitted dark gray tunic and cloak that blended into the shadowy twilight.

"Lord Archmage?" she said aloud as she spotted him standing at the door. "Archmage Bluestaves?"

"Yes?"

He didn't mean to be curt, but it had been a disappointing night. He sighed and shook his head.

"Apologies, miss," he said before she could reply. "Long night. Yes, I am Armand Bluestaves."

"My master, Archmage Portentous Blackshield, wishes that you do him the favor of joining him for a drink this night," the darvar told him. "He regrets that he was unable to attend your dinner, but thinks he has some wines that would be of interest to you."

Armand looked at the var in silence for a long moment. He was no true connoisseur of wine at the best of times…but after a second, he realized that the Blackshield was extraordinarily unlikely to be sending this kind of "right now" invitation over wine.

"I would be delighted to accept the Blackshield's invitation," he told the aide. "Now?"

"I can escort you to his tower now, if you wish," she confirmed. "The streets are safe enough, especially for an archmage, but I am used to watching the gaps in an archmage's vision."

That took Armand a moment to process, and then he smiled at the bodyguard.

"Of course," he conceded. "Lead on. I am at the Blackshield's pleasure."

None of the eighteen towers looked the same, yet they had enough in common that they weren't overly *different*, either.

To Armand, who lived in them, they were as easily distinguishable as his hands, but he'd known strangers to get confused. He'd never been inside the Blackshield's tower before, but he still instantly recognized it as his escort led him out of the dimly lit trails into the main courtyard.

She didn't knock at the tower door or even touch it. The massive double doors swung open as she approached, allowing her and Armand to enter a main hallway that *did* look exactly the same as all of the others.

The bottom two-thirds of each of the towers was a school, and those sections were near-perfect copies of each other. There were both conventional and magical ways of reaching the uppermost floors, and his escort led him to one of the latter—what looked like nothing so much as a closet from the outside.

The magic of the portal chamber pulsed as they stepped through it, delivering the pair to the top of the tower, and Armand swallowed a smile. Only in a place as suffused with magic as the towers would the portals be remotely useful—they were difficult to build, notoriously finicky, short-ranged, and required permanent installations on both ends.

But they were *much* faster than stairs.

"I leave you here," his escort informed him as they stepped into an entrance chamber with a gleamingly polished floor. "Through those doors. My master awaits…and I serve an archmage."

She smiled.

"I have learned to avoid being involved in the archmagi's affairs where I can."

Chuckling, Armand nodded to her and crossed the antechamber. There was...*something* in the air there, a powerful magic he wasn't familiar with. It wasn't hostile, but it created an almost-physical pressure that he had to push against to reach the doors.

It released as he passed through the outer boundary of whatever spell it was, and the doors swung open silently as he reached them.

"Well, don't just stand there, lad," a gruff voice declared. "Get in here."

Obediently, Armand stepped through the doors. They closed equally silently behind him as he looked around the library he found himself in.

Someday, Armand Bluestaves would have the library expected of an archmage. For the moment, his collection was focused on quality instead of quantity, centered on a collection of ancient halvar texts his family had been quietly acquiring for dances upon dances.

The Blackshield's collection had both quality *and* quantity. Heavily built wooden shelves towered three yards high along every wall Armand could see, dividing a room that filled most of that floor into a labyrinthine maze of shelves filled with books.

There was an open space in the center with a table next to a magically contained fire. Two chairs had been pulled up to the table, and a bottle and glasses had been laid on its top.

The var seated at the table was potentially the skinniest darvar Armand had ever met. He'd seen the Blackshield only once before, briefly at the ceremony for his elevation, and he'd been too stunned by the events of that clock-day to truly register the var.

Portentous Blackshield was past skinny and well into gaunt, with heavyset features looking sunken with age. His hair and beard were thick and well maintained, with finger-wide streaks of pure white running through otherwise jet-black hair.

He was sitting next to the fire with one leg tucked under the other, examining the containment magic as Armand approached the table.

"I am old," he told the halvar archmage. "And a fire helps warm my bones. But with a fire in the library, one must always be careful with the containment magic."

The Blackshield chuckled.

"There's only one magic I care about more these clock-days," he admitted. "Have a seat, lad."

There were very few people who could get away with calling *any* archmage "lad," but Armand couldn't dispute the Blackshield's right. The second-oldest archmage at the Towers could call Armand anything he wanted, and Armand wasn't going to do *anything* about it.

He took the indicated seat. A glass of wine slid over to him, a warm scent of mulling spice and alcohol wafting up.

"I'm too old for cold drinks," the Blackshield said drily, his tone making it clear he knew he was repeating the same point. "But mulled wine goes down well. Drink."

Armand drank. He wasn't sure if the underlying wine was any good, but the spice mix worked with it perfectly. He suspected the other archmage had spent a long time working on the recipe.

"You were missed at dinner," Armand finally said into the silence.

"Aye, but that's normal for us all," the Blackshield told him. "Be careful as you work toward your ultimate achievements, young Bluestaves. I have created a magic unheard-of before, unrivaled, achieving *exactly* what I set out to do…and because I have done so, I am trapped in this tower."

Armand didn't understand, but he took another sip of his wine to cover his confusion.

The old darvar chuckled.

"In these upper chambers, no one ages, lad," he told Armand. "So long as I remain inside the spell, I am forever preserved. But every clockday—every *tick* of the clock—that I am outside the spell, I age toward the final fate of all var.

"By remaining here, I can extend my limited remaining hours for a long, long time," the Blackshield continued. "But leaving costs me time I cannot get back. Forgive me, lad, but your dinner isn't worth that."

"I understand," Armand conceded. "You didn't need to explain that."

No one had told him that the Blackshield had achieved anything quite so impressive as that—which, given the degree to which the archmagi talked about their various projects, told him that very few of their fellows even knew about the Blackshield's spell.

"Perhaps not," the other mage told him. "But I *did* want to explain why I was eavesdropping on your dinner via my dear Patience's earrings."

Armand took another sip of the mulled wine to cover his surprise.

"That shouldn't have breached my defenses without my realizing," he murmured.

"Hence the earrings," the Blackshield told him. "They provide an anchor that enables a surprising degree of subtlety in the scrying. I *suspect* that Patience knows which of my gifts can be used for that, but she hasn't said anything in a hundred dances, so I figure she's playing along."

"So, you know what we spoke of," Armand said.

"I do. And unlike our friends, I recognize that you are very young, lad. They are correct that this is your task, for you to take on or abandon of your own accord, but that does not mean we stand on the shore and watch you drown."

"You can aid me? But you said you can't even leave this tower."

"I can't, not for long," the Blackshield confirmed. "But *that*, my lad, only means I have spent thirty dances finding ways to learn what goes on in the spheres without doing so. And I have my own powers of prophecy, if not of a type that lends itself to the observatory."

"You know something about all this?" Armand asked.

"Dragons have haunted my dreams for some time now," the older mage told him. "I had less detail than you. My foresight is my least controllable gift, so I have spent little effort on it until more recently."

He shrugged.

"So, I have researched our aether-born friends in some detail. They are an interesting race, one that the var are quick to ignore or dismiss as mindless beasts." The Blackshield chuckled. "Old Bloodscale alone should convince them differently, but even *he* is often dismissed as an outlier that shouldn't be counted.

"To do so is foolish. Dragons are less intelligent in their youth than most var, yes, but they grow to adulthood and their full mental faculties around their sixtieth dance…and do not die except by violence or misfortune.

"Old Bloodscale is the largest known living dragon and therefore, one presumes, the oldest. He stretches some five cables from nose to tail, larger than the largest aether ships. Others are smaller, but any adult dragon is large, powerful and intelligent.

"What I do *not* understand is why they would involve themselves in the affairs of var," the Blackshield noted.

"They breathe aether like elvar and gobvar," Armand noted. "They don't need the worldlets that we require."

"They are at their most vulnerable when exposed to lodestone and pinned down," the Blackshield noted. "Our wordlets are not only of no interest of them, they are active *threats* to the dragons. So, why would these most ancient and strange of beings choose war? Why would they ally themselves with the gobvar?"

"Perhaps because of Old Bloodscale?" Armand asked.

"Then why now? The two immortals of the Quadrumvirate have been among the Clans for a thousand dances, lad. Why would Bloodscale bind dragons to their cause *now*?"

"I had most of these questions already," Armand admitted. "But what do I do? Do you know any of these answers?"

"I do not," the Blackshield conceded. "But I know where you will find them, lad. In the Clan Spheres, beyond the border."

"Past the spheres where gobvar raiders and Her Crimson Sisters will kill anyone who sails," Armand said grimly. There were reasonable gobvar in the Clan Spheres; he was sure of it. But Her Crimson Sisters, the priestesses of the bloody-handed faith with an iron grip on the gobvar's cultural throat, didn't pick reasonable var to guard the border spheres.

"I do not know the answer to that," the Blackshield told him. "Few are those who have breached the border spheres and returned to tell the tale. I know…"

The darvar trailed off, staring into the fire for several seconds without speaking. Armand waited in turn. He saw no reason to prod the old archmage. Whatever was going on wasn't going to be decided by a few seconds here or there.

"It's funny," the older var told him softly. "Prophecy, scrying, foresight. They give us keys, but they don't always tell us the locks. I know that *you* have part of the answer. I know *another* part of the answer is the Monastery of the First Digger in the dark sphere of Brokenwright."

"Do I know what those parts of the answer are?" The Blackshield shrugged and took a long sip of his mulled wine. "No. I *do* know all of the pieces of one thing, though."

"And what is that?" Armand asked, trying to think just what *he* might have that would provide answers.

"As I said, dragons have haunted my dreams for a long time. I have agents across the spheres who know to report anything about them to me as quickly as they can. I learned of the battle in Shadowcastle a while ago.

"Cat Greentrees of the House of Forests was the commander of the surviving warship. Elvar being elvar, he was stripped of his rank and command for retreating from the enemy."

Armand considered what he'd seen of the battle in his vision and shook his head. Elvar adherence to codes and laws, above anything *he'd* call sense, was…nonsensical to him. Even stupid, at times.

"He may have information I need," he admitted.

"If nothing else, if you want to breach the Clan Spheres, you'll need a navigator, a captain and a ship—and Greentrees is at least two of those," the Blackshield told him.

"A ship with the right gear to carry me," Armand said grimly. Most aether ships had an air envelope to carry halvar and darvar passengers, but not all. "And a crew, for that matter."

He still wasn't sure what part of the answer *he* had, though the nature of the spheres gave him some places to start. The archives he'd inherited from his family included some very old charts, after all, and he had the observatory as well.

"I…*feel* that you will find all that you need where you find Captain Greentrees," the other archmage told him. "My agents tell me that he is in the sphere of Birdsbreath, living in a bar in the city of Rising Swallow on the worldlet of Blueswallow."

Armand chuckled.

"You know a lot about this var," he said.

"Few var have met dragons in battle and lived to tell the tale," the Blackshield noted. "Not least because the elvar are notorious about their oaths and their status and their obedience to their laws. For an elvar captain to retreat to save their crew, well. Let us just say that Captain Greentrees has a rare type of courage."

"That may be useful to me," Armand considered aloud. "Thank you, Archmage Blackshield."

"Thank *you*, Archmage Bluestaves," the darvar replied. "You and I have both seen or sensed what is coming. I cannot leave this tower, and

I know how difficult it is to convince our siblings-in-magic to act outside their particular projects."

He chuckled.

"A failing I am guilty of as well, if I am honest. The aid I can give is limited, my young friend, but I will do what I can."

"Even if that is to send me into the Clan Spheres with a crew of strangers to hunt dragons?" Armand asked drily.

The Blackshield chuckled again, his eyes crinkling with amusement.

"I can help you know where to look for the answers, lad, but it's going to be up to you to do the actual looking!"

CHAPTER

15

THE SALIENT HUNT WAS a nicer bar than Cat Greentrees had anticipated when he'd made the decision to go drink himself into unconsciousness for thirty dances and pay a friend for the privilege.

It was at the low end of the docks district of the city of Rising Swallow, far enough down the mountains that halvar and darvar could breathe in the bar but high enough up to make watching the aether ships come and go possible.

The main dining room of the Salient Hunt was on the outside of the mountain, opening out onto a balcony supported by trusses that held it in the air. While Oathsworn Lane and her staff were working, the balcony and dining room were fully open to allow the guests to look up and see the ships.

Shutters and awnings were in place to cover the area during storms or at night, and Cat had already been drafted to help close them a few times. It wasn't an arduous task, not compared to climbing the rigging of an aether ship—and Cat was hardly the only retired High Court Navy var working or staying in the Salient Hunt.

Most of Lane's staff were missing at least one limb, though Cat was surprisingly representative of the guests staying in the dozen rooms concealed under the bar. He'd paid for a full dance in advance, but otherwise he was a decent match for the collection of former officers and noncoms of the High Court's Navy.

Long-term guests, staff and clientele were all of a similar breed. The ones who weren't Navy were still aether sailors—and they were elvar to a one. It was as close to being back aboard an HCN ninesail as Cat could get now.

After a few weeks, he had a routine. It wasn't one even he particularly enjoyed, but it was a routine. He had a table in the corner of the bar that he dropped himself into, and one of the servers showed up a few moments later with a bottle of brandy, a pot of tea and a plate of eggs.

"Thanks," he told her. He poured tea, added brandy and then swallowed down most of the cup of steaming beverage. He wasn't drunk yet…but he wasn't planning on taking very long to get there.

His head hurt—and the magic he would once have used to cure his hangover required a focus. He still found himself absently reaching for a wand far too often. It was *hard* not to be a mage anymore.

Cat was…no longer a lot of things, a thought that saw him partially fill the teacup with straight brandy and swallow it back in a single gulp. His hangover faded a bit, enough that the eggs looked edible, and he slowly ate his breakfast while working his way through the pot of tea.

With the plate cleared, he leaned back in his chair and looked up. Rising Swallow's docks were busy today, with aether ships coming and going. Small skiffs, built of cloudwood and supported by magic to fly within the worldlet's lodestone field, ran between ships carrying messages and last bits of cargo.

There were even a handful of warships, smaller sixsails flying the black-painted swallow of the King of Birdsbreath. While they were in service to a halvar king, those ships would still be crewed by elvar.

The massive fortified Citadel at the peak of the southern mountain would be guarded by halvar and darvar, though. With air held in the fortress by magic, it mustered as many storm staves as half a squadron of ninesails. In theory, the Citadel would protect Rising Swallow from attack from the aether.

In practice, Cat could think of half a dozen ways he could have defeated the fort with a single ship. It would take a good crew, but *Running Fox*'s crew had been that good. Now, though, he supposed he could probably make some money walking the King's var through the weaknesses of their Citadel.

Of course, he didn't *need* the money. But he supposed that getting drunk in the corner of a bar could get old fast.

As if that thought had summoned her, Oathsworn Lane appeared out of the corner of his eye, hooking a leg under a chair and taking a seat at his table without saying anything.

"Good morning, Oathsworn," he greeted her. "It's your table, I suppose."

"It is," she agreed. "You pay rent for a room, not the corner table. Planning on anything except drinking away in this corner?"

"Not today," Cat admitted. "Mayhap tomorrow."

"You've said that five clock-days running," she pointed out. In the case of another var, Cat might have suspected either romantic interest or a more maternal concern. He knew, however, that Lane's interests ran solely to her own gender—and that she was far too cold-blooded for anything resembling maternal concern.

"My coin fills your coffers," he told her. "I'm not planning on dropping dead in your bar. What are you so worried about?"

She snorted.

"I'm not worried, Greentrees," she said. "Just keeping a finger on the pulse. Seen a few var like you... Well, it's a place where var do things like jump over that railing."

Lane gestured toward the thin wooden railing keeping people from accidentally falling over the edge of the balcony. From the Salient Hunt, it wouldn't be a very long fall—but Cat got her point. There were definitely balconies around there with longer falls.

"I'm not that far gone," he said. "There's an end point to my misery, at least."

"Thirty dances." Lane looked at him and shook her head. "So, you've what, ten thousand clock-days left?"

"Ten thousand seven hundred and fifty-six," Cat replied precisely. "You stand to make good coin off me for a while yet."

"Damn waste," she said. "You paid more attention than any other Court-born mage I was ever handed as a toddling officer. I had hopes for you, Greentrees."

"Sorry for shattering them," he muttered, half-turning away from her to look back up at the Citadel.

"'*Shattering* them,' Greentrees?" There was something in her voice, and he kept his eyes on the fortress. He wasn't sure how to read the older elvar's tone. It wasn't what he was expecting.

"You didn't shatter my hopes, Captain. You lived up to and exceeded them. Not many Court-born House mages would choose their var over their precious *status*. More than just your money that got a place in my house, Captain Greentrees."

"I'm not a captain anymore," he told her, still not meeting her gaze.

"That's what you get wrong, I think," Lane said, reaching over to squeeze his shoulder. "The Navy can say that you're no longer a captain of one of *their* ships—but to the var who crew the ninesails?

"You're one of our captains. In a way not every var who commands a ninesail can be. You understand?"

"Not in the slightest," Cat admitted.

She laughed.

"Fair. But trust that *I* do." She rose. "Someone in the city is asking after you, by the by," she warned. "I don't think I have the connections to lose them, so watch the door a bit more carefully than usual, will you?"

Cat wasn't entirely sure who would be looking for him, but he kept an eye on the door from the inside of the bar as requested. The *last* thing he expected to walk through that door, however, was a formally robed halvar archmage.

The stranger was short, though taller than many of the elvar in the room, and portly enough to give the impression of being significantly shorter than he actually was. His dark blue formal robes did him no favors, the austere lines and colors intended to announce his power and position only making him look softer in comparison.

The stranger looked around the bar and locked on to Cat instantly.

Cat wasn't a spy or anything of the sort, but he could recognize absolutely awful tradecraft and a complete lack of subtlety when he saw it. Whoever the stranger was and whatever he wanted, he wasn't dangerous.

For certain definitions of *dangerous*, at least. Halvar or not, the archmage could probably melt the city off the side of the mountain if he needed to.

He reached Cat's table, looking down at the elvar captain, and arched a visibly ungroomed eyebrow at the half-empty bottle of brandy.

"Captain Cat Greentrees?" he asked.

"I'm not a captain," Cat replied, pouring a generous allowance of brandy into his teacup. "But yes, I am Cat Greentrees of the House of Forests. What do you want?"

"May I join you?" the stranger asked, gesturing at the empty seat.

For a moment, Cat wondered what the halvar would do if he declined—but it was unwise to toy with archmagi that weren't his sister. He sighed and gestured the stranger to the seat.

"I am Archmage Armand Bluestaves," the stranger introduced himself.

"I recognized the robes, yes," Cat said drily. "I'm not sure what an archmage wants from me."

His hand grasped uselessly at where he'd have worn his focus once. Archmagi had two advantages over a mage like Cat. Bluestaves was both able to muster almost more power without a focus than Cat could *with* one...and the archmage could *make* a focus, given half a clock-day and just about any raw materials.

Technically, only the latter was required to be recognized as an archmage, but Cat had never heard of an archmage of any of the var who wasn't more powerful than any regular mage.

"You were the commander of the ship that survived the dragon attack at Shadowcastle, yes?" Bluestaves asked.

Cat considered the archmage for a moment, then swallowed the brandy in his teacup. He considered refilling the cup with brandy for several seconds, then sighed and poured himself more tea.

"I was," he conceded. "It's not a pleasant subject, Archmage, so I hope you have a point to this."

He had no real desire to talk about his discharge from the Navy with a halvar half his age, let alone the battle where he'd seen multiple ninesails destroyed with all hands.

"I am investigating the situation," Bluestaves told him. "I have had... visions, Captain Greentrees, of a future where these dragons do great harm."

Visions. That word reminded Cat, and he twitched, clenching his fist under the table as Crystal Voice's last warning and promise replayed in his head.

"Captain and Shaman; Shaman and Archmage. Your doom is to be one of them. All that passes until you meet the Archmage is nothing but shadow."

He studied the halvar archmage for a silent second, then swallowed half of his tea and poured brandy into the cup to fill it.

"I have little faith in prophecy beyond the next few hours, Archmage," he conceded carefully. "Short-term prediction is critical in sailing and warfare, but that only makes the failures of *prophecy* more obvious."

"Believe me, Captain, I am intimately aware of the flaws and failures of long-term divination," Bluestaves said. "But part of the reason for the limitations of that art is that we can change what we see.

"I saw all we defend destroyed, Captain," the archmage warned him. "I swore an oath to defend the Shining Kingdom and all var."

In roughly that order, if it was anything like the oath Cat had sworn as a captain of the High Court Navy.

"So, you want to stop that fate," Cat concluded. "What do you want from me?"

"I want to know what you saw," Bluestaves said. "I want to understand as much of the battle as I can. I have, via the magics at my command, *seen* the battle at Shadowcastle. But I am not an aether captain of any kind. I recognize that I do not have the skills to understand what I have seen."

Cat was taken aback by the archmage's comment. First, that the halvar had somehow seen the battle. That was a level of divination magic beyond anything he'd ever heard of—and he was vaguely discomfited for it to be in the hands of a halvar! But it was also rare in his experience with his sister for any archmage to admit that they had limits.

"I see," he allowed, taking a mouthful of his mixture of tea and brandy. "I..."

He wanted to refuse, but Crystal Voice's words echoed in his head. And Bluestaves himself had just said that diviners could change what they saw. He suspected now that Crystal Voice had told him what they had to make sure he *didn't* dismiss Archmage Bluestaves when the halvar came to him.

He exhaled a long sigh.

"I was told that I would meet you," he admitted to Bluestaves. "The seer on my ship said that there would be a...trio. A shaman, a captain, and an archmage. I guess I know which one you are."

"A shaman?" Bluestaves sounded intrigued. "That is...fascinating. You are but one part of the plan I am putting together, captain, but there are no shamans involved in any part."

"Then I suspect we still have a surprise coming," Cat told the other var. "As for the battle at Shadowcastle…"

He considered the contents of his table for several seconds, then picked up the bottle of brandy and took a long drink.

"It was a mess," he told Bluestaves. "The gobvar came on as they usually do. Their warlords and leaders know how we fight—and we know how they fight. No one involved in the conflict at the border is incompetent, Archmage.

"The gobvar do tend to overestimate their strength, however, which allows us to generally hold the line," he continued. "It was a usual three-phase attack, opened with fireships to force us out of position, followed by light warships and then heavy galleons.

"I cannot say when the dragons came through the strait," he noted. "They were well concealed by powerful magic. Their own, I suppose?"

"Which is concerning in itself," Bluestaves said. "Dragons possess powerful magical abilities, but they are rarely *subtle*. It is more characteristic for them to hold an aether ship in place with their magic than to conceal their own presence.

"Potentially, someone had to teach them the spell—though the dragons would then put far more power behind the magic than their teachers had."

"If someone is teaching dragons, we have a problem," Cat murmured.

"And there, Captain, you begin to understand my fears," Bluestaves told him. "Continue; I need to understand."

"There isn't much *to* understand," the captain admitted. "The dragon strike was clearly coordinated with the gobvar. I'm not certain the cutter crews were happy to be sacrificed to cover the dragons' arrival, but that is…their role in the strategy."

"Normally to cover the galleons, yes?" Bluestaves guessed.

"Exactly." Cat shook his head and considered what he'd seen. "Once the dragons closed, the cutters pulled out. They were expecting the attack. The galleons stayed in, but they were more careful with their storm strikes to avoid hitting the dragons.

"It was a carefully coordinated, preplanned strike," he concluded. "Potentially even practiced in spheres on their side of the border. The gobvar are a dangerous enemy, but working with dragons changes the threat entirely."

"Thank you," Bluestaves said. "But...as I understand, the dragons never appeared again?"

"The gobvar raided several spheres near Shadowcastle before falling back on that dark sphere," Cat agreed. "My information is incomplete after that."

He wasn't going to tell the archmage that he'd only learned *that* much during his trial.

"Thank you, Captain Greentrees," Bluestaves told him. "They were not seen again, as I have heard it. I would *guess*, myself, that they remained in Shadowcastle. Now...you saw the dragons. They were...young, yes?"

Cat snorted. That was utterly beyond his knowledge.

"I never studied the biology of dragons," he admitted. "I know they were smaller than many I've heard of, but that is all."

"I appreciate your honesty, Captain," the other var said.

"I have answered your questions," Cat said. Crystal Voice's vision or not, he wasn't sure what else he could do for the archmage, and he was *tired*. He didn't *want* to think about the battle in Shadowcastle or his trial or any of that.

He was also, he realized, significantly drunker than he had meant to be. The brandy bottle was empty now, and it normally lasted him the entire clock-day.

"You have," Bluestaves agreed. The halvar appeared to be studying him. "I have one more, though, at least."

"Then ask and be done," Cat told him.

"Do you really plan on sitting in this bar and drinking yourself unconscious for *thirty dances?*"

"I'm not halvar. That's just the blink of an eye," Cat snapped. The brandy was loosening his tongue, he realized too late. That was *not* something to say to an archmage!

"We both know that's a lie," said archmage replied gently. "It's one I suspect you're telling yourself to make facing that trial less terrifying, but it's a lie nonetheless."

"I've answered your questions," Cat repeated, letting fatigue and alcohol slur his voice. "What do you *want* of me, Archmage?"

Bluestaves grabbed his hand across the table and fire *burned* through Cat's veins, his skin crawling as the halvar's power flared through his body.

Cat was familiar enough with the spell—he'd used it on more than a handful of overly drunk subordinates over the years—and it was not *intended* to be pleasant. The alcohol in his body was swept up in the magic, concentrating into his lungs…and then releasing in an actively painful belch.

But he was also instantly, completely, stone-cold sober, and he glared at the archmage.

That was not a spell to use without authority or permission, and Bluestaves had *neither*. Cat grasped for a focus he didn't have and then realized he was trying to threaten an *archmage*.

"Get. Out," he growled.

"No, Captain Cat Greentrees of the House of Forests," Bluestaves told him. "I have an offer to make you, but I will not bind you to a promise made on the wrong side of a bottle of brandy. Will you listen?"

CHAPTER 16

Y*OUR DOOM IS TO BE ONE OF THEM.* Crystal Voice's strange prediction flickered in Cat Greentrees' memory, and he sighed.

There wasn't much point being angry at an archmage, anyway. Halvar or not, half his age or not, Armand Bluestaves could obliterate Cat with a word and a gesture, and no power in Birdsbreath would blink at his doing so.

"Speak," he growled.

"Thanks to divination magic and tools I have access to, I believe I know where to look for the dragons," Bluestaves told him. "A particular sphere in Clan territory."

"Good luck with that," Cat said drily. "Unless you have a fleet somewhere the High Court doesn't know about, you're not getting through the border past Her Crimson Sisters and their chosen Clans."

"I have no intention of breaching the defended border," the archmage said. "I *have* a plan. I *need* a ship, a crew and a captain."

Cat swallowed. Part of him wanted to leap at the chance to command an aether ship again. But…to command an aether ship and navigate the aether currents, he needed to be a mage. Without a focus, he could sense the currents and navigate, sort of, but he couldn't control a ship's magic.

With the brand burned into his palm, he couldn't use a focus…and an aether ship's control wheel *was* a focus.

"I do not have a ship," Cat told the archmage. "I don't know where to find a crew…and I am no longer a captain. I am not even a mage anymore."

"Give me your hand, Captain," Bluestaves ordered.

"I already made that mistake once," Cat pointed out.

"I needed you to be able to accept or reject an offer in the fullness of your mind," the archmage told him. "You have my word I will do nothing further without your permission. Now give me your hand."

Cat didn't even need to ask which one. He offered his right hand across the table, palm up.

Like Hearth had done just after he'd received the brand, Bluestaves looked at it carefully. He took Cat's hand in his and traced a finger over the magical mark.

"Clever," he finally observed. "Imperfect, but it serves the task quite well."

"So, you see that I cannot help you," Cat replied. "I suppose I could navigate for you, but I don't see why I would *want* to be back on an aether ship at this point."

"Would you rather drink yourself into a thirty-dance stupor here… or follow me, command an aether ship and potentially save all var?" Bluestaves asked softly.

"What I *want* is irrelevant. I am exiled from High Court territory and my magic is broken," he told the archmage. "If I return once my exile is complete, they will restore my magic and I will once again reclaim my place in the Houses."

Bluestaves chuckled bitterly.

"Do you want to know what is so *clever* about that brand, Greentrees?" he asked.

Cat didn't reply, and the archmage's chuckle turned even more bitter.

"The brand itself is an anchor," he told Cat. "It doesn't do *anything* on its own. If you went to a tattoo artist in Rising Swallow…well, none of them *would* touch a High Court magebreaker brand, but even if they *did*, it wouldn't break the magic.

"But…" Bluestaves shook his head. "They will heal the *brand* when you return to the High Court in thirty dances. But they will not give you back your magic."

"And what makes you think that?" Cat demanded. "The High Court obeys its own laws."

"Because the spell anchored on the brand will have failed long before you return to the High Court," the archmage said quietly. "They won't be able to restore your magic because it will no longer be broken.

"The magic in that brand will only last about thirty-five hundred clock-days. A bit less than ten dances."

Cat stared at Bluestaves in silence for several seconds.

"They rely on my not realizing that to keep me disabled for the rest of the sentence?" he asked.

"And that you will have lost most of the habits after ten dances," the archmage agreed. "But that also provides a small opportunity."

"What kind of *opportunity*?" Cat demanded, trying to swallow the sudden spike of hope.

"If you return to the lodeplates of the High Court in thirty dances, the mages of the Halls of Justice will be unable to tell if your brand ceased to function ten dances from now—or today.

"So long as the brand itself remains intact, they will have no grounds to doubt or challenge you. You are bound to your *exile*, Cat Greentrees... but it is within *my* power to give you back your magic.

"Here. Now."

Cat was tempted. There weren't words in the language for how tempted he was—but he *also* knew that regardless of the status of his brand when he returned from exile, if he spent thirty dances acting as an aether captain, word would get back.

And yet.

"Save all var, huh?" he asked quietly.

"I think so, yes," Bluestaves replied. "My vision was of dragon-led fleets crushing our defenses, bringing the Shining Kingdom, even the High Court, to their knees." The halvar shook his head. "And it wasn't a victory for the Clans, either. The gobvar weren't even first among slaves... simply the first slaves.

"For untold thousands of dances, dragons have wandered around the edges of var civilizations. They have raided us, dealt with us, negotiated with us...but they have never served us and, with one great exception, have never ruled us. Something has changed, Captain Greentrees."

Cat sighed.

"You don't even have a ship," he pointed out.

"I have a line on that," Bluestaves told him. "And on at least part of a crew, though I am hoping you can help me find officers."

Cat chuckled and gestured around the bar they were standing in.

"About the only skillset you won't find in the Salient Hunt is *captain*," he told the archmage. "Except I guess I'm here, so I suppose that's a lie. I can talk to Oathsworn Lane and find anything you need."

"The first thing I need is a captain," Bluestaves said with a chuckle. "A var who can navigate the deep aether, who has sailed through the dark spheres and waged war across the sky. A var who has commanded, led, bled and served.

"Such a var must be a mage, yes, but mere magic is insufficient for the task before us. I require a *captain*."

"Then you should be expecting to pay for the privilege," a new voice pointed out.

Cat looked up in surprise to see Oathsworn Lane herself standing at their table with a tray holding two dark glass bottles.

"You got well into it before we could even ask for a drink order, Lord Archmage," she told Bluestaves with a chuckle. "I took the liberty of guessing—and assuming you didn't have much of a worry about price."

She put the two bottles on the table and slid them over to each var.

"I couldn't help but hear you attempting to recruit my friend here," she continued. "I never served under Greentrees as captain, but I know var who did. And I can tell you that he *listens*, where a lot of var wouldn't. If you want a captain, you can't do much better—but I don't think he should come cheap."

Embarrassed, Cat raised his hand to try and head off Lane's praise. He didn't actually *need* money, after all. Just having his magic restored was more than sufficient payment for the mission on offer.

"No, Captain Greentrees, your friend is entirely correct," Bluestaves said. He inspected the bottles on the table and inhaled a sharp sigh.

"Red Oaks Ale," the archmage observed. "I was not aware that traveled this far from the Great Red Forest."

"It doesn't, as a rule," Lane told him sweetly. "I figured your budget could swing it."

"It can," Bluestaves agreed, popping the seal on the bottle and inhaling the aroma in a way Cat was more used to var doing with wine than beer.

"And it can cover the wages of an expert captain, the price of a ship and the wages of a crew," he told Cat. "Master Lane, the going rate for an aether captain these days, please?"

"I'm not master of anything but this bar nowadays," Lane told him. "But the best merchant captains I know of claim fifty gold swallows a clock-day as a base rate."

"Is that acceptable, Captain Greentrees?" the archmage asked. "Considering that I will break the enchantment on your brand and provide you with a new focus as well."

Cat was about to agree when the last piece registered.

"A focus, Archmage?" he asked slowly.

"You wielded a general focus in the High Court's Navy, I believe?" Bluestaves asked.

"A House focus, belonging to the House of Forests," Cat corrected softly as the archmage drank his beer.

A general focus could be used by any mage but was limited in how effective it was. The more matched a focus was to the mage, the more power the mage could wield through it. General focuses were the most common, followed by House focuses that could be used by anyone in a House—the elvar Houses were very large blood families, after all—followed by *family* focuses that could only be used by close relatives of a single line.

And then there were *personal* focuses, made specifically for a given mage by an archmage.

"A personal focus would allow you to serve our needs best, wouldn't it?" Bluestaves asked, echoing Cat's chain of thought.

"It would," Cat said levelly. "Your offer is acceptable, Archmage. Though I don't know where we're finding a ship or a crew."

"The ship I believe I have arranged. The crew we will need to recruit, though I have some feelers out."

"May I make one last interruption?" Lane said.

"Your aid has already been immensely valuable," Bluestaves told her. "If I thought you were interested, I would attempt to recruit you for our ship."

"I am content here," the bartender said with a chuckle. "But I owe a *small* favor that you may be able to help me repay."

"I am in your debt already," the archmage said. "How may I assist you?"

"There is a group of crewvar in town who were released from their ship in one go," she said slowly. "I know their captain. She didn't *want* to release them, but the requirements of commanding even a merchant ship left her no choice.

"It sounds like you will be somewhat less…dependent on the vagaries of the shipping community than she was, so you may be able to offer them employment. I am told they are highly skilled, but they have struggled for some time."

"If they are skilled, then why have they struggled?" Cat asked. "This seems like a strange—"

"They're gobvar, Cat," Lane snapped. "It's a small tribe of gobvar that has made their living working as the core of an aether ship crew for dances upon dances. But because our var are bigoted *fucks*, their last captain was forced to put them aground."

A chill of anger ran through Cat.

"I'm not sure we *want* to take on a gobvar crew," he said slowly. "If their captain had to put them aside…"

"I trust Captain Spherefox when she tells me that the Hammerhead tribe are experts at their trades, calm in their demeanor and have suffered for the bigotry of our var," Lane told him. "I can guess from the presence of an archmage that your mission will not be easy or simple.

"You need the best—and many of the best won't sign on for 'complex and messy,'" she continued. "The Hammerheads are desperate. They need employment…and they are among the best. Everyone wins, Cat…and you owe me. For more than this conversation."

Cat exhaled a long breath and looked over at the halvar archmage.

"I owe her," he conceded. He owed Oathsworn Lane a *lot*. Just because he'd been paying to live in her bar and drink himself stupid didn't mean she'd had to take him when he'd arrived on her doorstep. More than that, he owed her for taking a young idiot of an officer under her wing and showing him how to *be* an officer.

If he was unsure about how his career had ended, he was still proud of the captain he'd been—and he owed that to Oathsworn Lane.

"Then it shall be done," Bluestaves decided. "Come, Captain Greentrees. We have work to do…and I need a quiet space to heal your hand."

CHAPTER

17

"Do I want to know what happens when we run out of money?"

Windheart Hammerhead's voice was soft as he and Brushfire looked at the paltry-seeming spread of coins in her tent.

"We will shortly need to decide what is more important," she murmured. "Feeding our family decently or not being thugs for the local crime syndicate."

Various var from the organization that Virtuous Axhead represented had continued to show up every few clock-days to collect the "rent." Brushfire was well aware she was paying thinly concealed protection money…but at least no one had bothered their camp.

"We're pulling a swallow or so of silver every clock-day when we're lucky," Windheart noted. "It *costs* half a swallow of silver to keep us all fed."

"I've been doing the math," Brushfire agreed. It was why she hadn't taken the time to see if her shaman instructor could give her more training while they were stuck. If there was work she could do for the Clan, she needed to do it.

Gobvar or no, she was a Master of Sails, and that was a title that conjured some respect in a port town. The handful of clock-days *she'd* worked were the only ones they'd come close to breaking even.

"We're running out of money," she told the old gobvar sitting across from her. "Another twenty clock-days, maybe. Then we need to start asking for volunteers to break legs for Axhead."

"You're assuming Axhead will wait that long," her eldest family member warned her. "I didn't meet him, but I wasn't under the impression that he was really after our gold."

"No. But he's extorting protection money so that *we* make the call of when we're willing to get down in the muck with him," Brushfire said. "If it's our call, then we can't blame him, can we?"

She shook her head, running a hand along her silver-inlaid horns.

"We shouldn't need to be doing this," she murmured. "We have a hundred people, each of whom should be earning handfuls of silver a clock-day, not these scraps."

"We knew, those of us who fled the Clans, what we were getting into," Windheart told her softly. "We knew that the crimes of our entire var would be held against us, that the reputation of Her Crimson Sisters would undermine us, that the border wars would forever taint us.

"The other var hate and fear our people, and not without reason." He shrugged. "But we fled anyway. Not all who flee the Clan Spheres make it, eldest sister."

Brushfire chuckled softly at Windheart using that honorific. He was almost *six times* her age. The Hammerhead tribe had fled the Clan Spheres over two hundred dances earlier.

"Was it worth it?" she whispered. "Two hundred dances of being outcast and hated. How could it have been worth it?"

"It was worth it," Windheart told her firmly. "Every last moment. Every last insult and derision and lie and mistreatment has been worth it. You are the first daughter of this tribe with the gift in great measure since we left the Clans. You have been trained as a shaman by the scattered teachers of our people here.

"But your sisters before you were taken from us," he whispered. "Six daughters of the tribe—two of my mother's daughters—were taken by Her Sisters. We had no choice but to yield them, and they had no choice but to go.

"Blood of my blood now weaves the chains that bind our var, eldest sister," he told her. "They are either broken to Her Will or no more. This was not a fate we could accept for any more daughters of our tribe.

"So, we came here. And it has been unpleasant," he admitted. "It has been painful and it has been violent, at times. But the crimes of bigots pale in comparison to the sins of Her Sisters and the Quadrumvirate.

"Yes, my eldest sister, daughter of my first-sister…it was worth it."

Brushfire inhaled, considering the small array of gold and silver coins. She'd been told that she would have been taken by Her Crimson Sisters in the Clan Spheres, but she'd never realized that was part of why her tribe had left.

"If we have made it this far, we will continue to make it," she finally said. "Whatever it takes."

Even if it meant that *she* would have to become a crime lord's enforcer to spare her family.

Whatever it took.

Brushfire had just finished putting their freshly counted reserves back in the locked chest meant for them when a throat cleared at the entrance to her tent. She looked up to see her massive younger brother bent over in the flap.

"Eldest sister, you have guests," Fistfall told her. "Strange guests."

"Fistfall," she said slowly. "Now is not the time to play games. What kind of guests?"

"A halvar and an elvar," her brother said. "The halvar's in archmage robes... Not sure what the elvar's supposed to be."

Up until Fistfall mentioned the archmage, she'd been assuming that Virtuous Axhead's employers had sent another set of representatives... but no criminal organization commanded an archmage's service—and *no one* dressed in archmagi robes who didn't have a real claim to them.

Archmagi were not a group of people to piss off.

"They asked for me?" she asked.

"For the Master of Sails of the Hammerhead tribe," Fistfall told her. "Not by name, but that's pretty specific."

"Indeed." Brushfire sighed. She *wanted* to think this was good news, but she'd seen precious little of that in recent clock-days.

"I'll be right out," she told her brother. "I'd say get them drinks and chairs but, well...we don't have anything to offer."

"I can probably manage chairs," Fistfall told her. "Some of us carpenters had been working on a clever idea."

The words "clever idea" when it came to Fistfall, a var Brushfire would trust to be anything *except* clever, were worrying. Still...

"Chairs would probably be good," she agreed. "I'll be right there," she repeated.

Her brother stepped out of the tent and Brushfire took a deep breath. Covering the chest with her bedding again, she straightened as much as she could inside a tent made for halvar, rotating her shoulders until some of the tension released.

An archmage had no reason to be visiting her people. She couldn't think of any *bad* reasons the halvar could be in their muddy camp...but she also couldn't think of any good ones!

Brushfire wasn't sure where her brothers had found the wood, but she recognized the craftsvarship of the chairs that had been laid out under an awning on the edge of camp. It was a darker wood than she'd ever seen aboard ship—ships were almost universally built of cloudwood for its mix of strength and lightness, though the masts were often sturdier trees—but she could not only tell it was handmade by her tribe but *which* chair had been made by which brother.

She guessed they'd been making them for sale and had been planning on surprising her with the money. Depending on who they found to buy them, that would have been a pleasant surprise indeed—her carpenter siblings were just as good with furniture as they were with ship repairs, and it might have been easier to get money for goods than for gobvar labor.

Now the chairs served the purpose of hopefully keeping the tribe from completely embarrassing themselves in front of strangers. Somehow, Fistfall had managed to provide an awning and three almost-matching chairs in the minute it had taken her to finish covering up the chest.

As she approached the chairs, it swiftly became obvious that there was *no way* the halvar in the archmage robes was faking it. Power rippled out from the stranger in unthinking waves. She couldn't *miss* the strength of his magic—it was unlike anything she'd ever felt before.

The overwhelming sense of the portly halvar meant she almost didn't register the other stranger. The elvar could almost have been considered the quintessential image of his var, a slimly built figure with shoulder-length blond hair pulled into a plain ponytail behind his long ears.

Something about the way the elvar carried himself, though, made the plain ponytail and even the simple gray tunic and hose he wore feel *off* to Brushfire. He didn't radiate power the way the archmage did, but in his own way he radiated...control. Composure. Authority.

In a simple tunic, in a chair in a muddy field a clock-hour's walk from the nearest ship, there was no question in Brushfire's mind that the elvar was a *captain*.

Swallowing the momentary hesitation, she stepped under the awning and took a seat in the third chair, leveling her best confident and competent look on the two strangers.

"I am Brushfire Hammerhead, former Master of Sails on the aether ship *Skyfish*," she greeted them. "How may I help you?"

She realized that the elvar was staring at her... No. He was staring at her *horns*, in a way that suggested he knew what the silver inlay meant.

"*Shaman* Brushfire," the elvar said slowly. "Yes?"

"I am trained as a shaman in the traditions of the gobvar, yes," she said carefully. "I am sworn to use my magic only to heal and to help, never to harm."

"She's the one," the elvar said flatly, clearly expecting the archmage to understand.

"I thought you didn't think prophecy worked," the archmage replied.

"And you said it can help us make decisions, didn't you?" the elvar demanded. "Shaman, Captain and Archmage. It's her. Lane sent us to the right place."

He shook himself and bowed slightly in his seat to Brushfire.

"My apologies, Master Brushfire," he said. "I am Cat Greentrees of the House of Forests. Archmage Armand Bluestaves here has tasked me to assemble an aether ship and crew for a mission he feels is extraordinarily important.

"You and your tribe came recommended to us by Oathsworn Lane, and we are considering hiring you to crew our ship," he continued. "Why don't you do Archmage Bluestaves and me the favor of, say, listing what skills your people have?"

Brushfire might not have been prepared to pitch her people at that exact moment, but she'd been ready to do so at any opportunity for clock-days now.

"There are one hundred and four of us," she told them. "Basically, the entire deck crew and a portion of the rigging crew for a regular merchant aether schooner. We have carpenters, sailmakers, cooks, ropemakers and riggers among us. While I am the only one gifted enough to be considered a mage, all of my people have some level of magical power and can work with the usual arcane mechanisms of an aether ship."

Brushfire was strong enough to count as a mage, but without a focus, she wasn't truly considered one. Gobvar shaman traditions focused on a very different path than elvar mage schooling, learning to use the body as a focus to channel power. It was a far harder path to walk than that of a mage with a focus, though she understood that master shamans were more powerful, in many ways, than fully trained mages.

"What about weapons training?" the archmage asked.

"All of us have some degree of training with blades, battlewands and crossbows," Brushfire told them. "We aren't marines or soldiers, though. Just sailors with basic training."

"And storm staves?" the halvar said.

"We've never served on a ship with them," she replied. "And, in all honesty, few elvar captains in these spheres would trust gobvar with storm staves. It's not a skillset we saw value in acquiring."

"Nor one I thought we were going to need," the elvar captain murmured, then shook his head into silence.

Brushfire's potential employers did not appear to be on the same page yet. That had advantages, she supposed.

"What about repairs?" the archmage asked, as if he hadn't heard Greentrees' words.

"Anything a ship needs," Brushfire said instantly. "Our carpenters built these chairs, for example."

She tapped the arm of the handmade seat she was in.

"Given the right supplies and tools, my people could probably build you an aether ship," she told the two strangers. "Of course, it would be done *faster* by a yard, but we could do it."

The lodestone keel was the only part she wasn't certain her family could make, given an available *forest*, let alone anything more refined.

"*That* shouldn't be required," Bluestaves said wryly. "But I will admit that the ship I expect to have in hand is in…poor shape."

If Brushfire read the elvar correctly, that was something else he hadn't been told yet.

"Well, Captain?" the archmage asked. "I may pay the bill, but the ship will be yours."

Greentrees looked down at the chair he was sitting in and ran his fingers along the wood with a measuring expression.

"Scrap wood," he noted. "Pieces formed together with glue and magic, till most couldn't tell the difference. Sanded and polished by hand, basically no tools. These chairs were made with hands and a couple of knives."

Brushfire hadn't looked that closely at the furniture, but at the elvar's words, she did. He was right. That was part of her answer, she supposed, to where her siblings had found the tools and wood to make furniture: *they hadn't*.

They'd made furniture *anyway*, with sheer stubbornness and skill.

"Standard ship rate," Greentrees said, looking up at her. He...didn't look happy to be saying it. "I don't want a gobvar crew, Shaman Brushfire," he admitted to her. "But it's a lot easier to assemble *half* a crew from handfuls of var than to do the same for an entire crew.

"There's...prophecy in play as well," he admitted. "We'll explain as time goes on, but I was told that I needed to work with a shaman and an archmage. When it comes to divinations like that, I sincerely doubt in coincidental matches."

"I doubt all prophecy," Brushfire said. "But if it's in my people's favor, I'll make an exception this once."

Even Spherefox hadn't paid her tribe standard ship rate. It had been neither offered nor asked for. Windheart and the other old hands had considered it more than fair that the tribe had averaged three-fifths of the standard rate.

"I'm not enthused myself," Greentrees told her. "But we will hire your tribe. I think, though..."

He fell silent and turned to look at the halvar next to him.

"I think that Brushfire and I need to see this ship, Bluestaves," he told the archmage. "*Before* I start recruiting more crew. I...did not realize it was going to require repairs *or* that it had weapons."

"Of course," the archmage said calmly. "You will understand when you see it."

"I hope so," Greentrees said. "And I hope that Officer Brushfire understands as well."

Brushfire blinked. She had to have misheard him.

"Officer, Captain?" she asked, very carefully.

"All I know about gobvar is about fighting them," the elvar captain told her bluntly. "If I am to command over a hundred of your var, I must know them better. But until then, I will rely on you to keep them in line and to keep me from making critical mistakes.

"That is not a task for the Masters of Sails. That is a task for my first officer." He turned a sharp eye on the archmage. "Assuming, Lord Archmage, that making the good shaman a focus is an acceptable addition to their wages?"

Now she was even *more* taken aback. It wasn't that there were no gobvar mages or gobvar with focuses. But she was a shaman and had only a limited idea of what to *do* with a focus—and she wouldn't have expected an elvar to insist she had one.

"You will need to teach her to use it," Bluestaves said calmly. "It would be a good idea, if our new eldest sister is willing, to learn from her in turn. You each have things that you can teach each other, from different paths."

He smiled thinly.

"And you *can* teach each other," he noted. "I can provide some training as well, but I cannot make you archmagi. Convenient as that might be for our purposes."

Brushfire was beginning to realize she'd acquired some very strange employers.

CHAPTER

18

Like most halvar rulers, the King of Birdsbreath laid claim to a single aether sphere but made her claim to the *entire* aether sphere. Not all of those halvar kings could make that claim stick, and the fundamental barrier was that their main sources of soldiers, the halvar populations under their rule, could not breathe aether.

There were mercenary aether ships that placed themselves at the service of whatever halvar or darvar ruler could pay the most, but most rulers regarded those as extras. Any ruler that wished to not merely claim but *enforce* rule over an entire sphere required at least some aether ships.

Sensible halvar kings went for sixsails, lightly rigged ships that required far smaller crews than the full ninesail warships of the elvar Navy. There were elvar living in most of the halvar kingdoms, after all, but not many. Smaller ships were easier to crew.

The current King of Birdsbreath was a sensible var. Her father, on the other hand, had been…less so, in Armand Bluestaves' considered opinion.

The evidence of that lay in front of him as his two new companions stared at the ship in distaste.

"Her Majesty's father, Falcon the Third, purchased two ninesail ships of the line from the High Court Navy," he told Greentrees and Hammerhead as the two studied the ship. "So far as rumor has it, *neither* ship flew more than a handful of times, and Her Majesty formally decommissioned them as quickly as was…appropriate after her father passed beyond the spheres."

The hull of the big warship was still intact, Armand judged, but he wasn't qualified to say more than that. It had been landed in a valley on the opposite side of one of Rising Swallow's mountains, half a league beneath the Citadel that guarded the city.

"I am told that the storm staves were stripped from both ships," he continued. "But I have already negotiated to have a number returned to us."

Being an archmage opened doors that would never open for anyone else. The Royal Navy of Birdsbreath was a competent force, one disinclined to sell warships, let alone warship *weapons*, to strangers.

But there was a real question over whether the ninesail Armand was looking at even qualified as a warship. He suspected that even putting staves back on the old ship wouldn't make her a warship again—but she had the hull and spars and mechanisms to support them, where a merchant ship wouldn't.

"She's a wreck, Bluestaves," Greentrees said grimly. "Even if Birdsbreath was willing to sell her—and I can't see a halvar navy parting with her, wrecked as she is—I'm not sure we could get her functional. And... *why*?"

"For the path before us, even the *impression* of power will clear our way," Armand told his captain. "Damaged as she is, it will be easier to install an air envelope solid enough and large enough to carry me with you."

"I assumed we would be leaving you behind, Lord Archmage," Hammerhead said slowly.

"No, eldest sister," he replied. "Too much is at stake and I have put too many resources into this task. As we repair our ship, we will build her to include space for me. Since we won't be taking aboard a full ninesail's crew, there should be space."

There was a long silence as the two var studied the ship.

"You've already bought her, then," Greentrees concluded.

"I have," Armand confirmed. "And the supplies Birdsbreath had laid in for her repair. I doubt it's sufficient to the work, but I have more resources."

The resources of an archmage were not infinite—but they were large enough that he doubted he was going to run out of money. Even if he did, he already knew he could access an effectively infinite amount of credit from Birdsbreath's banks.

Everyone wanted archmagi to owe them favors, after all.

"We'll have to build a frame to lift her off the mountain," Hammerhead suggested. "Until we've got all nine masts clear and examinable, we can't speak to how long this will take. Safety will be key. Her lodestone keel is intact, and while Blueswallow's core overwhelms it, it still has an effect."

That all made sense to Armand, but he wasn't the expert. He glanced over at Greentrees and saw the elvar looking at Hammerhead in near-disbelief.

"She's a wreck," Greentrees repeated. "Her starboard masts have to be *gone* under there, or she wouldn't have settled the way she has. She has no staves, as the archmage noted. Even with supplies…she'll still be a wreck."

"Give me a lodestone keel, the storm staves, and a forest, Captain Greentrees, and my tribe could *build* you a new ninesail," Hammerhead replied. "This? This is a repair job. Yes, she's a wreck. But we can rebuild her."

"My divinations suggest that we will need a warship for the task ahead," Armand told them. His work with the observer before he'd left the Great Red Forest had been clear, in fact. He not only needed a warship, but it also needed to be *this* warship.

Of course, as warships in Birdsbreath went, there were only three options: this ninesail, her sister and a single aged sixsail that the King was considering having rebuilt into her personal yacht.

There was something about the other two ships that wasn't right, some factor of sturdiness or reconstruction that would fail. Armand didn't know what it was. All he knew was that his visions were clear: he needed *this* ship.

"You're certain?" Greentrees finally asked.

Armand realized the captain was ignoring him. The question was directed entirely at their gobvar companion.

"The question is not *can* we rebuild her, Captain," Hammerhead replied. "The question is only how long it will take. From what I can see, even the worst case is doable—but the more hands we have, the better. And, of course, the less damage she has taken underneath everything, the better as well.

"We can do this," she repeated. "You have to have faith in the crew you've hired, Captain."

"I'm not great at faith," Greentrees told her. "But let's give it a try and see what happens."

Armand looked around the valley. It was clearly a place where the Birdsbreath Navy sent their ships to rot. They'd passed a lightly patrolled wall to get there, but it wasn't really part of the Citadel or intended as a secure zone.

His money and status had got him the ship and a promise of supplies, but Rising Swallow's construction docks were full—and it wasn't like the ninesail could fly under her own power. Armand could move the ship himself, but he wasn't sure he saw the point.

"We'll want to set up here," he told his two hires. "Move your tent camp, eldest sister, and perhaps build some cabins as well. How long are we talking?"

"I don't know," Hammerhead admitted. "If there is no damage I cannot see, forty, maybe fifty clock-days." She chuckled. "But as Captain Greentrees said, most likely the starboard masts are gone, and we are planning to rebuild the interior to carry a halvar contingent.

"Fifty clock-days," she repeated. "Perhaps sixty, at the outside. I'll know more once we've got the frame and lifted her into it."

"Lifting her, at least, is a task the three of us will have no problem with," Armand pointed out. He still needed to make focuses for his two mages, though he could lift the ship into a frame on his own.

"That helps," the shaman admitted. "That may save us several clock-days, in the end. I was thinking of building a crane."

"You don't need a crane, eldest sister," Armand told her with a smile. "You have an archmage."

"And we may find more ways you can save us time as we go," she conceded. "Should I be getting to work?"

"As soon as you can get your people up here and under the protection of the King's var," the archmage agreed. He didn't *know* anything about the situation of her tribe at the bottom of the gobvar ghetto, but he had read the body language of the var around him when he'd arrived at the camp.

They were under threat, and the faster they were moved, the safer they were—and the more value they were to him.

"What's the ship's name?" Greentrees asked. "It's ill luck to change it, so I'd like to know."

Armand had to think for a moment. It had been mentioned, but he hadn't registered it as important.

"*Star*," he finally remembered. "A simpler name than I'm used to for elvar ships."

"Not everything we do is lost in intrigue and tradition, Lord Archmage," Greentrees said with a chuckle. "But in this case, tradition is the key. *Star* is an ancient and revered name, one with an honorable history.

"There would have been a new *Star* in commission within a few dozen clock-days of her being sold. The name has meaning to the High Court Navy."

"Is it bad luck for us, then?" Hammerhead asked.

"No," the elvar captain murmured. "No, quite the opposite. I think it might even be a sign."

For the first time since they'd arrived at the ship, Greentrees suddenly looked less worried. He walked over to where the port mast hung just above the ground near them, and touched the cloudwood.

"A sign?" Armand asked.

"If I've got my dates right, Lord Archmage, this is the *Star* I served on in my first training cruise, almost sixty dances ago," the elvar said softly. "So, I think she may serve us just fine."

CHAPTER

19

IT WAS IMPOSSIBLE for a var in Cat's position not to believe in divination. He was leery about prophecy and even leerier about fate. Still, he couldn't deny it was an incredible coincidence that put the ship he'd done his training cruise on, what felt like a lifetime ago, in the hands of Birdsbreath and then in a hollow on a mountainside for his new employer to purchase.

Star's presence in the middle of the mess was the only positive feeling he had about the whole affair. Getting his magic back was a big thing, but it was also a huge risk, something that could cause him problems down the line.

And now he had a gobvar crew and a gobvar first officer. He couldn't have done anything else with Brushfire Hammerhead, not and commanded her people in the way he felt was necessary. He just hated it.

Gobvar were the enemy. The Clans and the Quadrumvirate and the fleets they commanded—those were the threat he'd spent his life training to fight. Even the pirates he'd mostly fought over the dances, well… half of them were elvar, sure, but given how few gobvar there were on this side of the border spheres, that was saying a lot all on its own.

And the Hammerhead shaman was twice his size in any measure he cared to judge by. Her horns, her muscles, her…everything. He was guessing there was only one area of her body with *any* fat—though at that, her *breasts* were the size of his *head*.

Bluestaves was also taller and heavier than Cat, but at least the halvar archmage had the courtesy to be pudgy. Brushfire Hammerhead was simply a wall of walking muscle and horns, matched with a shamanic power he barely understood and had no choice but to augment.

Every one of the gobvar set his teeth on edge, and he'd made the most powerful of them his first officer. It was the *right* call, he knew that, but he'd be damned if he *liked* it.

Cat Greentrees cursed Fallen Crystal Voice of the House of Fires to void and darkness under his breath as he reentered the Salient Hunt alone. Without the seer's prophecy, he'd have at least tried to get out of hiring the gobvar tribe. With prophetic words around doom and "the Shaman, the Captain and the Archmage" echoing in his mind, he didn't see an alternative.

"Greentrees, how can we help you?" the bartender asked. "Drink? Food?"

It was the first time the staff had seen him leave the Salient Hunt for any extended period, and Cat could *feel* the elvar restraining their curiosity.

"Tea, roast grazer flank," Cat told the server. "Is Oathsworn around?"

"Not at the moment," the staffer told him. "She should be back by nightfall."

Cat looked outside and tried to read shadows to guess how long that would be. He'd been born on a lodeplate, though, and lodeplates didn't *have* night. He glanced back at the bartender and arched an eyebrow.

"About two hours by the clock," they said with a chuckle. "Brandy while you wait?"

"Just tea," Cat told them. The habits he'd planned for thirty dances of exile would not serve while he commanded an aether ship—and it was better to begin as he meant to carry on.

Somehow, he suspected that living with a crew of a var he hated was going to be the *easy* part.

The smoldering ember that lit the sphere of Birdsbreath was drifting behind the mountains when Oathsworn Lane finally returned to her bar. She didn't even wait for her staff to catch her up before she crossed the room and took a seat at Cat's table.

"So?" she asked.

"Bluestaves is crazy," Cat said bluntly. "But he's an archmage, so that's expected. He bought the hulk of one of the ninesails Birdsbreath used to have under their flag, and the gobvar tribe thinks they can fix it up."

Lane nodded slowly.

"I'd forgotten about those ships," she said. "They solid?"

"Might be," he admitted. "The one he bought…it's *Star*. The *Star* I did training on, back before even you got your hands on me."

"Makes sense, I suppose. The High Court keeps them in service for a hundred dances if they can, but sometimes it's not worth repairing a ship," Lane murmured. "But even an expensive repair is cheaper for a halvar king than a ninesail."

"I'm guessing they didn't serve him well."

"No." She shook her head. "Before my time here, I think, though they were probably around when I was falling in love with this rock thirty dances ago."

Cat had never asked his hostess why she'd picked Blueswallow, of all worldlets in the spheres, to settle on. He wasn't going to now, either. That seemed like the kind of thing she might keep to herself.

"You're not just back here for a meal and your stuff," she observed. "What do you need, Captain?"

"Var," he told her. "Var I can trust. We're rebuilding an old ninesail and taking her into the aether, Lane. There's no one out there to have my back. I trust the gobvar as far as I can throw the ship, and I'm not sure I trust Archmage Bluestaves any further.

"I'm following hints of prophecy from a seer aboard my last command, working with a crew that's going to be anchored on gobvar and a gobvar *shaman*, under the command of a halvar archmage."

He shook his head.

"I need stavemasters for fifteen storm staves," he told her. "And then at least another two hundred var beyond that. Two hundred and fifty var, mostly riggers."

"And var who'll tolerate working with gobvar," she noted. "You needed that chunk of hands to start, but it'll narrow the list of who'll work with you."

"We need them," Cat agreed. "This damn prophecy tells me that Brushfire Hammerhead's the right one, which means I'm taking her tribe on. But I still need those var."

"You're not going to like my advice," Lane said. "You're twitchy enough about Hammerhead."

"I have a gobvar shaman as my first officer," he pointed out. "Which means I'm having my archmage employer make a gobvar shaman a focus, which *I* then will have to train her to use."

"I can source you a navigator—though they won't be as good as you—a pair of surgeons, one a mage, and a couple of other decent officers I'll swear by," she said. "They'll each have a few var they trust themselves to bring along, to fill out the medical contingent and so forth."

"I'm hearing a *but* coming," he said.

"Your stavemasters will need to be elvar. I'll ask around; I think I can find them. But…if you've already got a hundred gobvar at the heart of your crew, you're going to be better off sourcing gobvar riggers than trying to find elvar who'll do more than rudely tolerate gobvar."

"Which is a recipe for mutiny in the deep aether," Cat said grimly. He swallowed a curse. "I don't *want* more gobvar on my ship, Oathsworn."

"You need smart and sensible elvar with the skills you need," she pointed out. "And, frankly, you need ones who aren't bigoted from here to the High Court. That's rarer than you think."

"So, instead of looking for these rare elvar, you think I should hire more gobvar?" he asked.

"I can find you *some* elvar who'll work with gobvar," she said. "If nothing else, any gobvar stavemasters we find would *definitely* be pirates. But if you're going to have any gobvar crew, you need to have a mostly gobvar crew."

"Okay." Cat growled. He hated it, but she was right. He had confidence in his ability to keep a leash on idiots, but not *that* tight a leash. "So, where do I find gobvar crew? I know the Hammerheads are too new to Rising Swallow to have made those connections."

He grimaced.

"And how do I make sure I *don't* hire pirates?"

"You can't," Lane told him flatly. "But, frankly, most gobvar pirates would *rather* be legit. There aren't a lot of good options for folks like the Hammerheads. I won't send you to anyone I know has been pirating, but I can't guarantee some of those we find won't be pirates anyway."

Cat swallowed a series of curses, staring down at his cup of un-doctored tea. It took a moment of sheer will *not* to order a bottle of brandy.

"Where do we find them?" he finally ground out again. "I could... No. No, I can't send Brushfire. It has to be me."

He was tempted to send his new first officer, but that wasn't fair to anyone—her *or* the var he needed to hire. Or to Cat himself, for that matter. He needed to judge the people he was hiring.

"There's a bar, much like the Hunt, in the gobvar ghetto," Lane told him. "The Fallen Anchor. The var who runs it was picked up by elvar after his cutter got torn apart in one of the attempts to breach the barricade.

"He either talked fast or got lucky, but he lived and got dropped off here," the elvar continued. "Worked his way up to running a bar for a halvar, then inherited the bar when the owner died."

"You trust him?" Cat asked.

"Broken Hand Oilfire is an asshole of the highest degree with a chip on his shoulder larger than some worldlets I've visited," Lane told him wryly. "But I know his priorities. His bar is mostly a flophouse, for gobvar stuck between ships. Gobvar that lose their ships are pretty hard done by, and he helps them as best as he can.

"You're offering them legit work? He won't sabotage that. Some of them might sabotage it themselves, though."

She considered silently, then sighed.

"Don't go the Fallen Anchor alone, Cat," she told him. "These var are used to High Court officers from the wrong side of your stave decks. They'll smell what you were, and they'll hate you for it. But I know you, Cat. You'll be starting from the bottom, but treat them fair and you'll earn their trust."

"I'm not going to treat them any differently than any elvar crew we get," he said flatly.

"And that, my old student, is why you're one of the few elvar captains I'd even *suggest* hiring gobvar to," she told him. "You don't have it in you to be unfair to anybody."

"Doesn't mean I like having the horned bastards on my ship," Cat replied.

"I'd have felt the same way once," Lane told him quietly. "But I spent way too much time in the ghettos of port cities not to understand where the gobvar in our spheres stand."

"I'm learning," he said. "But that doesn't mean I like them."

"You don't have to like them, Cat. Just treating them fairly puts you ahead of most of our var."

CHAPTER 20

There was at least a higher grade of dirt underneath Brushfire's tent now. She sat cross-legged in the entrance to the fabric structure, watching her tribe swarm over the hulk of *Star*.

Windheart and Axfall were her two elders, the two var who'd led the tribe until she'd become sufficiently a shaman that they'd deferred to her. Axfall was sixty or so dances younger than his lover, but that still made their senior carpenter the third-oldest member of the Hammerhead tribe.

The second-oldest, Faithful Hammerhead, was the senior cook of the tribe—and genteelly regarded by everyone, including herself, as completely lacking in anything resembling long-term planning skills.

It wasn't that Faithful was stupid or incompetent or even lacking in common sense. Something in how her brain ticked, though, meant that she had a hard time foreseeing consequences for even minor decisions, let alone major ones. Faithful was much beloved by the tribe, but even she didn't think she should make decisions for other var.

But even though Windheart and Axfall deferred to Brushfire on most matters of the tribe's future and survival, Brushfire knew better than to override them on their areas of specialty. That meant the two old gobvar would be the ones who decided how the tribe would approach repairing *Star* for their mission.

She had faith that they *could*—and they'd unleashed the entire tribe to go over every inch of the ship to get as many eyes on as many potential problems as possible—but she would admit that she had only the roughest ideas of how to begin.

As if summoned by her thoughts, the two white-haired gobvar appeared around the tents and walked up to her.

"It's still a tent city in a field of mud," Axfall groused.

"There's grass to hold this dirt together when it rains," Windheart told his lover with a chuckle. "And we have an end to living on dirt, too. One we control."

"I'm not sure whether to be flattered or frustrated with you, eldest sister," Axfall told Brushfire as he and Windheart pulled up patches of ground next to her. "You looked at *that* and went, 'Yep, we can fix it.' Are you mad?"

"No," she said, chuckling herself. Axfall was...not an optimistic soul, in her experience.

"I'm not mad," she repeated. "I know you and I know Windheart and I know my siblings of the tribe. We *can* fix her. My only question is how long and how much of the archmage's money we're going to need to spend."

"Wait, there's going to be *money* to spend on this?" Axfall asked. "I take that back; we might be able to fix her after all."

Brushfire rolled her eyes exaggeratedly, letting her two eldest tribesvar see her amusement.

"There's supposed to be a storehouse of supplies that the halvar had laid in for if they ever tried to repair her," she told them.

"Fistfall found that," Windheart confirmed. "It won't be enough, but it'll let us get started. I'm assuming the locals will be grumpy if we start cutting down trees around here?"

Brushfire looked around the mountainside. She'd seen thicker forests on other worldlets, but this was a decently dense one. None of it was cloudwood, either, which meant it wasn't immediately strategically valuable to the halvar.

Except...she suspected this wasn't the only valley tucked away in the middle of the mountainside forest, and the trees did a good job of concealing the others if they existed. The Kingdom of Birdsbreath could have more secrets than she knew about, and many could be hidden in this forest.

"Let's spend the archmage's money instead of the local King's favor," she murmured. "Bluestaves seems to think he has more coin than we could possibly need."

"Dangerous assumption on the halvar's part," Windheart noted. "We're going to need to replace every sail on her. The weave on the old aethercloth is worn out. Too long in too powerful of a lodestone field."

"We're going to have to replace a set of masts," she pointed out. "It's still cheaper than trying to convince an elvar to sell a halvar a ninesail."

"I'm impressed the archmage got a *halvar* to sell a halvar a ninesail," her sailmaker said. "The King here really didn't think she could get it fixed, huh?"

"Or that it wasn't worth it. I guess she figured she didn't need *two* half-wrecked ninesails sitting on a mountainside," Brushfire replied. "Can we fix her?"

"Yes," Axfall said flatly. "Better and faster if we can just buy cloudwood spars and such from the shipyard—but give me the supplies they've got here and permission to cut down the trees around us, and I can make it happen."

"We have Bluestaves' promise that we can buy whatever we need," she told them. "He's given me some coin to cover those costs, so let me know what you're thinking as you get it sorted out."

"I can tell you right now that they didn't expect to replace the sails," Windheart said. "There's no aethercloth in the supplies we inherited. I can buy pre-shaped sails at the yards, but we might be better off buying a few cables of raw cloth and cutting it into shape ourselves.

"There *will* be sails for elvar ninesails in the yard, but they expect to sell them to the High Court Navy, and they're priced appropriately," he concluded.

"Let me know when you're heading to the yards, and I'll come along to pay for things," Brushfire suggested, then she shook her head. "Or maybe we should wait until the captain is free and has picked us a few more elvar.

"We'll pay less for the same damn things if we sent someone with pointed ears and no horns."

"We'll pay less still if we send something with *round* ears and no horns," Axfall suggested. "Archmage robes will counter most of that, but if the archmage can find a halvar to put orders in for us once we've sorted out what we need…it'll save him some coin and headache."

"I know we're going to have more elvar officers, so we can count on having var with pointy ears," Brushfire told them. "We can't bring many halvar with us, even with the section the archmage wants us to install, so I suspect we may need to accept whatever price we can get through the elvar.

"Time is also a factor. And while I suspect we might find there is a limit to the archmage's funds after all, I suspect he'd rather pay extra than deal with extra hassle."

Another figure was moving through the camp, carefully keeping a measurable distance from tents and Hammerhead tribesvar alike. Brushfire watched her captain for a moment before she swallowed a sigh.

She doubted Greentrees *realized* how obvious his distaste for the gobvar was, but it grated. On the other hand, he was paying them more than any other captain ever had, so she'd bite her horns before she spoke.

"Captain's on his way to see me, I think," she told the two craftsmen. "Start putting together your plan and your lists. We have work to do."

"Brushfire," Greentrees greeted her, nodding calmly to the two older gobvar as they walked past him.

It was *fascinating* to her how polite the elvar was when he was directly interacting with her people. She could tell that just being around gobvar made his skin crawl, but he was surprisingly good at putting it aside for a var whose *job* had been to fight her people.

But it was a conscious effort, and it faded the moment he didn't think anyone was looking at him. It was fascinating...but it didn't do him many favors in her mind, either.

"Captain," she said. "What do you need?"

"A few things," he admitted, half-turning to look back at the ship. "We're still in the planning stages on *Star*, I'm assuming?"

"Aye. That was my senior sailmaker and carpenter you just walked past. *Our* senior sailmaker and carpenter, I suppose."

"You'll have to introduce me another time," Greentrees murmured, not quite meeting her eyes. "To everyone, ideally. I prefer to have names and faces lined up in my head."

"Of course," she agreed. "We'll have time," she continued. "We're looking at weeks' worth of work before *Star* is ready to fly again."

"I'm impressed that she's looking to fly again at all," he told her. "Would more hands help?"

"More hands, so long as they're skilled, will always help," she admitted. She wasn't looking forward to integrating elvar and gobvar crews, but she figured it was better to get started while they were on the ground.

"I have interviews scheduled for key officers over the next few clock-days," Greentrees said. "I'll need you to attend with me."

"Captain?"

"You are my first officer," he reminded her gently. "If that's going to be a problem for any of our potential crew and other officers, we need to know that before they join us, don't we?"

"Of course. Apologies, Captain; I'm still getting used to this idea," she admitted.

"Fair." He nodded crisply—though he still hadn't met her eyes the whole time they'd been talking.

At least he wasn't staring at her tits. Given the general build of most elvar, she'd met a few over the years who fetishized the more pronounced curves of halvar and gobvar women.

"How long, do you think, before we begin raising the ship?" he asked, looking back at *Star* again.

"A few clock-days. Not much more," she admitted. "We need to raise her relatively quickly to tell how much work it will take. The archmage promised to do the heavy lifting."

"By then, you and I should have focuses as well," he noted. "That will help."

That took Brushfire a moment to fully process, and she glanced at the captain's waist. She'd known he was getting a new focus from the archmage, but she'd assumed that was a personalized focus to replace his existing one.

Only now did she realized that the elvar wasn't carrying a focus at all. He'd picked up a sword and belt since the previous clock-day, but there was no focus scabbard on the weapons belt.

That was a question she didn't quite feel up to asking her new captain, so she simply nodded.

"It should," she agreed. "Though I only know a little about using a focus. My training has been centered on shamanic magic, which is a different path entirely."

"And mine has been centered on the focus, leaving me vulnerable without one," Greentrees told her. "Which brings me to my other need, I suppose."

"Of course." She waited.

"I am going to be visiting a couple of bars for recruiting, and I need an escort," he said. "Who among your people is best trained for that?"

Brushfire swallowed her initial response and took a steadying breath.

"My people aren't thugs or leg-breakers," she said flatly. "We're not going to press people into the ship's crew."

She wasn't sure whether she was more relieved or amused by the look of absolute *horror* in Greentrees' gaze as he finally met her eyes.

"I...intend no such thing," he told her. "I'm not even..." He trailed off and shook his head.

"I need an *escort*, Officer Brushfire," he continued after a moment. "Bodyguards, hopefully to prevent trouble by their mere presence. Not leg-breakers. *Marines.*"

"I apologize," Brushfire said. "We...have some bad experiences with people who assume gobvar are only useful as muscle."

"We hired you all to crew an aether ship," Greentrees noted. "I *hope* you are useful as more than muscle. Unfortunately, I'm going to be trying to recruit gobvar crew in a gobvar bar, and it strikes me that having some gobvar with me is going to help smooth things over."

"I wasn't aware you were planning to hire more gobvar," she replied, rolling his intent and words around in her head. "You're likely right that we'd smooth that path."

"Your tribe serves as an excellent cadre for crewing a ship," he told her. "I have hints from prophecy that I need *you* in particular. Given that criteria, I already have a third of my necessary crew as gobvar.

"And my var are not...*smooth* with yours," he conceded levelly. "I believe that I and Archmage Bluestaves are best served by recruiting more gobvar and being very specific in our elvar recruits.

"But I also believe that if *I* walk into a gobvar sailor bar on my own, I will either be thrown out or murdered before I can state my intent," he concluded.

The wryness in his tone belied his clear discomfort with the idea and the very real danger involved in what he was planning.

"I will accompany you myself, Captain," Brushfire decided. "And I think we have a few gobvar whose presence will help head off trouble before it begins."

And because she'd pick var like Fistfall, she knew the gobvar she was bringing weren't going to *start* trouble.

CHAPTER

21

Intellectually, Cat Greentrees had always known he lived a privileged life. Even the life of a sailor on an aether ship was privileged by many standards. The elvar who crewed them demanded a certain degree of accommodations and luxury, after all.

He'd been aware that the living situation of the average elvar was better than that of the average halvar or darvar, too. On the lodeplates of the High Court, the elvar lived at the center of a trading and manufacturing empire that directly or indirectly spanned over two hundred spheres. In the spheres of the halvar and darvar, the elvar had natural skills that were in high demand—and their connections to that sphere-spanning imperial power didn't hurt, either.

For all of that, though, Cat had only been vaguely aware that there even *were* gobvar on this side of the border. He knew there were gobvar pirates, of course—pirates were much of the High Court Navy's actual day-to-day work, and while most were elvar, there were enough gobvar to reinforce stereotypes.

Walking through the ghetto to visit the Hammerheads' camp had been an illuminating experience, but he'd still been in a daze and walking with an archmage. Bluestaves' robes brought out the best in people around him.

So did Bluestaves himself, in a way that Cat both enjoyed and was a bit confused by. Despite working for the halvar, he hadn't spent that much time with him yet. There was an odd but endearing not-quite-befuddlement to the var, one that seemed to bring out the helpful nature of a lot of people.

Including Cat and, he suspected, the gobvar they'd recruited so far. That had to be part of why Brushfire Hammerhead had agreed to accompany him and conjured three decently armed large sailors to walk with them as well.

Her initial reaction to his request worried him. He might not *like* his gobvar crewvar, but they were still skilled crew. Why would anyone look at them and just see leg-breakers?

Still, Cat appreciated their size as the five of them walked through the ghetto at a slower pace this time. Even down there, there were clear gradations of better and worse areas, and Oathsworn Lane's directions were leading him into one of the more run-down sections.

He suspected that just having four gobvar with him was buying their party a lot of grace—potentially even more than the fact that Brushfire and her first-brother were among the largest gobvar Cat had ever seen—and his first officer hadn't picked *small* gobvar for the rest of the party.

Feeling reasonably safe let him take in the context of the slum sprawled around the base of Rising Swallow's mountains. There were halvar and darvar there in the ramshackle mix of shacks, rotting older buildings, lean-tos and tents that lined roughly defined streets.

But the only gobvar he'd seen in the upper streets of Rising Swallow, even in the lower-class neighborhoods just above the slums, had been working or clearly on their way up to the docks. Blueswallow's var were prepared to hire gobvar for the tasks only they and elvar could do, but if any of them had been *allowed* to live in nicer neighborhoods, at least some would have found a way to afford it.

Instead, they appeared to all live there, where the large horned var made up at least half of the population on the muddy streets. Many of them were dirty and ragged-looking. Most looked skinnier than he thought was healthy for *any* var...and his bones themselves shivered as he realized a baby sobbing from hunger sounded the same regardless of their parentage.

Glancing at his companions, he saw the stony expression on Brushfire Hammerhead's face and recognized that what he was *just* realizing had been the entire lives of the people with him.

That was food for thought, and something he put away for later as they stepped into the square he'd been told to look for. A barely functional—but *functional*, which spoke to someone putting in immense effort—fountain burbled away in the center of the open space.

It might have once been decorative, but from the lineup of people filling containers with water, its water line now served a far more practical purpose. A pair of gobvar stood by the fountain, not *officially* organizing the line but definitely keeping an eye on it.

A third gobvar, with silver inlaid into his horns in a similar fashion to Cat's first officer, was kneeling at the far side of the fountain from the line, working with an incense burner and a collection of herbs—and a gentle sense of flowing magic that Cat could feel from a hundred yards away.

Whatever system of arcana or artifice that provided water to the fountain likely didn't purify it, he realized. Without *someone* putting work into the structure, the people who depended on it could easily get sick.

Instead, a shaman worked away to keep the water clean, and a pair of gobvar that could have passed for thugs stood guard to make sure nothing happened to the fountain—and no one was paying anything for water.

Across the square from them, on the far side of the fountain, was one of the more-intact buildings Cat had seen in the ghetto. It had been a grand house once, before the slums and ghettos had sprawled out over there, and the fountain had likely been a decorative part of its grounds.

Now a roughly lettered sign declared it the Fallen Anchor—and their destination.

Walking through the doors of the Fallen Anchor, Cat immediately realized both why the house had originally been abandoned and why the bar was named what it was. Aether ships used anchors to connect themselves to lodestone cores they didn't want to land on, keeping the ship itself out of reach of the pull without risking drifting away.

Someone had lost one of those anchors above Rising Swallow at some point in the past, and the three-yard-high piece of metal had fallen to the base of the mountain and crashed through the roof of the house.

Now it sat in the middle of what had once been a grand entryway, blocking the stairs up to the second floor and serving as the focal point for a surprisingly well-lit common room.

It was also a completely *silent* common room, as the several dozen occupants turned toward the doors and saw an elvar standing in the middle of them.

For a moment, Cat's fingers twitched toward the battlewand he was carrying. It was far from as useful as a focus, only being able to fire bolts of energy and nothing more complicated, but it *was* a weapon.

He'd have a focus soon, but for now he had a sword and a battlewand. With every eye on the room on him—and every head in the room except his surmounted by horns—he regretted not waiting for the archmage to finish his work.

Then Brushfire and her companions stepped in the room behind him. The shaman stood by his side and something in her body language calmed the room. He suspected that his first officer had just silently communicated *mine* to the entire room.

"Let's talk to the bartender over there," Cat suggested softly. "The proprietor should be around somewhere, but unless you know who to look for...?"

"I didn't even know this bar was here," Brushfire told him. "Would have been useful for us."

"We're here now," he said. "Come on."

Brushfire walked by his side across the room as their crewvar spread out behind them. There were still eyes on them, but the gazes weren't as hostile as they'd been when it had just been Cat in the door.

They were *curious* now, which he could live with. He suspected a number of the var he needed to hire were already in this room.

"What do you want?" bartender asked, glaring aggressively at Cat. "Not supposed to bring pets here, shaman."

"He's my captain," Brushfire told the gobvar. "And we need to talk to the owner. Are they about?"

The bartender looked Brushfire up and down in a way that made Cat's hackles twitch, but he *needed* these people. He kept his temper—easy enough after seeing the kind of area they lived in. The real anger he was sitting on wasn't targeted at the gobvar around him at all.

"Shaman with an elvar," the bartender finally concluded. "What do you want with the boss?"

"Business," Cat said swiftly. "I need to hire sailors."

"And what's an elvar doing looking to hire sailors *here?*" the gobvar asked, gesturing around the room with a horn.

"My first officer is a gobvar, and I figure I'm more likely to find var who don't have a problem with that here than up the mountain," he told the bartender. "Am I wrong?"

The gobvar laughed aloud and took a very different look at Brushfire.

"First officer, hey?" he asked.

"My tribe is half the crew," Brushfire told him. "Need to fill it out."

"An elvar captain with a gobvar shaman first officer," the gobvar chuckled. "All right. Follow me."

He gestured another gobvar to take over the bar and hopped over it with the clear ease of long practice.

"Where's the owner?" Cat asked.

"*I'm* the owner," the var replied. "Broken Hand Oilfire, Captain. Proprietor of the Fallen Anchor and absolutely *fascinated* with what's going on here."

The office Oilfire led them to had likely once been the receiving parlor of the grand house. Now it held a motley collection of chairs facing a large desk that had clearly survived at least one fire.

The gobvar pulled wooden cups from a side cupboard, and a young gobvar appeared at the door a moment later with a pitcher of water. Grunting his thanks, he poured cups for all of the members of Cat's party and gestured them to chairs.

Oilfire himself took a seat on his desk, pushing papers aside to clear space for him to perch and survey his guests.

"Brushfire Hammerhead, you are known to me," he told them. "I presume these are your tribesvar."

"They are," she confirmed, glancing at Cat. "And this is my new captain, Cat Greentrees."

Oilfire shrugged.

"I'm surprised you came down here yourself," he admitted to Cat. "But I'm not sure I'm willing to help an elvar captain save pennies by hiring gobvar. I'm not a job-posting board."

"I didn't know there was a sailors' bar down here," Brushfire admitted. "It would have saved my people some heartache if we had."

"The water is from the fountain outside," Oilfire told Fistfall, and Cat realized the big gobvar had been looking suspiciously at the cup. "My husband purifies the fountain every clock-day. He insists we give something back to the area, as best as we can, and the pumps and piping for that whole affair still work, given a few nudges."

Cat took as open a sip of the water as he could. If *he* got drugged, Brushfire and her tribesvar could drag him back up to the valley with *Star*—and he was the one who needed to show the most trust.

"I knew about your tribe," the bar owner continued to Brushfire after all of them had drunk. "But I'm never sure what to make of job lots like that. Not many of us this side of the border still *have* tribes."

He shrugged.

"Plus, with strangers who sailed for elvar, we need to be careful. Some are housegobs, more elvar with horns than our var."

"So, you don't know me enough to trust me, so helping the captain is a problem?" Brushfire asked.

"I'd rather be trusted on my own merits," Cat interjected before Oilfire replied.

"The only reason you even made it *to* the door, Captain Greentrees, is that your horned friends were with you," the bar owner pointed out. "But the eldest sister is correct. I *don't* know her. I don't know you either, Captain, but I was never going to trust an elvar.

"Her, though. Her I need to judge so I can tell whether *her* trusting you is worth anything."

Cat waved Brushfire to silence before she said anything. He could guess what the flash in her eyes meant, and that wasn't a fight they could afford to have.

"My first officer may have opened the doors for us, but I'm not leaving her to do the work here, Master Oilfire," he told the gobvar. "Perhaps you would do us the courtesy of hearing out my offer, what I'm looking for, before you dismiss us entirely?"

"Do you think fancy words and polite gestures are going to help you here, Captain?"

"No. I think a fair offer to hire people for real work is going to help me here," Cat said bluntly. "I also think you're being spectacularly rude to my first officer, and it falls to me to step in to protect her."

Cat didn't even need to be able to see his first officer to guess that she was bristling at the suggestion that she needed protection—but he figured he was right. It wasn't that she was physically or even *socially* vulnerable.

It was just that it was his job to stop her being continually prodded by the bar owner.

From Oilfire's lengthy silence, that was not the tack he'd expected Cat to take. After several seconds of quiet, he slowly nodded.

"You are not what I anticipated, Captain," he said politely. "I apologize, Officer Brushfire. While I have my concerns, I was indeed being rude to see how you both reacted."

He met Cat's gaze.

"All right, Captain, what is this 'fair offer' you want to make?"

Cat returned the other var's nod.

"We are in the process of refitting an old elvar ninesail to serve as a lightly armed exploration ship for a halvar archmage," he explained swiftly. "While we are recruiting elvar officers and elvar stavemasters, Officer Brushfire will be serving as my first officer, and we already have her tribe signed on as crew to complete the refit.

"Since I have to recognize the prejudice that exists between our people, I believe I am better served recruiting more gobvar for the deck and sail divisions than I am trying to convince elvar to listen to gobvar Masters of Decks and Sails."

He'd need an elvar Master of Staves, but he was already considering a plan for his Masters of Decks and Sails—observing the Hammerheads had already told him that the two elders of the tribe had the skills he needed.

He hadn't told anyone his plan yet, and he was still thinking about it...but he suspected admitting to it now would open a door that might remain closed despite everything.

"That is...likely correct," Oilfire said slowly. "Quite the savings you may make there."

"Not in the slightest," Cat told the bartender. "The money isn't mine, and I see no reason to treat var who sail under me unfairly. All var serving aboard *Star* will draw standard rates for merchant ship crew in their role."

"An archmage, huh?" the gobvar asked. "I guess he has the money."

"Any ship captain should," Cat said levelly. He had been sufficiently oblivious not to realize that there even *were* gobvar serving on civilian ships this side of the border—but he would never have considered paying gobvar less to do the same work.

"We need another two hundred riggers and deckhands," he continued. "They'll have to be willing to work under a mix of elvar and gobvar officers. My stavemasters will be elvar, but I will pick the elvar carefully; you have my word as a scion of the House of Forests."

The office was silent.

"It appears you were correct, Captain Greentrees, and your offer *will* make a difference," Oilfire finally said. "I will ask around and see who is interested. I believe I may be able to find you your var…but realize you're not getting a single tribe. They will need to learn to work with each other as well as your elvar.

"This is not the first aether ship I have commanded," Cat told the gobvar. "The first, perhaps, with gobvar—but I have the suspicion that sailors are much the same whether they have pointed ears or curving horns!"

CHAPTER 22

Finding a workspace in a strange city was never an easy task for an archmage. While Armand could make do with fewer tools than a more-conventional arcane artisan, he needed a larger safety zone.

He'd rarely had actual problems with a working, but the consequences of an *archmage* making a mistake were...dramatic. Armand's defenses and protective magics were enough that he would survive. The building probably wouldn't.

The heavily built stone warehouse on the lower end of the dock district he'd found was normally used for storing entire shiploads of explosives. Emptied of everything except a trio of workbenches, it caused every sound Armand made to echo in the open space.

But he'd inspected the construction of the space carefully. Designed to contain and control the detonation of tons of both conventional and arcane explosives, the warehouse *should* serve the same purpose for any accidental release of energy in his working.

The simple part had been setting up the workspace in the warehouse. Armand used the same tools and equipment as the arcane artisans who crafted the systems for aether ships and similar artifices. A city like Rising Swallow had hundreds of thousands of var-hours' worth of arcane workings woven through the districts.

The same mix of arcane and artifice that enabled travel between the spheres was used, at a different scale, for everything from street lighting to providing pure running water for the city's high-end residential districts.

The same crucibles, inlaying tools, woodworking equipment and so forth that were used for the arcane components of that infrastructure were what Armand needed for his own working. He worked on a smaller scale, but that was an adjustment he was used to making.

One workbench off to the side now held over a dozen general focuses. While even a general focus was expensive enough that a few of them would cover a good chunk of the expenses he was incurring for this project, they were also simple enough for Armand or another archmage to make in bulk—their price was driven by the fact that *only* an archmage could make them.

On the other hand, they lasted basically forever. There was a reason that there were enough general focuses around for every aether ship captain in the spheres to have one, after all.

At the opposite end of the spectrum were the two rods—not yet focuses—sitting on the other table in front of Armand. At first glance, there was no significant difference between them, but that illusion faded swiftly on close examination.

The general focuses were a simple wooden shape, tapering slightly over a twelve-inch length, with runes carved into the wood. To Armand's senses, they had an almost-heartbeat-like quality, a solid pulse of magic.

The two in-progress focuses still lacked that pulse. He had not yet opened the channel to the core essence of the universe that would give them their power. Even without activation, though, they showed their nature to those with the eyes to see.

The general focuses were all made of the same material, a local dark red hardwood. Cheap and easily accessed, it had served Armand's purposes—and he had more of it for once he was done with the personal focuses.

Cat Greentrees' focus had been easy. The moment Armand had seen *Star*, he'd known that cloudwood from an aether ship would be the right material for the elvar captain. Once he'd learned that *Star* had been the first ship Greentrees had served on, the connection was clear.

So the elvar's focus was a length of cloudwood carved down from a broken piece of *Star*'s hull the crew was replacing. It was exactly the length of Cat Greentrees' forearm from elbow to wrist, and its runes had been inlaid with a mixture of silver and green enamel.

Unlike the general focuses, it wasn't an even taper from base to tip, either. The intricate pattern of peaks and valleys to the carving wasn't something that Armand could even consciously map. He'd based it on his perception of the elvar captain, and he would adjust it slightly with magic when he paired the focus to his new companion.

For all of the complexity of the process and the final product, Armand had made personal focuses for elvar aether ship captains before. Many of the details were shaped by the nature of Cat Greentrees in specific, but the archmage knew the type of var he was creating for.

Brushfire Hammerhead, on the other hand, was an unknown quantity. A gobvar, a shaman…neither of these were things he'd worked with before. Even finding the base material had been a pain, a long and frustrating tour through the markets of Rising Swallow.

Even when he'd found the large horn from the local grazer population, he'd hesitated. Grazers were ubiquitous across the spheres, a general class of a dozen species and a hundred breeds of animals that were raised on local forage and slaughtered for their meat.

Blueswallow's particular larger form of the type was a four-legged beast with dangerous-looking horns that could grow to the length of most var's arms. There had been a stall in the market selling those horns, and one particular horn, either naturally tinted or artificially dyed black, had caught his instinct.

Armand could think of a few different problems with giving a gobvar, a member of the only var with horns of their own, a focus made of horn. Nothing else had spoken to him during his clock-day-long search, however, so that horn now lay on the table in front of him.

He'd *carefully* cut it down to the same length as Hammerhead's forearm, a good three inches longer than Greentrees'! Like the cloudwood focus for the elvar, it had been cut into an uneven pattern of ridges and valleys based on his read of the gobvar's aura.

The archmage had carved similar, though not identical, runes into the horn. They were inlaid with gold and green enamel, both contrasting and complementing the one for Cat Greentrees.

The green enamel was fascinating to Armand. He didn't really *pick* the colors for this process—instinct, magic and analysis of the recipients did that for him. That the two focuses both used the same green enamel in large chunks of their runes spoke to a greater compatibility between the two var he'd recruited than he would have guessed.

There was only one stage left before he would need to do the final map and link of the focuses to their owners—and it was the stage that *required* an archmage. A non-archmage could certainly do the carving and inlaying work necessary to get to this point. They might even have been able to learn how to judge someone well enough to make some of the choices.

Certainly, Armand knew of archmagi who worked with arcane artisans to forge general focuses that they then empowered. But only an archmage could make the final step that took a focus from a decorative object to a link to the power of the universe.

Exhaling a long breath, he extended his senses, sweeping the building to make sure that no one had somehow breached the locks or anything similarly stupid. The last thing he needed was distractions or interruptions now.

Once he was certain he wasn't going to be interrupted, he reached inside himself. At the center of his magic, beating just beneath his heart at a slightly different rate, was the link that made him an archmage.

Armand had heard a hundred names for it over the years. The Deep Magic. The Weave. The Source. The Weft. The Veil. The Song of the Spheres.

It was the underlying magic of the universe, the leftover energy of creation, the essence of the power that fueled spherelights and embers and great crystals. The true Source of all magic.

He called it the Source when he taught his students. All focuses contain a link to it and it was the creation of that link that only an archmage could do.

Drawing on his own link, Armand felt energy fill his limbs and lungs. His stress and concerns vanished into the beating pulse of the universe.

The focuses he'd already created were suddenly far more perceivable, their soft magical heartbeats now the only sensation he truly registered. Even his own body seemed to float, intangible and distant.

This was the act that made the difference between mage and archmage. Every student that Bluestaves had trained or studied with had hoped to attempt this process, forging their own personal focus—and a permanent link to the Source within themselves.

Less than one in a hundred who made that first attempt, known as the Archmage Trial, would succeed. Some would come away with their power greatly augmented, a few moments of sustained link to the Source enough to broaden their pathways for more ordinary magic, but unable to keep the link for long.

Some could neither withstand the link to the Source nor end it under their own control. The lucky lost their magic forever.

The rest died. More died than became archmagi—and *none* of the mages who attempted to forge a personal focus were mages their teachers wanted to lose. No one made it that far without being talented, intelligent and magically gifted.

But becoming an archmage was becoming something *more*—and it was something the spheres needed, so their teachers walked their students through the ritual of the Trial, helped them set up the space, even helped channel the energies that would make them archmagi.

And, more often than they honored new archmagi, they buried their finest students.

The Trial had been almost a full dance before for Armand Bluestaves, and he had walked out with a second heartbeat and an understanding of the spheres that no non-archmage could ever match.

Now he drew upon the pulse of that link and the energy of the Source, seeking through the intangible nature of the world around him for the anchors he'd forged. Cat Greentrees' focus came into clarity first.

Armand reached out his hand and laid his palm on top of the cloudwood wand. Drawing on the Source, he pulled out a piece of the essence of all creation. It began to pulse in his hand, separate from and yet forever linked to the heartbeat of the universe.

That fragment slid into the anchor he'd forged of silver and magic. For a moment, the focus and the anchor and the Source fragment were three separate pieces, overlaid on each other in reality.

And then there was only one. A focus, linked to the Source, awaiting only the final pairing to be linked to the var it had been forged for. Until that pairing, it was incomplete in a way the earlier focuses weren't...but it was done for now.

He turned his attention to the grazer-horn wand and plucked another fragment of the Source.

The two var who commanded Armand's ship were clearly expecting there to be more in the explosives warehouse than the handful of workbenches at the center. The archmage concealed a small smirk as Greentrees and Hammerhead walked across the empty stone floor to reach him.

"Please, sit," he instructed, waving a hand to pull chairs over to them. "Thank you for coming."

"We work for you," Greentrees said drily. "Your message said it was important, though I didn't know about this place."

The elvar was looking around curiously. Armand suspected that he, at least, understood what the place was for. Elvar aether captains were trained mages, after all, though he understood that the elvar were usually far more restrictive about who was allowed to attempt the Archmage Trial than his own school.

"I won't need it much longer," Armand told them. "I'll be joining everyone at the camp by the ship soon enough. If nothing else, I hope the frame is complete enough to need me soon."

"Within two clock-days," Hammerhead promised. The gobvar seemed subdued. Something about the stone structure seemed to concern her.

"I should be done here by then," he said. There was no need for him to explain to them what he was doing. Greentrees was eyeing the table of general focuses with enough curiosity to suggest he understood those, at least.

"But I promised you both a particular payment for your services," Armand continued. "It is a payment I cannot make without your presence."

He'd acquired silk bags sized to the two focuses, and he took them from the table.

"Captain, you first."

He passed the first bag to Greentrees. The elvar studied it silently for a few moments, recognizing it from its size and shape, the archmage guessed.

Then he drew the focus from the silk and ran his fingers along its surface.

"Spheres and void," he whispered. "I don't think I've ever seen a personal focus this close before."

"It's not a personal focus yet," Armand warned. "Right now, it's not even truly a focus. It is only…potential. But it only holds potential for you."

"Okay. What do I do?" Greentrees asked.

Armand produced a small knife and passed it over to the elvar.

"Cut your thumb, smear blood along the length of the focus, then hold it in both hands and let me work," he instructed. He glanced at Brushfire Hammerhead and smiled gently at the gobvar's discomfort.

"You'll have to do the same, Brushfire," he warned. "But you can watch Captain Greentrees first."

"Thank you," she whispered.

Returning his attention to Cat Greentrees, Armand saw that the elvar hadn't even hesitated. He'd made a tiny cut in his thumb, as instructed, and smeared blood along the full length of the cloudwood wand. Now Greentrees held the focus in both hands on his lap, his gaze firmly fixed on it.

Armand walked up in front of Greentrees and laid his own hand on the focus, between the elvar's. He touched the pulsating fragment of the Source in the focus and woke it up.

Power flickered out from the wand now, but Armand was there to guide it. The blood along the focus vanished, drawn deep into the wood and silver in a moment of magic. The curves turned into the focus shifted as the focus and Armand worked together, linking the arcane artifact to the elvar who would wield it.

A final flicker of power, and Greentrees hissed at an instant of pain.

"It is done," Armand told him. "Hold your focus, Captain."

The cloudwood gleamed in the warehouse's lamplight. Silver and enamel and pale-yellow wood shivered with the last pulses of magic as the focus settled into its owner's hand like a content puppy snuggling home.

Greentrees moved the focus through the air softly, tentatively, and Armand felt the other var's power. The captain was no archmage, nothing like it, but he was powerful as regular mages went. Armand had known mages who'd opened their magic channels with a partially successful Archmage Trial who didn't wield as much power as Greentrees.

He'd suspected as much before, but now that there was a *focus* in the var's hand, Greentrees' power was clear. Armand had chosen his captain well.

Greentrees flicked the wand gently against the cut on his thumb, healing it with a tiny spark of magic. Running the focus's tip over the smooth skin, he smiled and looked up at Armand.

"Thank you," the elvar whispered, the awe and gratitude in his voice recognizing that, economic transaction or not, making a personal focus for someone was a huge gesture.

"Now you, Hammerhead," Armand said, turning to the gobvar. "Are you ready?"

He produced a second knife—he could clean the knife Greentrees had used with a thought, but there was a certain propriety to be observed, even if they were dodging much of the usual ceremony of giving a personal focus.

Hammerhead took a shaky breath, then nodded. She accepted the knife and opened her silk bag, drawing out the black-dyed horn rod. She ran her fingers down its smooth fingers, an unconscious mirror of Greentrees' gesture a few minutes earlier.

"It's beautiful," she whispered.

"I try," Armand told her. "Now, as Cat did. Cut your thumb and run blood down the length."

The gobvar might have hesitated more than Greentrees had, but she was also more inured to pain and discomfort than he was. Her cut was wider and she smeared quite a bit more blood along the shaft of the focus.

She mirrored Greentrees' position from before and held the focus on her lap with both hands. Armand joined her, laying his hand on the center of the rod and waking up the power inside it.

Even now, he'd doubted his choice in the black grazer horn, but at the moment he tried to bind the focus to Brushfire Hammerhead, his doubts were proven wrong. He barely needed to guide the waking power at all.

The focus and its link to the Source *leapt* to her in a way he'd never seen before. The blood along the horn vanished, and the surface rippled for a single moment before settling into a new configuration.

There was no flicker of power or hiss of pain this time. Simply a deep, certain knowledge that the focus was Brushfire's now and always had been.

"It is done," Armand whispered. "Hold your focus, eldest sister."

She didn't even know what to *do* with a focus, not really. Armand was planning on training her himself, in coordination with Greentrees as they could, but right now she held an arcane device of immense power.

That energy flickered around her, and she looked at her injured and still-bleeding thumb. Mirroring Greentrees' gesture, she tapped the tip of her focus onto the wound.

And Armand realized she was mirroring more than the gesture. She had somehow sensed enough of what Greentrees had done that she was mirroring the *spell*. Her wound closed smoothly and she looked at the smooth skin in awe.

Armand looked at *her* in awe. He recognized that Greentrees was doing the same.

Healing magic was one of the most difficult things to teach, and whatever healing magic Brushfire Hammerhead knew didn't use a focus. Yet she'd healed a wound, having seen it done *once* and never having wielded a focus before.

Armand smiled.

"We're going to need to teach you how to use that," he told her. "But I'm suddenly suspecting that might be easier than I was expecting."

CHAPTER

23

A SINGLE CLOCK-DAY wasn't enough for Brushfire to get used to wearing a focus at her hip. Greentrees had helped her get the right size and type of belt to carry the wand, but it still felt strange. She'd worn a sword before, but she was constantly aware that the focus was far more dangerous.

Even with her nonexistent training with the device, she was certain she could duplicate the attack spell stored in a battlewand. What Brushfire *wasn't* sure of was whether she could do so in a manner that wouldn't take out a good chunk of whatever building was behind her target.

She had no real sense of her own power. She'd learned to work magic that didn't require a focus, spells that relied on subtle effects and both magical and physical leverage to achieve their goals. She'd long been used to seeing elvar mages casually do workings that would require her hours of preparation.

The benefit to that had been that she was far more capable of using magic without being *noticed*, and she was far more capable of using magic on herself than most elvar. Still, they'd always commanded more immediate power…and now, so did she.

Still, the focus's weight was strange on her hip. Plus, she could *feel* its magic in a way she'd never felt the focuses carried by elvar mages around her. Even Greentrees' focus didn't resonate in her mind the same way, though she definitely felt it more than she'd felt any other mage's wand.

Regardless of her distraction, she had work to do and she was out with the rest of her tribe.

She and Axfall were walking the edge of the frame that would soon lift *Star* off the ground and clear space for them to work on her underside. Currently, one of the ninesail's lower decks was pressed against the mountainside, and Brushfire was expecting to have to rebuild all three masts on that side.

"Tomorrow," Axfall finally told her as they stood at one end of the valley and studied the frame. "Assuming we can lift her into the frame without pulleys?"

"We'll have the archmage for that," she reminded her elder. "And Greentrees. That should make for any lift we need."

"It should, yes," the elder gobvar agreed. He lapsed into silence, studying the frame.

It was a temporary dock, one that would only ever hold one ship, but it was sturdily built for that. Ladders rose up the frame every twenty yards or so, connecting layers of scaffolding that would allow the crew to access all three sail decks and all three stave galleries.

"The captain offered me the Master of Decks job," Axfall said calmly. "Offered Windheart Master of Sails."

"I know," Brushfire told him. "He checked with me first."

She kept being surprised by Greentrees treating her as his first officer. He'd given her the job, but somehow she still didn't fully trust that. Yet she had to admit that he certainly *acted* like she was *Star*'s first officer.

"He thinks he'll find a Master of Staves among the elvar Oathsworn Lane referred to us," she told Axfall. "Sails and Decks, though, we're expecting to mostly be gobvar, and he wanted gobvar Masters."

"I didn't give him an answer," Axfall admitted. "Said I had to think about it. Meant I had to talk to you and Windheart."

"And?"

"Windheart said yes on the spot," her friend said, shaking his head at the thought of his lover's optimism. "He said, 'If we're going into the deep aether with this var as our captain, we'd better trust him enough to take his offers.'"

"Windheart is often the wisest of us all," Brushfire observed. "That's why you love him."

"Wise, yes. Overly optimistic, yes. He trusts beyond reason." There was a long silence as they studied the almost-complete dry dock. "And you?"

"I trust Cat Greentrees and Armand Bluestaves," she admitted. That was almost a surprise to *her*, let alone anyone else. "They've kept their word to us and proven themselves so far."

She shook her head.

"I think you should take the Master role," she told him. "There's no one better, and we both know it."

Axfall snorted.

"Guess I can keep you all out of trouble better if I run the deck than if I just do carpentry," he admitted. "Been a while since I ever thought I'd be a Master, though."

"I was surprised enough when Spherefox asked me to be Master of Sails on *Skyfish*," Brushfire admitted. "I wasn't quite sure what to make of it when Greentrees asked me to be first officer.

"But he seems to mean his word, which means that we'll be in position to hold a proverbial knife to his throat if he *breaks* it now," she said grimly. "Out in the deep aether, he can't betray the crew."

"Where are we even *going*?" Axfall asked.

"Bluestaves hasn't told us yet," she admitted. "But he will soon enough."

Before Axfall could say anything else, Fistfall emerged from the camp and waved up at them.

"Eldest sister," he called, projecting his voice to carry up the mountain. "We have company."

That could mean anything...except that Fistfall was Brushfire's first-brother and she knew his tone.

They didn't just have company. They had *trouble*.

Brushfire wasn't surprised to see Virtuous Axhead picking his way down the side of the valley into their camp. He was again dressed in the latest fashion, with mud splattered up his fine white trousers and several tears visible on his long white coat as he glared around the Hammerhead camp.

This time, though, he wasn't alone. Two dozen halvar and darvar followed behind him, spread out in a scattered line that clearly gave them enough space to reach blades and battlewands. At least two of the var pinged her other senses as well, warning her that there were focuses among the...gang.

Axhead might have been tasked to recruit leg-breakers from Brushfire's tribe, but he seemed to have quite a few of them to start with.

"You became a surprisingly difficult var to find, Shaman Brushfire," he told her as she met him at the edge of the camp.

His thugs stopped half a dozen yards back, inside easy reach for magic but far enough back to *pretend* they weren't threatening her.

"I wasn't aware I was under any obligation to make finding me easy," Brushfire said lightly. "We paid your rent and now we are no longer using your property. Our business is done, Axhead."

"Now, now, now," he said with a shake of his head. "We both know that tenants aren't supposed to just up and leave. There is *notice* to be given when you break a rental agreement like that, Shaman Brushfire.

"Plus, there is the damage your party did to our property," he continued. "Between that and breach-of-contract penalties, you owe my employers in excess of one thousand gold swallows. We are prepared to round down to merely one thousand, to make payment easier, but if you can't make prompt payment, we are going to have a problem."

Brushfire let the demand hang in silence. The tribe couldn't pay that amount if they wanted to, even if she thought that it would buy them peace. She might be able to get Greentrees or Bluestaves to come up with the money—it was only eight clock-days' or so of wages for the entire ship's crew, after all—but she wasn't certain that even paying the var would buy them peace.

"We both know every scrap of coin you have demanded from the beginning is lies and grazer offal," she told Axhead flatly. Behind her, she knew Fistfall would be collecting other members of the tribe and sorting out weapons.

Two focuses and twenty blades and battlewands. The hardened thugs were probably more dangerous than her crew, even when outnumbered several times over. Despite the numbers, Brushfire knew her tribe was in danger.

"You wound me, Shaman, but I suppose I am used to debtors trying every angle to escape their dues," Axhead told her. "If you don't have the money, we will need to come to alternative arrangements…or we will *force* alternative arrangements."

Brushfire might not have been used to carrying a focus yet, but she'd carried enough weapons over the years that the instinct of reaching for one put her hand in the right place. A warm shiver ran up her fingers from the arcane tool, a pulse of confidence and power that drove her one confident step forward, looming over Virtuous Axhead with every bit of her height.

"And just what kind of 'arrangements' are you thinking?" she hissed.

"One of your people will enter our service," Axhead told her, as if he was discussing the purchase of a grazer or a layer. "At a reasonable wage and providing them a living allowance, it should only take that worthy ten dances to pay off your tribe's debt.

"Who knows? After ten dances, they may choose to stay with us." The darvar smiled thinly. "We are not difficult employers, after all. The work is straightforward enough."

"And if I refuse to let any of my people sell themselves into slavery?" Brushfire asked. This was what Axhead had been after all along, she suspected. His employers had tasked him with acquiring gobvar slaves, to either be used by the crime syndicate itself or even sold onward.

"Then we will take by force five times what you will not sell," Axhead told her. "And your tribe will suffer for the refusal."

Fistfall was suddenly at her shoulder, his hand grabbing her arm before she did something precipitous.

"Carefully, eldest sister," he murmured to her.

"This brave lad would serve well," Axhead told them, gesturing at Fistfall. "I'm sure he understands well enough the danger to your tribe and people. We ask you to repay an honest debt with honest labor, nothing more."

Exhaling a sigh, Brushfire nodded to her brother.

"Thank you, little brother," she told him. "With certainty, then."

"With certainty," he agreed, his eyes flickering with mirth—and trepidation.

Brushfire drew her focus and stepped forward to clearly place herself between Virtuous Axhead and her family.

"You are a pathetic little wretch, a bottom-feeder in the service of monsters," she told the darvar. "By my oath and my power, you shall have not one moment of our labor, not one drop of our blood."

Several of the gangsters behind Axhead flinched at the sight of a focus in her hand. They clearly hadn't been expecting a mage at all. Their darvar leader simply stared at her, unintimidated by her size or the wand.

"A fancy toy, but do you know how to use it?" he asked. "You are trained as a shaman. You would have got that in the last few clock-days and it takes years of training to use a focus. Resistance will only harm yo—"

The *clunk-thwang* of a crossbow releasing cut off the rest of Virtuous Axhead's words—and a six-inch feathered quarrel sprouted from the gangster's throat.

"Loose!" Windheart's voice snapped. Another dozen weapons cracked in the quiet of the mountainside, though few of the shots were as perfectly accurate as the first one.

A dozen battlewands crackled as well, bolts of bright-red energy hammering into the ground and trees around the attackers.

Despite the volley fire, only a handful of the gangers behind Axhead went down. The rest went for their own weapons, and Brushfire *knew* there were mages with focuses among the crowd.

There were only a handful of spells she was certain she could use her focus with, and she went for the simplest. She trained her focus toward where she knew one of the enemy mages was, and she called the same bolt of heat and light the regular battlewand conjured.

She had no time to consider how much energy to summon—and no reason to limit her power. She wasn't expecting the result, though.

A flash of brilliant light split the air, and she threw a bead of red light at her target. It was brighter than the usual bolt from a battlewand, but it didn't otherwise look any different until it landed.

Then Brushfire and Fistfall were both thrown from their feet by the explosion of fire and force that ripped apart the forested valley. Light and fire rippled through the afternoon air and then silence fell.

"Crossbows are reloaded and battlewands are charged," Windheart shouted over everyone's ringing ears. "Plus, do you *really* want to bet the shaman can't do that again?"

"Time and past time you took your friends and went home," Axfall added. "This is *Star*'s dry dock and *Star*'s crew will defend her. So, get gone!"

Brushfire staggered back to her feet, the focus still somehow in her hand despite everything, and leveled her best glare on the scattered gangsters. Silence was the only answer to her two Masters' declarations.

Then the first gangster got back to their feet, their hands spread wide in surrender. Others followed. The point, it appeared, had been made.

CHAPTER

24

"Ready on port?"

"Ready!"

"Ready on starboard?"

"Ready!"

"Ready on the tops?"

"Ready!"

Shouts echoed across *Star*'s hull, and Cat listened to the practiced call-and-response with a sense of belonging he couldn't quite explain. The crew swarming over the ninesail's three sail decks were mostly gobvar, anchored on the Hammerhead tribe.

In the end, their only real elvar contingent was in the stave galleries. Eighty elvar, including four of the five officers and one of the three Masters, made up barely a quarter of Cat's crew. The presence of the horned gobvar on all sides still occasionally gave him shivers, but they were just as skilled as any elvar he could have recruited.

"Are we ready?" Cat asked his new Master of Sails.

Windheart was among the oldest var he'd ever commanded. He'd known that gobvar could live just as long as elvar in theory, but his understanding was that most of them died long before reaching their third hundred of dances. Even in the Clan Spheres, violence was part of their culture.

Working with a crew of mostly gobvar now, though, Cat had to wonder how much of that was as intrinsic to gobvar as he'd always thought… and how much it was traced back to the Quadrumvirate of beings who ruled the Clans.

"We are ready," the old gobvar told him. "It will certainly help if, say, you and the archmage are standing by in case something goes wrong."

"That is why Bluestaves is here," Cat replied, gesturing out at the set of tents positioned above their impromptu dry dock. The halvar archmage stood in front of them, at the edge of the hollow that had held *Star* for over a dozen dances.

If something went wrong, Armand Bluestaves' magic was ready to pull them out of the fall that would follow. The power of Blueswallow's lodestone core could be overcome by many means—and while Cat hoped not to need the magic of an archmage, it was definitely an option.

"There isn't much of a current down here," Cat warned the Master of Sails. "It will all be on the lift crystals."

"Of course," Windheart replied. "On your order, Captain."

Those words warmed Cat's heart in several ways, and he smiled as he looked out down the mountainside. A military dock at the Rising Swallow Citadel awaited *Star*, where they would receive the final pieces of their storm staves and the ship would become a true warship again at last.

For now, though, the locals had only provided them the frames of those staves. Without the central thunder crystals, *Star*'s weapons were nonfunctional. Of course, without the frames, the thunder crystals were useless to the King of Birdsbreath.

"Open the sails, Master," Cat ordered. "Stand by the lift crystals; let's see what we can get from the current."

Even here, barred by dirt and stone on one side and surrounded by air, there was an underlying layer of aether. *Star*'s sails could catch that aether and ride its current, which was almost inevitably up the mountain—that was part of why ports were built on mountains.

But no shipbuilder relied on that to lift an aether ship. Any smart var building a ship included enough lift crystals to carry the ship into the aether from the edge of the lodestone core itself. His new crew might not have built *Star* from scratch, but they'd made certain she had the lift for this.

Cat could only see one set of *Star*'s sails, the three masts of the upper deck. They opened above him, stiff fabric guided by ropes to form horizontal canopies above the ship and catch what current they could.

He felt the ship move underneath him as the lower decks spread their sails as well. All nine masts and twenty-plus actual sails would be aligned at much the same angle, catching as much of the aether current up the mountain as they could.

This part was a test. He *knew* the ship couldn't rise up the mountain on the aether current he felt. But if she could lift at *all*, it was a good sign for her speed and maneuverability in the long run.

And lift she did. *Star* shifted farther under his feet, and he whispered a soft prayer to the patrons of sailors and fools. His people *should* all be strapped in, but this was one of the most dangerous tasks for any aether sailor.

Star's lodestone keel was intact, a rod of forged lodestone half a yard across that ran the full length of the ship, but its power paled in comparison to the lodestone core of even a small worldlet—and Blueswallow was in the mid-range as habitable worldlets went.

They would need to be significantly farther up the mountain and supported by other magic before *Star's* crew would be safe to walk her lower decks without physical assistance.

But...she was in the air, hovering a handful of yards above the dry dock they'd built.

"We're alive, Captain," Brushfire told him, his first officer looking awed. "I knew we could do it, but it's still...impressive."

"I did *not* know that our people could do it," Cat admitted with a chuckle. "So, imagine how impressed *I* am, Officer Brushfire. If you would do the honors with the lift crystals?"

Any var could activate the lift crystals they were standing next to—there was that much spark of magic in even the dullest fool—but only a focus-equipped mage could use the links of crystal, copper and gold that linked together the arcane systems of the aether ship.

But Brushfire Hammerhead *was* now such a mage, even if her training in focus use still lagged behind what Cat would normally expect in a first officer. Her ability to blow up forests and attacking squads was proven, at least, though over forty clock-days had passed since that incident now.

She nodded at his command and stepped up to stand beside him, carefully judging the array of crystals and other paraphernalia next to the main wheel. She tapped three crystals in quick succession with her focus, channeling power into each of them, and the crystals began to glow a soft pink.

Cat *felt* his first officer's power flicker through the ship, magic running along those nodes and touching crystal after crystal in a flow of energy that seemed to bring *Star* awake in a way the hulk hadn't been since they'd set foot on her.

"Keep an eye to your sails, Master Windheart," he ordered as he laid his own hands on the wheel. "Because up we go!"

And in answer to his soft words, the crystals finished activating. *Star* leapt forward and upward at his touch, and for the first time since his arrest, Cat Greentrees took control of a ninesail.

Cat could tell that the guards on the Citadel towers were *not* happy when they realized his ship was crewed by gobvar. He sympathized to a point, but they had known what was coming.

Disgruntled or not, Rising Swallow's guardians ushered *Star* to the dock swiftly enough. The old ninesail's wheel responded swiftly to his hands, gently gliding the ship into the indicated space.

"Lock us on, Master of Decks," he ordered Axfall.

The second of his two elder gobvar started barking orders immediately, then personally led a team of half a dozen deckvar to the edge of the ship. Massive hooks locked on to brackets built for them, and Cat could feel the weight of his ship shift as the dock's magically supported framing began to hold *Star* up.

"Locked on," Axfall reported. "Should we check their safety netting?"

"Always," Cat told him. "I might not have the High Court behind me if I offend them this time, but we're still checking their safety netting." He smiled brightly, his mood buoyed by being once again in command of an aether ship.

"I'll risk offending our hosts before I'll risk the crew," he continued. "Get to it."

Axfall nodded and disappeared belowdecks. They were high enough now that, with a little care, the crew could walk on the sections of deck opposed to Blueswallow's lodestone core. Still, the safety netting that was spread out beneath them was critical to making sure everyone was safe.

"You can tune down the lift crystals," Cat told Brushfire. "We never completely discharge them in a core's lode field, though."

"I remember that," she said.

Despite his first officer's polite tone, there was an also an edge of "Of course I knew that" to her words. Which was fair: she might be new to being an officer and being a focus-using mage, but she'd been on aether ships for a long time.

Some things were obvious to anyone who spent time on a ship.

"Once that's done, I'll need you to double-check the air envelope," he told her with a nod that hopefully acknowledged her point. "I trust our crew, but I want to be *absolutely* sure the envelope is sealed, intact and working in every way before we put the archmage inside it!"

"Agreed," she said. "What about you?"

"I'm going to grab our Master of Staves and talk to the locals about getting our thunder crystals," Cat replied. "That's our most important need from the Citadel—and it will give them a chance to get used to the idea that we have gobvar aboard without rubbing you in their faces."

"Probably wise," she agreed after a moment.

"Wise, yes. Also frustrating," he conceded. "I'll step softly around the locals when we're under their protection; we have to."

"I understand, Captain," she said. "It's fine."

"No, it's not," Cat admitted. "You should be coming with me and Paintrock. But we can't risk creating trouble with the Birdsbreathers."

"I *understand*," Brushfire insisted, and something in her smile told him that he'd belabored the point enough…and that she actually *believed* him, too.

Cat was starting to understand the situation of the gobvar. Enough so, at least, that he wasn't sure he would have believed him in her place.

Despite his concerns around hiring gobvar pirates, Cat had to admit that he wasn't entirely convinced that Hunter Paintrock, the blue-skinned and black-haired elvar he'd hired as Master of Staves, *wasn't* a pirate.

The irony wasn't lost on him as he watched the gaudily dressed elvar out of the corner of his eye. Paintrock wasn't a mage, but he had no less than *four* battlewands distributed along a bandolier slung over his left shoulder, plus a sword and several grenades.

"We're not planning on trying to take the Rising Swallow Citadel by storm, Master of Staves," Cat observed wryly when he saw the last. "Grenades?"

"I learned the hard way you regret *not* having them more than you ever regret bringing them," Paintrock said cheerfully. "I'll leave behind anything the hallies ask me to."

Cat considered ordering the var to leave the bombs behind himself, then sighed and stepped out onto the drawbridge connecting *Star* to the suspended dock. A half dozen guards of three different var were scattered along the length of the pier, uniformly armed even if they varied in height and breadth.

That was one of the advantages of the weapon the guards wielded. A wand-halberd included both a battlewand's magical components, stretched over a longer shaft, and a wicked point with three different heads.

The three-yard-long weapon was also balanced and designed such that it was equally usable by a short darvar at four feet tall as by a tall halvar at six feet. While the guard squad's mixed makeup could still cause them problems in many ways, Cat was sure, they at least knew that all of the troopers had about the same reach with the weapon.

The closest trooper waved the two elvar through, gesturing toward the mountainside anchor of the floating pier.

"Commander's waiting for you," the darvar grunted.

"Thank you, soldier," Cat told her before setting off down the narrow spit of wood and iron and magic toward the Citadel itself. He'd known var to find the suspended docks disturbing, failing to recognize that the magic and engineering that allowed the docks to support an aether ship wasn't going to be bothered by the weight of one var.

And even if someone fell off, the safety netting set up to protect the ships' crews would serve just as well for clumsy world-dwellers.

Cat wasn't sure if their immediate host was one of those people, but the fancifully dressed halvar was waiting for them on solid rock. Birds-breath's military, he reflected, clearly didn't bother with such concepts as *uniforms* in any great measure.

The officer wore a knee-length crimson tunic only vaguely related in style to the outfits worn by the guards. To that eye-catching central garment he'd added a pair of stuffed shoulders that easily consumed his upper arms and concealed his neck.

"Think that's supposed to protect his throat?" Paintrock muttered. "Because I'm pretty sure I can put a knife through the puff and into his neck from here."

"Let's *not* find out," Cat said repressively, realizing that he hadn't even *seen* throwing knives on Paintrock's bandolier. His new Master of Staves was an…interesting individual.

From Paintrock's chuckle, that had been the expected response. Cat recognized when he was being played—but so far, at least, Paintrock appeared to be doing so for shared amusement rather than any ill intent.

It was still something he was going to have to watch.

Laying that thought aside, he inclined his head to the Birdsbreather officer.

"I am Captain Cat Greentrees of the House of Forests, Archmage Bluestaves' ship captain," he introduced himself. "This is my Master of Staves, Hunter Paintrock. We are expected, I hope."

"You are, you are," the officer confirmed. "I am Tower Commander Grazer Rainshower, son of Turtle Rainshower, of Clan Crimson Petal."

For a blink of an eye, Cat thought he was being made fun of. Then he realized that, no, that was how certain classes of Birdsbreather society apparently named their children.

And that he had no grounds to complain about anyone *else's* name.

"You should have fifteen storm-stave thunder crystals laid aside for my ship," Cat continued after a moment. "We will take them aboard as soon as you're ready for us. My archmage should also be joining us within the clock-day."

"The thunder crystals await only the hands of your var," Rainshower conceded. "My King has also asked me to extend her admiration for the work your crew carried out in rebuilding *Star* and constructing the dry dock to work on her.

"She has asked me to ask you if the dry dock is a permanent structure?"

"I would need to confirm with the carpenters who built it," Cat admitted. "My understanding is that it could both easily be turned into one or taken down."

"My King wishes to preserve the dock," the officer said stiffly. "If your carpenters and crew could provide drawings or other instructions to enable us to complete their work and move *Shadow* into the same dock, Her Majesty would arrange appropriate compensation."

"I will speak with my Master of Decks and see what we can arrange," Cat promised. "Her Majesty's cooperation and assistance in Archmage Bluestaves' project have been invaluable."

Of course, Bluestaves had compensated the King and her people more than generously for that assistance. Money would flow both ways, but that was the nature of the spheres.

"I also need to ask…you have gobvar aboard your ship?" Rainshower asked.

"We do," Cat confirmed. "The majority of our riggers and deckvar are gobvar. They are skilled sailors, and many were finding it difficult to secure proper employment for their skills."

"But they also bring trouble, do they not?" the officer said.

Cat's smile and eyes narrowed.

"The only trouble I've seen with my crew would have been prevented if the Citadel's patrols had done their job," he murmured. "Part of what my archmage paid for, after all, was a secure dock."

That was going to be a sore spot on both sides, he suspected. The thugs that had tried to extort his crew had walked right through the fences and gates and patrols that were supposed to protect the forest reservation *Star* had been rebuilt in the middle of.

The locals weren't happy that his gobvar had laid out a stack of corpses in the middle of their military reservation. *Cat* wasn't happy that his people had been *attacked* in the middle of the locals' military reservation.

Rainshower gave a dismissive gesture and sniff.

"Current past the sail, I suppose," he said. "Shall I show you to the warehouse where you'll find your crystals?"

"Please, Tower Commander."

CHAPTER 25

The air envelope was a fascinating piece of the ship to Brushfire. Every ship she'd been on had had one, but they'd only barely registered to her before *Star*. With the right plugs pulled in, the envelope became completely airtight except for a set of doubled doors to avoid losing too much of the air contained within.

Magic refreshed and replenished the air, but it could only replace so much when the ship was in aether, so they minimized the loss by having paired doors and by limiting the number of times people went in and out of the envelope.

On most ships, the envelope was a relatively small compartment: a few rooms for passengers and a mess that doubled as the ship's surgery and sickbay. While gobvar and elvar could breathe aether, it was a stress on their bodies, and they healed faster in air.

Aboard *Star*, the entire section that had once been the officers' quarters—underneath the captain's quarters in the aftercastle on the upper sail deck—had been added to that envelope. The officers' quarters had been moved into the starboard sail deck aftercastle, where *Star* had been built to host an admiral.

Since the officers traditionally had decent-sized quarters *and* a mess of their own, combining it with the usual passenger and medical space—still present on a ninesail warship, even before it had entered the service of a halvar king—had created an air envelope larger than some houses she'd been in.

The comparison was apt, she realized as she stepped into a room that was definitively Armand Bluestaves' *library*. The archmage had taken up less space in the envelope than she'd expected after seeing his specifications for its size, but he'd also apparently brought aboard a hundred or so books while she wasn't looking.

"These are all copies," he told her as she looked around in her surprise. "Still not cheap—none of these are printed—but some of the originals are irreplaceable."

"Irreplaceable?" Brushfire asked, realizing the two of them were alone in the room. Bluestaves was sitting in an overstuffed armchair pulled up to a table he'd covered in papers—some of which were definitely sphere charts.

"My family has collected rare books, texts and charts for as long as the Bluestaves line has existed," he told her. "We usually keep meticulous records, though we're not perfect, and the archive is about six hundred dances old. Older than the oldest living mortal var."

He shrugged.

"I am not the first Bluestaves to be an archmage. I probably will not be the last, though I believe my sister is currently expected to carry on the family name." He smiled sadly. "My own interests do not extend to children.

"But I am currently the custodian of the Bluestaves Archive. The books are in my tower in the Great Red Forest in the Shining Kingdom. These are…copies of a relevant selection."

"I've only ever seen printed books," Brushfire admitted, looking at the rows of clearly hand-lettered spines in awe. "This is incredible."

Bluestaves smiled, clearly touched.

"I'm not sure I have much here that would be of interest to you," he warned. "It's mostly very old history and some more recent pieces on esoteric cults of the spheres."

"An odd combination," she said.

"It will make sense shortly, once the captain is here."

As if summoned by his title, Cat Greentrees slipped through the door into the library.

"I thought I smelled books being brought aboard," the captain said. "But I wasn't expecting this many!"

"As I was just telling Shaman Brushfire, these are all copies," Bluestaves noted. "I keep an archive for my family. Not as old or as extensive as the archives of a High Court House, but…sufficient to the mystery at hand."

"You found an answer to why dragons are fighting alongside gobvar?" Greentrees asked.

Brushfire shivered as she took a seat. She'd never seen a dragon in her life and often allowed herself to forget just what the mission she'd signed her tribe up for was.

"No," the archmage conceded. "The histories of the spheres have not been that forthcoming. Only one dragon has ever worked with gobvar that we know of. Old Bloodscale inserted himself into Clan politics about nine hundred and fifty dances ago, burning and killing until he convinced the Clans to acknowledge him as one of their rulers."

"The Quadrumvirate," Brushfire whispered. That, like Old Bloodscale, was a name to conjure with even among gobvar exiles.

"The Quadrumvirate," Bluestaves agreed. "Old Bloodscale, Her First Sister, the Blood King and the Clan Warlord."

"It's telling that the *least* terrifying member of that group is the var considered the deadliest and most powerful commander in the gobvar spheres," Greentrees said grimly as he took a seat next to Brushfire.

"The only dragon to ever involve himself in mortal affairs, the senior priestess of a goddess that demands living sacrifice, an immortal mass-murdering demigod, and the deadliest living gobvar warrior," Bluestaves reeled off. "I'm not sure which of the other three is the most terrifying, but the Clan Warlord is definitely the most understandable danger."

From what Brushfire understood, Her Crimson Sisters were an ever-present part of life in the Clan Spheres. Old Bloodscale and the Blood King were more distant figures, feared and obeyed but without servitors to be present in the same way.

And every Clan had their warlord. And while only one was *the* Clan Warlord, every gobvar understood what the Clan Warlord did and how they got their place.

"If the Clans spent less time fighting over who got to be Clan Warlord, the High Court and the Kingdoms would be in real danger," Greentrees murmured. "They already test the border often enough, even if it's been a hundred dances since we had a real war."

"That was the thing I went researching," Bluestaves told them. "How long has the border existed in its current form?"

Brushfire looked over at the elvar officer. She didn't have the luxury of a wide education, but she suspected and hoped that her captain did. That question, however, had left Greentrees looking discomfited.

"I'm…not sure," he admitted.

"About four hundred and fifty dances, give or take," Bluestaves told him. "Very few elvar, even, remain from the era of that war. So, we think of the spheres as they are now as being the way they always were."

The archmage spread a large chart over the table. Brushfire leaned forward, following the familiar lines of a sphere chart.

"The spheres as they are now," he repeated unnecessarily. "Our charts cover about three hundred spheres on this side of the border, and eighty or so on the other side with…lesser degrees of certainty."

And nine spheres marked the only places those two regions intersected: the border spheres themselves, where elvar and gobvar fleets had skirmished back and forth for a long, long, time.

"The border is effectively impenetrable both ways," Bluestaves conceded. "There's a limited amount of smuggling, but even that is sparser than I expected when I started looking. I had hoped to charter passage on a smuggler ship, but it appears that even finding one was beyond my resources."

From what Brushfire had seen of the archmage's resources, that was saying something.

"Why does it matter?" she asked.

"Because we're not going to find our answers by sailing up to the gobvar flotilla in Shadowcastle and asking them why they worked with dragons to take the sphere from the High Court," Bluestaves said grimly. "We're going to need to enter the Clan Spheres to search out information—potentially, we will even need to speak with dragons as well as negotiate with gobvar.

"We cannot do any of that from this side of the border."

Greentrees was studying the chart, though he had to be just as familiar with it as Brushfire was.

"The High Court has half their fleet along the border," he noted. "They're not going to let us pass those straits without a good reason—and even if your archmage credentials can get us past the Navy, the border Clans are…"

"More directly controlled by Her Sisters than any other," Brushfire murmured. "The Sisters would turn *Star* into our funeral pyre and laugh."

"Exactly," Bluestaves agreed. "Passing through the border isn't a practical answer to the problem. But we need to investigate in the Clan Spheres, or we face a potential dragon-led invasion that will overrun everywhere."

Brushfire swallowed. She'd been shown bits of the archmage's vision. Enough to terrify her. She didn't know how to stop what was coming—but she'd committed herself to helping the archmage try.

"I was told by a friend that I had part of the answer, so I went looking in the records my family kept," Bluestaves told them. "And I found what may be that 'part of the answer.'"

He spread a second sphere chart across the table. The basic geometry and layout of the spheres was the same, but the labeling, symbology... even the script was different. Even the *language* was archaic, Brushfire realized after a moment.

"This is a copy of a copy of a copy," the archmage said quietly. "The version in my family archives was copied from a degrading chart a hundred and fifty dances ago—and our records show that *that* chart was a copy of a previous chart acquired when the archive was established.

"And that chart was at least two hundred dances old when my ancestor acquired it." He shook his head. "Fortunately, the influence of the elvar has kept our main trade languages and writing styles consistent enough that I can follow the notations."

"This chart is...what, seven hundred dances old?" Greentrees asked, eyeing it carefully.

"From the iconography, language drift and writing style...more like twelve," Bluestaves admitted. "I only know its history after it ended up in my family's archive. But this chart predates the border as we know it."

"It predates the Clans as we know them, I think," Brushfire murmured. "Certainly it predates the Quadrumvirate."

"It is old enough that no mortal has seen the spheres as it portrays them," the archmage told them. "The Blood King, for example, probably saw the spheres this way. I don't know how old Old Bloodscale is, either, but it's probable that some of the elder dragons like him were around twelve hundred dances ago."

Greentrees was examining the map carefully, and Brushfire found herself following his hand as he traced individual spheres he recognized.

"What is the Ironhand Imperium?" the elvar finally asked, tracing a boundary drawn on the chart in dark red ink. "I've never heard that name before."

"The spheres are not always as they are now," Bluestaves repeated. "But since they live longer than everyone else, the elvar find it convenient to pretend the High Court has always been the supreme power in the spheres."

"Where the High Court itself is on the edge of this chart," Greentrees said slowly. "Far from the center."

"One of the reasons my family's archive exists is that an ancestor of mine realized the High Court was using their political and economic influence to quietly suppress pre-Court-era history," Bluestaves told him.

"At this point, they've been so successful that I don't think any of the current generation of *elvar* realized it ever happened," he continued. "There are records of the Ironhand Dynasty, but they are scattered, and it's honestly not very relevant to anybody. A thousand dances is two full lifetimes even for elvar and gobvar."

The archmage shook his head.

"No one living even had *parents* who lived under the Imperium. We have some records, like this chart, *of* the Imperium. But we don't know what happened to it."

Brushfire followed Greentrees' pointing finger and then traced the boundary herself.

"This chart includes more of the gobvar spheres than the modern one," she observed. "And almost as many of the Clan Spheres were part of this Imperium as the Court and Kingdom spheres."

"I knew that about this chart," Bluestaves told them. "I spent some time digging into the Ironhands during my studies. We have some information of their rule and existence but nothing about their fall.

"I *believe* they were overthrown by twin rebellions, one from the High Court and one in what is now the Clan Spheres," he continued. "But…all of this is only somewhat relevant to why I'm showing you this.

"Look here."

He stabbed a delicate finger down on the map.

"Brokenwright," Bluestaves noted. "Captain, if you could pull the current chart out?"

Greentrees obeyed and Brushfire helped lay the two charts next to each other, drawing a mental line between the two representations of the sphere of Brokenwright.

"It's a backwater with no habitable worldlets," Greentrees said. "A small ember that doesn't provide enough light for anything."

"Agreed, but look at it on the old map," Bluestaves told them.

Brushfire's rough reading of the notation suggested that nothing had changed, except...

"Wait, this mentions a fortress citadel?" she said. "And..."

"There's an aether strait that isn't on the current map," Greentrees finished for her.

The elvar's finger traced the route, but Brushfire's eyes were on the map as he did it. From Brokenwright, the strait linked to a sphere that didn't exist on the modern map. Then another. Then two more—before it finally linked back into a outerlit sphere in the territory of the gobvar Clans.

"Spheres don't just go away," Bluestaves told them. "Those four spheres *have* to still exist."

"If I'm reading this right, this sphere"—Greentrees tapped one of the four missing places—"was a major location for the Ironhands. Multiple worldlets, fleet bases... This was their core, the anchor of their industry and military.

"Perhaps even their equivalent of the High Court itself."

"And it's gone," Brushfire murmured. "No wonder their Imperium vanished with barely a whimper."

She was looking at the modern chart again, studying the icons on Brokenwright, and shivered as she recognized one. It wasn't a common one, but she'd seen it before.

"There's a void strait in Brokenwright," she told them.

"A what?" both of the other var asked in near-unison.

"They're rare, but *Skyfish* used to make a run that brought us far too cursed near to one," she told them. "So, we learned to recognize it on the charts and make sure we could avoid it in the aether."

"A void strait," Greentrees echoed. "I'd heard them mentioned, but never..."

"It would be an aether strait except it links into nothingness," Brushfire explained to Bluestaves as the archmage still looked confused. "It pulls aether into it, so they're unsafe to travel near, but otherwise, they have all the magical properties of an aether strait."

The captain had followed her gesture and was carefully reading the notes on the two maps, a dark expression falling over his face.

"It was the strait to this sphere," he told them both, tapping the first missing sphere. "That's why these spheres aren't on the map, Archmage."

"Because they no longer have aether," Bluestaves said calmly. "They are void spheres. I established that much through divination, though I expected the aether strait itself to remain much the same."

"So, you *knew* you needed to cross four spheres of void?" Greentrees asked. He was reading the old chart now, running his fingers down ancient numbers. "Thirty-six *thousand leagues* with no air. No aether. Nothing."

"It is that or somehow breach the Clan's border spheres in the face of Her Crimson Sisters," the halvar replied. "I believe this option may be easier."

"No, no it isn't," the elvar captain snapped before Brushfire could say a word. "Even if we somehow build some super air-envelope to cover the entire exterior of *Star*, we still wouldn't be able to travel those spheres, archmage.

"*Star* is an aether ship. Without aether, we can't maneuver. I can do a lot to make up for uncooperative currents, but I can't make the ship move with *no* currents—and I need riggers to navigate uncooperative ones.

"Riggers I can't send up if there's no aether for them to breathe."

"He's right," Brushfire said softly. "No aether ship can make the journey you're asking, archmage. You'd be better off gathering a fleet and breaching the border. We..."

She didn't want to say that they'd all wasted their time. If nothing else, there were a lot of sailors aboard *Star* still expecting to get paid. Bluestaves would *probably* pay them out, no matter what, but they'd been expecting real work.

"I am not that foolish, my friends," the chubby archmage told them, leaning back in his seat. "I recognized this difficulty and sought answers before I ever came here."

"And you still had us refit a ninesail for you?" Brushfire asked.

"*Star* is a beginning," Bluestaves told them. "But she is not the ship that will carry us through the void. We needed an aether ship for the next step, and I needed a crew I could trust—and while my visions are unclear on many points, I suspect we're going to need a *warship* before we're done."

"Six spheres and fifty thousand leagues to Brokenwright," Greentrees said slowly. "Forty clock-days just to get there, depending on the currents. But there's no point with a ship that can't enter that void strait."

"The last piece of the puzzle was delivered into my hands by a colleague, shortly before I left the Shining Kingdom for here," Bluestaves told them. "It's not exactly a secret—but it was not easy to learn for a non-darvar, either."

Brushfire looked at the archmage questioningly. What did darvar have to do with this?

"What was?" Greentrees asked the question she was thinking.

"Brokenwright has inhabitants," the archmage told them. "According to the information I was given, a sect of the worshippers of the First Digger have set up a monastery inside an airless worldlet in Brokenwright, to allow them to 'meditate on creation and the Digger's Will' away from the interruptions of modern life and Court and Kingdoms."

Brushfire was passingly familiar with the First Digger, a god worshipped by a minority of darvar that supposedly had carved the spheres out of some greater infinite expanse of stone that had later turned to the void. Some of them believed that if they meditated on the spheres for long enough, they would be able to find a way to turn void into stone or even lodestone—or just find a way for darvar to breathe aether. That meditation required isolation, though most wouldn't abandon all civilization to do it.

"They've certainly found a spot for that," she observed. "Not even the spheres linked to Brokenwright have anyone else living in them. You have to pass a true dark sphere to enter Brokenwright, and these notes suggest its ember is almost burnt out."

"And that is not entirely out of character for the most austere sects of the First Digger's worshippers," Bluestaves said.

"But you don't think that's what's going on?" Greentrees asked.

"I *suspect*, given the charts and information in my family's archives about Brokenwright, that the sect has actually set up in the old Ironhand fortress citadel that Shaman Brushfire noted. While it would be within the capacity of at least some Digger sects to repair such a structure..."

"It would be a great triumph, one to be shouted about in the circles of darvar artisans and builders, if they'd done such a thing," Greentrees observed. "If they kept it *secret*..."

"But presumably someone is supplying them?" Brushfire asked.

"There are a handful of aether ships contracted to bring them supplies, yes," Bluestaves agreed. "But how many elvar could tell the difference between a monastery dug into the side of a small worldlet and a fortress citadel that honeycombs the entire interior of such a world?"

"Not...many," Greentrees admitted. "Not least because most who would command aether ships would not actually *care*."

"So, I believe they have kept the true nature of the Monastery of the First Digger secret, which makes me wonder what other secrets they keep," Bluestaves told them. "My own divinations remain...foggy. But I believe there is *something* in their monastery that will allow us to traverse the void.

"I have dreamt a ship like none I have seen in my waking hours," he continued. "I know nothing of it, only that it is in that monastery and that I believe it can travel the void. But that, combined with the other secrets being kept by the sect, leads me to a conclusion I dislike."

"They are not meditating on creation's beginning," Brushfire said softly. She knew what the archmage was talking about. She'd had the misfortune of encountering His Brothers in the past.

"They are meditating on its end, on the void and its slow spread through all spheres," Bluestaves agreed, his tone equally soft. "I fear they are not worshippers of the First Digger. They are worshippers of Her Dark Brother."

Brushfire wasn't sure who the "she" in the titles was, but Her Crimson Sister and Her Dark Brother were twin gods, believed to be the last-born of the divine children of the spheres and bitter in their late coming to the universe.

Her Crimson Sister was the goddess of strife, bloodshed, violence and murder. Worshiped by Her Crimson Sisters, the priestesses of the gobvar, they had shaped the Clans into the nation that the High Court feared.

Her Dark Brother was the god of endings, deception, betrayal and death. His Dark Brothers were creatures of the shadow and the void, sliding unnoticed through the cracks of all var and killing anyone who identified them.

A cult of Her Dark Brother would find all too many uses for a void strait and a ship to traverse it, even if was only for the relatively innocent purpose of meditating in an area of true void.

"If they are His Dark Brothers…they will not lightly allow us to use their ship," Greentrees warned.

"And that, my friends," Bluestaves agreed softly, "is why I fear we're going to need *Star*'s storm staves before this is over."

CHAPTER 26

It took two entire clock-days for the crew to bring the thunder crystals for fifteen storm staves aboard the ship and fit them out—two clock-days Armand Bluestaves spent bringing other supplies aboard. The books and charts he'd used to find their destination had been critical, but he wasn't going to miss his food if he could avoid it.

Without access to the kitchen in his tower, he'd had difficulties sourcing even the right kind of magical stoves and ovens to run aboard an aether ship, let alone the right supplies. He'd cook his own meals, he was fine with that, but he needed a lot of supplies to make that happen.

He wasn't expecting to be able to acquire much in terms of spices, specialty flours, sweet glazes or even anything but standard layer eggs in the aether. Fortunately, while crystal-chilled storage boxes were expensive, they were acquirable and didn't impede the ship in any way.

Several of the gobvar crew eyed him askance as they helped him set up the array of cold-storage containers, but they'd done the work without much question. They all knew he was the one paying the bills for the ship, after all.

Armand wasn't sure he'd have much luck moving the cold storage to the void ship when they acquired it, but that was a problem for then. He'd live on regular rations if he *had* to, but until then, he had a chilled wine and beer cellar, a stockpile of eleven different types of flour, four different glazes, seventy-three spices and eggs from nineteen varieties of layer.

He was pulling a tray of sweet rolls from the oven when someone knocked on his kitchen.

"Enter!" he shouted. Or tried to, at least. Given the mouthful of bread, it might not have sounded coherent to whoever was at the door.

Greentrees came in anyway, the elvar surveying the now-fully equipped kitchen with an odd look.

"I'd been told you were bringing gear aboard," he noted. "I wasn't expecting…this."

"I acquired my midsection by dint of heroic labor, Captain," Armand said with a chuckle after swallowing his test roll. "These rolls could have used a bit more sugar. With the artifice-driven pressure in here, things don't bake quite the way I expect.

"The glaze will help make up for that, though."

He slid the tray onto the counter, where a mixing bowl held that addition.

"What do you need, Captain?" he asked.

"To give you the final warning, I suppose," Greentrees told him. "The last thunder crystals have been installed and *Star* is officially ready to sail. I've given the locals notice that we will be departing in two hours.

"If there's anything else you need before we sail, now is the time to make sure of it."

"I believe I have arranged everything," Armand said before he tested the taste of the glaze. It would work perfectly, even with the rolls being less sweet and fluffy than planned.

"I would love to watch the flight out into the aether, but I am sadly aware that would be…unwise for me."

"It can be done," Greentrees said. "But it would require a great deal of effort to prearrange—or a prodigious display of magical strength on someone's part."

Armand chuckled, carefully brushing glaze over the first sweet roll.

"My part, you mean," he guessed. "I should perhaps preserve such displays for less-frivolous uses."

"Perhaps," the elvar agreed. "But then, I've made hundreds of ascents and it still awes me every time. The aether is something else. The fundamental connective tissue of the spheres."

"Where I would argue that the fundamental connection of the spheres is magic, the Source of all things," Armand replied. "A philosophical discussion in some ways, an eminently practical one in others."

"From what I understand of what you do, I can see why you think that way," Greentrees agreed. "But as a sailor, I must always remember that we can go wherever there is aether. And the absence of aether marks the limits of the spheres."

"That's what makes our destination fascinating, isn't it?" Armand asked thoughtfully. "It *was* a sphere. Now it is void. I wonder what remains."

From Greentrees' expression, the aether ship captain wasn't enjoying that thought.

"Sweet roll, Captain? These first few are ready."

CHAPTER 27

*A*SCENT.

It was a simple word, one that said everything that needed to be said about the process of taking an aether ship up into its natural habitat.

And yet...it didn't convey anything near the reality of the event. Cat Greentrees had left dozens of worldlets behind in his career, but it still struck pure awe into him each time.

The slim elvar stood on the wheel deck, watching Brushfire Hammerhead guide the wheel with a cautious eye. He'd walked the gobvar officer through the process and he had faith in his instruction, but it wasn't a fair expectation that she'd get it right the first time without help.

Most of his attention was on the mountains of Rising Swallow as they fell away from *Star*. The aether ship drew back and up, away from the Citadel guarding the halvar city. The lift crystals were being watched by their fourth officer, a young elvar mage of no House, named Bogsong Smallwolf.

Smallwolf was only forty or so dances old, making her roughly the same age as their archmage employer. An age that was considered *experienced* for a halvar was fresh-faced and barely out of training for an elvar.

Still, she seemed to know her way around the lift crystals and had been prepared to sign on with a crew of gobvar. Cat would keep an eye on her, but he was used to playing mother-layer to young mages.

"We're clear of the mountain," Cat murmured. It wasn't an instruction, just an observation, but there was a small point to it. Lift crystals could hold *Star* up against the worldlet's lodestone field, but it would take both the crystals and an aether current to lift the ship all the way out of the field.

And the best currents ran up mountains—which made the ascent a careful balance of being clear enough of the mountain for safety and still close enough to rise on the current that wove up the rocky slopes.

His new first officer nodded silently, her focus still on the wheel. She adjusted its angle, first slowly and then with more assurance as the sails above and around them responded to her movements.

Within a few moments, *Star*'s sails went from nearly vertical to nearly horizontal, and their ascent began to gain speed. Rising Swallow began to drop away beneath them, and Cat watched the city shrink with an odd feeling.

He'd paid for a full dance in advance at the Salient Hunt. That room was still his, acting as a catch post for his mail. He didn't want to draw even his family's attention to his absence from Blueswallow.

Cat had planned and expected to be in Rising Swallow for a long time. He'd never *truly* intended to spend the full thirty dances in the halvar city, but he hadn't had any plans to leave, either. He'd taken the room in Oathsworn Lane's bar, planning for it to be his home for some dances to come.

Instead, he was leaving the entire worldlet behind after less than half a dance. To do so, he'd defied his sentence and his House. That went against the grain for an elvar of the Houses, but what could he do?

Prophecy said he needed to be here. An archmage said that the fate of all free var rested on his mission. Cat knew all of the arguments, and he'd make them eventually, at least to his family.

But in truth, he knew he would have taken Bluestaves' offer no matter what. In that moment, watching a worldlet fall away beneath his aether ship as they rose to the sky, he knew the reality.

He was an aether ship captain and he would have done almost *anything* to stand on the forecastle of a ship rising into the space between worlds.

"No more air," Brushfire observed, even as Cat's breath caught in his throat. "The archmage is stuck in his quarters for a while now."

"We'll have to make sure to visit," Cat said wryly. He held out a hand in the aether, feeling the currents. They weren't clear of the lodestone field from Blueswallow yet, but they were on their way.

"I have the course you charted," the gobvar told him. "Any changes?"

He paused thoughtfully, considering the currents he could feel.

"Not yet," he said. "Once we're a bit farther from Blueswallow, the currents become a touch more variable and I can find us some speed. For now, the chart will serve."

The spheres they would travel to reach Brokenwright were charted, at least. Those charts laid out the primary currents of the aether in those spheres and allowed a course to be planned well in advance.

Cat, on the other hand, could sense the currents of aether around him and adjust his ship's sails and course to match them. Not every aether navigator had his sensitivity, which allowed him to shave time and distance from trips that other captains couldn't.

"Ship to port," Smallwolf shouted down to him, the fourth officer standing in the watch post on the forward upper mast. There was a gobvar watcher up there with the young elvar mage, but Cat took it as a good sign that Smallwolf was willing to climb the masts at all.

And that the watchvar didn't seem to mind her presence, either.

"I've eyes on her," Cat replied loudly, his attention falling on the approaching sixsail. A bit over half a cable long, the smaller warship's sails bore the black-painted swallow of the King of Birdsbreath on their white aethercloth.

"Run up the sphere flag and the blue pennant," he ordered after a moment.

While *Star* was now definitely Armand Bluestaves' ship, she remained home-ported in Birdsbreath. That meant they would fly the flag of that sphere, the same black swallow emblazoned across the sixsail's sails.

The blue pennant that would fly *above* that flag marked the ninesail as the personal ship of an archmage, to be challenged at the peril of the archmage's ire.

"Straightening us out," Brushfire noted, clearly leaving the local guardian to Cat's judgment as she focused on the task of flying the big ship.

As the flags ran up the poles on the central masts, *Star* shifted under Brushfire's hands. So far, she'd risen from the surface of Blueswallow in the same orientation as she'd rested at the docks: roughly parallel to the worldlet's surface.

Now the sails shifted slowly back toward vertical relative to the decks—except if Brushfire had done it *right*, the sails would have stayed in the same place and the *ship* would have rotated up around them.

But she'd rushed it and the end result was somewhere in between. Instead of *Star* putting Blueswallow behind her stern, the worldlet was still partially beneath them, and Brushfire cursed.

"If that's all you mucked up on your first ascent, Officer Brushfire, you did much better than I did," Cat told her with a chuckle. "Take a breath, straighten us out. We're all but clear of the lodestone core; turning us about is easy now."

With Blueswallow's core pulling them toward the worldlet, rotating the ship was easy enough. As Cat glanced back at the controls, his second officer, Faith Streamwater, tapped her focus along the lift crystal controls.

The pink light faded out and *Star* settled into her sails. The worldlet was shrinking behind them, and Cat took a glance down and backward to take in the expanse of blue-green—still a world, but no longer seemingly the entire universe.

"Birdsbreather ship has matched course at four cables," Smallwolf called down. "Our blue pennant is flying."

"Any message flags?" Cat called up. Half of his attention was on Brushfire now, watching as his first officer worked her way through the straightforward, if embarrassing, process of slowly orienting the ship.

"Nothing so far," the fourth officer told him.

"Testing to see what we do," Streamwater observed. She was an older elvar, probably into her third hundred of dances, though still spry enough to climb a mast. Houseless and Kingdom-born, she'd slowly worked her way through the ranks as first a sailor, then a Master of Sails and then an officer.

"They know who we are and what we're doing," Cat pointed out.

"Different rules for the High Court Navy than for a merchant ship," Streamwater reminded him. "Even with the archmage's pennant, we're still near the bottom of the heap. And local warships are near the top."

"Right." He eyed the ship, barely a toy by the standards he was used to, and shook his head. *Star*'s reduced armament was only slightly inferior to the local ship, and the ninesail could handle hits better.

No sensible sixsail captain challenged a ninesail in any state...but that was a question of weapons and not of face and stature.

Cat might be used to being on the "top of the heap," as Streamwater put it, but he knew the games of face and stature by heart. He was an elvar of the Houses, after all. And as a High Court Navy officer, he supposed he knew the respect *he* would have expected.

"Smallwolf, send up a flare salute, please."

The fourth officer didn't verbally acknowledge the order, but her focus sparked magic a few seconds later and a blast of blue light blazed into the aether. Two more followed at an even pace, the young elvar knowing *how* to do the salute if not necessarily *when* to.

Which, to be fair, was an etiquette Cat wasn't used to being on this side of.

"Return salute from the sixsail," Smallwolf reported as a single blue flare flashed above *Star*'s upper deck.

"She's breaking off, falling back into guardian orbit," Streamwater reported as the sixsail's course shifted. "Just making sure we knew our place."

"And what would she have done if we *hadn't* saluted?" Cat asked.

"Kept closing the range until she was basically on top of us," the second officer said grimly. "Only the fact that they *know* who we are and that we serve the archmage would have stopped them boarding us and imposing a dozen frivolous 'inspections.'"

"And the gobvar crew would have borne the brunt of those," Brushfire noted. "I've corrected our orientation, Captain."

"Well done, Officer Brushfire," Cat told her. He paused for a moment, studying the body language of the two var on the forecastle with him, then swallowed a concern.

His first and second officer hadn't had a chance to work together much yet. Time would smooth away the inevitable friction.

He hoped.

"Let's be on our way."

CHAPTER

28

Brushfire had spent the vast majority of her adult life on aether ships. The dimensions and realities of intersphere travel were burned into her brain, and they were all, by and large, pretty standard.

Most air-possessing worldlets were between a thousand and two thousand leagues across. Most spheres were between ten and twenty thousand leagues across, with the distance between aether straits usually somewhere between eight and ten thousand leagues.

Based on her experience, the journey from Blueswallow to the Monastery of the First Digger in Brokenwright should have been around forty clock-days, averaging a bit under a league a minute once they were fully into the aether.

By the third time Greentrees walked out onto the forecastle, held a hand out into the aether, and adjusted their course based on some factor Brushfire couldn't see, they were starting to come up on the aether strait out of Birdsbreath.

"Hold this course until we hit the strait," Greentrees instructed her and Streamwater. "Once we're through, I'll take a look at the currents in Shatterlight."

"Of course, Captain."

Brushfire checked the log and did mental math. Across four thousand leagues, their captain's instinctive course adjustments had cut four full hours off their trip. Over forty-five thousand leagues remained of their journey, and if Greentrees kept up this rate, he'd carve multiple full clock-days off the journey.

That did make it easier to handle when he simply nodded to the two of them and walked away, leaving flying the ship to them. He'd taken his turn at the helm, but it very much felt like she and Streamwater were carrying the main weight of flying the ship.

Brushfire had never been an officer before, though. Spherefox had handled most of the key moments of the journeys aboard *Skyfish*, though she presumed the other officers had handled moments like the long trips between worldlets and straits.

Giving her head a small shake, Brushfire turned her attention back to the wheel. Keeping the ship on a given angle was easy enough, after all. Once the ship was on the course, the wheel was locked in position, anyway. It would take *effort* to cause a problem.

Brushfire was there in case the watchvar spotted something requiring immediate response. Streamwater…was there because she chose to be.

The ninesail's second officer had her own shift watching the wheel, but she always seemed to be either on the forecastle or nearby while Brushfire had the watch. The gobvar hadn't minded the first two clock-days.

Now they were on the third clock-day of their journey and Brushfire had held down her watches without any issues. She'd made a minor mistake handling the ascent, but that had been her first ascent ever.

But still, every time she was on watch, the second officer was there.

Despite her spike of irritation, Brushfire had long before learned to control her actual actions and expressions—anything else would have ended poorly for a gobvar serving on elvar ships.

She kept her attention on the wheel, checking and rechecking the locks.

"Stop *poking* at it," Streamwater suddenly snapped. "You'll unlock it and make an ass of yourself again."

Brushfire bit her metaphorical horn and turned to study the elvar officer. Streamwater, it seemed, had never learned the same restraint a gobvar needed to survive in the elvar's world. Thankfully, there were no crewvar on the forecastle right now, though the watchvar in the masts could *see* their argument, at least.

"What makes you think I'm likely to unlock it by accident?" she asked, her tone level and calm.

"You have no idea what you're doing with any of this," the elvar second officer said with a gesture around the forecastle. "The only reason you're an officer at all is to keep the rest of the horns happy. Don't go thinking you're *actually* the second-in-command here!"

Brushfire straightened and turned to look down at the elvar. Streamwater was broad-shouldered and tall for an elvar…but Brushfire was broad and tall for a gobvar and dwarfed the other woman in every dimension.

She also knew she was a more powerful mage than the other var. Streamwater was more experienced and better trained with her focus, but Brushfire had a personal focus and commanded more magic.

"I have spent weeks rebuilding this ship from a hulk embedded in the side of a mountain," Brushfire told Streamwater. "There is no piece of this forecastle I have not touched, did not help build. I know these locks like the back of my hand. I know those control crystals like the beat of my heart.

"Half this crew is my blood. Our Masters, my sworn brothers. Our captain, my teacher in magic."

Streamwater, to be her credit and detriment, didn't quail under Brushfire's derision.

"You are untrained and unprepared," she snapped. "And no horn will *ever* be able to grasp the intricacies of this ship."

"I would choose your words very carefully, Officer Faith," Brushfire said softly. "I don't overly care if you call *me* a 'horn,' but insult our crew and I will break you."

"You wouldn't dare," the elvar sneered. "You, of all var on this ship, should know your place."

"I swore service to the Archmage Armand Bluestaves and to obey the orders of Cat Greentrees of the House of Forests," Brushfire pointed out. "You are neither of those var, Officer Faith. You are, frankly, a redundancy present in case something happens to both the captain and me.

"I *am* inexperienced and would value your advice and assistance. But I will not see our crew insulted and I will not be bullied. If you have a problem with me, tell me. But I know, as sure as I breathe aether, that you were hired for this ship because you told Greentrees you could work with gobvar."

"I can work with gobvar that *know their place*," Streamwater told Brushfire. "And the captain understands that. *I* am this ship's true first officer. *You* are a figurehead, in place to keep the rest of the horns happy."

Brushfire's fingers traced the base of her focus, and magic flooded her body as she moved. The skills of a shaman, backed by the power available to her through the focus, let her *blur* across the deck with a speed Streamwater couldn't match.

Before the elvar even realized Brushfire had moved, the shaman had both of Streamwater's arms locked into one of hers and her knee pressed into the small of the elvar's back.

Slow, steady pressure forced Streamwater to her knees as she hissed in pain.

"You are our second officer," Brushfire told Faith Streamwater. "Backup navigator, backup watch officer, backup mage. *Backup*. Never first.

"If you can do that job, you're fine. If you're going to cause trouble, I'll chain you in your quarters until we're in Shatterlight and we'll dump you on Iodestone at the first chance.

"Or do you *really* think that the captain will choose you over the three-quarters of the crew you're determined to insult, Officer Faith?"

She leaned forward to whisper in the other var's ear.

"As you say, *know your place.*"

Brushfire released Streamwater, stepping away from the elvar as the older var rubbed her forearms and glared at her.

"Well?" she asked.

Brushfire was surprised that the second officer didn't immediately leave the forecastle after their confrontation. Instead, the elvar retreated to a corner by the stairs but still remained present, keeping an eye on everything as Brushfire continued to hold down the watch.

She wasn't sure if that was a good sign or a bad sign, though Streamwater seemed to be taking her warning to heart so far. It was hard to tell.

Still, the forecastle was filled with an icy silence as the clock ticked toward their exit from Birdsbreath. Aether was never warm, though it was rarely intolerably cold, either. The edge to the presence of the second officer seemed to chill things even further, and part of Brushfire was expecting to find ice on the ship's wheel.

She wasn't expecting the captain to appear on the forecastle deck just as the aether strait began to grow into a visible streak of orange light in the distance.

Greentrees didn't announce himself, just stepping up onto the deck with a heating flask and three cups in his hands. He cleared his throat to get their attention, then laid the cups out in the air and poured a thick black liquid into each of them.

"Hot sweetbark," he told them as he floated the cups over to his two senior officers. "Take the drinks, officers."

Brushfire had rarely had a chance to taste the cloyingly sweet beverage, but she recognized the scent as the cup reached her. Waiting for the captain to say something, she took a careful sip. The flask had done its job and kept the sweetbark at a drinkable temperature, and the warmth helped wash away some of the cold of the aether.

Greentrees sipped his own drink, clearly waiting for Streamwater to have some of hers.

"We hit the strait in an hour," he observed when she finally did. "We're not planning on making landfall in Shatterlight unless something comes up, so I hope that the discussion I heard is the end of that particular conflict, yes?"

Brushfire tried to cover her surprise by taking another sip of sweetbark. She wasn't even sure *how* the captain had overheard their "discussion." They'd kept things relatively quiet, though she suspected the watchvar in the masts had seen her physical demonstration at the end.

Greentrees smiled calmly and pointed his sweetbark cup at Streamwater.

"Officer Faith, your experience is hugely valuable to us all, and I know that Officer Brushfire appreciates your knowledge and advice," he said calmly. "But you are not this ship's first officer in any sense. You convinced me that you could work with gobvar and under a gobvar officer.

"I am...*disappointed* in your interpretation of that concept," he told her. "Either you can work with gobvar as if they were elvar, or we may need to make landfall in Shatterlight and find a replacement officer.

"Am I clear, Officer Faith?"

Streamwater glanced at Brushfire, then back to Greentrees, and nodded silently.

The captain then turned his level gaze on Brushfire.

"That said, Officer Brushfire, I am unenthused with officers who find it necessary to resort to threats and application of violence to get their way," he told her calmly.

His tone was soft and unaccusing, and yet Brushfire felt his disappointment down to her bones. She met his gaze levelly and nodded her understanding.

The captain waited a moment for either of them to speak, then smiled and took another sip of his sweetbark.

"We haven't even left Birdsbreath yet," he observed. "I think we can chalk everything prior to entering that strait down to lessons we needed to learn and forget about it all going forward, can't we?"

Brushfire met Streamwater's gaze. The elvar glared at her for a moment, then glanced aside.

Swallowing her pride, the gobvar crossed the distance between them and offered her hand.

"Peace, Officer Faith?" she offered. "We have a job to do, after all, and the archmage tells us it's bloody important."

She could feel Greentrees' eyes on her. She was surprised by how much she found herself hoping that the captain approved—she might have broken another var in half for how he'd approached the conflict, but this seemed to have worked for him.

"Peace, first officer," Streamwater finally acknowledged, gripping her hand for a firm shake.

"All the elvar on this ship are learning to swallow their pride and work with our gobvar crew," Greentrees told the two officers. "It's no excuse and it's something you and I, Faith, need to watch more above all else.

"*We* have to set an example to the rest of the elvar crew. If the three most senior officers on this ship can't put aside our var's grazer shit and work together, how can we expect the rest of the crew to do the same?"

CHAPTER 29

CAT STOOD ALONE on *Star*'s forecastle, his hands outstretched in front of him as he sought any consistent current that could guide his ship more quickly through the sphere of Skyford. He'd carved ten hours off their journey through Birdsbreath and Shatterlight, but the third sphere of their journey was being frustrating for him.

The current charts of Skyford were a mess, and he'd thought he'd be able to save them even more time there. Instead, he was finding that the charts understated the chaos of the aether currents in the sphere, and the brilliant light of the source of that chaos was getting on his nerves.

Living spheres generally were either spherelit or they had an ember or they had a great crystal. There were *very* few dark spheres that were occupied, not least due to the difficulties of growing crops without light.

On the other hand, Skyford had *both* an ember and a great crystal, the flaming star and the glowing gem each providing enough light for var to live and work by on their own. With the two sources of light sitting roughly ten thousand leagues apart, most of the sphere was too brightly lit for most var's tastes.

The presence of the two light sources seemed to have a huge and unpredictable effect on the aether currents as well. While the charts allowed him to plot *a* course through the mess, his ability to sense the flow of currents at some distance usually let him plot better courses.

Instead, it was just giving him a headache. He'd never felt such a tangled weave of aether currents before.

Still...*there*.

He adjusted the wheel slightly, angling *Star* a bit downward and to port, then sighed and locked the wheel in place. Inside the distance he could sense, there wasn't going to be much benefit to actively navigating the ship.

"Sails ho!"

Cat looked up at the watchvar's shout, scanning the distant aether for what the sentry had seen.

"Starboard and up," the watchvar continued a moment later. "Coming from the Ford itself!"

He followed the directions and spotted the brilliant white speck of an oncoming aether ship. A chill of anxiety flickered through him, and he wished they'd managed to hire a seer. Somehow, even with four mages—one also a gobvar shaman—and an *archmage* aboard, they still lacked enough foresight for some of the knowledge of what was coming he'd been used to aboard *Running Fox*.

Now he knew where the ship was, he could feel her presence in the aether currents. Often, he'd sense that *before* he could see the ship, but with the chaos in Skyford, it wasn't as clear.

The sense was familiar, though, and his anxiety solidified. He crossed to the back end of the forecastle and called one of the sailors over.

"Get the officers," he instructed the gobvar. "All four of them."

There was another ninesail approaching through the aether, and Cat guessed that Skyford's rulers weren't going to let an unknown ninesail pass through their sphere without challenge.

"She's still over half a dozen leagues away, but she's definitely closing," Cat confirmed to his officers as he put the spyglass away.

"Skyford is elvar territory, right?" Brushfire asked. "I've never been here before."

"Neither have I," Cat admitted, looking to the three junior officers. "The Ford is independent of the High Court, unlike most elvar spheres."

"They're only as 'independent' as the halvar kings," Streamwater pointed out, the broad elvar studying the speck of white in the distance that was the approaching ninesail. "But they aren't part of the system of House and Court, which puts them aside from the rest of our var."

Cat nodded thoughtfully. "The Ford" itself was the feature Skyford was named for, a single lodeplate forever suspended between the Skyford's ember and its crystal with two worldlets close enough to share air.

Both sides of the lodeplate were habitable and inhabited, and the shared air allowed halvar and darvar to travel from worldlet to lodeplate to worldlet without needing the magical envelopes of air required elsewhere.

"I haven't been here either," Smallwolf admitted, the youngest officer looking worried. "Are they going to be trouble?"

"We're flying an archmage's pennant," Hammerhead reminded the elvar youth. "They'll challenge us because we're flying a *ninesail* and we're not High Court, but Bluestaves' authority will carry us through."

Cat was amused by the irony of his gobvar officer reassuring the elvar junior about the approach of an elvar warship. His crew was starting to come together, realizing that they had more in common as aether sailors than they had differences in var and culture.

But his first officer's words reassured *him*, too, though he couldn't show it. Archmagi were respected and honored *everywhere* in the territory of Court and Kingdoms. No one was going to give too much trouble to a ship under the blue pennant.

"We fly under the blue pennant," he reminded his officers, putting his thoughts into words. "We'll be cooperative and helpful, because this is their sphere, but we are on a mission of the greatest importance.

"We aren't making landfall in Skyford and we can't be delayed for long." He smiled thinly. Whatever deadline hovered around Bluestaves' visions of doom, it wasn't *soon*—but Cat couldn't help but feel that only necessary delays could be tolerated.

Rebuilding the ship had been a necessary one. Playing politics to calm Skyford's ruling Council? That wasn't—and it was a delay Bluestaves' rank should cut right through.

"The blue pennant should open any doors that need to be opened," he concluded. "So, let's see what happens."

While Cat wasn't going out of his way to be uncooperative to the local ship, he also didn't divert from his course to meet them. If he'd redirected *Star* toward the other ninesail, they'd have closed the distance in a couple of minutes.

As it was, it was almost ten minutes before Smallwolf, watching through the spyglass, could read the signal flags the Skyford ship was putting up.

"Flags are orders, Captain," she reported as soon as she *could* read them. "Strike sail and hold for them to haul alongside."

Cat's original feelings of trepidation returned in full measure. That wasn't an *unusual* order, per se, but it meant that the Skyford captain wanted a closer look at *Star*. It was the prelude to an inspection—or even a boarding action, though he couldn't see any reason for the last.

The thought still hung in his head as he stepped back to the inner edge of the forecastle.

"Master of Sails," he called.

Windheart, of course, was faux-lazily leaning against the closest mast. The elder gobvar straightened at Cat's call.

"Captain," he replied crisply.

"Strike all sails, Master Windheart," Cat ordered. "We're going to meet the locals."

"Aye, aye, Captain."

Windheart turned away, gesturing for the riggers to converge on him as he started to bark orders. Some of the gobvar were moving immediately, heading up the masts even as they listened to the specifics of ropes and aethercloth. Others listened longer, taking in instructions that they would pass on when they reached the other decks.

The arcane wheel on the forecastle could change the angle and tilt of the masts and redirect the ship in any direction, but it took hands on the masts and cloths to adjust how much sail was hanging on *Star*'s nine masts.

Striking all sails took several solid minutes, by which point the closing ninesail was clearly visible in the distance. She was still small, still a dozen cables distant, but close enough that Cat could make out details.

The Skyford ship had a fish of some kind as her figurehead, and her white sails were painted with a trio of bright blue stylized waves. The same sigil was on the flags that flew from her mainmasts.

A series of pennants hung underneath the flag of Skyford. They were enough different from the High Court Navy's equivalent that it took Cat a few moments to interpret them, then he sighed.

"Captain?" Brushfire asked.

"She's the squadron flagship and her Lord Commander is a member of a Council family," Cat told his first officer quietly. "I'm not sure if that means they're related to a current Councilor or just that their family often holds Council seats... I'm not as familiar with Skyford as I'd like to be."

He shook his head.

"A similar pennant on an HCN ship marks someone in the core line of a House," he concluded. "That means this is political no matter what we do."

Cat, for all of the wealth and power of his family within the House of Forests, was of a tertiary lineage of the House. He'd never have had the right to fly a House pennant on his ship. While he wasn't sure if the pennants worked quite the same way for the Skyford fleet, at the very least it marked someone of major importance.

Or, at least, *related* to someone of major importance.

That was always going to be a complicating factor.

Now Cat could see the elvar aloft on the other ship setting to work lowering her sails as she drew closer to *Star*. The ninesail's name, *Charcoal Sky*, was now visible on her bow as she drew level with *Star*.

Charcoal Sky was a newer and bigger ninesail than *Star*, even before *Star* had been stripped of over half her armament. If Cat's estimating eye was correct—and he was rarely wrong—*Sky* had fifteen storm staves in each broadside. That was as many as *Star* had in total.

There were also, he noted with interest, a trio of gobvar-style flamethrowers mounted on each of the forecastles. The High Court preferred to keep their distance from gobvar ships and stick to the storm staves. Skyford appeared to have decided on a different style.

Charcoal Sky finished striking her sails and drifted in less than a cable away from *Star*. They were still flying the same instruction flags as before, ordering *Star* to strike sail and allow them to come alongside.

At least one officer on *Sky*'s forecastle was studying Cat's decks with a spyglass as the distance between the two aether ships slowly shrank. Something in their body language made Cat twitch, especially when they suddenly raised the spyglass to focus directly on Cat's face.

"Captain?" Brushfire asked softly.

"It's nothing," he told her. "Just the first time someone has ever been boarding and inspecting *my* ship."

As if they'd been listening, the flags came down and someone handed the Skyford captain a speaking trumpet.

"*Star*, prepare to receive inspection party," he bellowed through it. "We're throwing over ropes."

"Master of Decks," Cat shouted, leaning back over his own decks. "Prepare to receive ropes from *Charcoal Sky*."

He nodded for Brushfire to follow him and descended to the main deck as the crews set to work.

Heavy long ropes were thrown between the two ships and attached to capstans on each side. Ever so slowly, the two ships were winched together until the local ninesail's crew dropped half a dozen gangplanks down to link the two ships.

Cat had been expecting a small party of sailors led by a single officer, an inspection that only required a single bridge. The half-dozen gangplanks took him by surprise.

A surprise that made him wish he'd listened to his paranoia as a dozen elvar marines surged across each gangplank with battlewands and swords in hand!

CHAPTER 30

"Hold your hands!" Cat bellowed as his own people started to go for anything that could be used as a weapon. "Hold your bloody hands!"

He strode forward to stand in front of the nearest party of marines.

"What is the meaning of this?" he demanded. "We sail under the pennant of an archmage! This is a deplorable violation of the archmage's privileges."

A focus was trained on him before he'd even finished speaking, and Cat glared at the pup of a mage holding it with contempt. He could feel the weave of aether and magic around the younger var, and the youth had missed that Cat's fingers were resting on his own focus.

Cat had no need to *point* his focus to attack the other var. Brushfire probably would, but that was why his first officer was behind him.

If push came to shove, if this was the only mage in the boarding wave, Cat could probably disarm and contain all of them on his own. Of course, there would be more mages back on *Charcoal Sky*…and the politics were a concern.

"Stand back," the officer ordered. "Everyone *stand back.*"

Cat ignored the order and stepped into the elvar's personal space, forcing the officer to backpedal.

"This is my ship," he pointed out calmly. "A ship under the blue pennant. You have violated the privileges granted to the archmagi by all spheres. *You* stand back and explain yourself!"

The focus was still pointed at Cat, an explicit threat that he was ignoring except to weave a concealed defensive spell in front of himself. The Skyford mage didn't seem to be skilled enough to recognize his threat had been countered, which also suggested that none of this was the youth's idea.

"You will surrender your arms and your ship," the local mage ordered, trying to enforce a level of authority his retreating away from Cat had already thrown away.

"I am Captain Cat Greentrees of the High Court House of Forests, in the service of the Archmage Armand Bluestaves of the Shining Kingdom," Cat stated slowly and loudly, projecting his voice so that all of the boarders and all of his own crew could hear him.

"By the ancient rights of the archmagi, I will surrender neither my arms nor my ship. I *suggest* that you and your marines return aboard *Charcoal Sky* before my crew is forced to disturb the archmage from his studies."

Cat figured it was at least half-likely that Bluestaves was baking, not studying, but that wasn't a distinction the Skyford marines needed to be aware of.

"I know who you are, Captain Greentrees," a new voice said loudly. The marines split to allow a squat and scarred elvar in a simple black tunic uniform to approach behind the junior officer. Only a gold chain hooked to the shoulders of the tunic gave any indication that the battered old var was the Lord Commander aboard *Charcoal Sky*.

It was enough for Cat to give the var some credence, though, and he leveled his best captain's glare on the stranger.

"You are in command of these fools?" Cat demanded.

"I am," the Lord Commander agreed. "And I am disappointed, *Captain* Greentrees, that a scion of a House of such stature as yours would stoop this low. Even branded, broken and exiled, I would expect better than for a captain of the High Court to become a figurehead for pirates flying under a false archmage's pennant.

"We are not fooled by your deceptions, Captain," the elvar said flatly. "*You* have no magic, and no archmage would hire a crew of gobvar. This is a pirate ship, whatever illusions you seek to weave of fabric and lies, and I am ordering it interned by the authority of the Council of Skyford."

Of course the news of Cat's sentence would have spread to other elvar worlds, he realized. And the presence of a mage who shouldn't have commanded magic had clearly been one of the markers against this stranger believing *Star* to be a pirate ship.

But given how the stranger was eyeing Brushfire and the rest of the gobvar, Cat realized that his own official status was almost irrelevant.

Star had been judged to be pirates solely and entirely because the crew was gobvar.

Cat fingered his focus again, drawing calm and energy from its gentle pulse of magic as he met the stranger's gaze and glowered back at them.

"And you are?" he finally asked.

"I am Lord Commander Evening of the Mountainbirds," the old officer told him. "I know gobvar pirates of old, Captain, and your service as their figurehead does you no credit."

"And your bigotry does you even less," Cat said, letting his anger run through his words. "You have neither evidence nor grounds to intern my ship, Lord Commander, and by the ancient rights of the archmagi, I have every right to defend my crew and my master with all necessary force.

"But since I have no desire to inflict harm on var merely following the orders of a commander who cannot see past my crew's var, I *suggest* that you meet with Archmage Bluestaves before you take a step that you will not live long enough to regret."

Mountainbirds glowered at Cat's description of his reasoning.

"Do you know who I am?" he demanded. "My judgment is more than sufficient to impound all of your pirates!"

Power flickered up Cat's fingers in response to his anger, but he controlled himself for at least a few moments longer.

"If you are *wrong*, Lord Commander—and you *are* wrong—you set your crew and your marines against the wrath of an archmage," Cat warned him. Not that Cat figured he needed Bluestaves. Brushfire had fallen back slightly, and his four officers were now positioned to blockade each of the boarding parties.

Knowing where his officers were told him the situation was at least partially in hand. *Not* knowing where his Master of Staves was gave him faith that the rest of the backup he'd need was already in place.

There was only one person on his ship he was reasonably sure *had* been a pirate, and it was Paintrock. If Paintrock hadn't worked out what was going on and started organizing the crew under the decks, Cat would eat his own focus.

"This is my sphere, Captain, and I *know* what you are," Mountainbirds told him. "I am disinclined to believe that an archmage, even a *halvar* archmage, would stoop so low as to have a ship crewed by gobvar and commanded by a captain with no magic.

"Surrender. Your. Arms."

Unlike his young officer, Evening of the Mountainbirds hadn't touched his magic up to that point. Now, though, he went for his focus—a House focus like Cat's old wand, though the terminology was almost certainly different there.

He didn't reach the focus. Cat's magic snapped across the deck in a moment of release, tearing the Skyford officer's weapon belt from his waist and hurling it back onto *Charcoal Sky*.

The whole scene froze and Cat smiled as every eye snapped onto him. He drew his own focus for the first time, the gesture making it clear that he'd been touching the arcane implement the entire time.

"You are aware, Lord Commander Mountainbirds, of the penalty for striking an archmage's sworn servants, yes?" he asked.

Cat, as a personal servant of the archmage, actually held much the same level of diplomatic immunity as he'd held as a captain of the High Court Navy. If Mountainbirds had pulled a focus on *Bluestaves*, that was instantly punishable by death.

Attacking Cat fell more into the category of "irritating an archmage," and the official penalty was the general equivalent for attacking the guards of a king or Councilor. In the High Court, it would have been ten dances of imprisonment at least—and the *true* penalty tended to be "whatever the archmage asked for."

Cat wasn't sure what the listed penalty was in Skyford, but he doubted it was any more pleasant than imprisonment in Heartfall. The pale looks on several of the marines implied it might be worse.

"Since you have not actually managed to touch me," he continued, "I suggest that you send your marines back to your ship and that you and I meet with my master."

He glared at the now-disarmed Skyford Lord Commander.

"And I also suggest that you consider that your bigotry against my crew may not be shared by the archmage."

It definitely, Cat realized, was no longer shared by said archmage's *captain*.

CHAPTER 31

ARMAND BLUESTAVES wasn't *entirely* unaware of what was going on around *Star* outside his carefully maintained bubble of air. He had a magical warning net woven across the decks, allowing him to know if strangers came aboard the ship. His short-term divination wasn't up to the task of maintaining the early-warning net a High Court Navy ship would prefer, but he was alerted the moment Skyford marines stormed his ship's decks.

Unfortunately, as he and Greentrees had discussed when they'd first ascended from Blueswallow, it would take a massive amount of effort, even for an archmage, to maintain a traveling pocket of air to allow him onto the deck.

Enough effort, in fact, that Armand couldn't do so and fight. Even talking would be a strain through the demands of just staying *alive* on the decks of the aether ship.

That left him watching as Cat Greentrees fielded the Skyford Lord Commander and cursing the limitations that prevented him interfering—as well as the interruption that was causing the problems in the first place.

He had a new appreciation for his captain, though, as the elvar led their new "guest" into the aftercastle and toward the air envelope where Armand waited.

The archmage took a quick glance around his receiving room. A wave of magic swept away crumbs and empty dishes, clattering plates and cups into a cupboard out of sight. Furniture sorted itself into the appropriate position for giving an audience to a supplicant, and Armand fixed his grimmest expression on his face.

It wasn't hard. He'd heard enough of the conversation on the deck to be utterly furious—and while being trapped in the air envelope limited his ability to act, bringing *Star* to the Ford would remove that limit.

A removal Lord Commander Mountainbirds would have lived to regret. Probably.

As it was, the Lord Commander had been sufficiently intimidated by Greentrees' show of power that they were *hopefully* going to be able to defuse the situation—though the Skyford marines were clearly ready to resume their assault at a moment's notice.

In Armand's opinion, that would be a mistake—and not just because aggravating an archmage was generally considered foolish. He had enough awareness of the *interior* of the ship to know what the three ship's Masters had been doing while Greentrees and the deck crew had been facing off with the marines.

The next push would be met by several times their own numbers of fully armed sailors. The marines were probably better fighters, but *Star*'s crew were fighting for their own ship.

He suspected it would be a bloodbath—a bloodbath his plan could ill afford, bringing his attention back to the entrance to his receiving room as the outer doors swung open.

A moment later, he heard them close again and the inner door opened, allowing Cat and two of the gobvar crew to escort Evening of the Mountainbirds into the air envelope.

"Captain," Armand greeted Greentrees. "Is this gentlevar still refusing to believe you?"

His arched eyebrow at Mountainbirds hopefully made it clear that he'd been watching most of what had occurred.

"According to Lord Commander Mountainbirds, our gobvar crew are pirates, using me as a figurehead and a false blue pennant to cover our crimes," Greentrees said calmly.

"And then Lord Commander Evening of the Mountainbirds drew arms against my ship captain," Armand observed, studying the elvar. The local only looked skinny compared to the gobvar flanking him. He was broader and more muscular than Armand himself—hardly a challenge—and radiated righteous anger.

"I am hardly to be fooled by blue robes and an arrogant tone," he snapped.

Armand gestured, sending a chair flashing across the room and hammering Mountainbirds into it with a crushing blow of magic.

"You are so far beyond a *fool*, Evening of the Mountainbirds, that I am not sure there are words for the depths of your idiocy," he told the elvar. "I am disinclined to anger and, in general, quite concerned about the privileges that my siblings-in-magic have ordained to ourselves over the dances.

"But you try my patience," he warned. "With no grounds and no reason, you have concluded the worst of my crew and officers and continued to maintain it even in the face of my own person. You have insulted me and, worse, insulted var who have pledged their lives to my service and my mission.

"I have listened, Lord Commander, to every excuse and justification you have slobbered at my captain," he continued. "And they all ring *empty*. From the moment you saw gobvar in the masts of my ship, you were convinced of our sins.

"Based on no crime but the horns of our crew, you would have condemned every hand on this ship and seized the vessel for your Council." Armand held the Skyford officer's gaze.

"And if I were not an archmage, you would have succeeded," he whispered coldly. "There are no words for my anger and disgust at you, Evening of the Mountainbirds. You are a bigot and a thug, and I fear for the fate of any innocent ship that passes under your gaze."

He watched as the elvar officer tried to speak, then held up a hand to silence the Lord Commander.

"You should have listened to Captain Greentrees, Lord Commander," he told the other var. "You *should* have recognized the blue pennant and gone on your way—in the best of all spheres, you would not have prejudged my crew by the presence of their horns!

"But you did none of those things. Instead, you boarded the ship of an archmage and drew arms against my crew and my officers," Armand ground out. "Captain Greentrees?"

"Lord Archmage?"

Greentrees had clearly sensed that this was a moment for formality, far beyond anything Armand usually asked for. Armand did not *like* the position the archmagi had put themselves in in the societies of the spheres, but sometimes it served his purposes.

And Armand Bluestaves wasn't a fan of bullies.

"Chain this var," Armand ordered. "I will seal his manacles myself and he will bear my letter to the Council of Skyford."

It wouldn't take Armand long to write that letter—and in the writing, he would end Evening of the Mountainbirds' career.

"I will not stand for this!" the Lord Commander bellowed, lunging to his feet. "You make a mockery of the blue robes, a mockery of—"

Armand woke the link to the Source that rested beneath his heart. He let pure *power* fill the room, hammering the local elvar back into the chair with an invisible blow as Armand rose to his feet.

"I am an Archmage of the Towers of the Great Red Forest," he whispered. "The rights of the blue robes include a claim to your *life*, Evening of the Mountainbirds. I have chosen mercy.

"Do not make me reconsider."

CHAPTER 32

Brushfire watched the Skyford ninesail drift away from *Star* with a strange feeling. She'd run into the locals' assumption with regard to her var before, if rarely quite with the determination and scale that Mountainbirds had brought to it.

On merchant ships, there'd been enough elvar crew and officers to smooth over the problems. She'd often had to humiliate herself in one way or another to help convince local officers that she and her tribe were obedient and well behaved.

Part of her had hoped that the blue pennant would evade the worst of those problems, but in truth, she'd just been waiting to see how bad it got. The Skyford ship's reaction had been even worse than she'd anticipated, but the *type* of reaction wasn't a surprise to her.

Her new captain's response had been a surprise. Greentrees had unhesitatingly leapt to the defense of his gobvar crew, to the point of challenging Lord Commander Mountainbirds and disarming the local officer.

She wasn't sure what the consequences of Cat revealing that he had his magic back might be, but she did know that he had accepted those consequences to protect her tribe.

And Bluestaves had backed him, sending the Lord Commander packing in enchanted manacles and carrying a letter to the Council of Skyford.

Brushfire's impression was that Cat wasn't entirely over his own biases against gobvar, but he was starting to separate *his* gobvar from the rest of the var. She suspected he'd give any new gobvar he encountered more of a chance that he would have before—but she *knew* that it was more important to her boss that his crew was *his* crew than what var they were.

"Keep an eye on *Charcoal Sky*," the captain ordered her. "I'm going back down to talk to the archmage."

"Everything okay?" she asked.

"Bluestaves has been calm and generous the whole time I've known him," Greentrees confessed quietly. "I was not prepared to see him become the archmage of myth and terror at someone. Even a shared enemy.

"I'm more comfortable, it seems, with carrying the chubby diviner who bakes sweet rolls than I am with carrying a living demigod."

"He was always an archmage," Brushfire pointed out. "I never forgot."

"True. He was just always so…harmless that it was easy to forget *why* we fly a blue pennant."

"It's not to protect us," she murmured. "It's to protect idiots like Mountainbirds."

Greentrees snorted.

"Those manacles won't come off until he stands before the Council of Skyford," he noted. "Do not meddle in the affairs of archmagi, for they are irritable and far from subtle."

"My sympathies for the Lord Commander are limited," Brushfire admitted.

"As are mine," Greentrees agreed. "I won't stand by while people insult our crew."

He nodded slightly to her and walked away, heading for the doors into the forecastle—leaving Brushfire with the spyglass to watch an enemy ship and consider the changes in her captain.

The clock ticked over another hour, and *Star* was now out of sight of the Skyford ship. Their latest difficulty seemed to have faded away, though Brushfire could see ways that the dismissal of *Charcoal Sky* could come back to bite them.

Still, her sweeps with the spyglass didn't see any other ships approaching them as they sailed toward the next aether strait. Thousands of leagues still lay between *Star* and their flight from Skyford.

Then more spheres and more thousands of leagues to reach Brokenwright. They were barely halfway through the first phase of their journey—and yet she was feeling more confident about the trip than she ever had before.

A throat cleared behind her, and she turned to see the blue-skinned Paintrock had joined her on the forecastle.

"First Officer," he said respectfully, standing to attention. "Do you want a report on how our counter-boarding preparations went?"

She chuckled.

"May as well, Master of Staves," she observed. "It likely won't be the last time we're accused of being pirates."

Paintrock shook his head and ran his finger along one blue ear, tucking hair behind it.

"Almost as insulting to pirates as to our crew," he noted. "*Pirates* don't put gobvar in the rigging, to avoid just this trouble. Plus..." he shrugged. "If I've got an elvar and a gobvar, and I need one to handle the rigging and one to lead a boarding party, I'm putting the elvar in the rigging.

"Assuming equal skill with a blade and wand, anyway," he concluded after a moment's thought.

"Don't admit to piracy where the captain can hear you," Brushfire said drily. He hadn't *quite* done that—but it was close enough to probably make Cat twitchy. "He was High Court. The rest of us...not so much."

"He wanted officers and stavemasters who were willing to work with hor—gobvar. He had to figure at least some of what he was getting was trouble," Paintrock observed.

Somehow, *Paintrock* almost calling her people "horns" didn't bother Brushfire much. There was no...contempt or derision in the word as he used it.

"I'm not going to ask," Brushfire said firmly. "But it will bother the captain if you're too blunt about it. So, don't be."

The blue elvar nodded his understanding, looking out into the aether and studying the distant lights of Skyford's ember and crystal.

"Against another ninesail, we're almost better off letting them board," he told her. "All the crew were quick to wake and ready to hand when we mustered them under the deck. We've blades, wands or bows for all var, too."

"Not all of our people are trained on any of those three," Brushfire pointed out.

"But they're willing," he replied. "We can work with *willing*. I can train them, if you give the order."

"Even the gobvar?" she asked.

"Won't be the first gobvar I've trained to the blade," he said genially, though he was a bit more circumspect about saying *why* this time. "Captain's orders say I shouldn't train any of the gobvar as stavemaster backups, but I've picked out half a dozen good var to run a training program for the weapons we've got."

Brushfire nodded slowly. There were only four types of weapons on the ship, excluding the mages' focuses: swords, battlewands, crossbows, and the big storm staves themselves.

Most of the Hammerhead tribe had some training with the first three, but many of their other gobvar crew didn't. Most of the elvar aboard were stavemasters, trained to use the big magical wands, but they potentially *weren't* trained on smaller arms.

"Make it happen, Master of Staves," she ordered. "I'll confirm with the captain, but I don't see any problems."

She turned back to the spyglass.

"Even if we somehow make the rest of the voyage without incident, we don't know what's waiting for us in Brokenwright. But somehow, I doubt it's going to be a polite negotiation with ascetic monks."

If nothing else, Bluestaves had admitted at least once that his divinations had told him he was going to need a warship before they entered the void spheres.

CHAPTER 33

Darkness.

Cat had made certain *Star* was equipped for the problem after seeing the charts and course that Bluestaves wanted them to pull, but the dark sphere still sent shivers down his spine. There was still aether there, but it was chillier than usual.

There was even dirt and stone here, according to the charts. Half a dozen worldlets charted lonely, dead courses through the aether, as frozen and lifeless as the aether they drifted through.

But the extra-large lamps and reflective mirrors mounted on *Star*'s masts cut through the dark like blades of fire, illuminating the space around them as they swung toward their destination.

Only the tiniest spark of orange and purple marked the strait they were headed for so far, but less than a clock-day remained before they would enter Brokenwright.

Six spheres and forty-six thousand leagues lay behind them now. A few hundred more leagues there in the darkness, then thirty-five hundred between the aether strait and the Monastery of the First Digger.

He'd carved four clock-days from their journey, bringing them this far in thirty-three clock-days instead of thirty-seven, and he suspected he'd save them some more hours before they reached the Monastery. Without the need to stay in formations or follow orders, he'd been able to give his sense of the aether currents full rein.

"Three clock-days," Brushfire Hammerhead's voice said behind him.

"Three days," he confirmed, nodding for her to join him at the prow railing. "Then we find out how crazy our employer actually is."

He'd sworn an oath to the archmage, but that had been as much to put himself under the protection of the blue pennant as anything else. Bluestaves didn't *want* to be called *master*—and Cat was finding himself surprisingly uncomfortable with the idea of accepting another strict authority over himself.

That would be a problem when he returned to the High Court, he supposed. The rules of House and politics and stature on the lodeplate swarm were only slightly less strict than the rules of hierarchy and rank that defined the High Court's Navy.

"At least the Monastery will have air and we can bring him with us," Brushfire observed. "Though I wonder now if we should have hired some darvar to help smooth the way."

"And to make sure we had *every* var aboard?" Cat asked with a chuckle. "I hope, at least, that having an archmage will open more doors than carrying a few darvar with us would have."

They watched the aether in silence for a few minutes. The advantage of the somewhat more informal nature of *Star*'s crew versus the HCN was that no one was going to bother them unless there was an actual report to give.

The HCN would have had regular reports given for the sake of following protocol and procedure. Even Cat, who saw the value in fixed procedure, didn't see the need for as much as his old Navy had called for.

"Are we ready?" he finally asked her.

"We've trained the crew in every weapon we have," she said quietly. "I've studied the magic of this focus as best as I can."

Which was better than any other student Cat had ever worked with. He'd had junior officers who'd been swift studies before, but he'd never seen someone who was quite so much a "show me once" student as Brushfire Hammerhead.

He was still the more powerful mage, but the margin was thinner than he would have expected. If she was an elvar, she'd have been tested to see if she was ready for the Archmage Trial.

The elvar had learned to eliminate most of the mages who would completely fail the Trial. Unfortunately, they hadn't managed to identify the ones who would die versus the ones who would become archmagi.

Cat knew, from those tests, that he almost certainly *could* form a connection with the Song of the Spheres. Given that his sister *was* an archmage, though, he was actually *forbidden* from attempting the Trial.

His chances of dying were in some ways *worse* than a halvar student. Because the elvar could eliminate most of the complete failures, he had a better chance of being elevated as an archmage—but the elvar Trials produced the same ratio of bodies to archmagi as halvar or darvar Trials did.

The Houses wanted to preserve the bloodlines that produced archmagi. Only one child of a generation was permitted to attempt the Trial. It was a theory that have worked better if Cat or Hearth had been inclined toward children, but he accepted it anyway.

His impression was that *Brushfire* should have been permitted the Trial. But he couldn't see a version of the spheres where any of the academies of the elvar would train a gobvar as a potential archmage.

"Paintrock has been a gods-send," his first officer said into the silence. "He rubs me the wrong way sometimes, but at least it feels like he rubs *everyone* the wrong way."

Cat snorted.

"I hired a void-cursed pirate," he admitted. "After everything I did to try and avoid gobvar pirates, I hired an *elvar* one."

"He seems to be...loyal and useful so far."

"He does," Cat agreed. "Just...rubs me the wrong way, as you say. I spent sixty dances hunting pirates, elvar and gobvar alike. Employing one now...and seeing how your var are treated, too..."

He trailed off, staring off at the multicolored spark of the distant strait.

"I understand better how gobvar end up on that path," he murmured. "My var, especially, have done your kin ill. I have less sympathy for the *elvar* who have chosen that route, but, as you say, Paintrock is useful."

Cat shrugged.

"And I don't *know* he was a pirate," he conceded.

It was Brushfire's turn to be silent, and he eventually glanced over at her.

"What is it, Brushfire?" he asked.

"I never expected to hear *you* admit that my var are pushed into things like piracy," she told him. "When I met you, all you saw was my horns."

"More than that," he protested. "But..." He sighed. "I spent my time fighting pirates in our spheres and watching for gobvar on the border. I had *reason* to see you as the enemy. The rest of my var... They have even less excuse."

"And I'm not sure I'd trust most of them to give us the chance and the trust you did," Brushfire said. "You made me your first officer, even then."

"I told you why," Cat reminded her. "I couldn't safely command a crew of gobvar without accidentally pissing them off. I needed someone in between. You needed to keep your people safe and *I* needed them to serve.

"Having you as the first officer aligned your goals with mine."

It sounded so cold-blooded when he said it aloud—and it had been pretty cold-blooded in truth, too. But Fallen Crystal Voice's prophecy of "Shaman and Captain and Archmage" had driven it as well.

"I've known too many captains, even if all of them were merchants, to think that calculation holds true as much as you think it does," Brushfire told him.

"Then they're fools," he said without passion. "Letting their hatred overwhelm their good sense. I…"

He sighed.

"I didn't like having a gobvar crew, but if I was going to take you on, you were going to be *my crew*. That gave me responsibilities—but more than that, it meant I needed your people to work and serve."

"And now?" she asked.

"You've repaid any fragment of trust or faith I extended a hundredfold," Cat told her. "You and the rest of the gobvar crew have *earned* my trust. I extend no credit now, no faith. Only the trust and value that my judgment says you've earned."

"Our people repay that, you know," Brushfire said. "Trust with trust. Faith with faith."

"That's good," Cat admitted. "Because we're about to sail up to a fortress citadel we know nothing about, filled with darvar members of a religious sect we know nothing about, to attempt to purchase a ship we know nothing about, and enter a series of spheres filled with void…"

"That we know nothing about," she finished for him. "The void spheres aren't even in my thoughts yet, Captain. The Monastery, though…"

"I believe the archmage has a plan," Cat told her. It didn't, sadly, involve a surprise attack and taking control of the fortress monastery. They *probably* didn't have the information and hands for that, but he still wasn't sure that talking to the monks first was the best plan.

If the Monastery was what they said they were, they *still* might not want to sell the ship. If they were void-worshippers, His Dark Brothers… even asking might get whatever party went ashore attacked.

And all of that assumed the ship that Archmage Bluestaves wanted even existed!

CHAPTER 34

After thirty-plus clock-days of travel, Brokenwright itself was disappointing to Cat. He'd known what to expect from the charts, but it was still anticlimactic to emerge from the aether strait into a sphere that was only barely brighter than the dark sphere they'd left behind.

The ember that burned at the heart of Brokenwright was more than half-dead, the bright orange-yellow of most living embers having faded to a bruised-looking purple and green. It still provided light to the entire sphere, but it warped colors and softened shadows, resulting in everything looking odd.

The currents in the sphere were simple, at least. *Simple*, though, did not mean *ordinary*. If Brushfire hadn't told him about the nature of void straits, he'd have been holding *Star* at the entrance to the space while he worked out just *what* he was seeing.

Every aether current he could feel was warped, twisting toward a single point on the far side of the sphere. With a chart of the sphere pinned to a draft table on the forecastle, he traced the currents he could feel on the map and ended at the strange symbol he hadn't seen before this mission.

"Every current leads to the void," he said aloud.

"Sir?"

He looked up to see Smallwolf looking at him from the ship's wheel in concern.

"I'm tracing the currents to see if I can find a swifter route," he explained to the younger elvar. He'd probably told her this two or three times at that point, but he'd rather overexplain than under. "Most spheres, the currents are basically circles, wrapped around the ember or crystal."

He shrugged.

"There are always variations to that," he noted. "Every worldlet has its impact; every strait has its impact. But except in spherelit spheres, the central light is always the largest impact.

"In spherelit spheres, the end result is much the same, but the outer sphere has much more impact than in innerlit spheres." Cat studied the chart. "Aether straits are usually on par with midsized worldlets, and most spheres will have some big dead rock causing interference."

"But here?" his most junior officer asked, her gaze flickering to the strange purple fire warming Brokenwright.

"Here, *this* is the biggest impact," he told her, tapping the marker for the void strait. "More even than the ember. All of the aether in this sphere is being slowly sucked through that hole into the void."

The small elvar shivered and it wasn't just at the cold.

"This whole sphere feels *wrong*, Captain," she admitted. "What is this place?"

"The end of our spheres," he told her. "Only one way in and only one way out—except for the void strait itself.

"And that strait is *hungry*," he whispered.

He realized he was scaring the young elvar and forced a smile.

"It's a natural phenomenon, Officer Smallwolf," he continued. "A bit discomfiting in its nature, but natural enough for all that. And strange as it is, it's still a strait. Given the right kind of ship and the right kind of navigator, it can be traversed."

"But if there's only void beyond it…why?"

"Because beyond the void are the Clan Spheres," Cat said. "And somewhere in the Clan Spheres is the answer to the doom that Archmage Bluestaves foresaw."

"Is it going to be worth it?" she murmured.

"I know that Bluestaves foresaw the fall of the Court and Kingdoms, Bogsong," he reminded her gently. "So, while I *know* that the course we are taking is risky beyond all belief…I also know that *not* taking this path risks all that I am sworn to defend."

Smallwolf grimaced, but she nodded and turned back to the wheel.

"Any change to our course, Captain?" she asked.

Cat considered the currents sweeping around them and looked at the chart again. Like most spheres, there were multiple worldlets of potential value here. But the Monastery of the First Digger was at least marked on the charts, which made it a destination.

Now that he was *in* Brokenwright, he could understand something that the maps could never make clear. The Monastery was close to the void strait—and now that Cat could feel the impact of the void strait across the entire sphere, he was beginning to realize just how insanely dangerous having a settlement there was.

"Let's adjust course over three degrees to port and up fifteen," he told Smallwolf. "If the currents all head to the void strait, they're at least going to make it easier to get to our destination if we ride them."

"Yes, Captain."

Star shifted under Smallwolf's hands, and Cat looked out into the dimly lit aether. The strength of the void strait's impact was underestimated on the charts. He'd save another third of a clock-day before they reached the Monastery.

He had to wonder, though, just how much the darvar monks were paying the ships who supplied them. *He* wasn't sure he could have been paid to sail this sphere, not without oath and honor to compel him!

"And there it is."

Cat passed his spyglass over to Streamwater, directing her toward what he'd seen. Once she had a solid grip on the device, he touched his focus and summoned magic to show her what he'd seen through the telescope.

The spyglass was useful most of the time, not least because it *didn't* require any arcane ability. The collection of officers on *Star*'s forecastle were all mages, but what Cat was doing wasn't as simple as he made it look.

Once he'd recreated his view of the spindle-shaped worldlet, he expanded the end of the spell aboard *Star* with a gesture of the focus, spreading it out to allow his officers to see what he had seen.

Someone *else* had been paying attention too, and he registered Paintrock, Windheart and Axfall stepping onto the forecastle as well. He acknowledged the ship's Masters with a nod as he focused his attention on the illusion of their destination he had conjured.

The worldlet was strangely shaped, but that wasn't overly unusual. Cat had been born on a "worldlet" that was a thousand-league-square sheet of lodestone, after all. A planetoid that looked like it had been spun on a lathe to create the support for a railing wasn't particularly out of place.

"Scale is hard to tell at this distance," Streamwater observed. "How big is the worldlet?"

"We're still six hours' sailing away, almost three hundred leagues," Cat pointed out. "With magic and optics…we can see them in some detail, but we're a long way away."

"Charts say it's three hundred leagues from top to bottom, fifty leagues across at the thickest points," Brushfire told the second officer. "I'm not sure *I* believe that it's constructed."

"Those same charts put the Monastery on the large nodule at the northern end," Cat added, gesturing toward that part on the illusion. "Or, well, *in*."

There wasn't enough detail, not yet, for him to say where on that chunk of stone the entrance to the darvar monastery was.

"We don't have much more than what's in the charts," he warned. "Archmage Bluestaves promised to do some scrying of the worldlet before we made landfall, so we're waiting on him for whatever details his magic can conjure.

"But…this is our destination," he told them all. "And according to the archmage, somewhere on that worldlet is a ship built specifically to pass through the void strait."

Even he shivered at the thought. They were within a thousand leagues of the strait now, but he still couldn't see it. It blended into the background, but *all* of them could feel its effect on the surrounding aether.

Cat could sense the currents that propelled his ship and predict them, but this was almost a literal breeze in the aether, a pull that most of his var would normally only sense on a worldlet with air and weather.

Weather in the aether wasn't *unknown*, but it wasn't normally this constant. The void strait was a strange and terrifying thing, and every var on the ship could feel its pull now.

"I'm not sure how anyone could live here," Smallwolf muttered.

"Bury yourself under a few cables of stone, on the right side of a magically sealed air envelope, and you'd be fine," Paintrock told her. "It's the poor bastards who run them supplies who bear the worst of it."

"I'm not sure what would bring the students of the First Digger out to this...place," Cat murmured. "But I can damn well see what would bring the students of Her Dark Brother here."

"We can still hope all of this is innocent, yes?" Windheart asked. "Plan for the worst, hope for the best?"

"Even if they are Dark Brothers, we may still be able to buy or rent their ship," Paintrock observed. "Even His Dark Brothers are not immune to money, in my experience."

Cat swallowed his initial response and simply nodded his understanding.

While he didn't want to know *how* Hunter Paintrock had met His Dark Brothers before, the Master of Staves made a useful point—and Paintrock's experiences would serve them well out there in the dark.

As *Star* drew closer to their destination, Cat's illusory telescope began to show more detail of the worldlet. Lights began to appear on the "top" of the spindle, near where the maps said that the Monastery was located.

The crystal lamps drew the eye, helping to pick out the artificial lines where eight fortified towers rose from the surface in a perfect octagon. Each of the eight had a single dock extending outward, supported by a mix of magic and careful stonework, Cat presumed.

"Clever," Brushfire said. "The towers all have lights on them, making it clear where the settlement is and drawing the eye. But I'm guessing the darvar don't normally *live* in the towers, right?"

"No," Cat agreed. "If you look around the base, you can see that the ground there is basically untouched—and I don't see any entrances. The real monastery is underneath that plain of stone, and the towers are just the way in.

"You're right that the lamps draw the eye. That's why you'd have light towers like that on most airless worldlets. Makes sure people know where to land."

"And it helps keep people from looking too hard at the rest of the rock," his first officer said. "If we're focused on the Monastery, we're not noticing any strangeness elsewhere. If we were delivering supplies or lost or..."

"Unless we're *looking* for something unusual, we have no reason to do anything except head straight for the lights," Cat agreed. "Of course, we *are* looking for unusual things."

"But we're also heading for the lights?" she said.

"Exactly." He gestured for Streamwater to step up. "Second Officer, do you think you can maintain the telescope?"

The older elvar studied the spell for several moments before she grimaced.

"I could try," she said. "But I think I'd need to be taught before I could do it myself."

"A lesson I didn't think to teach anyone," Cat conceded. "Use the spyglasses, then. You, Smallwolf and Crane keep an eye on the worldlet, let us know what you see."

Emberlight Crane was their third officer and surgeon. Crane was rarely on deck, but he'd use the mage now for eyes.

"Brushfire and I need to talk to the archmage," he told the officers. "Hopefully, by the time we reach the Monastery, we'll have enough information for a final plan."

CHAPTER 35

Armand walked around the illusion hanging in the middle of his library, studying the monastery worldlet with a cautious and cynical eye. The charts and books he'd found that referenced Brokenwright were scattered around the room, and he was comparing the strangely shaped planetoid against the information from them.

He'd added illusory lights highlighting key places on the rock. The books flagged some points. He picked out others by examination—others came from the divinations he was intermittently stopping to do.

Several different varieties of runes, a crystal ball and a deck of oracle cards were intermingled with the books. A pair of translucent winged lizards, roughly the size of a house cat, fluttered around the illusion, the oracular spirits occasionally hissing to draw his attention to a point.

"Archmage?" Greentrees asked from the door.

"The spell will survive you coming in, Cat, Brushfire," Armand told them absently as he prodded another octagonal set of towers. This one was completely in ruins and was only distinguishable from the debris-strewn plains around it by the now-recognizable pattern.

His two allies entered the room, both studying the illusory replica of their destination with awed eyes.

"I thought I was doing well with my telescope," the captain said drily. "But that was nothing like this."

"Illusions are my specialty, Cat," Armand reminded Greentrees. "Come, sit." He looked at the chairs in the room and sighed. A wave of magic relocated enough of the books to create spaces for them to sit.

"We left the other officers looking for strangeness on the surface of the worldlet," Brushfire told him as she carefully took a seat. "That may be unnecessary, it seems."

"They are looking with their eyes and I am looking with my magic," Armand replied. "Each of us may well see things the other misses. Every set of eyes and every mind that is turned upon this stone may reveal new secrets."

He shook his head.

"This place has *many* secrets," he observed. "Each of these lights you see marks an octagon of docking towers, like the one the Monastery is underneath. This fortress could have anchored sixty-four ninesails, at least. Several of the tower structures I've found are utterly ruined; it is difficult to tell their original scale."

One of the oracular spirits hissed again, curling itself around one of those ruined tower sections and cutting through the air with its translucent claws. A hazy image of the towers as they had once been appeared in the air above them.

"Thank you," Armand told the spirit. "As you see, not all of my magic is entirely obedient," he observed with a chuckle. "But they do try to help."

"So, there were eight complexes like the Monastery itself?" Cat asked. "But the underground structures…are they as pervasive as the original charts implied?"

"Yes," Armand said bluntly. He gestured and a crisscrossing network of dark gray lines appeared inside the worldlet. They faded into translucency and then vanished as they went deeper into the rock.

"The stone was chosen well," he warned. "It blocks divination of the depths of the citadel. I have not found the ship yet, though I have my guesses as to where it must be."

"It's not docked at one of the towers?" Brushfire asked.

"That was my first guess and what I had these two"—he gestured to his oracular spirits—"looking for. But they found nothing at the towers— but the towers are only the most obvious of the surface structures. This worldlet may have been rebuilt to the whims of the Ironhand Dynasty, but it also appears to have been heavily populated. For an airless rock, at least."

"Three hundred leagues from top to bottom," Cat noted. "Are we sure it's a construct?"

"Oh, no," Armand said. "It's a natural worldlet. They just made it exactly what they needed, including reshaping the lodestone core as well as the exterior shape. The docks were towers, but there are also sets of three towers scattered across the surface that clearly held weapons of some kind—I presume some precursor to our storm staves."

He gestured, and an image of one the sets of defensive towers appeared next to the main illusion. Their roofs had clearly been built to open up once, though most of them that Armand had looked at were collapsed in now.

The Ironhands had reshaped the lodestone core, but they hadn't *removed* the core. That downward pull over hundreds of dances had worn down even stone, pulling structures and roofs and walls to the surface of the worldlet.

"The positions are big for storm staves," Cat murmured, studying the defensive towers. "Or, at least, the storm staves we have now. A thousand-plus dances ago…who knows? The entirety of the tower could be a single stave, no more powerful than the magic we command today."

"Or a single stave, vastly more powerful than any magic we can construct today," Armand pointed out. "We know so little of the Ironhands. They were overthrown, yes, but we know at least one of their major spheres is past the void strait."

He sighed and gestured toward the monastery at the top of the worldlet.

"Our first step is to visit the monks, and they have made that very straightforward," he told the others. "I hope they will be cooperative, but I have to admit that I have not fo—"

One of the oracular spirits suddenly started chirping excitedly, the winged creature fluttering down to a spot on the wide top of the worldlet—the far side of the top from the Monastery but still "only" forty or so leagues away from the lit-up towers.

Armand crossed the room to see what the magical being had located and smiled as he saw it. There was very little visible on the surface, but he hadn't released the illusion of the underground tunnels.

The spirit had found a spot where the "underground tunnel" was a cavern at least three cables across and half a cable deep, covered by a relatively thin layer of surface rock.

"Perhaps indeed, my little friend," he told the oracle. "That cavern looks like the kind of place you might park a ship when the crew doing repairs needs air, doesn't it?"

Cat and Brushfire joined him in studying the cave.

"You'd need a way out," Cat observed.

"We already saw the opening roofs on the towers," Brushfire pointed out. "Could this be a larger version of the same?"

"Potentially," Armand agreed. Power flickered through him as he focused on the spot, flinging his magic and attention across the leagues of empty aether to *see* what he could find.

Almost unconsciously, his hands twisted in front of him, weaving the magic to recreate what he found.

"There is air in the cavern," he said slowly. "Light, too. And...*something*."

He couldn't call it a ship. It didn't look like any ship he'd ever seen. It was a long cylinder of metal and wood, sealed by magic and steel with strange open barrels on one end.

"That has to be it," Cat said. "It's a strange creature, but it...feels right to be a ship."

"So, now we know where it is," Brushfire noted, studying it. "And we know it exists. I..."

"You doubted," Armand said, pulling his attention back to the room and looking at his new illusion of the cavern. "I know you did, both of you. But now we have found what we need, the answer to passing through the spheres of the void.

"Now we just need to buy her."

"What happens if they don't want to sell her?" his ship captain asked.

"That, Cat, is why we needed a warship," Armand admitted.

CHAPTER 36

Brushfire stood on the port side of the upper deck, leaning over the edge with Axfall as *Star* swung ever closer to the monastery docking tower.

"I sure hope they mean the same thing with the big green lamp that everyone else does," the Master of Decks said drily.

The light in question now burned in the middle of the roof of the tower they were approaching. The other seven towers in the cluster still had their presumably normal blue-white lights, but the green light stood out and, hopefully, marked where they were expected to dock.

In the purple-green light of the sphere's slowly dying ember, it all looked weird and alien. The pattern was still distinguishable, though, and Greentrees was bringing the ship slowly in.

"There," Axfall said, pointing. "The dock is covered. That has to be the one; we can link our air envelope to it and take the archmage in that way."

"Makes sense," she grunted. "Unless they keep a few gobvar or elvar in the Monastery to talk to visitors, they need an air envelope just to say hello."

And, to her knowledge, no non-darvar worshipped the First Digger. While there were all kinds of theological arguments matching the darvar creator-deity to the pantheon of "known" gods worshipped by the other var of the spheres, the First Digger's claim to be the sole creator and shaper of the spheres ran counter to the aggregate myth of the rest of the pantheon.

Even to Brushfire, who was neither particularly religious nor well educated outside her specialties, the fracture lines where at least five pantheons had been rammed together to create the shared collection of acceptable deities were clearly visible. Those shared pantheons, though, all at least accepted that the creation of the spheres had been a group effort, which allowed for everyone to be "known to exist" and for long-standing and unresolvable debates over *which* gods, exactly, had built the universe.

The First Digger was part of a second tier of divinities whose stories and mythologies simply could not be fitted into the combined cosmology of the spheres. Those deities still had worshippers but tended to be far less important than the core accepted pantheon.

"Get the ropes and brackets ready," Brushfire told Axfall. "Captain is bringing us in."

She considered the dock thoughtfully.

"How would you hook up the air envelope to the dock?" she asked.

"Easy enough," Axfall said instantly. "We've got enough spare aethercloth to put together a tunnel of it. We'd need to seal it with magic, but we'd make an airtight tunnel for the archmage.

"Anyone else would have to enter the tunnel through the envelope, though," he said after another moment's thought.

"Once the crew is ready to tie us down, get a party working on that," Brushfire ordered. "Captain and I will go in with the archmage."

"And the rest of the crew?" Paintrock asked.

She hadn't even seen the Master of Staves approaching, her focus had been so strongly on the darvar monastery.

"Be ready in case something goes very strange," she said drily.

"If I may make a suggestion, First Officer?" the blue elvar asked.

"Suggest away."

"Take an escort," Paintrock told her. "Blades and 'wands. All sheathed, of course—we don't want to be *threatening*—but we are a long way from civilized spheres, and a show of force won't be offensive.

"And the extra hands may prove necessary."

Brushfire grunted and ran a finger down her focus.

"Put together a party," she told Paintrock, echoing her words to Axfall. "All elvar. Let's not trust the ascetic monks in the middle of nowhere, who only deal with their own var, *not* to be bigots, shall we?"

Axfall and Windheart had clearly put some thought into getting the archmage out of the envelope. Thought, Brushfire realized, that *she* probably should have at least asked for, if not engaged in herself.

They produced a nearly complete airtight tunnel of aethercloth in under thirty minutes, only needing her to seal the connections against air loss to make sure that it was safe for everyone to pass.

Both were standing at the entrance to the air envelope as she and Cat surveyed Paintrock's party of elvar escorts. None of the half dozen sailors were dressed any differently from the rest of the crew, but there was something in how they wore the weapon belts with the swords and battlewands now that was quite...*distinctive*.

From the way Cat stood, he'd picked up the same thing she had. But they had to trust their crew—after thirty-plus clock-days in the aether, there'd been a lot of opportunities for betrayal along the way.

"The rest of the crew is turning out and arming," Windheart told them. "Hopefully, it won't be a problem, but we'll be ready."

"There's no one else out here to save us if something goes wrong," Cat agreed. "Thank you, Masters. Your foresight is appreciated."

"I was planning on bringing the archmage in aboard a litter," Brushfire murmured to him. "I didn't think about the fact that the monks would *also* need air."

"But this works, and it helps protect us from them," her captain replied. "Cut it up once we're aboard and we're safe from them following us.

"Unless, of course, they have some monks who can breathe aether."

"All things are possible," Brushfire said. "Shall we go see if the archmage is as silver-tongued with darvar as he was with us?"

"He had prophecy on his side talking to us," Cat replied. "Well, me at least. You were just desperate."

He wasn't wrong, but Brushfire had to wonder what was bothering her captain. Potentially just...fear? Nervousness?

The whole situation was strange, she had to admit that, but they'd made it this far.

She followed him into the archmage's air envelope, hoping that the captain's nerves were just that. Half a dozen armed elvar followed her—and Bluestaves wasn't alone inside the envelope, either.

Half a dozen armed and armored halvar wearing the blue sashes of an archmage's personal guard and holding wand-halberds at the ready were waiting in the space as well.

"I don't recall bringing guards aboard," Cat said mildly.

"Illusions, but there's some real force behind them too," Bluestaves said brightly. "There are sashes for the entire party, though I don't have many extra."

He was taking the seven elvar escorts in as he glanced around. "I only brought a dozen or so. If I'd known I was going to have an army, I'd have asked Master Windheart to make some more."

Paintrock collected the cloth strips from where the archmage had indicated.

"Illusions and hidden magics go some way, Lord Archmage," he said stiffly. "But half a dozen var at your back with real blades and real arms—that'll take you the rest of the way, won't it?"

"We've connected a tunnel of aethercloth from the starboard entrance to your receiving room across to their covered dock," Brushfire told Bluestaves. She wasn't entirely sure what "real force" might be behind an archmage's illusions—but she doubted that the darvar monks wanted to find out!

"Clever," the archmage said. "I was planning on bringing air with me by magic. That will definitely save me some energy."

Everyone, it seemed, had come up with their own plan for getting Archmage Bluestaves from his sealed compartment aboard *Star* into the darvar's sealed monastery. At some point during the journey, they probably should have compared notes.

"This is your show, your mission, Archmage Bluestaves," Greentrees noted. "We follow your lead and wherever you go."

"Well, then, we should be getting started, shouldn't we?" Bluestaves replied. "If someone can grab that case there"—he pointed—"it should open some doors and ears that might remain closed if their bellies weren't full."

"What is it?" Brushfire asked as Paintrock picked up the large case. It looked like a smaller version of the magically chilled storage units they used for food.

"Sweet rolls," the archmage said cheerfully. "I didn't *just* spend the trip baking for myself, you know. I don't know if the monks of the First

Digger are allowed alcohol, but I suspect supplies and food will loosen some tongues here."

CHAPTER

37

With real elvar sailors leading the way and illusory halvar halberdiers bringing up the rear, Armand Bluestaves left the suite of rooms that had been his world for the last thirty-odd clock-days and entered the tunnel *Star*'s crew had created.

The tube of stark white aethercloth was *fascinating*, a tremendously clever solution to the problem at hand that Armand hadn't even thought of. By and large, halvar and darvar contingents boarded and left aether ships after they'd descended into air those var could breathe.

There, though, the Monastery of the First Digger itself was buried inside an airless rock. Arcana and artifice could create air inside the underground structures of the Monastery itself, but filling an airtight compartment was a vastly different task from providing air to the entire surface of the worldlet.

Sealed litters were the usual solution for that situation, though Bluestaves had planned on carrying his own air bubble as a demonstration of power.

His small squadron of real and illusory bodyguards made a decent show of power, though, he hoped, and he was *extremely* pleased by the thoughtfulness of his crew.

"Was this your idea, Officer Brushfire?" he asked the gobvar walking beside him.

"Master of Decks Axfall came up with the plan," she told him. "Master of Sails Windheart and his people did much of the work."

"I am impressed," Armand told her.

"So am I," she admitted.

"And I," Greentrees added. "Every time the clocks turn over, Archmage, I am reminded that we owe Oathsworn Lane quite a bit for directing us to the Hammerheads."

"A debt I will be delighted to discharge when all of this is over," Armand replied.

Assuming they made it back. Without the observatory in his tower, he was limited in his ability to project the future. As he'd demonstrated to his allies on their approach to the Monastery, he could spread his magic across a single sphere and learn what *was*, but to learn what *would be* was always harder for him.

Seers were more common than archmagi, but being an archmage did not guarantee the full panoply of their skills. Armand had more *power* but less skill and training than, say, the seer serving aboard an elvar ninesail.

He wished he'd had a chance to meet with the seer who'd sent Cat Greentrees to him. For now, though, he needed to handle the work in front of him.

"This is the edge of our tunnel," Brushfire warned as they reached a heavy curtain of aethercloth. "We tied it into the cover over their dock, but we needed to make sure it was airtight on our side, too. We'll lose a bit of air pushing through, but you should be fine."

Armand nodded with a small smile. He was the most powerful var on the ship by most measures, but he was also the only var on the ship who couldn't breathe aether. His people were mother-layering him, and he couldn't even argue.

"Ready?" Paintrock asked, the armed Master of Staves putting his hand on the curtain. "Hopefully, they won't be waiting to ambush us!"

"We are here to talk and make a deal, not wage a war," Armand told the elvar. "Lead the way, Master Paintrock."

The curtain swept aside, and Armand shivered as he *felt* the air get thinner and colder on his lips. Still, he strode forward with purpose, following the elvar sailors out of the aethercloth tunnel and into the permanently sheltered dock.

He summoned power to himself to keep a bubble of air around his head, just in case, and continued to move. His bubble carried him several yards into the sheltered dock, and he felt magic settle around him.

A mental poke confirmed what Armand suspected, and he released his bubble of air.

"Impressive," he told his companions.

"They've added a magical field containing the air at this end," Brushfire agreed. "Makes sense when you're darvar trying to deal with elvar, I suppose."

"Gives them options," Cat said, his voice a growl.

Armand suspected his captain was feeling more paranoid about the situation than the rest of the crew—which was a *good* thing. Armand himself had his suspicions about the monks and what their reaction was going to be.

Running into complex magic there at the docks wasn't reassuring, either. While this was a critical piece of infrastructure for the locals, one deserving of attention and power, an air bubble like the one they'd entered was difficult to both create and maintain.

Its presence spoke to the sophistication and power of the mages present in the Monastery of the First Digger.

"Come," Armand ordered. "Let's not keep our hosts waiting."

The monks might have created a bubble of air to make it *possible* to meet visiting var closer to the ship, but they didn't appear to be using it today.

The covered dock led into one of the ancient stone towers. The stone plinth that served as the dock's main structure merged smoothly into the tower itself, with no lines to mark where tools or magic had shaped it.

What little they could see of the tower itself was equally smooth, and Armand was impressed. It would have taken thousands of laborers and dozens of mages to raise even the single tower they stood outside. The sheer effort inherent in the task of reshaping the worldlet that held the Monastery of the First Digger was immense—and to have then taken the extra time and magical power to merge the stone was mind-boggling to him.

It had probably made the structures stronger, though the ruins he'd seen across the worldlet spoke to the limits of the Ironhands' building methods. There was a reason the elvar built simple and short, after all.

Here, though, the only break in the smooth exterior of the tower was a set of double doors that easily gave to Paintrock's push, revealing a matching set of interior doors. The same logic governed the design as had called for doubled doors in the air envelope on *Star*, Armand presumed, which suggested that the dock had not always been encased in a bubble of magical air.

Still, they let the outer doors close behind them before the Master of Staves pushed the inner doors open and led his sailors into the tower.

"Ah, greetings," a surprised voice said. "I was not expecting, uh…"

At the sound of a local host at last, Armand pushed his own way through the inner doors, holding them open behind him with a flick of magic for the others.

The interior of the tower was one large open space. A wide ramp started at the far side, descending smoothly toward the surface at a rate that would easily handle carts and bulk cargo transport.

"I apologize for the abruptness of my var," Armand told the single darvar standing just back from the entrance, looking uncomfortably at the armed elvar spreading out across the tower floor.

"They feel obliged to make certain of my security at all times," he continued, inclining his head to the stranger.

"I am Archmage Armand Bluestaves, and all of these var are sworn to my service," he explained. "And you are?"

"Ah, welcome, Archmage," their host said swiftly. "I am Senior Excavator Steadfast Miller. I welcome you and your people to the Monastery of the First Digger. Please, tell me…what brings you so far out in these remote spheres? Are you lost?"

Armand shook his head.

"No, my friend," he replied. "We were here looking for your monastery, in fact. I wish to speak with your High Excavator, on a matter of the fates of var and spheres."

Miller blinked in surprise and took a moment to find an answer to that.

"The High Excavator does not, as a rule, speak to strangers," he admitted. "It is my task to deal with visitors to our monastery and the supply ships.

"For an archmage, though…" Miller seemed to consider. "She may make an exception for an archmage. Follow me."

"Of course, Senior Excavator," Armand said with a nod. "We are at the High Excavator's convenience."

"I cannot promise that she will see you," the monk warned. "She rarely speaks with anyone outside our order. Her task is the contemplation of the First Stone."

"I understand," Armand said. "I would not seek to interrupt her contemplation unless I thought it was important."

The First Stone was the material from which the First Digger had supposedly carved the spheres, only to see the remnants turned to the void by the actions of traitors. Like most educated var, Armand found that myth required a great deal of twisting to fit the known reality, and the shared myth of the generally accepted pantheon made much more sense to him.

But he was not rude enough to say so to a monk of the First Digger's faith, merely following the darvar toward the center of the tower.

A gesture from Miller woke the magic there, lighting a circle of runes that pulsed with a familiar power to Armand. The archmage concealed a moment of surprise as he recognized the spell.

Even in the Towers of the Great Red Forest, short-range teleportation magic was used sparingly and required a fully contained space. Armand, who had walked among the most powerful and trained mages in the halvar kingdoms, had never seen the equivalent of his tower's transportation closets created as simply a circle of runes on the floor.

"You will need to leave your escort behind," Miller told him as the darvar stepped into the middle of the runes. "There isn't enough space for them all."

Armand surveyed the size of the circle and smiled.

"I will bring some with us myself," he told the monk, gesturing his illusory halvar guards back. There was *just* enough space for the elvar sailors and his two officers to squeeze in around him.

The monk looked concerned—and just a little claustrophobic, almost certainly not used to this many var—but he nodded and activated the circle with another gesture.

The room flickered around them and vanished, replaced by a near-identical one. The immediately identifiable difference to Armand was that the ramp now came down from above instead of descending from the floor.

A moment's thought and the illusory halvar bodyguard flickered back into existence around them. Miller looked at them with concerned eyes but then shook his head.

"Very well, Archmage," he allowed. "If you and your var will follow me into the monastery."

From the bottom of the docking tower, Miller led them into what Armand presumed to be the crossroads where the access from all eight docking towers converged. The wide tunnel descended gently into a large open space that had been subdivided with storage racking.

Barrels and crates of supplies stretched in every direction, sufficient stockpiles to feed a town for years. The area was chilled, presumably to help preserve the supplies, and Miller sped up his steps as he led them through it.

At the center of the warehouse, another wide ramp descended in a downward circle—and another teleportation circle had been built in the middle.

Armand repeated his trick with moving his illusory escort, but he found himself blinking against brilliant crystal light as the teleporter finished its work.

They'd moved from a very clearly underground cavern, surrounded by boxes and supplies, to a wide-open space that took him a moment to take in. The immediate clue that he was still in the Monastery was the stone ramp descending around them. Looking up, he could see where it emerged from the cavern ceiling.

There were no walls around the ramp there, though, allowing the light from the massive crystal lamps providing full daylight to the cavern to fill where they stood.

Armand surveyed their location and had to admit he was impressed. Farm fields spread in every direction around him, fueled by the magical light and heat filling the space. Roads formed cardinal lines through the cavern, splitting it into four segments.

One of those roads led to what appeared to be a brewery, a low stone building surmounted with massive barrels. Two others led to similar structures that were less clear in their purpose, and the last, opposite from the brewery, led to a set of gates at least ten yards high.

The gates were currently wide open, but Armand guessed they were the entrance to the main underground monastery. They didn't look easy to move, rendering the Monastery almost invulnerable to outside attack if closed—even assuming there were no barriers that had been bypassed by Miller's use of the teleportation circles.

"Come," the monk ordered. "It's still quite the walk from here."

CHAPTER 38

The underground farms gave the Monastery an oddly rural feel as Miller led the way down the road toward the gates. There were other darvar working in the fields, but they didn't so much as raise their heads to acknowledge the presence of strangers in their midst.

"Tell me, Excavator Miller," Armand eventually had to ask. "We spotted other towers, ruined ones, on the surface. Was all of this here when the Order of the First Digger arrived? Or did you dig out the complex under the tower yourself?"

Miller looked back over his shoulder at the archmage in surprise.

"Most visitors don't realize there are other structures here," he finally allowed. "The farms and apiaries and such are all us, including the lights."

"I presumed that," Armand agreed. "I was thinking about the underground caverns themselves. They seem…out of character for the Ironhands."

Now Miller was *definitely* concerned.

"I don't know," he admitted. "Our Order's arrival here was long before my time. That is not a name I've heard often—and never from visitors."

Darvar were longer-lived than halvar but shorter-lived than the two aether-var. Miller didn't appear to be much past a hundred dances, making him early middle age for a darvar—and almost certainly too young to have been present when the Order of the First Digger had first resettled the ruined citadel.

"I am a student of the Ironhand Imperium," Armand told the monk. "That is part of the business that brings us here."

"I…see," Miller acknowledged. "That will fascinate the High Excavator, I believe. Even here, there are few who know much of that ancient empire. I do not know if you will find the answers you seek, Archmage Bluestaves."

Armand smiled and shook his head at Miller.

"I know what answers I am seeking, Excavator, and I do believe I will find them here," he told the monk. "Merely the presence of the ancient citadel itself answers some questions while presenting others.

"I look forward to my conversation with your High Excavator. I would hope that the Digger's children, more than any other, will have dug deep in these stones to find answers."

"We have many purposes here," Miller replied as they reached the open gates. "But we are mostly here to meditate upon the universe in private, away from distractions. Investigating these stones is not part of that task.

"It would be a distraction of its own, in truth," he admitted.

"Perhaps, but there are prices to be paid for all kinds of isolation," Armand said.

The gates loomed above them now. Unlike most of the rest of the cavern, *this* was definitively Ironhand work to his eyes. No var of the current age worked in ironbound stone in the same way as the Ironhands had. There were few ruins left of their work after a thousand dances, but the distinguishing characteristics were clear to Armand's eyes.

The darvar had replaced the ancient machinery with more recent mechanisms, but Armand doubted that the immense doors closed quickly. Or at all. The monks would, presumably, have hours or even clock-days of warning before needing to close them, but even the "new" machinery appeared to be rusted in place.

Once through the gates, the Monastery became more what he had expected of the place. The entrance hall inside the gates would have seemed immense and grand if they hadn't just passed through the massive farming and storage caverns outside.

"We mostly eat in here," Miller told the *Star* crew, gesturing at the long and unadorned stone tables and benches that were the room's only furniture.

"Then this is the place for our gift, I suppose," Armand said, gesturing for Paintrock to lay out the case of pastries. "I did not expect as much agriculture here as you have, I must admit, and took the liberty of bringing you several hundred frozen pastries.

"If they are left out to thaw, they should be at a perfect temperature by your evening meal," the archmage promised.

"We make our own breads and beer," Miller said slowly. "But while we are expected to maintain a certain level of asceticism in our food and drink, your gift will be appreciated, I promise."

The monk bobbed his head.

"Please, take a seat at the tables," he told them. "I will ask the High Excavator if she is willing to meet with you.

"You may have come all this way to be disappointed, I warn you," Miller continued, "but for an archmage, I will ask on your behalf."

"That is all I can hope for, Senior Excavator," Armand said. "I hope that we will be permitted a tour of the Monastery either way, but I will not press my presence upon the Excavator."

With a tour, he could try to match up his divinations from the surface with the reality of the underground. That would let him locate the strange void ship with more precision.

He still hoped to cut a deal, but the more information he had on what was there, the more alternatives he would be able to conjure.

"There are fewer people here than I would have expected," Brushfire admitted after their host had disappeared. "Those farms and supplies… They appear to be ready to feed a city's worth of people for a long siege."

"I was expecting to be under constant guard," Cat added, nodding in agreement. "I can see some logic behind the supplies, but the farms are strange."

"We are being watched," Armand warned, reminding his var that while they might be *alone,* they were not in *private.* "Several scrying sensors are in the room. I suspect we are under careful guard indeed, if not necessarily a guard we can see."

"A lot of mages for darvar," the captain murmured. "I wouldn't have expected monks on the end of nowhere to have the skill, let alone the hands, to maintain multiple teleporters."

"Those circles are an advancement of the art beyond what I am used to, as well," Armand warned. "Not only are there more mages here than I expected, they are capable ones."

"A danger?" Brushfire asked.

"I don't think so," he replied, looking around the empty hall. "I think they are judging to see if *we* are a danger. A place like this has many secrets, however quiet and meditative the current residents are."

"Do you think the High Excavator will meet with us?" Cat asked.

"I hope so, but I'm not certain if admitting I knew about the Ironhands helped open the door or close it," Armand admitted. "A shadow falls over my divinations."

"Choices unmade?"

"Exactly," the archmage told his captain. "I don't believe even the High Excavator knows if she will speak with us yet. Time will tell."

"And if they don't…" Brushfire was clearly thinking of Armand's mention of the scrying when she trailed off. "What if they can't help us?" she finally corrected herself.

"Then we return to *Star* and consider our next steps," he told her. "We have many options for what we seek."

Unspoken was that the "options" were only around how they *acquired* the void ship. So far as Armand Bluestaves knew, the ship there could easily be the only void ship in existence.

If the locals were truly worshippers of the First Digger, he wished them no ill will…but he *needed* that ship.

Or Court and Kingdoms would fall, and one Armand Bluestaves would die. He had no intention of allowing either of those things to happen.

CHAPTER 39

EVERYTHING ABOUT the situation was making Cat nervous. They'd brought every tool and trick they could really risk bringing without making it an open assault, but he couldn't help but feel completely exposed as ten var—and half a dozen illusions—sat alone in the middle of the Monastery's grand hall.

Nothing about the place, from the unusual nature of the teleporters to the ancient Ironhand ruins to the way the monks didn't even *look up* when strangers walked by, felt right to him.

If the Monastery was as self-sufficient as the farms suggested, why did they have the massive quantity of supplies stored in the warehouse above the farm cavern? If they needed as much food as the supplies and farms implied, *where were the monks?*

Their party, including the illusions, easily filled half of one table. There were only five tables, which meant the hall had enough space to sit maybe two hundred var. The "Senior Excavator" had implied that the monks all ate there, together, which suggested there were under two hundred monks.

Cat had seen maybe a dozen in the fields, but the fields alone were enough to feed at least a thousand. There were supplies in the caverns to feed a thousand for several complete dances.

Self-sufficiency and reserves against crisis or loss of connection made sense for a sphere so disconnected from Court and Kingdoms, but this was far beyond anything necessary for that.

They couldn't turn back or leave, and Cat was determined to see Bluestaves' mission through, but the monastery didn't feel right. If the monks were actually what they said they were instead of what Bluestaves feared they were, they were very strange var.

More than anything else, though, the nature of the aether currents throughout the citadel worldlet had been strumming on his nerves since

Star had docked. Every worldlet had currents in the aether, shaped by the worldlet itself as well as all the forces that shaped the aether away from worldlets, too.

He'd expected that the currents would be pulled toward the void strait, like everything else in the sphere…and they *were*. But they also swirled around the worldlet itself in a way that was unlike anything he'd ever experienced.

Aether curved around lodestone cores…but this pulled the aether in, accelerated it and curved it around the worldlet again and again. If it wasn't for the void strait, he suspected the worldlet would have drawn the local aether into itself in much the same way as the strait did.

But there was no void at the heart of the Monastery of the First Digger. The void ship wouldn't cause the effect he was sensing. He suspected it was something the Ironhand Dynasty had done, potentially part of how they'd reshaped an entire worldlet to match their design.

Neither of the other mages seemed to have noticed it, and he was considering raising it with the archmage—whatever ancient arcana was impacting the aether could be dangerous—when a set of doors to the great hall swung open.

A trio of darvar in the same robes as Miller came through. All were strangers, but they approached the table with *Star*'s crew, clearly having expected to find them.

"I am Senior Excavator Virtue Advisor," the central darvar introduced herself. "This is Senior Excavator Crystal Builder"—she gestured to her left—"and this is Senior Excavator Victory Towers"—she indicated the last darvar.

"The High Excavator has agreed to meet with you, but she is occupied with meditation and ritual for some time yet this clock-day."

"We await the High Excavator's convenience, of course," Bluestaves replied instantly. "I understand that var such as Her Holiness have many duties, both religious and secular, to occupy their time."

"She asked that we"—Advisor gestured around at the other two senior monks—"give you and your officers the tour of the Monastery you requested. We fear you will find it far less exciting than you may expect or hope, but what little we have, we are delighted to share."

"So long as you can respect our siblings-in-faith's need for privacy and quiet," Towers growled. "Internal reflection can be difficult without distractions, let alone the reflection upon the First Stone."

"Of course," Bluestaves agreed.

"We also must ask that your escorts remain here," Advisor said. "Only you and your two officers. More would be an unavoidable disturbance."

Cat did *not* like that. While he was mostly confident in the ability of the archmage to defend them, let alone his and Brushfire's ability to defend themselves, dividing the group went against the grain.

Especially when he was as uncomfortable with the entire situation as he was.

To his surprise, Bluestaves slid his hand over to grip Cat's forearm firmly.

"Again, we understand," the archmage said, his grip on Cat's arm surprisingly communicative. "This is your home, Excavators, and as guests, we are more than willing to abide by your rules."

The archmage had…a point, Cat admitted silently. Until and unless they actually decided they were taking the ship by force, they had to go along to get along.

And if the halvar's warm hand lingered longer than was required to communicate his intent, Cat was surprised to find that he didn't mind at all.

Cat hung back as Brushfire and Bluestaves followed the Excavators, bringing up the rear of the group so he could watch his companions' backs.

It also allowed him to keep half an eye on Bluestaves' illusory halberdiers. He wasn't particularly surprised that the illusions remained sitting at the table, engaged in much the same small entertainments as the elvar sailors. Knowing that the halvar were illusions, he could tell that they weren't interacting with the elvar—but that could easily be put up to some of the inevitable standoffishness between different var serving the same master.

He was impressed, though. Even with an archmage's power, maintaining that kind of fidelity once out of eyeshot took skill and talent. Bluestaves' capabilities were both terrifying and reassuring, especially this far away from any other source of support.

"Through these doors here you can see our kitchens," Advisor told them, holding a swinging door open and gesturing through.

Warmth and the scent of fresh-baked bread billowed out of the room in question. Even if the Excavator hadn't told them what they were looking at, it would have been obvious—but Cat found himself immediately looking beyond the obvious.

The nature and structure of the big room wouldn't have looked out of place on any worldlet in any sphere he'd ever visited, but what he started estimating was the *size*. How many ovens. How many hearths. How many prep tables.

Half a dozen darvar monks were silently going about their work, which was currently emptying bread out of the ovens. Cat quickly estimated the number of rolls and loaves compared to the size of the kitchen.

It was more food than needed for, say, two hundred mouths. But not by much. If they were baking bread for tonight's dinner and tomorrow's breakfast, with an allowance for the guests that had arrived...

The amount lined up relatively neatly with the number of darvar Cat was estimating. And left him, once again, questioning just what the monks were growing all of that grain in the farm cavern for.

It wasn't like they were *trading* it, after all.

The tour continued on and Cat kept his concerns to himself. Their three guides weren't being subtle about the fact that they were keeping their eyes and ears on everything the three visitors did and said.

The elvar captain couldn't blame them. He was counting and calculating in his head as they went on, and each piece of information fit the picture. There were about two hundred darvar in the Monastery—maybe a dozen more or less, but roughly two hundred var.

If there were any more var—and he wasn't ruling that out!—they neither ate nor slept nor made their clothing there.

The Monastery seemed to be self-sufficient in almost every way. The grain they grew became beer, bread, clothing... The tour eventually led them to a section off to one side of the farms that held a large array of layers of half a dozen breeds to provide both eggs and meat for the Monastery.

Without knowing exactly how much meat the monks ate, he couldn't say how many var the layer coops could feed...but assuming they were eating meat and eggs every clock-day, the flocks were large enough to support over two hundred var. Maybe as many as two hundred and fifty.

Cat counted layers and coops in silence as Excavator Towers waxed rhapsodical about the breeds of layers they raised in the cavern. One breed, apparently, turned feed into meat with a significantly higher efficiency than any other breed—they laid fewer eggs, so the monks had to make sure their eggs were fertilized and incubated to keep up the meat supply.

He recognized the *value* of layers, in an intellectual capacity, but he found the birds in all of their varieties to be noisy and dirty. At that moment, he was more concerned about the math he'd run in his head.

There were *definitely* only two hundred var in the monastery they'd been shown. He figured they hadn't been shown all of it by any measure, but the eating and food preparation spaces only really served two hundred.

But the layer population could provide a luxurious level of egg and meat for more var than that—and the monks were supposed to live a relatively ascetic lifestyle. He doubted that covered a diet that would put the one served by the High Court Navy to their *officers* to shame.

So, there were another hundred darvar somewhere *else*. Maybe two hundred...which made sense, since *Star*'s crew knew the void ship was at least forty leagues away. Unless there was a teleporter link—possible, though that was a strain for the permanent teleporters *Cat* knew of—they'd want to have anyone working at that cavern living there.

"Now that Excavator Towers has exposed us all to his vast knowledge and great fascination with our birds, we'll continue on a bit farther," Advisor said with a chuckle and a smile at her counterpart.

It was oddly out of character for the stoic monks, but Cat suspected that *everyone* on the citadel worldlet had been thoroughly exposed to Senior Excavator Towers' feelings and research on the layers.

Even among monks, that kind of enthusiasm could only have two reactions: utter hatred or bemused exasperation. Senior Excavator Advisor, at least, had clearly chosen the latter.

"Now, over here you can see our granaries," Advisor continued, leading them around the back of the coops and gesturing to the circular structures. "This far out from our home spheres, we have always judged it wise to maintain several years' reserve of all of our needs.

"You saw the warehouses when Excavator Miller brought you in. We keep the grain we grow here—and keep a careful watch for vermin making it in on the aether ships," she noted. "Currently, there are no grain-eating vermin here, which makes storage much easier."

There were an even dozen silos, each about the size Cat would expect to hold enough grain to feed a hundred var for a year. He wondered if the Senior Excavators even realized how many secrets they were giving away.

"You do a lot of things with one grain," he observed, studying the silos.

"It's a versatile plant," Advisor agreed. "Excavator Miller could give you almost as long a lecture on our grain as Towers can on our layers, but we use it for almost everything. The chaff gets divided into fibers long enough to be woven—you saw our looms—and compost that helps fertilize the fields for the next crop.

"We grow a few species of ground cover as well, to rest the fields every few crops. Those also help keep the dirt suitable for farming." She shook her head. "The actual farm soil is imported from several spheres and needs to be refreshed every ten dances or so despite everything we do.

"But the grain, as you say, serves most of our needs. It makes our bread and our porridge, it feeds our layers, it ferments into our beer, it distills into our…liquor."

Cat was listening for a misstep and still barely caught the pause when she talked about distilling the grain. He'd only heard mention of beer so far—and they'd only been shown a brewery. He hadn't seen any kind of distillery, though any ship captain knew that a still could be surprisingly small.

But if they weren't distilling *liquor*, what were they distilling?

Before he could think of asking that question, they were interrupted by the return of Senior Excavator Miller. The darvar monk clearly knew exactly where to find them, as he cut a straight line—or as close as he could without crossing the grain fields—toward them from the Monastery.

"Her Holiness is ready to greet her guests now," he told the other three senior monks. "Come, Archmage Bluestaves. We appreciate your patience, but I must warn that the High Excavator has little time to spare for you.

"We must not delay."

The monks of the First Digger, Cat reflected, apparently took their scheduling lessons from the High Court Navy.

CHAPTER 40

Armand had definitely noticed the thoughtful expression on his captain's face throughout the tour. He'd done his best to catch what was bothering Cat, though the inability to *talk* while being shadowed by the locals definitely limited it.

While he still wasn't entirely sure what the elvar was seeing, he'd caught the unexpected pause in Excavator Advisor's comments on distilling the grain into liquor. He hadn't so much as seen a bottle of whisky in the entire place, only beer.

That curiosity carried the archmage back to the great hall of the Monastery, where their escorts were waiting for them. It was a relief to finally be able to see his illusory guards again. He'd left them running a cycle of motions, but if anyone had been paying too much attention, they'd have realized that the illusions repeated themselves after about half an hour.

Hopefully, none of the monks had been watching that hard. All but one of the scrying sensors had followed him, Brushfire and Cat on their tour, so he guessed that their guardians had been mostly ignored.

"Fall in!" Paintrock ordered crisply as he spotted the officers, the Master of Staves almost leaping to his feet.

Bluestaves and the others had been on the tour, but the Master and the rest of the escort had been left sitting in the great hall with nothing to do. The noncom looked bored out of his skull.

"We would prefer that your escorts not—"

"They can accompany us to the audience chamber at least, yes?" Armand interrupted Miller smoothly. "These var are sworn to see to my protection, after all. They don't like leaving me alone."

There was a long silence, then Advisor sighed and nodded.

"The High Excavator will only see the three of you," he noted, gesturing to Armand and his officers. "But I suppose the rest can accompany us there."

"I appreciate the accommodation," Armand said. "I do not wish to stress those charged with my protection; you understand."

"I do," Miller agreed. "We feel much the same about the High Excavator."

"Of course. And we do not wish to keep her waiting. Lead on, Senior Excavator."

All four of the Senior Excavators escorted them from the great hall. Unless Armand badly misunderstood the ranking structure of the Order of the First Digger, there would only *be* five or six, at most, Senior Excavators in a monastery like this.

Armand suspected that the presence of so many of the senior monks was more to do with keeping the strangers under control and away from the rest of the Monastery than it was about showing respect or anything of the sort.

Or, of course, they were just being lied to about the ranks. That was also a possibility. It would be a stupid and pointless lie, but that hardly put it outside the realm of likelihood.

The four Excavators led them along a path that he'd spotted a few times during their tour, one that intersected several of the hallways they had seen, and then turned to the left and sharply descended.

The corridor never became stairs, but Armand couldn't help but feel that it *should*, given how steep the incline became as the corridor spiraled down beneath the sections of the Monastery they'd been allowed to see.

If he'd judged it correctly, in fact, the tunnel had wrapped around to put them directly beneath the great hall when it opened up into another cavernous space.

This one was smaller—but Armand judged that was only because it was split in two. The area they'd just entered was clearly an antechamber, decorated with gorgeous tapestries hanging from the ceiling to the floor and covering chunks of the room.

The far end was a visibly mortared wall, one that stood out compared to the smooth lines of the tunnels and structures carved by the Ironhand mage-engineers who had dug the original caverns.

The wall was new, as was the three-yard-high set of double doors in the center of it. The tapestries, with their scenes of great crystals and embers and mason-work and similar markers of light and industry, all guided the eye to that pair of doors.

"Your escort will wait out here," Miller announced. "I'm afraid there is no seating, but we were expecting them to wait in the main hall."

"We'll be fine," Paintrock assured the monk. "We don't want to be too far from the archmage, after all."

Armand nodded his head to the Master of Staves. There were few threats he couldn't protect himself from, but having the backup was still welcome.

He then turned to Cat and Brushfire.

"Shall we?"

Armand stepped through the doorway and immediately lurched backward to avoid falling. His initial impression was of a vast pit sweeping away for leagues in every direction, which made…very little sense.

A gravelly chuckle greeted his reaction.

"It is safe, Archmage," the speaker told him. "Come, all three of you. The glass will not fail today. I promise you that."

Carefully, oh so carefully, Armand obeyed. The "pit" was real, if smaller than initial impressions and mirrored walls had made it appear, but covered in a thick, transparent floor.

The room was only slightly bigger than the antechamber on the other side of the wall. Black cloth and ceiling-height mirrors were interspersed along the walls, giving an impression of both darkness and vastly increased size.

None of that helped the fact that the entire floor of the space—which had originally been only half of a larger room but, with the new additions, was an entire space on its own—was made of glass and hung over a pit that had to descend leagues into the heart of the worldlet.

To the lodestone core, at least, if not *into* the core itself.

"What is this place?" Armand asked aloud.

"A drain for aether currents," Cat Greentrees said sharply. "Everything is coming here before it's pulled away by the void strait."

"Your captain sees what many do not, Archmage," the robed figure sitting in the middle of the floor said. "This was once the Seventh Ward of the Ironhand Imperium. All of its arms and fortifications were secondary to its true purpose: to blockade the access to the Ironhand core at the whim of the Dynasty.

"I have no idea how that feat was achieved," she continued calmly. "But I know that this 'drain,' as Captain Greentrees called it, was a key component of the magic that allowed them to protect their spheres."

"Not that it saved them in the end," Armand observed, watching the glass beneath his feet as he crossed toward the figure. He realized that neither the monks nor the scrying eyes had followed him and his companions into the room. It was just the three of them and the High Excavator.

A situation that would have been far more dangerous to the var they were speaking with if he couldn't feel the pulse of the link to the Source under her heart. Like him, she was an archmage.

"I am Archmage Armand Bluestaves of the Towers of the Great Red Forest," he introduced himself. "This is Captain Cat Greentrees of the aether ship *Star* and his first officer, Brushfire Hammerhead."

"Please, Archmage, my monks are not incompetent enough not to have passed on your names," she told him with a chuckle. "I am the High Excavator of this Monastery of the First Digger. I have surrendered my name in the service of my god and bear only that title.

"So, tell me, what brings the Shining Kingdom's newest archmage to our distant corner of the Kingdoms?"

That wasn't information Armand had given the monks. The High Excavator knew more than she was giving herself credit for.

"The past," he murmured, stopping about two yards from the darvar woman. "The future. The fate of the spheres and the var. I have foreseen a great doom to fall across our realms, and I seek a way to turn it aside before all that I am sworn to protect is enslaved or broken."

"You have come to a strange corner of the spheres for that, I am afraid," she told him. "We deal little with the future here, Archmage Bluestaves. We cannot avoid dealing with the past, not when we have taken up residence here in the Seventh Ward, but the fate of all spheres rarely rests on a place so distant from so many of them."

"Frontiers are like that," Armand said. "The borders between two places are rarely at the center of either of them."

"Brokenwright has not been a border for two lifetimes of the elvar," the High Excavator replied. "The Ironhand Imperium *fell*, Archmage. The dynasty consumed their own subjects, their own worlds. There is nothing left of the Imperium but *hunger*, Archmage Bluestaves. A hunger you do not wish to challenge."

"I do not wish to challenge anything," he said. "I *need* to pass through. Four spheres through what was the Ironhand Imperium's core would bring me to the spheres of the gobvar Clans. Those spheres still exist, even if the aether is gone from them.

"If they can be transited, that passage will allow me to seek answers among the gobvar. And if I find those answers, spheres that might burn may be saved. I have seen a future that I know has already been set in motion, First Excavator.

"I can turn it aside. But only with your help."

The robed and hooded var didn't move at all for several moments. Then she rose. Even for a darvar, she was short. Stocky like all of her var, she still seemed small and frail against the immense chasm beneath her feet.

"I sympathize with your desire to achieve an impossible mission, Bluestaves," she told him. "But the Order of the First Digger has no answers for you. There are no secrets here except the one beneath your feet—and that ancient magic is the opposite of what you seek.

"From these stones, the Ironhands' mages could seal those spheres. But even if you gathered a hundred archmagi, I do not believe we could warp that spell to somehow open a channel through the spheres of the void.

"There is no passage from here except back the way you came. No aether ship can transit the strait into the Ironhand Imperium. Those dead spheres are forever barred to your eyes."

"No aether ship can make that passage, no," Cat Greentrees said from behind Armand. "But there are other kinds of ships, aren't there?"

"At least one," Armand said, challenging the other archmage. She had yet to even turn and face him. "There is a vessel on the Seventh Ward, forged of artifice and arcana and designed to breach that very strait. I have seen this ship; its power flies across my visions of the now and the future.

"It was built to breach the void, and it can make the journey I need to make. I need that ship, High Excavator, and I will pay any price you ask of me for it."

"You know nothing of what you speak," she whispered—yet her words echoed around the chamber as if she had bellowed them. "That is a sacred thing, forged to bring His children closer to His Divinity.

"I will not permit you to profane it at any price. That you even *know* of what you speak is a failure of our magics, a violation of our oaths, *blasphemy* against His Will."

She was *shaking* under the robe, Armand realized—with anger, he suspected.

"You will burn as well if what I have seen comes to pass," he warned. "Someone has roused a desire to *rule* rather than ignore the var among the dragon kin. They will break the gobvar to their will, and they will come for everyone.

"They will come for *you*."

"We are of no interest to anyone here," she snapped. "Except, it seems, archmagi who know more than they should and not enough to watch what they demand."

Armand let her words hang in the dark room for a dozen heartbeats.

"I need that ship," he told her. "I *need* to pass through those void spheres."

"You ask for one who understands nothing to board a ship built by the faithful to serve a purpose most sacred, to be carried through spheres sanctified by blood and destruction, to prevent a future that may never come to pass but will serve His Will regardless," she told him, still facing away from them.

"You have come to the wrong place and asked for the wrong things, Archmage Bluestaves."

"'His Will'?" Armand asked softly, taking a step backward and reaching out to draw strength from his companions. Both Cat and Brushfire stepped into reach, allowing him to clasp their forearms.

"I am no worshipper of the First Digger, but I do not remember His Will calling for the enslavement of the darvar and all other var," Cat Greentrees said.

"Nor for the purification of spheres by blood and destruction," Brushfire continued.

"Nor, in any of my research, have I have ever heard of High Excavators being asked to surrender their names in the service of their god," Armand concluded. "In fact, only *two* gods have ever demanded that of their worshippers.

"The Crimson Sister demands that as part of the sacrifice to forge Her Sisters into Her *weapons*," he noted. "But they would never have even permitted us to land.

"Only His Dark Brothers walk enough in shadow to have attempted to deceive us and yet worship the void itself. Only His *Seekers* yield their names as a sacrifice for power."

The darvar turned and the robe rippled away as the light finally shone on the Seventh Ward's ruler. Her skin was pale as aethercloth in sunlight, almost translucently white, and her hair was long gone.

Only one color marked her face: the pitch-black voids where her eyes should have been. The voids that confirmed that the archmage who led the monastery they had come to make a deal with was *everything* that Armand Bluestaves had feared and more.

An archmage who was one of His Dark Brothers would have been bad enough. But a Void Seeker was armed with an entirely different kind of power, a channel from the void that defined the younger of the divine twins. *Combined* with the power of an archmage…

The Void Seeker commanded both arcane and profane power, and he *felt* her summon it to her as she faced them across that glass floor and that ancient pit.

"You should have stopped asking questions, Archmage," she snarled. "Now you have condemned every var you brought. You have breached the secrets of the Seventh Ward…and you will *die among them*."

CHAPTER

41

BRUSHFIRE DID NOT KNOW what a Seeker was. Even without the threats, the connection to Her Dark Brother or the fact that they stood over a pit of empty void, she would have guessed that the darvar priestess was bad news simply from the pitch-black abysses that should have been eyes.

Something about that space underneath the surface of the Seventh Ward had helped conceal the priestess's power, but that veil shattered now, and Brushfire almost flinched backward at the sheer waves of energy that rippled away from the darvar before she even acted.

But she drew strength from Armand's hand on her arm and grasped her focus as the trio stepped back as one. The archmage's magic flickered in front of them in a wispy-feeling tracery of magic that she *hoped* belied its power.

"We didn't come here to fight you," Brushfire told the priestess. "We can come to a deal."

She shivered as she spoke—and realized that the wisps of magic she was feeling in the room were Armand and the Seeker *already* dueling. The temperature around *Star*'s retreating officers was plummeting, a chill sinking into her flesh and bones that no mortal heat could dispel.

Brushfire *focused* and channeled energy through her own wand. Her magic flickered across herself and her men, a personal and powerful warmth that drove back the chill of the Seeker's magic.

Armand's magic wove between them, scraps of light that each held as much power as Brushfire's entire warming spell. Scraps of darkness challenged those sparks, and the gobvar shaman shivered as she recognized the level of arcane might those *sparks* entailed. A dozen attacks and counterattacks flickered in the cavern in every blink of the eye.

All of that was going on even as the Seeker was continually trying to chill the entire space and freeze out her unwelcome guests. It was taking all of their archmage's strength to hold off the direct attack—and the Void Seeker was *still* managing an indirect attack!

Even as Brushfire realized that, a more solid magical shield slid into place around the trio, just in time to catch one of the sparks that slipped past Armand's interception. The entire chamber rang like a bell as Cat's shield threw off the Seeker's strike.

Brushfire *knew* her limitations as a mage, and this duel was out of her depth. She had the *power* to contribute, but she didn't have the *knowledge*. Her hundred or so clock-days of training with a focus left her as undertrained as a mage as she was as a shaman—she was qualified to call herself both, but she lacked the knowledge necessary to even fully *understand* how Armand was dueling the Seeker, let alone contribute.

Even as she thought that, though, the chilling spell increased in intensity. Ice crystals began to appear in the air around them—and Cat's shield rang again as another attack made it through.

Between them, Armand and Cat were keeping the direct attack at bay, but the trio had taken half a dozen steps back toward the door now, and Brushfire suspected that walking out among the monks while still fighting their mistress was a *bad* idea—and it was *taking* an archmage and one of the strongest mages she'd ever met just to hold their own against the Seeker.

Her own contribution, as she wove a warming spell strong enough to stand against the void itself around her companions, barely registered to her. She had *power* left. What she didn't have was the skill to weave a defensive shield that could stand off storm-stave strikes or to forge semi-living sparks of magic to seek their prey across the battlefield the glass-floored room had become.

The glass floor.

Only lightly protected by Brushfire's warming spell, the transparent floor was frosting over except directly around them. It had endured a thousand dances of sitting above a pit that drew aether and mass toward it.

It would endure this battle, too. Mere cold and heat wouldn't break the artifice of the long-dead Ironhand mage-engineers who had reshaped an entire worldlet to their whims. The handful of sparks of magic that missed their targets hammered into the walls around them—if the monks in the next room hadn't realized something was going down before, they probably had when one of the Seeker's bolts tore a yard-high hole through the mortared wall behind them.

But if Brushfire Hammerhead didn't have the skill to unleash complex battle magic as her partners were doing, they'd *both* told her she had a more powerful natural gift than Cat—and Cat was the brother of an archmage.

"Hang on," she told her companions. "And be ready to run."

"Whatever you're doing, do it *fast*," Armand hissed. She'd *never* seen him even gesture to use magic before, let alone wield a focus.

Now, for the first time, she recognized that the three rings on the archmage's right hand were *all* focuses. He held that hand up in front of him, channeling power in a way no regular mage or shaman could match, hurling a dozen thinking magical bursts at their enemy in every breath.

She couldn't do that. But she could do *this*.

It was the same spell as the regular battlewand. She'd used it once to blow up two dozen gangsters without trying to augment its strength. Now Brushfire threw every scrap of energy she could spare through her focus on that same spell, targeted not at the Void Seeker but at the *floor*.

The glass exploded. It was designed to endure a perpetual pull, to withstand time and weight and pressure. Its designers had even considered *some* allowance that it might take damage, but they'd never accounted for it to take the full power of an angry and terrified mage.

Shards of glass the size of daggers smashed into Cat's shield, and an ear-tearing scream suggested that the Void Seeker had been underprepared for a physical attack. The sensation of power in the room winked out—and the sensation that the floor was disintegrating replaced it.

"*Run*," Brushfire snapped, suiting her actions to her words and *pulling* Armand with her as she bolted for the gate through the darvar-built wall.

A blast of magic from her focus threw the door open, and she half-pulled, half-hurled the archmage through the gate—and then turned back to look for Cat.

She barely registered that he was right behind her before *he* grabbed her, pulling her through the door and onto solid stone before a rapidly spreading crack tore the last glass next to the gate to pieces.

Looking back over the pit, Brushfire tried to find the Void Seeker… but there was nothing there. Half the floor was gone, the rest was already coming apart and there was no sign of the darvar priestess.

Gasping in a desperate breath, she turned to see what new trouble was waiting for them. There had been three darvar monks in the room, monks they now knew were His Dark Brothers.

The illusory halvar halberdiers were gone, unfortunately. So, it seemed, were the three Senior Excavators. It took Brushfire a moment to locate the monks—one of the tapestries had been pulled down to cover their bodies and give the sailors access to a statue they were dragging toward the door.

"You know, I'm glad I guessed right when I started hearing explosions and the halberdiers vanished," Paintrock said drily. "Because murdering three priests was going to be a *real* pain on my conscience if I was wrong."

He chuckled and gestured at the statue they were moving—a statue of an elegant-looking elvar in white marble with black opals where his eyes should have been. A statue, very clearly, of Her Dark Brother.

"Of course, *that* was reassuring even before someone blew the wall open."

CHAPTER 42

Cat was awestruck and terrified. Terrified of the Void Seeker, because she was something *entirely* outside his experience, and because he wasn't entirely sure the darvar priestess was dead. He was in awe of his companions, because for all that he *knew* the power of an archmage, he'd never seen one in action.

And Brushfire, for all the incompleteness of her training, had seen straight to the solution she *could* execute and saved them all.

The elvar captain also *hurt*. It was always a fascinating discovery, where he would feel the ache from magical exertion. This time, it was his right hamstring, the entire leg trying to seize up as he walked over to check in on his crew.

"Report, Paintrock," he ordered, old habits kicking in.

"We sat here and exchanged grumpy faces with the monks while you were chatting in there," the elvar told him. "I figured things weren't exactly aboveboard when they were *very* clearly keeping us from poking at the tapestries.

"So, when we heard explosions and our illusory halvar friends went *pop*, I moved before they did."

Cat glanced over at the three dead monks. All three had been taken out by sword strikes at close range—and there was only one piece of bloody cloth tossed by their bodies.

"Before *anyone* did," he observed to his Master of Staves. "I think you've been holding back in the swordfighting lessons, my friend."

Paintrock shrugged.

"Follow orders, be loyal, keep an ace up your sleeve," he told Cat, as if reciting a mantra. "You're not paying enough for *all* of my secrets, captain."

"They know what happened here," Armand warned, the archmage stepping up to join the conversation. The halvar was still catching his breath, his hand pressed to the top of his stomach in a way that worried Cat.

"They had scrying eyes in the room," Cat agreed. "And there are a lot more of them than us—and plenty of mages, even if the Void Seeker is out of the picture."

"For now," Brushfire added. "We dropped her into the pit, but I wouldn't want to assume she's dead."

"Void Seekers are reputed to be very hard to kill," Armand said. "I was expecting one here…but I had never heard of a Seeker who was *also* an archmage. I did not anticipate that danger."

"So, we need to move, and we need a plan," Cat said. "I can get us back to the teleporter in the farm cavern, but they used those to make sure we *couldn't* easily find our way out."

"Then they made a mistake," Brushfire told him, smiling as Cat remembered his first officer's key talent.

She was a "show me once" student. He or Armand could probably figure out how to activate the teleporter given time, but Brushfire would be able to duplicate *exactly* what the monks had done to bring them down.

"Can you do it?" he asked her. "It won't be exactly the same; we're going the other way, after all."

"I think so," she promised. "It's that or walk, isn't it?"

"Even assuming that the teleporters are only going up and down, we don't know how far they moved us," Armand warned. "It would be easier to tell the alignment if it was a full teleporter chamber, but the fact that I've never seen circles like that means I don't know their limits."

"Either way, we have to go up," Cat said. "And we have to go *through* whatever monks decide to try to stop us. Paintrock? Are we ready?"

"You three don't need weapons," Paintrock replied. "The rest of us have blades and battlewands. I should lead the way though, not you."

"I can find the teleporter easily," Cat said.

"So can any aether sailor," the Master of Staves replied. "And *you* aren't expendable, *Captain*."

"Fine," Cat snapped. "We need to stick together, watch for threats, keep behind what cover we can as we move."

"A few more of those halberdiers wouldn't go amiss for cover," Paintrock said, glancing at the archmage. "Are you still up for that, Master Archmage?"

Armand nodded.

"I can do that," he promised. "It's a…codified thing, so it's an easier form of magic. I can't do many or much more. I need to preserve my energies. I'm already fatigued, and I do not trust that the Seeker is actually dead."

"I'm just hoping she's out of things until we can get clear of the Monastery," Cat said grimly. "Because at this point, I think we have to keep moving. No matter what."

He didn't like that. The High Court Navy had fewer virtues in hindsight than he'd thought when he'd served it, but they would only leave their dead behind in absolutely dire straits.

"Understood," Paintrock said softly, glancing at his sailors. Cat didn't think any of the elvar had missed their captain's meaning. They knew what they were in for now.

The six wand-halberdiers popped into existence again, standing next to the door and waiting for the sailors to open the way.

"I am ready," Armand declared.

"Anyone *not?*" Cat asked, looking around his people.

Brushfire held his gaze for the longest, her fingers white with strain around her focus, but she nodded firmly to him.

"Then let's go home."

Cat threw the doors from the lower hall open with a flick of magic and then watched Armand's wand-halberdiers charge through. Only silence answered the initial exit of the illusions, but he still waved the sailors to wait for a few moments more.

When no one opened fire or attacked the first wave, he gestured for Paintrock to lead on. He promptly found himself blockaded by Brushfire to stop him from joining the sailors immediately—which was fair, because *he* was blockading Armand for the same reason.

Though Cat, at least, had already conceded the point that Paintrock could find the way as well as he could. He wasn't going to change his mind now. He didn't trust *Armand* not to do something foolhardy and brave, though.

It took the three mages a few moments to sort out their particular order and follow their crew out into the hallway.

"Nothing so far," Paintrock told them. "How far ahead of us can the halberdiers get?"

"They have to be within eyesight or ten yards," Armand replied. "And I need to know the layout to manage ten yards in a way that doesn't put them inside walls."

"One curve ahead of us, then?" Cat suggested.

"I can do that," Armand agreed. "That should give us some warning. The halberdiers have very little autonomy, but they have certain…reactions."

"I'll take anything that makes noise," Paintrock replied. "Send them ahead, Master Archmage, if you would be so kind."

The halberdiers calmly walked forward. To Cat, their parade-ground line made it obvious what they were—but he suspected that anyone who assumed that *Armand Bluestaves*' illusions were harmless was going to have a very bad time.

"We're being watched," Armand warned. "Scrying eyes just reappeared."

"Then let's give them something *to* watch," Cat said. "Move, everyone. The sooner we're back in the open aether, the happier everyone is."

He paused.

"Well, maybe not you, Armand."

"I will be happier back aboard *Star*," the archmage said wryly. "Even if I quite enjoy being somewhere with air I can breathe."

The ascent up the spiraling corridor continued. Cat kept his focus in his right hand, and his left hand was never far from the hilt of his sword. His magic was woven around the group as best as he could manage, a defensive shield that would buy them a few seconds if someone bypassed the illusory halberdiers.

The question in his mind was whether His Dark Brothers would attempt to intercept them in the spiraling tunnel rising up to the main caverns, or if they would wait until the party was about to enter the great hall.

The answer, as it turned out, was "Hit them at the top of the ramp." With the highest point of the spiral at an intersection of corridors, there were three different directions for the monks to attack from.

The crackle of battlewands was sharp and sudden, clearly audible from beyond the curve as the halberdiers reached the top. A moment later, *screams* echoed back down the tunnel—and Cat doubted the illusions were *that* extensive.

"Go!" Cat snapped—but he realized he didn't need to. Paintrock was already charging, the sailors right behind him.

Cat and Brushfire were only a few steps behind the elvar sailors, emerging into absolute chaos. Cat's shields were still mostly in place on his people, enough to absorb a handful of blows or a battlewand blast.

There had been over a dozen of His Dark Brothers spread across the three corridors, and they'd even thrown together some rough cover. The path forward, toward the great hall, was just debris and chaos. The halberdiers had done *something* explosive, and those defenders were dead.

To Cat's left, five of his sailors were dueling a trio of the void monks. Several more monks were sprawled out on the ground, taken down by the sailors' battlewands.

To his *right*, Paintrock and a single other sailor were tangling with five monks—and the sailor was mostly trying to stay out of the Master of Staves' way!

Paintrock was a blur of blade and motion. As Cat hustled to join the blue elvar, a monk fell backward in a spray of blood—and a second exploded backward at the same time as one of Paintrock's bandolier of battlewands was discharged directly into the darvar's face.

Cat twisted power through his focus, and precise bolts of lightning flashed past the two elvar sailors. Two darvar monks crumpled, the smell of ozone and burnt flesh filling the hall—and the third, the monk he'd missed, fell as the sailor watching Paintrock's back took advantage of everyone's distraction.

Something *thundered* behind him, and he turned to see that Brushfire had cleared the last corridor by creating an explosion of fire *behind* the darvar defenders. Silence filled the corridor, and Cat shook his head to clear the ringing in his ears.

"Everyone still with us?" he asked loudly.

"Not even a scratch," Paintrock said after swiftly examining the var. "Whatever that shield you used was, Captain, I think I want every mage I fight alongside to know it."

"Fight alongside more professionals," Cat suggested. "Every High Court captain should know it."

Should didn't necessarily mean *did*, Cat knew. There was an entire panoply of defensive and offensive magic that every High Court Navy officer was supposed to know before they even made first officer, let alone captain.

In practice, reliably commanding all of that magic wasn't a requirement. They were *taught* it, but they weren't required to prove that they'd *learned* it. Plus, Cat wasn't sure many of his former fellow captains had possessed the will and power to suspend individually sustained fields over even a handful of others.

If the idea had even occurred to them.

"I'll keep that in mind," Paintrock said drily. His tone suggested that he'd definitely encountered High Court captains that *hadn't* been capable of it, but having seen the var fight…Cat resolved never to ask Paintrock questions about his past.

So long as Paintrock was loyal and followed orders, Cat didn't need or want to know if the var had been a pirate.

"We need to keep moving," Brushfire told them. "There were no mages in this group, which means they're still out there."

"We're still being watched," Cat agreed, sensing the particular eddies in the aether that he was now matching up to Armand's scrying eyes.

"No more surprises," Armand agreed—but as he said it, he conjured another half-dozen halberdiers. "That just means they now know my halberdiers explode. They *can't* ignore them."

Cat snorted and looked directly at one of the scrying sensors.

"We're just trying to *leave*," he told it. "Stop getting in our way and no one else has to die."

Shaking his head, he turned back to his companions.

"Lead on, Paintrock," he ordered. "We're getting out of here. If they want to watch the whole bloody process, then I hope they're entertained!"

Cat wasn't sure if it was his threats or the damage they'd already done, but they made it through the rest of the monastery itself without further opposition. Anyone still in the underground structure was clearing out of their way, letting them make their way to the exit to the farm cavern.

"Wait at the door," Cat instructed as they made their way slowly through the great hall, watching for any kind of trap or ambush among the long stone tables. "Armand, you said you could send the illusions forward so long as you could see them, right?"

"Not infinitely, but yes," the archmage confirmed. "What are you thinking, Cat?"

"We send them forward across the fields, see what happens," Cat suggested. "We all wait here, behind my shield, while we try to trigger an ambush with the illusions."

"They know they're illusions now," Brushfire pointed out. "I'm guessing you can't see through them."

"No," Armand agreed. "So, if they decide to be clever…"

Cat looked up at the scrying eyes and sighed.

"I dislike my plans being listened in," he observed. "It makes it difficult for *us* to be clever."

The only one of the three of them capable of creating a scrying sensor like the ones watching them *was* Armand, and Cat was worried about the archmage's fatigue levels. *Cat* had three separate sections of muscle strain now, informing him that he was pushing hard.

Armand Bluestaves had far higher reserves than Cat did, he had to assume, but the archmage had also done far more than Cat or Brushfire had done.

"It'll help, anyway. Check the door," Armand ordered.

Paintrock obeyed, a battlewand in his hand as he poked his head around the massive gates.

"Nobody right here, not yet," he reported. "But I can see movement in the fields. We're being watched in more ways than one."

"As expected," Brushfire said. "Cat, I can probably blow a few holes if we want…"

"So can I, but I'm wondering if they're willing to let us get out of here without any more bloodshed," Cat murmured.

"They're not," Paintrock said grimly. "I *know* His Dark Brothers, sir. Once they've gone this far, they will not stop until we're dead or we're out of their reach. We know who they are, and that's anathema to them."

"Then we see what we can draw out," Cat said with a sigh. "Armand?"

Six illusory halberdiers marched out the massive gates of the underground monastery. A moment later, six more appeared and followed them. Then six more. Then six more, as four carefully staggered lines of wand-halberdiers advanced along the road toward the teleporter circle.

As Paintrock had pointed out, Cat could see movement in the grain fields. None of it was distinctly people, and he didn't *really* want to kill someone who was just trying to stay out of the way. He wasn't entirely convinced that any of His Dark Brothers would avoid the fight, but even among void worshippers, there had to be a few people who were too valuable to use as battlewand fodder.

The other thing he realized as he watched the illusions advance down the road was that there was a breeze in the cave. He wasn't sure what its origin was, but it was responsible for at least some of the movement in the crops.

With Armand focusing entirely on the illusions, they were a step above what they had been before. They were sweeping the surrounding fields with their wand-halberds, clearly searching for threats as they advanced.

The mages might be telling His Dark Brothers that the halberdiers were illusions, but even *Cat* had moments where he forgot. The question wasn't whether the Brothers were aware that the advancing halvar soldiers were false—everyone present knew that.

The question was whether that knowledge was enough to keep the monks hiding in the fields and outbuildings, none of whom were actually soldiers, under control as the halberdiers completed their advance.

Cat's fingers shifted on his focus as he traded a glance with Brushfire. He was picking out what he thought were clusters of Brothers, and he figured she was doing the same. Paintrock and the elvar sailors were limited to blades and the slow-charging battlewands.

The three mages could probably manage to burn the entire farm cavern to bare stone in short order—and only the problem that would give *them* crossing it was keeping Cat from going for that plan.

The platoon of halberdiers almost reached the central ramp wrapped around the teleporter circle before someone's nerves finally snapped. A single battlewand cracked in the near-silence, the blast not even *hitting* the halberdiers on the main avenue.

But like someone had opened the gates to a grazer herd, dozens more weapons opened up in the silent cavern. The battlewands were the most distinctive, but Cat was sure he heard crossbow fire as well.

This time he got to watch what the *reaction* Armand had given the illusions was. As each halberdier was struck, they fell like ordinary var—but as they fell, they rippled and shrank inward, coalescing into a blue dart roughly the size of a fist.

Those darts blazed brilliant trails of light back to the attackers that had "killed" them and then exploded with the force of a portable storm stave. Not all of the halberdiers were struck and not all of the darts managed to land accurately, but *enough* struck home to leave a massive chunk of the farm fields devastated and burning.

"*Now*, Brushfire," Cat ordered.

He stepped out around the monastery gate and channeled power through his focus. Before meeting Brushfire, he would never have thought to duplicate the magic unleashed by the assorted weapons built of arcane artifice.

Now he duplicated the strike of a storm stave, summoning bolts of lightning that tore yard-wide paths of destruction through the farm fields toward the ambush positions he'd picked out. Half a dozen bolts flickered out from his focus in as many seconds—and then several new muscle knots in his back informed him that he was *definitely* overdoing things.

Fortunately, Brushfire had engaged at the same time as he had. Her overcharged fireballs struck with even greater force than Armand's halberdiers' counterstrikes, blasting away the positions she'd flagged as targets.

"Go!" Cat snapped.

Paintrock leapt forward like he'd been held back by chains, a battlewand in each hand as he led the way out of the Monastery. The elvar's wands crackled sharply as someone moved in the chaos, and Cat watched the clearly well-practiced maneuvers as Paintrock holstered the wands he was holding and drew another pair.

The sailors spreading out behind the noncom weren't as smooth or instantly deadly, but their wands barked as well as Cat and the other two mages followed them out.

Cat was worn by the amount of magic he'd already used—but he could almost *feel* how haggard Armand was looking. That last round of illusions had taken more out of the archmage than Cat had expected.

"Move, move, move!" he bellowed, gesturing for the sailors to keep going. "Don't slow down; don't stop until we reach that teleporter. They *will* have reinforcements."

He had no idea how many people had already died in the no-longer-golden fields inside the Seventh Ward. His Dark Brothers had chosen to make a fight of it when all he wanted to do right now was *leave*.

Despite his fatigue and aches, he moved forward at a brisk walk himself, reweaving the defensive shields around his people as he looked for any signs of new dangers. The fires in the grain fields were a defense of a kind, but the Brothers definitely knew this cavern complex better than he did.

Once they reached the ramp, they'd have cover. But it was several entire cables between the Monastery and the structure at the center of the cavern. Even sprinting, that would take time—and they couldn't afford to sprint, not when a new wave of attackers could emerge at any moment.

They'd crossed almost half the distance when the hamstring that had seized up after the fight with the Void Seeker registered its final complaint and just...*stopped*.

One moment he was moving forward, long practice allowing him to push through the aches and pains of heavy magic use. The next, sustaining the shield used up just a little too much power, and his entire leg spasmed and collapsed underneath him.

He threw his hands out in front of him, barely managing to hang on to the focus as he broke his fall.

"Voidshit," he cursed, trying to rise.

"Cat?" Brushfire asked, stepping in to check on him.

"Magic fatigue," Armand said before Cat could answer. "You'll be fine, but you can't walk on that leg for at least half a clock-hour."

"That's not going to wo—*urk!*"

He made an ungraceful sound as Brushfire scooped him off the ground. There was no way to be elegant or to exude power while draped across someone else's shoulders—and he was still taken aback by the sheer *physical* power his first officer possessed.

Cat had been impressed enough by her *magical* power, he'd forgotten that she was *also* one of the largest and most physically powerful var he'd ever met!

CHAPTER 43

Even with the training that Brushfire had been doing with both Cat and Armand, she'd never pushed to the point of suffering from casting fatigue before. Now, as she carried her captain on her back with the sailors spreading out around her, she was definitely starting to feel it.

Thankfully, hers had so far manifested as *just* fatigue. There was a bit of stiffness to her jaw, but not the kind of full lockup that Cat was clearly dealing with.

There was no time for any solution *except* to carry the captain, graceless as that solution was, and thankfully, Cat didn't weigh very much and was being as cooperative as he could be.

"We're clear; get inside the ramps and use them for cover," Paintrock barked to the sailors. "Officer, Captain, Archmage, you all good?"

"We're good, Shipmaster," Armand confirmed from behind Brushfire. "Put the captain down, Brushfire. We need you to make the teleporter work."

Brushfire nodded to her employer. Cat grabbed her arm to help her unload him, and she sat him down against the interior of the ramps.

"I don't know how long this will take," she warned Paintrock and the sailors. "Cover us. The captain isn't able to fight—and the archmage needs to save his strength in case that Void Seeker comes back."

She could tell that Armand was suffering from the earlier duel and his exertions with the illusions, but she wasn't sure how fatigued the halvar archmage actually *was*. Potentially, Bluestaves could *still* clear their way to the ship without being slowed by the remaining Dark Brothers.

"There are no scrying eyes left now," the archmage warned. "That means either the mages were in the fields…or they're coming now."

"Paintrock, keep an eye open," Cat ordered. "I'm not useless yet; I'll just need someone to help me stand when the bastards come."

Brushfire *wanted* to tell him to sit his butt back down and rest, but she knew her captain was right. *She* had a job to do—and it wasn't protecting the crew around her this time.

A flicker of magic traced out from her fingers and lit up the runes on the floor. Etched into the stone in gold and platinum, the characters were completely unfamiliar to her. That was strange in itself—the Court and Kingdoms shared a single language and script, even if not every dialect was entirely understandable to everyone else.

Even the gobvar Clans used the same language, though most Clan gobvar would find their accent and dialect impenetrable to most in the Court and Kingdoms. Now that she reflected on it, she wondered if that language was a leftover of the mostly forgotten Ironhands.

If that was the case, though, she should have been able to read Ironhand script. Enchantments weren't written in the common language, but they were usually anchored, at least, on understandable characters.

This teleporter circle had nothing she recognized at all. If she hadn't seen Senior Excavator Miller activate it coming the other way, she'd have had *no* idea what to do with it.

As it was, she concentrated, recalling the gestures and flow of magic and aether that Miller had woven around himself and his guests. Holding that memory, she touched her focus and channeled power.

Her magic flickered out into the circle and the runes flashed awake. Energy spiked up and the universe vanished for a split second…and then the farm cavern reappeared around her.

"Okay, so, now I could bring us *here* from the other side," she muttered. "Next steps."

"Fires are starting to die down," Paintrock reported. "No rushing you, First Officer, but we just burned down a good chunk of their food supply, killed a bunch of their friends and disrespected their high priestess.

"Even *rational* folks would want to take us down now—and these guys are *anything* but rational! Without the fires to keep them back…"

"You'll have to," Cat said grimly. "It's going to take Brushfire what it takes, Master Paintrock. We'll hold."

Brushfire shook away the distractions and focused on the runes under her feet. She didn't have time to experiment a thousand different ways.

Given a chance, she was certain that she and Cat and Armand could sort it out well enough to duplicate it.

Right now, though, she needed to get them all out before His Dark Brothers made sure they *never* left. What had the spell for the *first* teleporter been, again?

Running the two pieces of magic through her mind, she realized they were almost identical. They were primarily an activation code, a bit of ritual and gesture that anyone with even a tiny scrap of magic could trigger.

Since almost all var had *some* magic, they didn't even need Brushfire to turn on the teleporter. The only reason she was the best choice was because she could remember what Miller had done to get them down.

She didn't even need to recreate the flow of magic. The runes would do that on their own, in response to her gestures so long as she fed it a little bit of power. She started to run through the gestures in her mind and paused.

Could it be that simple?

"We've got movement from the brewery," Paintrock warned. "Wands are charged; we'll hold them off."

Brushfire swallowed a curse. She was out of time.

Stepping back into the middle of the circle of runes, she fed them power again and then repeated the exact same gestures Miller had used to bring them down here—except with the palms of her hands facing up instead of down.

Energy spiked up around her again and the universe flashed around her—and the farm cavern was replaced by the dimly lit warehouse amidst the docking towers.

"Yes!"

There was a lot to be said for idiot-proofed magic, she reflected as she summoned the magic to take her back down to the farm cavern.

"Everybody on the circle," she ordered as she reappeared in the farm cavern. "We're getting out of this place."

Two of the sailors grabbed Cat, one on each arm, as he helped them lever him up. The other four were clustered behind the rising ramp with Paintrock, and Brushfire heard the crackle of battlewands as they sent magic flickering through the air to keep the Brothers back.

Brushfire waited until Cat Greentrees was on the circle and Armand had joined them.

"Get over here," she snapped at the sailors. "It's time to go!"

Paintrock and the others half-stumbled, half-crabwalked backward to reach the circle without exposing themselves. Flickers of battle magic struck the ramp as they retreated, but none of the crew were injured before they were in the circle.

For the fourth time, Brushfire summoned the circle to wakefulness. It was harder this time, the light flick of magic she'd used the last time barely rousing the magic. It clearly wasn't intended to cycle this rapidly—which would hopefully slow His Dark Brothers down when they tried to pursue.

The circle might not have had enough power of its own to carry them up, but Brushfire Hammerhead had enough power left to make up the difference, and the void worshippers' burnt-out farm cavern vanished behind them.

With everyone safe, hopefully, in the warehouse cavern, Brushfire took a moment to take a deep breath and take stock of the situation.

Cat was still unable to walk. The two elvar sailors supporting their captain were a poor substitute for a working leg, but as Brushfire watched, his leg spasmed again and he nearly fell.

Armand was there, though, the halvar getting an arm under Cat's shoulder and lifting him up. Armand probably wasn't nearly as physically fit as the elvar, but he was enough broader and heavier to support Cat anyway.

Paintrock was surveying the rows of shelving and storage while he checked his battlewands. The ex-pirate seemed to have a better sense for danger than most of the party they'd brought into the Seventh Ward, so Brushfire followed his gaze.

"It's not a question of expecting trouble," Paintrock told her quietly. "It's a question of what *kind* of trouble they have waiting for us. There will be something between here and the ship."

"Assuming they haven't done something to the *ship*," Brushfire observed. That thought was...disturbing. Their party had caused a lot of havoc on their way out, enough to make certain His Dark Brothers killed them slowly, but if *Star* was gone, they were doomed.

"I'm *hoping* that they don't have anything in the dock towers that can harm her," the Master of Staves said. "A ninesail is a tough nut to crack, even for major fortifications. We didn't see anything when we came in, so I think we might be okay."

"Or they're concealed to keep people thinking they're innocent," Cat suggested, leaning on Armand as the archmage joined the conversation. "But they'd need air envelopes to operate anything."

"The teleporter is completely drained," Armand noted. "That buys us some time, but they are going to come after us. We need to move."

"Can you walk?" Brushfire asked Cat.

"Not without help," he admitted.

"I've got him," the archmage told them both. "We get out together."

"Agreed." Brushfire nodded, meeting Cat's eyes and seeing the same determination there.

"Together," the captain agreed.

CHAPTER 44

Armand was starting to think they might have made it when the first howl echoed through the cavern. They'd cleared most of the storage area, and he could *see* the tunnel that linked back to the tower and its teleporter.

The first howl was answered by another. Then another. Then *another*, and he watched as Paintrock faded toward the shade of ice.

"You know what those are?" Cat asked, trying to straighten away from Armand but only ending up falling into his side.

Armand shifted his arm to prop the captain up more, and to free his beringed right hand.

More screeching howls echoed through the cavern, and the entire party seemed to unconsciously accelerate. The exit wasn't *that* far away, after all.

"Wyverns," Paintrock said grimly. "Carnivorous lizards about twice the size of a big dog. Can breathe aether and are fast as lightning. I've seen them raised as var-eaters before…and I'm guessing if His Dark Brothers just released them into the caves…"

"These ones will be var-eaters," Cat concluded.

Supporting Cat this closely, Armand could feel the tension underneath his captain's usual mask of competence. The competence was very real, but so was the tension. It was a fascinating contrast, though Armand would have been happier if the elvar *wasn't* completely done as far as magic went.

Or if Armand himself had been further away from ending up in the same state. The duel with the Void Seeker had drained much of his power, and he was feeling his exertions more than he wanted to show anyone.

"We can't outrun them," Paintrock warned. "The teleporter will buy us time if we can get to it, but they are *much* faster than var."

"Watch our backs," Cat ordered. "Everyone head for the teleporter but keep your eyes open. They're coming."

"They sent them to slow us down," Armand said grimly.

"Probably." Cat tried to straighten again, only to grimace in pain. "Sorry to lean on you like this."

"Together," the archmage told him. "Come on."

He shifted slightly, helping Cat straighten out his overwhelmed leg, then tried to move faster. Armand was well aware he and Cat were slowing everyone else down—not that anyone seemed inclined to leave them behind!

"There!"

Paintrock's battlewands crackled and something *screamed* behind them.

"Keep moving, Archmage," the Master of Staves barked as a second set of battlewands crackled. The other sailors fell in with Paintrock, and more battlewands echoed in the caves as Armand obeyed, continuing to carry the captain forward toward safety.

"I can walk," Cat assured him.

"No, you can't," Brushfire disagreed. "But I can't stop those wyverns, so I've got you."

Armand gave Cat's arm a squeeze of reassurance as the gobvar shaman-mage roughly took over propelling the captain forward, and then turned back to see how the sailors were handling this.

That gave him his first look at a wyvern. Paintrock's rough description hadn't quite prepared him for what he saw. The wyverns were lizards, yes, but in the same sense that the Seventh Ward was a rock floating in the aether.

The smallest of the creatures was two yards from nose to tailtip, with the tail only a third of that length. A ridge of spines ran along their backs, and their forelegs were equipped with dewclaws Armand could see from thirty yards away.

Their fangs were no smaller than the front dewclaws, either, and their black-and-green hides were *deflecting* any battlewand blasts that didn't hit perfectly. Two of the beasts were on the ground, wounded or dead, but half a dozen more were closing on Paintrock.

The Master of Staves had hung back, making himself the target of choice for the animals, and he dropped his last pair of battlewands and rolled aside as the lead wyvern lunged at him. There was a flash of steel in the dim light, and the wyvern hit the ground, its stomach opened from throat to tail.

But there were five more beasts directly behind that one, and Armand threw his hands wide. The rings on his right hand flared with power, and so did the link to the Source under his heart. He didn't have much power left, but he had enough for *this*.

Five of the same thinking sparks of power he'd summoned against the Void Seeker flared to life. Without another archmage to challenge them, the seeking spells couldn't miss—and they were *far* more dangerous than the blasts from battlewands.

Two wyverns were attacking Paintrock as the elvar's blade flickered in front of him. One of them caught his sword in its mouth, allowing the other to lunge straight for Paintrock's throat.

Armand's spell caught that beast in mid-lunge, picking it up and hurling it a dozen yards across the floor in a heap of burnt meat. The one distracting Paintrock joined its partner a moment later, and the remaining wyverns fell simultaneously.

And then Armand's lower back seized up, driving him to his knees with a sharp exhalation of pain. Even for an archmage, overuse was a problem. An archmage, though, had *answers* to that.

He focused on the Source in his chest, drawing on the energy of the spheres, channeling it out to suffuse his limbs and wash away the feeling of running without breathing.

"You good?" Paintrock asked, the elvar offering him a hand.

"I'm good," Armand replied, realizing that the *lack* of respect in the Master of Staves' words *was* a sign of respect. He took the proffered hand and levered himself back to his feet, looking at the scattering of dead creatures.

The wyverns hadn't chosen this—but their fate had been sealed when His Dark Brothers had chosen to raise them as var-killers. There was nothing Armand Bluestaves could have done for them but end them as swiftly as possible.

"Those might not be all of them," Paintrock warned.

"Then we should catch up with Greentrees and Hammerhead," Armand said. "We want to get out of this place."

He was already thinking about what the next step was going to look like. Escape was one thing—but to succeed in his mission, they were going to have to come back.

Armand suspected that he had significantly less emotional attachment to *Star* than most of the var who were living aboard the ninesail. He, after all, had to spend his time aboard her stuck inside an enclosed suite of rooms with no view. He didn't—*couldn't*—see the ship the same way the var who worked aboard her and wandered all of her sails and rigging did.

Still, he was *ecstatic* to reach the stone quay with its enchanted cover and see the ninesail floating at the end.

He could tell the moment that anyone aboard the ship got a good look at them, too. They were less than half a dozen yards along the dock before a dozen heavily armed gobvar, led by Fistfall, were swarming it from the other direction.

"Eldest sister, are you okay?" Fistfall demanded as they met in the middle of the dock.

"We're almost certainly being pursued, but they won't be close behind us," Brushfire told the gobvar. "I discharged the magic in the teleporter circle, *intentionally* this time," she added to Armand, "so they're going to have to walk up the damn tower."

"I measured its height," Fistfall said drily. "I don't envy them that. Go, we'll watch behind."

Armand gladly listened to the younger Hammerhead. He'd taken over supporting Cat while Brushfire was activating the teleporter, and now supported the captain as they approached the ship.

"Feel like I should walk onto my ship on my own two feet," Cat muttered under his breath, and Armand smiled, shaking his head gently at the elvar.

"All three of us have pushed to the limits of our abilities, Cat—and it *took* all three of us to get everyone out," he told. "We're…probably safe now."

He didn't want to tempt fate, but as they stepped into the aethercloth tunnel, he figured he could *finally* breathe. Brushfire and Paintrock were right behind them, and the white cloth shifted under their feet as they boarded their ship.

"What do we do now?" Brushfire asked.

"You and I get to the wheel and get *Star* moving," Cat replied. "Even if I'm leaning on someone, I'm the best navigator we've got. We need to get clear of the Seventh Ward."

"Let's not get too far away," Armand said. "We're not done here yet."

Both his senior subordinates looked at him in silence for a long moment.

"No, we're not, are we?" Cat said. "Well, we still need to get far enough away to make a *plan* before we come back for the void ship, don't we?"

"A plan sounds fantastic." Brushfire sounded exhausted.

"Get clear," Armand agreed. "Then *rest*. Then plan. *Then* come back."

Cat slumped against Armand for a few seconds, a solid reassuring weight, then nodded and straightened—using Armand's shoulder to do so instead of trying to stand on his own.

"Whatever we do, I think I understand why your divinations said you needed a warship," Cat said. "I just wish we could have known instead of just suspecting that His Dark Brothers controlled this place."

"Even if we had known, I would have tried to cut a deal," Armand admitted as they finally stepped back into his air-enveloped quarters on *Star* and he took a deep breath of his own air. "We didn't need new enemies, after all."

"Her Dark Brother is everyone's enemy, regardless of whether we're thinking about him at a given moment," Paintrock said grimly. "These aren't the first Brothers I've dealt with…and the only question in a deal with His Dark Brothers is when they'll stab you in the back, not if."

CHAPTER 45

The retreat from the cavern had been embarrassing for Cat, but he drew comfort from the fact that his companions, even his crew, seemed to regard it as an acceptable price for his help. He'd drawn strength and support from leaning on Armand Bluestaves, too.

It was still a relief to reach *Star*'s wheel and support himself on the cloudwood frame.

"Report, Second Officer," he told Streamwater.

"Everything has been silent up here," she replied. "We've been waiting for your return; there haven't even been birds to watch to break the monotony."

"Things weren't quiet in the Monastery," Cat said drily. "Master of Decks, get us free!"

Crewvar were already in position, pulling the aethercloth tunnel back aboard the ship and removing the hooks and ropes linking *Star* to the Seventh Ward's docks.

"Watch for attacks," Cat ordered. "They have aether-breathing beasts; they loosed them on us in the tunnels, and there may be more."

"Staves are charged," Paintrock shouted up from the stave galleries beneath him. "Let them come."

Cat reached out, sensing the aether currents around him and shaking his head. The pit underneath the Monastery wasn't the only thing warping the sphere's currents, but here, it offset the usual flow of aether around and away from worldlets.

"Lift crystals to full," he ordered Streamwater. "There's not enough current to get us clear on its own."

"Creatures on the docks!" one of the riggers barked.

"I see them," Paintrock replied. "Hold us steady for one…two… three…"

A single storm stave thundered in the aether, a bolt of lightning blazing down the covered dock as another dozen wyverns charged toward the ship. The creatures didn't survive a weapon meant to shatter ninesail hulls—and neither did the cover on the dock.

"The air envelope is breaking," Smallwolf reported. "The darvar won't be able to reach us without it."

The control crystals next to the wheel lit up under Streamwater's magic as the fourth officer spoke. Cat adjusted the wheel to ride the currents as best as he could, but it was the crystals that finally lifted *Star* away from the Seventh Ward.

Cat's focus was on the ship herself, letting that concentration cut away such minor concerns as a leg that didn't want to work and a back that was shot through with muscle knots. The currents that swirled around the Seventh Ward were twisted, broken things, warped by both the void strait and the ancient magic had once allowed the Ironhands to seal the gateway to their core spheres.

Still, for a captain who could sense the currents and kept his hands on the wheel, there was *always* an advantage to be gained. The sails spread out above him, the riggers waiting for further orders, and he twisted the wheel to catch the scraps of aether moving away from the Ward.

"Watch for staves as we rise," he ordered. He had to trust the crew and the watchvar in the rigging to tell him if there was a threat. Except for a few attacks that would flare in the aether first, he wouldn't be the first to see a surprise attack.

"It looks like nothing in the dock towers," Smallwolf said. "They must have wanted those to pass inspection at close distance."

"They needed supplies after all, whoever they were," Streamwater added. "Who *were* they, Captain? Not monks of the First Digger, I'm guessing."

"His Dark Brothers," Brushfire said quietly, stepping up to stand next to Cat. "They're going to have their defenses around the airdock cavern. That's not officially part of the Monastery and not anywhere they draw attention to."

"I'll worry about that when we're planning for it," Cat admitted. "Right now, I just want to get us clear of this cursed rock."

He kept expecting *something* to go wrong. Anything from an unexpected elvar contingent of His Dark Brothers with another ninesail to a dragon would have fit his anticipation.

Instead, their ascent from the Seventh Ward was surprisingly calm. The chaos they'd left in their wake didn't seem to have followed them into the aether. For several whole minutes, *Star* accelerated away from the worldlet, Cat catching what few currents he could but mostly relying on the lift crystals.

The crystals' force was directly proportional to their distance from a lodestone core, though, and it slowed as they got farther from the Seventh Ward. There weren't enough currents to move the ship apace, and they were only a dozen leagues from the surface of the Seventh Ward when the aether *shifted* around them.

Suddenly, *all* of the aether currents were directly toward the Ward. The pit in the Ward's heart was awake—and even with the lift crystals, Cat felt *Star* begin to fall back toward the worldlet.

"Strike the sails," he bellowed. "Strike all sail!"

They lost a full league of distance before the crew managed to obey, and he could *feel* the lift crystals straining.

"We're too far for the crystals to have much effect," Brushfire warned grimly. "But they're straining. What the void?"

"The pit inside the Ward is awake now," Cat growled. "It's pulling all of the aether around the worldlet into it, and it's doing so strongly enough to affect the ship with every sail struck."

"Not all around the Ward," his first officer said. "Just around us, I think…"

Cat swallowed a curse and broadened his awareness. She was right. The currents that were being drawn in were those around *Star*. They were hitting the pit under the Monastery and then coming out the far side of the worldlet.

Not only was the pit active, but it was being *targeted* at his ship—and that could mean only one thing.

"The Void Seeker lived," he concluded aloud.

"At least she was out long enough for *us* to get out," Brushfire told him. "But if she pulls us back down to the worldlet, we are in trouble."

"We'll hit the rock hard enough to break the ship and kill everyone aboard." Cat listened to the keening of the straining lift crystals and eyed the distance.

They were gaining distance again now, but slowly. Oh so slowly, compared to the league-eating pace they could sustain under sail. They were too close for him to try and ride the currents and dodge the Seventh Ward, too.

Five leagues wasn't enough space for him to swing around the side of the rock. If he tried anything clever, he was going to ram *Star* into the surface at sufficient speed that the warship would *splash*.

"How long will the crystals withstand this?" Brushfire asked softly.

"Axfall!" Cat called over to the deck. "How long can she take this?"

The gobvar Master of Decks was standing next to the forward upper mast, his hand on the lift crystal embedded in the artificial tree. He looked up at Cat and Brushfire and shook his head grimly.

"Maybe ten minutes," he told them. "Maybe twenty."

"Not enough either way," Cat concluded. "That's what I needed to know, Axfall. Thanks."

The gobvar tilted his horns questioningly at them, and Cat chuckled. The var appeared equally thrown that Cat took the announcement that they were going to die as he was to the fact that Cat had *thanked* him by name.

"What do we do?" Brushfire asked.

Cat looked around the forecastle silently for a moment. Brushfire Hammerhead and Faith Streamwater were both standing around the wheel, Brushfire looking almost as concerned for Cat's *still*-failing leg as for the ship. Bogsong Smallwolf was at the very front of the ship, the young elvar mage balancing carefully on the railing to let her see more of what was going on beneath the ship.

"Get Crane up here," he ordered.

Emberlight Crane would be in the aftercastle of the starboard deck, prepping the ship's secondary air envelope to act as a surgery. But they were also the third officer—and the fifth aether-breathing mage aboard the ship.

"On it," Smallwolf replied before anyone else could say anything, the elvar off the railing and across the forecastle in a flash.

"Her enthusiasm is touching," Streamwater said slowly. "May I ask what the plan is?"

"We're going to match five mages against an ancient artifact of a fallen empire and an utterly furious high priestess of the god of death," Cat explained brightly. "And if we fail, said priestess is going to crush us into splinters."

By the time Smallwolf returned with the fourth elvar mage, Cat had taken the time to consider and, unfortunately, reject the idea of having the archmage help. Armand was at least as powerful as any three of the other mages on the ship, but this kind of working required the ability to *see* the outside of the ship.

And if the halvar was on the deck, he'd be dedicating much of his power to just being able to breathe. There was no point in getting him involved. Either it would work with five regular mages, two of which Cat would consider unusually powerful, or it probably wouldn't work with five and an archmage.

"This does make us all a rather fine target, doesn't it?" Crane observed as the gaunt elvar stepped delicately onto the forecastle.

"No one is throwing lightning at us, Third Officer," Cat pointed out, gesturing for the officers to gather around the wheel with him. "Our problem is of a grander scale than that."

"What is going on?" Streamwater asked. "I...have *heard* of Void Seekers. Her Dark Brother's chosen priests, yes?"

"Exactly," Cat told them all. "So, there's two parts to this mess. One is that the head of that monastery is a Void Seeker who is *also* a darvar archmage. Thanks to her divine patron, she is probably the single most powerful mage any of us will ever encounter in our lives.

"Fortunately, she's buried under a league or so of rock a dozen leagues behind us. *Unfortunately*, her chosen sanctum is a chunk of magically activated void put together by the Ironhand Imperium when they ruled these spheres.

"It's a piece of magic that neither I nor the archmage fully understood, but it supposedly used to allow the Ironhands to close the aether straits out of Brokenwright."

Cat gestured toward the Seventh Ward.

"And she is now using it to force every aether current on this side of her worldlet to pass through that rock," he explained. "We can't get out of the aether whirlpool she's conjured on sails alone—and the pressure is going to break our lift crystals long before we escape.

"So, we need to help the crystals ourselves. Combine our magic with the crystals and carry *Star* to safety by *our* power."

He shrugged, as if moving ninesails by magic was something mages did all the time instead of an act of utter desperation.

"Anyone who cares to throw rude hand gestures back toward said high priestess as we leave is *more* than welcome," he added. "But for now, draw your focuses and direct your minds."

"Let's leave the hand gestures to Paintrock," Brushfire suggested, drawing her black horn focus and presenting it.

Cat drew his own Armand-forged focus and touched it to Brushfire's. An almost-visible spark of power flickered around them as they touched. A third, plainer, focus joined them—Smallwolf, as usual, the first to obey.

Streamwater and Crane were quick enough to join, though, the five focuses and their mages forming an evenly spaced wheel on the forecastle deck.

Cat still had an arm hooked around the wheel, but there was a purpose to *that* too, beyond holding himself up. The wheel controlled the ship by both arcane and artifice means—and among those was a general focus embedded in the center of the wheel.

Cat concentrated and felt the wills of his mages gather around him. Now that his mind was in the field of magic and power, he could *feel* the untrammeled rage and will of the Void Seeker rippling through the surrounding aether.

He'd never been able to sense a mage's emotions wrapped into their power like that. Her rage fueled the magic she'd unleashed across Brokenwright, driving it that much farther and with that much more power.

The impact of her rage was nothing against the power lent her by Her Dark Brother, but Cat could feel *both* woven through the magic she'd created. The aether across three thousand leagues bent to the will of the Void Seeker.

Cat concealed his sheer terrified *awe* of the power his enemy commanded—and reminded himself that he didn't need to match the power of the Seventh Ward.

He just needed to *escape* it.

With the focuses touching, Cat didn't even need to give verbal instructions to his officers. He just showed them the way, weaving a net of magic that he threw out into the aether. Each of his mages added more strands, the net growing thicker as it fluttered in the aether currents that were trying to doom *Star*.

None of them, not even him, had finished weaving their portion of the net by the time it was strong enough to at least start. With a thought and a will, he snapped the net of magic taut and tight, wrapping it around the stern of *Star*.

Pulling it tight along the lower decks without injuring crew or damaging masts was a careful task, one demanding more concentration than he'd realized.

"If we ever do this again, we're sending the crew belowdecks," Brushfire muttered, clearly struggling with the same task as he was.

Grunts of agreement suggested that if anyone wasn't actively adjusting the weave to slide around crewvar, they were aware of the other four mages doing it. It took a full minute to wrap the net of their power around the aether ship, and Cat could already feel the strain starting to hit him.

He'd done a *lot* today—and so had Brushfire; even if the gobvar shaman-mage seemed to have an inexhaustible supply from outside, he *knew* she was feeling it.

But if they failed, every var on the ship would die and Armand's mission would fail. Cat didn't know what weight of fate and doom was behind the vision Armand had shown him of the possible future—but he suspected that their failure there would only make it easier for Court and Kingdoms to fall before the dragons.

"With me," he murmured once the net was tight, and began to *pull*.

Like pulling oneself up by one's bootstraps, this was something that was arguably impossible. At least unlike pulling by strings attached to himself, Cat could anchor his magic against the aether.

But that same aether was dragging them down. The current pulling on them was strong enough that he could have put them on the Seventh

Ward in under a minute if that was his destination. The Void Seeker had broken the fundamental force of the spheres to her will, and Cat wasn't sure if it was even *possible* to escape.

He only knew that he wasn't going to die without trying.

Magic pulsed along his lifting net, drawing on his subordinates' strength more than his. Drained as he was, Cat's main job was to act as a guide for *what* to do. He was still contributing as much as, say, Crane—but he was *significantly* more powerful than the ship's surgeon.

Slowly, ever so slowly, the ship began to accelerate. The lift crystals had kept them from falling so far, but now the officers' power added to that impulse. It wasn't the swift rush of being carried before the aether currents by sails of aethercloth, but it was movement.

For a minute they accelerated away. Then two. Then three.

And then the Void Seeker realized what they were doing. She couldn't strike them directly at this distance, only a tiny tendril of power could reach across twenty leagues…but that tendril was enough to slice into the edge of the fragile net of power lifting the shift.

"She's unraveling the spell!" Brushfire barked. "I'm taking over that side."

It was a sudden shift, one that Cat was barely able to compensate for, as Brushfire's magic slid around, smoothly moving Smallwolf's power into the center. Cat followed suit, backing up his first officer's magic with his own—rather than leaving their youngest mage to face the wrath of the Void Seeker alone.

The darvar archmage's power buffeted him and Brushfire as they solidified the edge of the net. She couldn't hit hard—she could barely "hit" at all—but it was enough to unravel loose threads, pull away strands of magic, potentially unbalance the net enough to doom the ship they were trying to lift.

Cat and Brushfire mentally danced along the line, replacing and retying strands of magic as their junior officers focused on lifting the net. They held the net together and the others moved it…and it was working.

But not well enough. They were losing pace. Cat could feel the current weakening, but their lift was weakening faster. They were slowing…and slowing meant doom.

Then a new source of power snapped through the spell. Inside *Star*, Armand Bluestaves had realized what was going on, and he'd found an answer to the problem Cat had foreseen.

The archmage couldn't see what was going on…but he *did* have access to the lift-crystal network. His power pulsed through those crystals, calming their keening strain with a subtle caress even Cat could never have matched.

Through the lift crystals, Armand touched the control focuses on the forecastle—the same focuses Cat was using to direct the power of his assembled officers.

A critical thread began to unravel—and then suddenly snapped straight, its color shifting to a brilliant blue in Cat's mental view as Armand's magic reinforced theirs.

He couldn't see what they were doing, not in the same way as the aether-breathing mages on the forecastle could. But he *could*, through their shared link to the ship, lend each of one a fraction of his strength.

Enough of his strength, Cat realized, to tip the balance in the struggle. *Star* was accelerating again, swinging away from the Seventh Ward at respectable speed.

They weren't clear of the Void Seeker's reach, not yet…but between the six of them, even Her Dark Brother couldn't stop *Star*'s escape now.

CHAPTER 46

Armand woke up with a start, banging his head against the wall he was leaning on.

"Ow."

His eyes refused to open for a moment, until he rubbed the accumulated crust off of them. Even once he could see, his vision wavered with migraine aura.

Headache or not, he slowly processed where he was and what had happened. He'd reinforced the spell Cat and the officers had been casting, holding it together as the Void Seeker had tried to unravel it.

When they'd broken free of the magical trap the Seeker had unleashed, he had…slumped against the wall where he'd been connecting to the lift crystals and passed out.

Graceful and intimidating, the picture of power and wisdom. That was archmagi, definitely.

Groaning against his pounding head, Armand slowly levered himself up the wall, cataloging his aches and pains as he did so.

Other than banging his head against the wall as he woke, he didn't seem to have any external injuries. Everything else was magic fatigue.

As an archmage, he could draw on the Source to sustain himself through feats of magic a regular mage couldn't match. The dark side of that was that it was more in the nature of a loan than a gift, and he paid for that power just as thoroughly in the end.

Every inch of his body felt like he'd been pummeled with hammers, and every one of his muscles complained as he slowly pushed himself away from the wall and took a tentative step.

Walking *hurt*, but he could do it. He was intimately familiar with the kind of concentrated fatigue that had temporarily crippled Cat while they were fleeing the Seventh Ward, and in many ways this kind of broad "everything hurts but everything works" crunch was better.

Or so he told himself, anyway, as hauling his body to a chair sent tremors of agony through him. Gesturing brought a pitcher of water floating over a sideboard, and he didn't even check the temperature before pouring and draining a glass.

He grimaced afterward. The water was on the unpleasant side of lukewarm, but chilled water would require him refilling the pitcher from the cooled tanks next to his bakery supplies.

Shaking his head, he determinedly swallowed down a second glass. A third finished off the pitcher, but was also about as much tepid water as he could stand.

Armand's body still ached, but his mind was now sufficiently present for him to check the time. He'd been passed out against the wall for about four hours. He could see a long list of reasons why he should check in with Cat or the crew or…

But truthfully, Cat and Brushfire should still be sleeping, and *Star* would just be holding position, a thousand leagues from the Seventh Ward. At that moment, if things *weren't* under control, Armand Bluestaves would be dead.

So, he did the only rational thing to do when overwhelmed by magic fatigue that made the worst hangover look like a stubbed toe: without even undressing, he fell onto his bed and passed out again.

When Armand woke up again, almost twelve hours later, at least some of the aches and pains had lifted. He was able to get himself fresh water from the tank and even start brewing some tea as he scavenged some leftover sweet rolls.

He was on the right side of half a dozen rolls and three-quarters of a pot of tea when a crewvar knocked on the door to his bedroom.

"Yes?" he answered.

"Lord Archmage, Captain Greentrees wishes to know if you have recovered sufficiently to discuss our strategy," the gobvar asked.

Armand swallowed a sigh. Of *course* the battle-hardened elvar captain had recovered faster than he had. If nothing else, he suspected that Cat's ideas of appropriate presentation of himself would require the captain to fake being at full form as soon as possible.

"Inform the captain that I will be ready to host him and Officer Brushfire for a discussion of our plan in a clock-hour," Armand told the crewvar.

That would give him time to clean himself up and find a fresh robe that he hadn't gone to war and slept in.

Another lizard-like translucent oracle spirit wound its way around Armand's hands as he dealt the cards. The summoned critter wasn't attached to the particular oracle deck that he was working with—its main job was to point out the parts of a reading or conjuration that he'd missed.

A secondary role was to be adorable and stress-placating when divinations proved difficult, as this particular work was turning out to be. With a muffled curse, Armand stared down at a collection of contradictory oracle cards, topped by one that in its current orientation explicitly *said* the divination had failed.

He swept the cards from the desk to a concerned squeak from the spirit, which promptly dove onto the floor and scooped up a single card to drop back on the desk.

Lifting even one of the expensively gold-foiled and hand-calligraphed oracle cards was easily at the limits of the spirit's ability to affect the real world, and the not-entirely-real flying lizard squeaked with satisfaction as it dropped the card on the table.

Armand stared at it. Each of his oracle cards was a work of art, as befitted an archmage. This deck had been a gift from the Shining King on his ascension, which put it leagues ahead of any of his other tools in terms of value.

The cost of a single card in the deck of a hundred and one would easily pay the salaries of *Star*'s entire crew for ten clock-days. Archmage or not, Armand would never have bought it himself—he'd rather have had a dance's worth of hand-crafted cakes and a much cheaper deck.

Calligraphed and metal-foiled or not, though, it was not difficult to recognize the Fortress of Shadows. In the position he'd dealt the card in the initial spread, it meant that his divination of what would happen when they reached the dry dock had been blocked.

As a single reading, on its own, it projected conflict. Violence. Challenge—and death.

It also, he realized suddenly, very strongly resembled the octagonal collection of towers that had marked the entrance to His Dark Brothers' monastery on the Seventh Ward. An ancient Ironhand fortified dock.

The oracular spirit trilled happily at him—it was sufficiently an extension of his consciousness as to follow his thoughts—and then vanished as the inner doors into his receiving room swung open.

"Am I…interrupting?" Brushfire asked, the gobvar clearly taking in the scattering of runes and oracle cards around Armand's desk as she and Cat stood in the entrance.

He sighed and gathered the divination tools back up with a wave of his hand.

"The dry-dock cavern is sealed against divinations through both time and space," he told them. "I cannot predict how they will react when we attack."

"They need to have made their decisions already for that, don't they?" Cat asked. "My understanding is that you can't foresee what decisions they're *going* to make unless they're already fixed."

"Yes and no," Armand agreed. "I should get *some* sense, some ideas of their weapons, their doctrine. Nothing."

"Was it that way before?" Cat said.

"No," he admitted. "I think the Seeker has woven new defenses around her ship. She knows what we want. She can guess that we already know where it is, but without the ability to survey their defenses, it's more difficult to plan."

"What about the divinations you did before? Can you recreate them?" Brushfire asked curiously, looking at where the illusion had hung before.

"A bit." Armand recalled the oracle lizards, the winged spirits popping into existence on his shoulders. Both leaned against him for a moment, infinitesimal but detectable weights, and then sprang into the air as he tried to rebuild an illusory model of the Seventh Ward from memory.

The lizards weren't just extensions of him, though they weren't truly permanently existing creatures, either. In this case, their memory of the divinations he'd done on the worldlet was fresher than his—but the spirits' memory wasn't great at the best of times.

They were things of magic that appeared and disappeared as he needed them, after all, and they could only remember so much when they didn't exist.

Still, their memories and his combined to give them the image of the Seventh Ward, the spindle-shaped worldlet hanging in the middle of the receiving room.

Cat walked over to join Brushfire in studying the illusion, stumbling for a moment on the carpet and grimacing.

"Take a chair, Cat," Armand ordered. "If you insist on maintaining face in front of me at this point…"

The captain chuckled as Brushfire pulled a chair over to the illusory image of the Seventh Ward—but he gratefully took the seat from the gobvar.

"To show…a *limit* in front of the crew, after achieving great things, is acceptable," he said slowly. "But to show *weakness* is not. I trust our var enough to do the first, but I need them to see me as the captain, formidable and unshakable."

"I'm not arguing that, Cat. I'm telling you that you do *not* need to maintain a false image for *me* to see you as formidable and unshakable," Armand told him.

The elvar captain chuckled and nodded—and he'd already taken the seat, so Armand let it go.

Turning his attention on the illusion, Armand waved away most of it with a gesture, giving them an aerial view of what they knew of the dry-dock cavern itself.

There wasn't much to see on the surface. Underneath, he'd layered in what he remembered of the underground caverns, but even matching those two up, the archmage wasn't quite sure how the ship was supposed to get out.

"Is it possible they're still building the ship and it won't leave from here?" he asked.

"No, it leaves," Cat said grimly. He started to stand but wilted as both Armand and Brushfire directed hard glares at him.

Instead, he conjured a ghostly illusion of a hand that flickered up to highlight a section of the surface. Armand didn't see anything there and raised a questioning eyebrow.

"They did a good job concealing it, but I think this whole complex was built as a shipyard," the elvar told them. "So, what looks like just a hill here was a major surface structure. It was probably designed for aether-breathers, so it didn't really cost His Dark Brothers much to ruin three-quarters of the exterior walls and bring in extra rubble to pile around it.

"But if you look *here* and *here*, you can see the straight lines of the structure's original outline." The illusory hand ran along the walls and Armand finally saw what Cat meant.

"So, there's a link that the divination of the tunnels missed," he guessed. "And a door in the upper structure that's big enough for the ship?"

"Probably a double-door structure, same as entering this envelope," Brushfire suggested. "And if you look at the position of the ship inside the cavern…it's angled upward enough to make it almost a straight line out if there's a door *here*."

She was standing basically *in* the illusion and ran her hand along part of the wall that Cat had indicated.

"I can't imagine it's going to be easy to open," Cat noted. "We can probably breach it with the storm staves, but if we try to take *Star* herself inside… I don't know what defenses they have, but I doubt that tunnel is large enough for us evade their weapons."

"And that is why I was trying to divine their defenses," Armand told them. "But the Seeker now knows what we're doing, and she is preparing for us."

"Which means, if nothing else, we're facing *her*," Brushfire said grimly. "That took all three of us last time, and we barely held our own."

"We can hope that she was weakened by that encounter," Armand said. "But most likely…not."

"I can't speak to the Void Seeker," Cat told them. "But I can speak to the defenses."

The archmage turned to look at the aether captain. "How?"

"Because unlike either of you, *I* was a Navy officer," Cat pointed out. "And while it's not something anyone ever said, I can *see* the lineage from the fortifications here at the Seventh Ward to how the High Court Navy builds our bases and harbors.

"If *we* were building a concealed dry dock, to hold and repair a ship we didn't want anyone to see but wanted to be able to deploy, well..." He considered the illusion of the dry-dock cavern for a few seconds.

"We'd usually use surface connections, but if we needed to work with local non-elvar troops at a location without air, we'd have tunnels as well," he observed. "We'd have a central access structure, a giant shed over the exit as much as anything. Assuming that the big structure is equivalent to that working shed, defensive towers would be..."

The illusory hand broke apart as Cat concentrated. He wasn't as good with illusions as Armand—but few were. Armand knew that his conjurings had few equals among *archmagi*, let along regular mages.

Cat was still able to generate translucent golden towers marking the six spots where he would have put the defenses. And as Armand looked at the divination he'd done of the surface and compared it to Cat's projection, he sighed.

"Again with extra debris piled around them, but they're there, aren't they?" he asked. "I wish we could inspect them more closely."

"We can," the elvar replied. "Well, *I* can, from the ship's deck. But if they're the size I think they are, His Dark Brothers have probably armed them with weapons we'll find familiar: storm staves and flamethrowers.

"It won't matter, though." Cat sounded calmly confident as he dismissed six eighty-yard-high defensive positions laid out in a pattern that even Armand could see allowed them mutual support.

"It won't *matter?*" Armand asked.

Cat shrugged.

"I spent a lot of time thinking about how to defend a hexagonal defensive citadel at various times," he pointed out. "That means I had to think about how to *break* them—and *these* towers are missing a thousand dances of very smart var thinking on how to take or hold surface defensive structures against attack from the aether.

"They probably have four or five times our staves," he continued. "But we can handle the defenses. The question, Armand, is how the hell do we get *inside* after that?"

The three of them looked at the illusion as the oracular spirits flitted around it.

"What about the pinnace?" Brushfire asked. "We haven't found much other use for it, but we do *have* it."

It took Armand a few seconds to even remember what the first officer was talking about, and he'd specifically *paid* for the pinnace carried on the starboard deck.

It was a small ship, intended to allow for landings when they didn't want to bring the ninesail in close. Only about fifteen yards long and with only three sails, it could make the approach without risking *Star*.

But…

"It can maneuver more easily in the approach tunnel, but it has no air envelope," Cat said slowly. "We can improvise one to protect Armand, but it will be vulnerable. The pinnace's hull is too thin to take even a single hit, and they have almost certainly mounted defenses inside the tunnel."

"If they didn't have them before we arrived, I imagine the Seeker is having the Brothers move staves around as we speak," Armand agreed. "She recognizes our objective. She'll be there herself, more likely than not, and I will *need* to be on whatever ship enters."

He considered for a moment, then chuckled.

"I suppose that does provide a solution to the vulnerability of the pinnace," he continued. "I can conjure a defensive shield that will stand off storm stave bolts. Not the full gallery of a ninesail, but hopefully enough to get us through a tunnel where they can only mount so many staves."

All three of them were quiet for a moment as they studied the drydock cavern.

"What happens if we fail?" Brushfire asked slowly. "When do we accept that we can't manage this with one ship and break off, go get help?"

"The option exists," Cat agreed. "An archmage's word that the Monastery has been overtaken by His Dark Brothers should suffice to bring a squadron of the High Court Navy here."

The ex-Navy officer shook his head, looking down at the brand in his palm. Breaking the spell had been a moment's thought for Armand, but they'd left the brand to cover him in future. Anyone watching him command or use magic, though, would realize what had been done.

"That might cause problems for *me* at this point, and they may cause difficulty over our crew as Skyford's people did," he warned. "But we *can* go for help."

"There are too many shadows in my divinations for me to want to bring in more var unless we must," Armand admitted. "The Void Seeker is powerful and clever. I worry about what His Dark Brothers may do, given time."

If nothing else, they could move the ship somewhere else, which would render the entire affair pointless for Armand's mission.

"No, we have to strike now and succeed," he told them. "If we fail, then we can consider other plans, but we *need* that ship."

"All right," Cat said calmly. The captain looked over the illusion again and smiled thinly. "Then I'll need to get back up on deck and see what I can see with the spyglass. Then I'll confer with the other officers and the Masters, but I think I know what we're going to do."

"And that, my friend, is why I know you were the right one to hire for this," Armand murmured.

CHAPTER 47

STAR SPENT a full clock-day arcing away and around the Seventh Ward, keeping a distance of at least twelve hundred leagues from the ancient fortification as Cat positioned his ship outside the cone where he knew the Seeker could drag his ship down.

Everything "above" the spindle was vulnerable, which meant he had to come in from the side of the elongated worldlet. That would keep them out of the danger zone for the ancient Ironhand weapon—and, conveniently, outside the line of sight for the defenses built into the sealed towers around the dry dock.

"The currents do make this easier, don't they?" Streamwater asked, standing next to him. "Everything is headed toward the cursed rock."

"We're avoiding the worst of it by coming in from the side," Cat confirmed. "But yes, we're still picking up speed and coming at almost two leagues a minute."

Slowing the ship *down* when they reached the destination was going to be a pain, but Cat had a lot of ways to use those currents to serve his purpose and keep his ship safe. They would cross the distance to the Ward in ten hours.

"Windheart is busily building the new envelope on the pinnace," Brushfire reported, the gobvar stepping up onto the forecastle with smooth ease. "Axfall figures he can add some bulwarks on the bow, give her the chance to take at least one hit from a stave if Armand slips."

"Let's hope Armand doesn't slip," Cat said. "This is going to require careful work from all of us."

He looked at his two senior officers.

"Both of you will have to go with the pinnace," he warned. "And… Smallwolf, I think. I'll keep Crane aboard to act as surgeon, and I have to handle the wheel and the ship."

None of his officers had his hand with the wheel or the currents, and it was going to take every scrap of his skill and experience to take one ship against six ground fortifications and fly away intact.

"I trust you to judge the right thing to do once you're inside," he continued. "The archmage wants that ship—but *our* first priority is to keep Armand alive. Achieving his mission comes after protecting him.

"Killing His Dark Brothers isn't even on the list, understand?"

Brushfire chuckled bitterly.

"I don't think any of us much like killing anyone, Captain. But I hear you. Get the archmage out alive on the ship he wants."

"Exactly." Cat snorted, turning back to study the rock in the distance. He'd done his examination of the defensive towers—with rubble piled up around their sides to help both seal in air and conceal them, they looked like nothing so much as particularly steep hills—and he'd found much what he expected.

"There are sixty storm staves in those towers—and we have fifteen," he observed. "I can even those odds, but it's going to take time. The question, I suppose, is if we want to send the pinnace in *before* we've taken down the towers."

"They know what we want," Brushfire pointed out. "And as I understand it, His Dark Brothers are not known for being *optimists*. If they think we'll succeed, they may destroy the ship before we can seize her."

"If half of what the archmage has told us will come to pass comes if we fail is true, that isn't something we can allow," Streamwater noted. "But I hesitate to load the archmage himself onto the smallest vessel I've ever sailed the aether on and charge into the teeth of enemy lightning, too."

"Bluestaves can shield the pinnace from storm staves, to a point," Cat replied. Or so Armand had assured him, anyway. He'd never known a mage of any kind who could do that. *He* had always figured he could stop a single stave blast if he needed to, but he'd never tested that theory.

Archmagi played by different rules, though. If Cat could stop one, then maybe Armand could stop a dozen. The problem was that the archmage would *also* have to duel the Seeker when that was over.

"I think we have to drop the pinnace as *Star* is still bombarding the towers," Brushfire agreed. "We can ask Bluestaves?"

"The archmage is powerful, but he is no tactician," Cat said. That was the problem Cat was dealing with all around, at the moment. He was the only Navy-trained officer aboard the ship. The only other var aboard who seemed to have any idea of tactics was Paintrock.

"We send in the pinnace," he decided. "I look to you two to keep Bluestaves and Smallwolf safe, but we know our duty."

"How bad can it get, Captain?" Brushfire asked softly. "I've never seen ninesails fight."

"Few people on this ship have, I fear," he admitted. "And it can be bad, first officer. *Star* is sturdy enough after her rebuild, so we should be able to take a few hits without being crippled, but..."

He looked over the main deck of the ninesail, watching the var going about their duties as the aether ship sailed toward her fate.

"Even hits we survive will cost us lives," he whispered. "The survival of an aether ship is generally bought with the blood of her crew. Not all of us or our friends will survive what is to come. We have been lucky so far."

"Luck be cursed to the void," Brushfire snapped. "We had Armand and we had Paintrock and we had you, Captain. *Luck* didn't get our party out of the Monastery. You three did."

"You had your own part in that, Brushfire," Cat countered. "And I look to you to do it again. Talk to the Masters; put together a landing party to go with you and the archmage. The pinnace should hold three mages, an archmage, and three dozen var...easily, if not comfortably.

"Hopefully between you all, you can manage to fly the void ship."

Both his senior officers were silent at that; until Brushfire shook her horns and grinned toothily.

"At this point, Captain, I believe I have learned to speak fluent *ship*. If she was built to sail at the hands of var, I will move her. Maybe not well, maybe not efficiently, but I will move her."

"I'm relying on that and on you," Cat told her. "You two keep the course on *Star*," he ordered. "I need to talk to Paintrock."

Star's starboard stave gallery, the traditional post of the Master of Staves, felt strangely empty to Cat. Aboard *Running Fox*, there had been twelve storm staves mounted in an only slightly longer space. *Fox* had only been one hundred and eighty yards long to *Star*'s hundred and seventy-five.

Lodestone keels were the main limit on the length of a ninesail, and the skills and techniques around casting them improved only slowly over time. Even having seen magical techniques far beyond the current High Court on the Seventh Ward, Cat would have been willing to bet a significant amount of money that the Ironhands' ninesails or equivalent had been *smaller* than the current HCN ships.

A hundred dances older than Cat's last command or not, *Star* still had a gallery that should have held far more than the five storm staves currently placed evenly along the openings above his head.

"Captain, welcome to the gallery," Paintrock said brightly.

The elvar studied Cat for a few seconds after speaking, then turned to the team of stavemasters he'd been talking with when Cat entered.

"Clear the gallery, folks," he ordered gently. "Captain needs a word."

Cat hadn't been *planning* on asking for privacy—or about anything needing privacy, for that matter—but he didn't object as the dozen elvar swiftly exited the space, leaving him and his Master of Staves alone in the stave gallery.

"I figure you have questions, after the Ward," Paintrock said. He pulled a pair of stools out from beside a storm stave and slid one over to Cat. "May as well take a seat, Captain."

"'Follow orders, be loyal, keep an ace up your sleeve,'" Cat quoted back to him after a moment's thought. "You going to keep doing the first two?"

"Unless you give me a reason not to or stop paying me," the blue var said instantly. "Though I suppose not paying me would be a reason to stop, now I think about it."

"If you follow orders and you're loyal, I don't need to know your secrets, and your aces serve my needs as often as yours," Cat replied. "That's a mantra I can accept when I know the var saying it has my back."

There was a long silence in the stave gallery, and then Paintrock nodded.

"I appreciate that, Captain," he admitted. "I…wasn't entirely sure how you'd handle a var with skills and a past that…suggests things, let's say."

"I might have raised more questions if I wasn't quite certain you'd saved my life, the life of my first officer and the life of our archmage," Cat pointed out drily. "In truth, though, that has nothing to do with why I wanted to talk to you."

"Well, then, I'm curious, I'm pleased and I'm at your service, Captain," Paintrock said. "What do you need?"

"I need to be able to take down a fortified tower in a single salvo," *Star*'s captain said swiftly. "Five storm staves won't do it. We can't rotate the ship fast enough to put all three galleries on target as we pass by.

"Suggestions?"

"What are my resources?" Paintrock asked, turning around on his stool to survey the full length of the gallery. "And what risks are we prepared to take?"

"About eight hours and anything we have on the ship that isn't in use," Cat said. "Not sure about risks; why?"

"Navy says a storm stave needs seven yards of clearance either side," the Master of Staves told him. "When *Star* was built, they wanted that almost entirely clear for each stave. They had a bit under fourteen yards between the staves."

Cat looked around the gallery, following Paintrock's line of sight. *Star* was a hundred and seventy-five yards long, seven-eighths of a cable. The stave gallery was one hundred and sixty yards long, and the actual storm staves themselves were a bit over two yards wide with their support structures.

Space was needed on both sides of the big thunder crystals and their iron-and-lodestone frames. Var needed to move around, the stave needed to draw on the aether to recharge, and even aiming and discharging the crystals took space.

When Cat had done his training tour aboard *Star*, she'd mounted ten storm staves in this space, with, as Paintrock observed, fourteen yards between them. Aboard *Fox*, though...

"We've cut that space down now," he observed. "*Running Fox* had twelve storm staves in a hundred and sixty-eight yards. We only had twelve yards between staves. But you need that space for var to move and for the aether crystals to draw in energy to recharge the assembly."

"So, in another life, we didn't have much concern for our own lives and did a bunch of experimenting that was bloody stupid," his Master of Staves said. "You only need *three* yards of space on either side of the stave for crew to operate her.

"The seven yards is for the aether crystals, and seven is...conservative. The charge isn't noticeably slowed until the crystals are *ten* yards apart. Eleven, for example, is fine."

"There's only ten stave ports on the gallery," Cat observed.

"Give me a box of saws and ten of Axfall's carpenters, and we'll have all the ports we need," Paintrock told him. "Fifteen staves on this gallery means less than nine yards' spacing. Charging time *will* change, but if we're coming in fast and low, we're not going to have a chance for a second shot anyway."

It took a var's hand on the crystal to fire a storm stave. That made testing things like how close storm staves could be to each other *extremely* risky, something the High Court Navy only did in minuscule amounts, if at all.

"How much of a delay?" Cat asked. If Paintrock knew the timing...

"You lose a lot at nine yards," the Master of Staves admitted. "You're up to almost five minutes a discharge—and you *cannot* bring them much closer together. At about eight yards, the charge time is more like an hour.

"At seven, they interfere on release, and you get a chain detonation as they all backfire."

Cat had seen *one* storm stave backfire, ever, in a career that had spanned over fifty dances. That one had been damaged, and the stavemasters hadn't inspected their weapon properly before activating it.

Seventeen elvar had died that clock-day, and a ninesail had been sent to the yards for major repairs. He could only imagine what having *fifteen* backfire would look like.

"But fifteen on this gallery is safe?" he asked.

"Should be," Paintrock confirmed. "I mean, there's all kinds of screwy things going on in this sphere, so...might not be. No way to guarantee it, not at under nine yards of spacing."

A fifteen-stave gallery would probably dismount every stave in a defensive tower and breach the air envelope, even if the tower itself survived. That was worth *some* risk...

"Everything we're doing here is a ridiculous risk," Cat admitted. "Do it, Master of Staves. We need to clear a path for our pinnace to land."

CHAPTER 48

It had been a long time since Cat Greentrees had looked at an oncoming worldlet and thought he was falling. Lodestone keels provided a solid-enough sense of *down* at any distance to allow the conscious mind to overrule any foolish instincts.

But as they made their approach toward the Seventh Ward, he felt a tiny tremor of that age-old fear. Riding the aether tide forged by the ancient Ironhand arcana at the heart of the Ward, *Star* was traveling faster than he'd taken any ship before.

They hurtled toward the stone at almost three leagues a minute, according to his sextant, a speed close enough to the normal maximum speed of an aether ship to be fully understandable—and all the more terrifying for it.

If he misjudged his maneuver, they were going to slam into the side of the Seventh Ward and explode. There was a reason that Cat was the one standing on the forecastle with his hand on *Star*'s wheel.

If anyone was going to wreck his ship and kill all of his crew because they misjudged an angle, it was going to be him. That might not say pleasant things about him as a person, but he'd rather die by his own mistake than someone else's.

"Staves ready?" he called out.

"Starboard gallery ready," Paintrock called back.

Cat only had one broadside today, not three. On the other hand, that broadside was more powerful than anything he'd ever commanded in the Navy. Assuming it survived firing, that was.

"Pinnace ready?" he asked.

"She's ready," Windheart told him, the Master of Sails standing at the rear of the forecastle. "We'll drop her off on your order."

Cat checked and adjusted the sextant again. The pinnace wouldn't be able to keep pace with *Star* once they dropped her, but he also *wanted* the smaller ship to come in behind the ninesail. It was all a question of timing and distance.

And he couldn't even see his destination yet. The worldlet was barely two dozen leagues ahead of them now, but he was coming in underneath the wide head of the spindle. The dry dock, like the Monastery, was on the top.

"Not yet," he told the old gobvar. "The crew, Windheart?"

"Everyone knows what the archmage saw, captain," Windheart said. "Court and Kingdoms may not have treated the tribe right, but we remember why we left the Clans. And it didn't sound to me like the Clans came out ahead in what the archmage saw, either."

"It didn't sound like anyone did," Cat agreed.

"The crew is with you, with the archmage." Windheart snorted. "With my first-sister's daughter. To the end. To the void."

"'To the void' quite literally, I'm afraid," Cat replied. "But thank you. Today, I needed to hear that."

"I've been a gobvar aether sailor in the Court and Kingdoms for longer than you've been alive, Captain Greentrees," Windheart pointed out. "You're the first captain I've ever had to just treat gobvar crew like crew.

"Every var aboard this ship will fight for you. You've my word on that."

Cat chuckled.

"Let's see if everyone still thinks that way *after* the stunt we're about to pull," he reminded the Master of Sails.

"All hands!" he bellowed. "Prepare for lodestone field maneuver!"

Everybody aboard the ninesail and the pinnace should have been strapped in, but there were warnings called for in the High Court Navy's book that Cat thought were only sensible. If there was any chance of losing people overboard, he wanted to be *absolutely* certain everyone was tied down.

There wasn't time for him to wait for confirmation, though. *Star* was in the final stages of what would either be a descent or a crash, depending on how well Cat Greentrees handled the next few minutes, and his focus had to be absolute.

"Stand by lift crystals," he ordered Crane. The third officer would be a surgeon for most of today, but right now Cat needed another mage on the deck to handle the crystals.

"Ready," the elvar told him.

"And...lift *now*."

He felt Crane's magic flickering into the ship's lift crystals at the same moment as he pulled on the wheel. Timing was *everything*—because neither the mechanical nor magical workings that allowed the wheel to control the ship were instant.

Nor was the ship's response to the reorientation of the sails. They were five leagues away when Cat gave the order and pulled the wheel back. Four leagues by the time the sails were angled enough to even begin to slow their hurtling approach to the rocky surface beneath them.

They were only three leagues away by the time the lift crystals kicked in—and under *two* at the moment the angles were where Cat wanted them to be and the horizontal tack caught the aether currents exactly how he was planning.

Star turned her speed from a headlong crash into the Seventh Ward into a high-speed dash eight thousand yards above the surface of the worldlet. Cat could see the battered ruins of another docking fort forty cables beneath him as he directed his ship across the surface, angling outward as they headed toward the head of the spindle.

"Crystals are holding," Crane reported.

Cat didn't reply. He needed that report, but his attention was on the surface beneath them. They had to get this right, and there were too many stages left. Too many places for it to go wrong.

An overwhelming sense of dread suddenly washed over him—and he *heard* Windheart and Crane both groan behind him. It wasn't natural.

"The Seeker is playing games," he shouted. "Hold your will. Don't let Her Dark Brother's power overwhelm you. You're better than that. *You are my crew.*"

The sound that came back wasn't coherent, but it told him what he needed to know—his people were with him.

"Windheart, drop the pinnace on my command," he barked. "And... *now*."

Riding the line between aether currents, the lift crystals and the inward pull of the Seventh Ward's lodestone core, Cat took *Star* around the edge of the spindle's "head." Even he felt the strain of an almost-complete inversion, but now they were heading toward their destination at last.

He felt and heard more than saw the pinnace release. The perpetual sense in the back of his mind of the archmage's power began to lessen swiftly as Armand and Brushfire and the rest of the landing party fell behind.

"Straight ahead!" bellowed the watchvar in the front upper staff. "I see the towers!"

"Stand by, stavemasters!"

Cat's command overlapped with Paintrock's, both of them giving the same inevitable order. They'd only have a few *moments* to take the shot as they swung by—and if they missed their target, Brushfire and the pinnace crew would be coming into the dry dock in the line of sight of every storm stave in the west tower.

He wasn't going to let that happen.

Star hurtled across the surface of the worldlet, the aether currents whipping the sails above his head and beneath his feet as he guided her. He'd adjusted for the chaos of the currents around the Ward, and even the moment where the Seeker intensified the downward pull as he approached didn't faze him.

She could only pull the currents "above" the spindle into the Ward, and he'd expected it. *Star* jerked downward for a moment, only to spring back away from the surface and twist to present her one full stave gallery to the towers as she continued to rush across the rock toward the fortress.

Cat could count on his fingers the number of times he'd ever flown an aether ship *sideways*, but it was the perfect answer for this moment—and lightning bolts crashed through the air where *Star* would have been if she hadn't bounced through the Seeker's attempt to pull her to the ground.

The closest tower was the one he knew would threaten the pinnace, and everything he'd done served one purpose: to line the fifteen storm staves up with the crenelated top ten yards of the structure.

Those slits had just spewed lightning at him, and that made them the targets. *Star* slid sideways and tilted, providing Paintrock's stavemasters with a perfectly level sight line for two seconds. Maybe three.

It was enough. Fifteen storm staves thundered as one, and the ninesail lurched backward, missing a salvo of lightning from another tower. Cat couldn't even count how many bolts hit, but it was enough.

More than enough.

The top ten yards of the defensive tower exploded, stone shattering under the multiple impacts. A secondary explosion was tinted with the sharp green of a backfiring storm stave, spinning the last few intact portions of the top stories away onto the stony surface.

Twisting the wheel again, Cat lifted *Star* over the wrecked tower and spun her around to accelerate away along the surface currents.

The price of the perfect shot became brutally clear almost immediately. The tower they'd destroyed had already fired on them and missed. A second tower had missed as they bombarded the tower.

Four more defensive towers remained, and their storm staves filled the aether above the dry-dock entrance with a hail of lightning. Cat had *Star* moving with enough speed to throw off the aim of His Dark Brothers, but with forty storm staves unleashing hell, they only had to get lucky once.

They got lucky three times.

Star lurched underneath his feet, and only the straps held Cat at the wheel. The smell of burning cloudwood and crystal filled the aether—with a sharp undertinge that he recognized as burning flesh.

But just as *Star*'s staves couldn't recharge to launch a second salvo before clearing range of the towers, the defenders couldn't recharge their weapons in time to catch her. Those three hits were it, and the ninesail was clear.

"Crane, get to the surgery," Cat ordered—and then glanced over his shoulder and chuckled bitterly.

Windheart had taken the surgeon's place at the lift crystals already. Crane was well on her way to do her main job on the aether ship.

And Cat trusted her skill. Var under his command had just died… but unless he missed his judgment, the stave gallery was intact—and Emberlight Crane would make certain anyone who was still alive stayed that way!

CHAPTER 49

To Brushfire, the pinnace more resembled the aerial skiffs used for transport between cities on a given worldlet—or even a bird—than the ninesail that carried it. It had three sails, yes, but it only had one deck and the slimmest of lodestone cores.

The main sail was rigged above the single deck to provide propulsion. The two secondary sails were at right angles to the main sail, extending directly to port and starboard. This close to a worldlet, the sidesails were horizontal, helping the lift crystals keep the small craft aloft with billowing white wings of aethercloth.

There was a single storm stave positioned forward, most easily aimed by turning the entire pinnace. Like the ninesail, a single wheel controlled the positions of the sails and allowed the ship to fly with as few hands as possible on the rigging.

Given that the pinnace had just dropped off *Star*'s stern and was struggling to remain airborne, let alone move forward, having everyone strapped in struck Brushfire as a great idea. They had barely three leagues to cross to reach their final destination, but the longer they took to cross them, the more danger they were in.

She could practically *feel* Streamwater's urge to take the wheel, but the second officer remained silent, strapped to her own post and watching the pinnace struggle forward against the twisted aether currents of the Seventh Ward.

"Say it, Streamwater," Brushfire finally snapped as another unexpected curve of current threw the pinnace a dozen yards to port.

"Dive," the elvar told her. "Go down, ride the current, don't fight it. The aether around here is *fucked*; get close enough to use the lift crystals against the rock for power."

She snorted.

"And so we can use the whole damn worldlet for cover against the towers!"

Brushfire had never flown a pinnace before and realized, in hindsight, that she *should* have had Streamwater pilot the craft. Too late now, with both of them tied into position to keep them from flying off in the turbulence of the Seventh Ward's twisted aethersphere.

But she listened to the other var's words and tilted all three sails forward. For a moment, the pinnace hung in the aether like a floating kite, and then she dove.

It wasn't the uncontrolled fall Brushfire had feared. With her hands on the wheel and riding the currents that *wanted* to go down, she finally started to move the little ship forward. They were gaining speed as they glided downward, and a rush of exuberance ran through her.

So, *this* was why some pilots loved the small ships.

That one piece of advice was the key she'd been missing, and now she took the pinnace skimming across the surface, far closer than she was truly comfortable with, riding the line between the lift crystals pushing against the Ward's lodestone core and the downward pull of the local aether currents.

There *should* have been more upward and sideways currents. But the Seventh Ward's aether wasn't normal, and Brushfire angled her side sails to take as much advantage of the strange pull as she could.

"You're heading *for* the tower," Streamwater observed. It wasn't even a complaint.

"I know," Brushfire agreed. "*Star* blew that one to void, but the others still can't see through it."

If she could make the turn, she'd swing around the wrecked tower and be right on top of the dry dock entrance. Then the real problem would arise.

Armand couldn't do much yet. The archmage was belowdecks, in an air envelope made by the simple measure of covering every hatch and port with aethercloth. There were no doubled doors or anything similar. As soon as they opened the envelope, the envelope was gone.

That meant that Brushfire had to get the pinnace *into* the dry dock before they could unleash the archmage for more than the crude defensive shield he planned—which meant that Armand couldn't be the one to open the hatch.

There were almost certainly mechanisms to open it, but with five defensive towers still able to lash them with lightning, Brushfire wasn't going to try to figure *that* out.

"That tower is getting, uh, rather close," Streamwater said. Her voice was a bit less calm now, and Brushfire grinned.

"I'd have made you fly," she told the second officer. "Except that both the captain and I figured that this particular trip was going to require a certain type of crazy we didn't think you had."

"Thanks, I think," the elvar said drily. "Can we please *not* fly into the—"

They reached the distance Brushfire was waiting for, and she twisted the wheel as hard as she could. The pinnace went up on its side, a mix of straps and the lodestone core keeping the passengers on board as she swung hard and practically orbited the wrecked tower at less than twenty yards.

Then they were in the most dangerous part of the trip. For the last two cables, they were crossing an open field with line of sight from at least two intact towers. Lightning began to flicker out, ranging strikes from the first stavemasters to see the oncoming ship.

The key to making it through this part was surprise. They'd been hoping to get there before the staves recharged, but the mess that was the Seventh Ward's aethersphere had prevented that. Now it was down to unpredictable maneuvering, speed and the hope that the towers hadn't seen the pinnace coming.

There were few enough lightning bolts initially to suggest they'd hoped right.

"Are you ready?" Brushfire asked Streamwater as they hurtled toward the hill containing the dry-dock entrance. She could make out the big hatch, she *thought*. It was probably big enough for a ninesail, but she agreed with the assessment that *Star* would have been vulnerable making the entrance.

"For the var," Streamwater replied, stepping forward with one hand on her safety strap and the other holding her focus.

Brushfire had never heard that particular oath before—most likely, she realized, because most people would use "Court and Kingdoms" instead of "var." "For the var" included *everyone*, including not only gobvar but the gobvar in the Clan Spheres.

And it covered the point of this mission, why Brushfire and her tribe were as committed to the task as Armand Bluestaves or, well, Faith Streamwater.

"For the var," Brushfire agreed, drawing her own focus. The inlaid black horn was cool to her touch, even as its internal pulse beat against her hand.

The riggers knew what to do, and the sails were already furling in as the pinnace plunged toward their destination. They were losing speed and altitude at about the same pace, but they were still going to hit the hatch at stride.

"*Now*," Streamwater barked, and her focus flared with power in Brushfire's senses.

A moment later, Brushfire channeled energy alongside her. Magic flashed out from both of them, intertwining into a braid of force that latched on to the top of the hatch and *pulled.*

There was no time or space for subtlety or experimentation. There was time for brute force and every scrap of it they could muster. As the hatch resisted their strength, a third strand added itself to the braid, Smallwolf taking a moment longer to join the more-experienced Streamwater and more-powerful Brushfire in the attack.

The young elvar might have been one of the weakest and least experienced mages aboard *Star*, but that was the *only* standard she fell short by. As Smallwolf's energy joined with the two other mages', the braid of force twitched slightly toward the pinnace—and then snapped backward as they yanked the multi-ton, cable-high hatch clean out of the hillside.

They'd hit at its strongest point and ended up snapping the main mounts and hinges, Brushfire realized as the entire plate of metal and stone lifted up and plunged down toward the surface. The entrance into the dry dock was now wide open, and she could *feel* the air rushing out of it as their pinnace dove in.

"The archmage's shield is up," Streamwater reported. "Fistfall has the stave. We are ready."

Brushfire's brother had been the most eager of Paintrock's gobvar students on the big weapons. He'd been an eager student of other things too, Brushfire suspected, that might or might not prove for the best—but the two were getting along.

And with Paintrock still on *Star*, he'd lent Fistfall his bandoliers of battlewands. Brushfire hoped that would help keep her brother alive through everything.

"Taking us deeper," Brushfire declared aloud, her hands on the wheel. The tunnel was a straight dive, a clean angle leading deep into the Ward. She'd been expecting a second hatch, but as they flew deeper, she realized that powerful magic held air inside the worldlet.

"The aether currents cleared up," Streamwater observed. "They're more normal in here."

"They may be more normal everywhere," the gobvar said grimly. "I suspect that means the Seeker has abandoned her pit and is coming here. For us."

As if to punctuate Brushfire's fears, they reached the first storm-stave position in the tunnel, and lightning crackled in the enclosed space. The bolt lit up the dim cave and hammered into an invisible barrier half a dozen yards in front of the ship.

Their own stave spoke in instant response, following the exact same path backward—and without an archmage to protect His Dark Brothers. An explosion tore out a chunk of the side of the tunnel, and the pinnace flashed past the wrecked position.

"Let's move quickly," Brushfire told Streamwater. "Is there enough air to get Armand out?"

She grimaced as the tunnel extended before them.

"We need to get through this *quickly*, because I do *not* want to fight the Seeker again!"

The tunnel was almost a thousand yards long, with a defensive position every cable or so. The first two hadn't managed to be ready to fire by the time the pinnace reached them, but the last three each took at least one shot at them as they flashed by.

None of them hit anything but the shield. The pinnace's storm stave only fired at the first and last, but Fistfall didn't miss either one.

The light of the exploding defensive position was behind them as Brushfire finally brought the pinnace out into the dry dock cavern. She pulled the small craft up and brought it to a halt in the air, surveying the massive open space.

The long and cylindrical void ship didn't look any less strange in person than it had in the vague haziness of the divinations and illusory projections. It had no sails, no aethercloth, nothing she recognized at all.

Instead, it was built of smooth, gray-painted metal. Brushfire couldn't even see an *entrance* from the air.

She also couldn't see that many var in the cavern, to her surprise. She'd expected that His Dark Brothers would have fielded an army to protect the void ship, but there was only a scattered handful of darvar, none of whom looked armed.

"I'm bringing us down," she told Armand and Streamwater. "Get everyone ready."

Landing the pinnace, she made sure she wasn't blocking the line between the front of the void ship and the tunnel outward. The ship was on a cradle that pointed her bow directly at the tunnel, which suggested she flew in a straight line, like a regular aether ship.

Brushfire just couldn't see how the thing *moved*.

Battlewands crackled behind her, and she turned to see Fistfall and two of her tribesvar taking cover on the edge of the pinnace, blasting away in response to an incoming attack. Silence fell as she looked, and her brother met her gaze.

"Some of them have weapons," he observed. "We'll need to be careful."

"They'll have reinforcements on their way," she agreed. "The Seeker herself is coming."

"Let's not wait for her," Armand told her, the archmage putting a hand on her shoulder. "Do you see an entrance to the ship?"

"No, but it *should* have some kind of ramp or stairs," she pointed out. "The whole thing is elevated, after all."

"Then we move and see what we find," he suggested.

"What about the pinnace?" Smallwolf asked.

"She's served her purpose," Brushfire admitted. "We can't leave *with* her, but I don't want to wreck her until we know we have a way out. She's useless to the darvar, at least."

"This way!" Streamwater called to the crew. "I see movement along the ship!"

Brushfire grabbed a rope and slid down to the ground, surveying the area for immediate threats.

Unfortunately, His Dark Brothers had clearly decided to fall back and gather numbers and weapons. Apart from the handful that had blasted away as they tried to dismount, the dry dock was now completely empty.

"Keep moving," she told Armand as the archmage landed next to her. "Can you sense anything?"

"The Seeker is getting closer," he said grimly.

"Is she still blocking divination?" Brushfire asked. "Or did that require the pit as well? One of your spirits might help us?"

Armand's expression was priceless. She suspected that the archmage was not used to feeling like an idiot.

"Let me check."

The translucent winged lizard popped into existence, chirped loudly and then bolted away faster than anyone could run.

"What's it looking for?"

"I'm...not sure," the archmage admitted slowly. "I didn't get a chance to tell it to find the door. The spirits have some level of awareness of their own, most oracular and divination tools do, and it must have decided there was something we needed—"

"Get it off, get it off!" a high-pitched voice shouted. "Get away from me!"

Streamwater was close to the voice, pursuing the movement she'd seen, and Brushfire didn't even need to give the order for the elvar mage to gesture and yank the speaker out of the dry-dock assemblage they were hiding in.

A darvar worker, clad in a blacksmith's leathers with an artificer's arcane monocle, fell out of the framework of the dock. Something in his build and dress told Brushfire he was definitely *not* one of His Dark Brothers.

Which raised the question of just what in void the artificer was doing *there*.

CHAPTER 50

The last thing Armand had expected to find in the middle of His Dark Brothers' secret shipyard on the back end of nowhere was a befuddled-looking mage-engineer who looked like he belonged in a smithy at the Towers of the Great Red Forest.

"Um." The darvar looked up at the landing party and adjusted his monocle. "You are...not what I was expecting. Who are you?"

"Who are *you*?" Armand asked, stepping past Brushfire and Streamwater to look down at the darvar. "I am Armand Bluestaves, Archmage of the Great Red Forest."

"Um. Stonefire. Um. I'm Alloy Bellowforge," the darvar said, his monocled eye flexing weirdly as he focused it on Armand. "Yep, Archmage. You shouldn't be here. Nobody should be here. They didn't tell me... They don't tell me anything."

Bellowforge suddenly straightened.

"You're not with them," he realized aloud. "What do you want?" He turned to look at the ship. "What am I saying, if you're here, you want the *Flyer*."

"The what?" Armand asked, a bit taken aback by the speed the darvar had just changed topics.

"The *Void Flyer*, the cursed *rocket ship*," the darvar said sharply. "It's the only thing in this particular hole in the ground anyone would be here for. My doom, my baby, my dream, my nightmare."

"We don't have time for this," Streamwater suggested. "We need to take the ship and get out of here."

"Luck with that," Bellowforge told her. "Do you know what a rocket is, miss elvar? Do you know the right proportion of magically produced air to distilled ethanol to propel her at appropriate thrust? Do you even know which valve not to fully open to make sure you don't ram her into the side of the launch tunnel?"

"You do?" Armand asked.

"I designed the *Void Flyer*," the darvar replied. "She was a thought experiment that got stuck in my head. Built a prototype for the University of Hammerhome. Then…well, His Dark Brothers kidnapped me and made me finish the *Flyer* for them."

"Can you help us?" Armand looked down at the darvar hopefully. The var seemed confused, but he also seemed like he could be very, *very* useful.

"You want to take *Flyer* out of here? Piss off His Dark Brothers, the Void Seeker? Be chased across all spheres and time by the furious worshippers of betrayal and death?" Bellowforge snorted. "I *can*, yes."

"That's about the plan, yes," Armand told him. "We need the void ship for a mission. The fate of all var and spheres may ride on it."

"That's great. Then you'll want to make a deal."

Armand could *feel* the Void Seeker growing closer. There didn't seem to be any teleporters directly from the Monastery to the dry dock, but from the speed of her movement, there was both a tunnel and either mounts or mechanisms to cross the distance swiftly.

"We don't have time for this."

"Easy enough. Save my family and take us with you, I'll get the *Flyer* out of here for you and teach your crew how to fly her."

"Your family is here?" Fistfall asked, the massive gobvar materializing with a silent step that Armand didn't hear coming.

"How do you think they made me build the *Flyer*?" Bellowforge asked. "We have a little suite that they've rigged with poison gas. My wife, my daughters. They have…made threats, if things go wrong.

"They may kill them out of sheer spite! You must hurry!"

Armand looked over at Brushfire. She looked steadily back at him and he shrugged.

"We'd help him either way if we can, and we need him," he conceded. "Let's make it happen."

The gobvar nodded sharply and turned to her brother.

"Fistfall, go with Streamwater and Smallwolf and half the sailors," she ordered. "Find the access to the ship, get aboard, make sure there's no one waiting for us.

"Everyone else"—she turned to the other dozen sailors with them—"we're going to find the Bellowforges. With me and the archmage, let's move."

"Show us the way, Alloy," Armand told the darvar. "But realize that the Void Seeker is coming and even I don't want to fight her."

Armand had researched His Dark Brothers sufficiently, after being warned that they might be in the Brokenwright sphere, that the thought of an innocent family in their hands was terrifying. Her Dark Brother did not teach virtues such as compassion or patience.

His Dark Brothers at least did not generally engage in the sacrifice of living var to their deity, as Her Crimson Sisters were known to. But given that they regarded both lying and torture as sacraments to Her Dark Brother, they weren't much better to be in the clutches of.

At least imprisonment by Her Crimson Sisters would *end*.

Now, as Bellowforge led the way through the workings of the dry dock, it took an effort of will *not* to unleash his magic. Armand could clear the way through the scattered defenders with ease, but he limited himself to a trio of oracular spirits that highlighted the attempted ambushers before they could attack.

That was more than sufficient for Brushfire and Streamwater to explode any of His Dark Brothers before they could lay a finger on the landing party, but he worried it was slowing them down.

Everything was a balance, though. If he threw all of his power into clearing the way, they might retrieve the Bellowforges and get out before the Void Seeker made it to the dry dock. If his power *didn't* buy them enough time, though, he'd end up trying to fight off the chosen archmage priestess of the god of murder, having already exhausted himself.

"This way," Bellowforge urged them. "Our rooms are on the west side of the cavern. They may already be dead—the rooms are rigged to flood with poison gas!"

"Right," Armand murmured as the darvar repeated that claim, his voice growing higher-pitched with panic. There was a time to conserve resources for the battle to come...and there was a time to save lives.

"Point the most direct path," he told the mage-engineer.

It was a sign, Armand knew, of the darvar's imprisonment that he hadn't been allowed a focus. Bellowforge could build and maintain the void ship without the ability to directly use magic—but without that ability, it would be far more difficult for him to escape.

As it was, Alloy Bellowforge clearly knew the entire layout of the drydock cavern like the back of his hand. It took him a moment or two to realize what Armand was thinking, but he then pointed at a set of shelving racks holding assorted consumables. Those shelves rose ten yards high and were blocking the direct path to the engineer's room—and Armand doubted that barricade had been unintentional.

It was exactly the kind of overcomplicated cruelty and protective measure His Dark Brothers would delight in. It would make the engineer have to walk farther every clock- and slow down any attempt to reach his family like this.

Unfortunately for His Dark Brothers, Armand Bluestaves was finally out of patience. The shelving was sturdy, full of combustibles and potentially dangerous items. Brushfire could probably have blasted her way through it, but it would have been draining and dangerous.

Armand put two parallel blades of force into the shelving and pushed them all the way through—then swept them apart, flinging dozens of yards of shelving and tons of supplies apart to create a passage through the cavern more than wide enough for the landing party.

A dozen black-robed darvar looked up in shock as their shelving barrier collapsed. They'd collected weapons and were hauling three roughly bound darvar of various ages.

Given a chance, Armand knew the Brothers wouldn't hesitate for a second to use the three Bellowforges as living shields. He didn't give them that chance. A dozen lethal sparks blazed from the rings on his hands, seeking attacks that flashed across the wreckage to strike eyes and throats with perfect precision.

The energy cost of those spells wasn't immaterial, and Armand sagged as his targets fell. He stabilized himself with a deep breath—and drew strength from the way the four Bellowforges ran into each other's arms.

He and Brushfire crossed the debris he'd created a bit more carefully, leaving Streamwater and the sailors to watch from closer to their destination.

"I hope we found the right family," Armand noted as the engineer's wife lifted a tear-stained face from her husband's head.

"I don't know what's going on," she told him. "But if you can get us out of here…"

"We're already on it," Brushfire promised. "But Alloy said he was the only one who could fly the void ship…"

"I exaggerated a *bit*," the mage-engineer admitted stiffly, looking away from his wife and daughters but not releasing them. "I'm sure you could fly her once you got the *Flyer* into open aether. The tunnel is the only real problem."

"Then we should all get out of here," Armand suggested. "Because I think *all* of us will be happier when we leave the Seventh Ward behind." He sighed. "Though I have to warn you: we're going into the void strait. We won't be able to return to the Court and Kingdoms to get you to safety."

"You saved my family, archmage," Bellowforge said. "I'm your var now. Forever and always."

"Let's think about what that might mean when we're a good distance from here," Brushfire suggested, the gobvar looking around nervously. "Because *I'm* starting to feel the Void Seeker, and that means she's close."

"Too close," Armand agreed. "Let's move."

The path back to the ship wasn't as clear as the path that Armand had blazed to the Bellowforges' rooms—and he muttered a quiet prayer of thanks to whatever sane divinity had made His Dark Brothers decide to move the family rather than gas them—and he couldn't blast his way through fuel tanks.

"The *Void Flyer* is ready to go," Bellowforge told them as the engineer led the way. "Once you've got me to the control room, I can have us out of here in a few minutes."

He paused.

"It'll be a bit awkward in there at first," he admitted. "The lodestone plate is just above the engines and completely overwhelmed by the Ward's core. The ship is built to be vertical, but the Brothers figured keeping her hidden was more important.

"Even *after* they crashed the first one and killed fifty of their people trying to land it," he concluded grimly.

"It can land safely?" Armand asked, suddenly concerned.

"Oh, yeah," Bellowforge confirmed. "The current *Flyer* has made the journey through the void strait and back six times.

"Landing it in *this cave* is a nightmare that their pilot spectacularly failed once, but it can be done."

"A few minutes might be too long," Brushfire warned as they *finally* reached the stairs up to the door.

Armand cut off what she'd been about to say as he saw the chaos around the steps. Some of His Dark Brothers had tried to hold the ship there—and it looked like even more had tried to retake it.

Fistfall was standing at the bottom of the stairs, looking exhausted—and with a massive splotch of blood covering his clothes and bandoliers.

"Brother!" Brushfire shouted, running over to him.

"I'm fine," he insisted.

"Just don't let him tell you that isn't his blood," Smallwolf said bluntly. The elvar mage was sitting behind the massive gobvar, her focus in her hands as she watched past him grimly. "I healed the big lug enough to keep him upright, but since he took the wand-blast aimed at *me*, that is most definitely *his* blood."

"Oh, you big…" Brushfire trailed off and embraced her brother. "We need to get everyone aboard. Bellowforge here says he can fly the ship."

"I can do that," the darvar confirmed. "I don't have the touch, don't have the extra *bit* a good navigator has…but I built the *Flyer* and I can still make her dance."

"Then do it," Armand ordered. "Brushfire, Streamwater, Smallwolf, get everybody aboard."

He turned back to study the surrounding cavern. His oracular spirits were swirling around him, clearly distressed, but he didn't even need their warning.

"Armand?" Brushfire asked softly.

"Get everyone else aboard the ship," he repeated. "Go."

"She's here, isn't she?"

CHAPTER

51

A RMAND BLUESTAVES, an Archmage of the Towers of the Great Red Forest, walked away from the *Void Flyer*. The strange cylindrical ship behind him was hope. Hope for the var who'd sworn him service. Hope for the strange mage-engineer and his family His Dark Brothers had imprisoned and force to work on it.

Hope for Court and Kingdoms and var for freedom from the future he'd foreseen.

But that hope would only be born if his people got her out of the Seventh Ward—and they weren't going to do that in the face of the Void Seeker.

He knew precisely where she was. Whatever mechanism had carried her from the Monastery stopped in a side cave, some distance from where he'd sent his people aboard the *Flyer*. She hadn't entered the main cave—

The moment she did, he knew. The same way he'd opened a passageway through the cavern's machinery and supplies to protect the Bellowforges, the Seeker opened one to him. He'd done it with walls of force, minimizing the damage and limiting how far his power went.

The Seeker did it with a ram of pure dark energy, a spike of void power that was aimed directly at him. Fuel tanks exploded and machine tools scattered as it hurtled at him, but he simply held up his hand and stopped it in front of him.

"You should not have come back."

"What did it matter?" Armand asked conversationally, stepping forward to face the black-eyed darvar.

She'd discarded illusions and disguise now. Her pale skin gleamed in the light, blending into the brilliant pure-white robes she wore. As her eyes were the only color in her face, the only color in her clothing was a black stole wrapped across her shoulders.

"You were already furious; blood had already been shed," he reminded her. "Would His Dark Brothers truly have let that go?"

"No," the Seeker agreed. "You have angered Him, not just me. His power would have hunted you across all spheres, all kingdoms. No power, mortal or divine, can save you now. You have chosen your doom, Archmage Armand Bluestaves."

"I swore an oath," he said. "To stand between the Shining Kingdom and all var—and those who would do them harm. It's hard to claim you don't qualify, even if you weren't the point of this."

"All of this." She gestured around at the wreckage of the cavern. "You don't even know how much of His Dark Brothers' work you've ruined. Dance upon dance was spent to restore this fortress to even this fraction of its ancient power.

"Even if you had not struck against us, I would be driven to destroy you," she told him. "You seek to breach the void straits, to walk the hungry worlds beyond. You have no concept of what you court, and there is no path to salvation for you.

"Her Dark Brother demands your life. Your power will feed His power. Your blood will repay our blood. You will not walk the hungry worlds. You will not forge answers from lies. You are doomed, Bluestaves of the Towers of the Great Red Forest."

Armand could live with that, so to speak, if it got the *Void Flyer* out and his mission continued.

"You have no concept of my power," he told her softly. "We are not done here yet."

"I am a Seeker of the Void, my eyes and name sacrificed on the altar of Her Dark Brother's will," she told him, the debris clearing away from her feet as she walked toward him. "My mind is His Mind. My will is His Will. My power is His Power.

"You have chosen to defy the void, and you and all who follow you will die. This ship will not escape here. It will continue to serve its sacred purpose."

The Seeker smiled coldly.

"Perhaps I'll mount your skull on the prow," she told him.

A flame flickered behind him, a soft and growing thunder marking that the void ship was preparing to escape.

"Do you think you're buying time?" the Seeker asked. "The *Void Flyer* will go nowhere without my permission. All the fury of her engines are nothing against the power of Her Dark Brother.

"Beg for mercy, Armand Bluestaves, and I may kill you swiftly."

"No."

Sparks of living magic flared out from his rings again, circling him in a rising tornado of power as he called on the Source and faced the Void Seeker.

"No," he repeated. "If you want my skull and you want my people, you're going to have to come through me—and then we'll see if you have enough guts left to stop the *Flyer* then!"

Armand flung his hands forward, unleashing his horde. Normally, the kind of attack spirit he was summoning was also instructed to defend him.

Today, they were purely tasked with attack. His only defense was the three oracular spirits he still had around him, and he listened to their squeaks and dodged sideways.

The Seeker's spirits had been given the usual dual order, and only a handful had reached him. They smashed into the ground around him as he took his clumsy body through a twisting dance guided by the oracle lizards.

His power flickered out, conjuring attack spirits by the half dozen and sending them flitting at the Seeker. Her own attacks paused for a moment, and she stepped back as his own unrelenting assault battered her defenses.

Armand had a good idea of how long he could keep this up before the debt he was accruing with the universe became unpayable. He could shield himself from backlash via his link to the Source, but that loan had to be repaid.

Sooner or later, it would just kill him. But for now, he drove the Void Seeker back, her stance surprised as she found herself focused on defense.

Then she released a blast of energy that wiped away all of Armand's attackers and flung him to the ground. The entire cavern shook and the engines roared again. Armand knew nothing about rockets, but he suspected that meant Bellowforge was now trying to escape in earnest—and failing.

"I am impressed," the Seeker told him as he struggled to get back to his feet. "But you have only the power of a mortal frame. I channel the power of a *god*."

Armand only made it back onto his knees, but he attacked anyway. He needed her to stop holding the *Void Flyer*. He needed her to focus on *him*.

So, he hit her with everything he had. A single beam of pure power blazed out from his focus rings and hammered into her defenses. There was no complexity or art to what he was doing now—and there was no art to how to stop it.

It was power against power. There was no room for Armand to tell if the *Void Flyer* was moving. Every scrap of magic, every scrap of focus, every drop of energy in his body was focused on that one beam of unquestioned and untrammeled pure power.

He pushed her back. Step by step, his power drove her back as she tried to divide her attention.

Then she stopped. He had her *full* attention now, he could tell… because he was now losing the battle of will and power between them. She'd grabbed on to his channel of power and used it to pull herself up.

Her power was pushing against his and he was losing ground. Still trying to break her, he found himself sliding backward across the rough ground, his robe tearing on the rock.

"You die now," the Seeker hissed.

And then fifteen storm staves sounded as one, the rage of an angry god in the confined space, and *Star* careened sideways into the cavern, just barely missing the top of the *Void Flyer*'s dry dock as she *obliterated* the Void Seeker with a broadside meant to take down fortifications and battleships.

CHAPTER

52

Cat clung to *Star's* wheel like the lifeline it was. There were no defensive towers left outside, but the ninesail hadn't carried the day unscathed. Only the concentration of storm staves on a single gallery kept her in the fight—especially since the *port* gallery was just... gone.

There was a massive gash in *Star's* side where the ceiling and mountings of that weapons deck had been. A chunk of the port side of the main upper deck was missing too, and Cat had seen several of his var vanish in that blast of lightning.

But *Star* was still flying. Still fighting. Right now, she was fighting *him* as he tried to keep her hovering inside a dry-dock cavern that wasn't really big enough for both her and the fire-spewing void ship.

"Please tell me that was enough," he half-gasped as he finally stabilized the ship, the upper deck level to the floor of the cavern.

"You tell *me*," Windheart replied. "I can't feel her presence. But I'm guessing, since we're still *alive...*"

Cat hadn't expected it to work. They'd made the descent down the tunnel into the dry dock as quickly as they could after leveling the defenses, but he'd been able to feel the Void Seeker the whole way in.

She was gone now. She might have run—he wasn't going to put escaping that broadside past the high priestess of Her Dark Brother—but she wasn't in the cavern anymore.

The strange thundering fire of the void ship slowed before the vessel could leave the cavern, but she was precariously balanced on the drydock frame as Cat studied her.

"Permission to come aboard, Captain!" Brushfire shouted up from the ground. "Pinnace is wrecked."

"I'd love you all to come aboard," Cat shouted down. "But the air envelope is breached. You need to get Armand onto the void ship, so the rest of you may as well go with him."

"The *Void Flyer* moved off the stairs," his first officer warned him. "May take us a bit, and you only blasted *one* Brother."

"We'll watch your backs. Get on the damn void ship," Cat ordered.

The *Void Flyer*, apparently. He didn't know how his crew had learned the cylindrical vessel's name, but he was pleased to *have* a name for it.

"Paintrock, Windheart, get some hands with wands on the railings," he barked.

His blue, definitely-not-a-pirate Master of Staves was already emerging onto the main deck as he shouted, at least a dozen battlewands tied together in a bundle in his arms. Var gathered around, taking the weapons and moving to cover the cavern below.

"Move," he whispered, knowing no one could hear him. He didn't know *anything* about the ship they were about to entrust their lives to, but he needed her to *move*. He needed his archmage and his officers safely clear of this place.

"Incoming on the le—"

The *twang* of a crossbow firing interrupted the shouted warning, followed by the *crack* of battlewands.

"Ain't incoming anymore!" the watchvar concluded with a loud chuckle. "Archmage has conjured stairs; everyone is moving up."

Cat didn't need to be told when his people were aboard the *Flyer*. Whoever had their hand on the void ship's controls clearly got the notice before he did, because the engines flared to life once more, thunder echoing through the dry-dock cavern as *something* burned with immense force.

He'd been the commanding officer of an aether ship of the High Court Navy. He'd seen, he thought, every type of aether ship to exist. On a few memorable occasions, he'd even encountered the paddlewheels, fully enveloped ships with small aether sails attached to pivotable wheels designed by halvar and darvar mage-engineers.

The void ship was completely unlike anything he'd ever seen before. A gout of flame, smoke and thunder erupted from one end—into an open area that appeared to have been left clear for just this purpose, with barricades to keep people out of it.

Cat wasn't sure exactly how the whole thing worked—but it *worked*. The *Void Flyer* moved with surprising alacrity, gaining speed as she blazed across the dry dock and into the launch tunnel on a pillar of flame.

"Hold on to yourselves, people," he ordered. "We're going up after her, and with that much heat, air currents are going to be a problem!"

Half-wrecked or not, *Star* still responded to the touch of the wheel with an eager cheer that warmed his soul. Her enthusiasm didn't necessarily translate into swift movement or tight turns, but the ship was *trying*.

And she was doing enough. No more of His Dark Brothers emerged into the cavern before Cat guided his ship back into the tunnel in the wake of the rocket.

"Hold everyone on the deck for a bit longer," he told Windheart quietly. "But I need you and Axfall to start thinking about how to connect *Star* to that thing and transfer over expeditiously."

"Just me, Captain," the old gobvar told him. "Axfall is with Crane."

"Void," Cat cursed softly. "Is he going to be okay?"

"He's a tough old sailor and Crane is a good doctor, so I think so," Windheart said. "But you want boarding bridges, Captain? We'll make them happen."

"I know you will." Cat adjusted the wheel, avoiding a piece of debris falling from one of the wrecked defensive positions in the tunnel. "I owe you and your tribe a lot. You've all made this happen."

"Not everyone would give us credit for it," Windheart told him. "Amazing what respect gets from a crew, isn't it?"

Cat chuckled.

"I learned *that* lesson a long time ago—with elvar. Sailors are all the same, whether they've got pointy ears or pointy horns."

"My experience as well, sir. I should get on those bridges for you."

"And get the hands packing," Cat warned. "We're going to have to leave *Star* behind for this next stage."

Even Cat had to exhale a sigh of relief when *Star* finally broke clear of the Seventh Ward's tunnel. The dry dock had been big enough for the ninesail, but an aether ship didn't belong underground. She belonged in the sky, in the open aether, surrounded by nothingness for leagues in every direction.

His first step was to catch up with the *Void Flyer*. The strange tubes on the back of the void ship, the ones that had belched fire to push the vessel out of the Seventh Ward, were silent and cold now, but the ship was still drifting through the aether—in the rough direction of the void strait, even.

It made perfect sense that the exit tunnel for the *Flyer* had been aimed at the void strait. Cat wasn't entirely certain *why* His Dark Brothers would have wanted to visit the dead spheres beyond it, but they clearly had.

He worked his sextant for a few moments, confirming distances and speeds. The *Void Flyer* would pass the strait in about two clock-days if her course didn't change. She'd *miss* it by about fifty leagues, of course, but they already knew the ship *could* move under her own power.

Hopefully, she could continue to do so in the void. Even the paddle-wheels Cat had known in the past needed aether to move, but that was why they'd come for the *Flyer*. His Dark Brothers clearly had used her to enter the void spheres.

The question, Cat realized, was more how *long* the *Flyer* could travel through the void. Magic would allow the crew to breathe perpetually, but every way he knew to move a ship magically required aether.

"It'll be about an hour to come alongside," he turned to tell Windheart.

That was when he realized he was alone on the forecastle, and he sighed. With most of his officers already aboard the *Flyer*, Axfall injured and Paintrock looking to the ship's arms and security, only Windheart had been present before—and he'd sent the Master of Sails off to other tasks.

Standing on the forecastle, he could look back across the main deck to the aftercastle holding his own quarters. The sails were still flying, with riggers doing their best to compensate for missing sails on the other two decks.

The other thing he could see, though, was the slowly growing row of white shapes where Windheart's sailmakers were sewing the dead into body bags. Many of their dead had been vaporized or blown into the aether—and many of their wounded would live.

The emergency healing of an ordinary mage was a draining thing for both healer and healed, but the practiced magical surgery of a doctor like Crane was a more measured thing, one that would allow the third officer to save almost any var who made it to his table.

But there were already over a dozen bodies laid out on the deck, and Cat was all too aware of the dead they no longer had bodies for.

He turned back to the wheel, keeping an eye on the not-so-distant shape of the *Void Flyer*. He'd bring them alongside, and Windheart would provide him with bridges to move his people and their things onto the void ship.

No one else aboard could fly the ninesail—and Cat was going to make it one of his first orders of operation aboard the *Void Flyer* to learn how to fly the void ship!

CHAPTER 53

Once they were clear of the lodestone core of the Seventh Ward, the vertical orientation of the *Void Flyer* became immediately clear, turning floors into walls and vice versa.

The furniture aboard the *Flyer* was mostly pegged to the floor, Brushfire realized, to avoid exactly that problem. No one would live on the cable-high void ship while she was docked on her side—and in Bellowforge's hands, she suspected it would never be docked horizontally again.

She ducked her head through another door that had been built too small for gobvar—she could *tell* that the ship had been built for darvar, though at least the individual *floors* were high enough to let her walk—and finally entered the control room.

There'd been a *lot* of ladders to get there. The ship was *very* tall, compared to what she was used to. Nothing on the ship was much like she was used to, and the control room didn't break that pattern.

The exterior of the void ship might have been metal plates, but the interior had been lined with wood—a backing for the metal to keep it in place and reinforced against any troubles, she presumed.

In the control room, those wood panels were broken up by a lot more bare metal. Interwoven with metal and wood alike were at least *some* systems that Brushfire recognized—there was a set of control crystals linked to lift crystals, for example, and there was *a* control wheel.

The wheel was a third of the size of what she was used to, and surrounded by knobs and dials unlike anything she'd ever seen. The knobs were mostly pushed in at that moment, with many of the dials all the way over to the left.

"I didn't catch your name, lady mage," Alloy Bellowforge told her. The darvar was calmer now, standing in front of the wheel and running his gaze over the dials and knobs in a clearly practiced manner.

"I'm Brushfire Hammerhead, shaman of the Hammerheads, first officer of *Star* and in service to the Archmage Bluestaves," Brushfire reeled off, then paused with a chuckle. "I guess that's everything of importance, right?"

"Probably," Bellowforge agreed. "The archmage?"

"We found a kitchen on the way up, and I left him there with Smallwolf and my brother to make sure he eats," she told the darvar. "He's busily pretending he isn't dead on his feet and that he wasn't planning on sacrificing himself to get us out."

"I'm glad that wasn't necessary," Bellowforge said. "I'm...still nervous over how far I had the engines open while we weren't moving."

"That was her," Brushfire said softly. "She was holding us in place."

"And we burned far too much fuel trying to escape," the darvar warned. "I don't know how far the archmage wants to go once we're through the void strait, but we might not be *able* to make it."

"Alloy...none of us know how this ship works or what her limits are," Brushfire warned. "You're going to be explaining a lot over the next few clock-days while we get settled."

She was...mostly sure there was enough space on the void ship for all of *Star*'s crew. The plan had been to park the ninesail there in Brokenwright and transfer everyone over—but what she'd seen suggested that *Star* might not be in a state to *be* parked anywhere.

"Okay." The mage-engineer exhaled a sigh, then gestured around him. "Basic principle: everything that moves does so by pressing on something else. Make sense?"

"That's why our aether ship won't work in the void," she agreed. "There's nothing to push against."

"Exactly. So, in the void, we need to provide our own push," Bellowforge told her. "We do that with a rocket—we burn a fuel, in this case alcohol, and focus the smoke and fumes from that out the back of the ship.

"That pushes the *Void Flyer* forward in the direction we have her pointed. These throttles here"—he waved his hand at the knobs—"control how much fuel we're feeding into the combustion chamber."

"What about navigating?" Brushfire asked.

The darvar chuckled.

"Look up, Officer Brushfire."

She did and swallowed a start of surprise. From the outside, the top of the void ship had been the same metallic plating as every other part of the exterior. From the *inside*, however, it was transparent.

"I don't know or really *want* to know where His Dark Brothers sourced the twenty-yard-wide circular crystal I needed for that," Bellowforge admitted. "It's about four inches thick, twenty yards across, and I cut it into a perfect circle.

"There are runes on the side you can't see in silver and gold that create the illusion, pulling the light from outside the ship to give us a vision like we were standing on a forecastle."

He tapped a set of devices she hadn't noticed.

"These are basically sextants, let us measure and estimate everything. She's not designed to fight, though," he warned. "I know that your captain's ship is coming up behind us, but I can't see her. If it isn't in front of us, we have problems seeing it."

He shrugged.

"There are a few smaller observatories in the lower decks," he continued. "The Brothers insisted. The purpose of the ship, after all, was to take them into the void and let them commune with their god."

Bellowforge was silent for several seconds before Brushfire reached out and put her hand on his shoulder.

"You're free now," she told him.

"Thanks to you and your friends," he agreed. "I'm the archmage's var now, till the end. But if you're wondering why I don't seem bothered by the gobvar crew, well… I was a prisoner of His Dark Brothers for three dances, Officer Brushfire. My *daughters* were prisoners of His Dark Brothers for three dances.

"I don't care *what* you are. I care that you saved us."

By the time *Star* finally pulled alongside, Brushfire had made a survey of the ship. The *Void Flyer* might be two hundred yards from bottom to top, but only the top half of that was livable space. The bottom half had access ladders, allowing crew to descend into the "depths," but it was fuel tanks and rockets, systems that only Bellowforge understood.

They'd fix that, she was determined, but it would take time. For the moment, the important part was that there were thirty decks of ship, each a perfect twenty-yard circle, in which she was going to be putting her crew.

There were several decks with extra height and more crystal panes on the exterior, allowing people to observe what was going on outside the ship. One had already been made up as a set of luxurious quarters, probably either the Void Seeker's own space or that of whoever commanded the *Flyer*.

Brushfire had put Armand in those rooms and covered him in a blanket. He'd been too tired to even protest before passing out.

While part of every floor was taken up by ladders and machinery, there was more than enough space for the three hundred var from *Star* to live aboard in comfort. The supply situation aboard was better than she'd feared, if not as good as she'd hoped—but they'd bring over everything from *Star*.

By the time an impromptu bridge of wood and aethercloth connected the two ships, Brushfire had a solid plan of how to bring people aboard the *Void Flyer* and where to put them.

What surprised her most of all, though, was just how claustrophobic the whole ship felt. She'd spent much of her life living *on* the decks of aether ships, but she'd also spent a lot of time inside the wooden sailing ships, too. Their spaces were more cramped than the *Flyer*'s—but on an aether ship, she'd known that she just had to go up a few decks to see the great openness of the aether.

Inside the *Flyer*, there were no open spaces. She was a sealed environment, with arcana and artifice to provide her air. Once they were in the void, especially, there would be no access to the outside.

That left Brushfire standing on the flimsy-looking bridge, taking in the aether for a few last moments before crossing to *Star*.

Cat was waiting for Brushfire on the ninesail's deck, the Captain projecting his usual aura of calm competence and command. Unfortunately for him, she was learning to see through her captain—her *friend*—and his projections. She could see the fatigue in his eyes—and the grief as his gaze flicked back to the white-wrapped bodies on the deck.

"You came at just the right time," she told him. "Armand was going to get himself killed…and the Seeker would have kept us from escaping, anyway."

"Frankly, Brushfire, I didn't have it in me to sit in the aether above the Ward, waiting to see what had happened," he admitted. "I *had* to see what was going on. And now…we seem okay."

"We do," she confirmed. "Armand is passed out in what I think were the Void Seeker's rooms on the *Flyer*. What's the next step?"

"We move everything we can use from *Star* aboard the…*Flyer*?"

"The *Void Flyer*," she confirmed. "We found her designer and builder on the Ward. His Dark Brothers had kidnapped him and his family and were holding his wife and kids hostage. We put a stop to that—and he's sworn himself to Armand's service.

"They're coming with us, unless we've got a way to get them home?"

"*Star* isn't up for a long flight," Cat warned. "In fact, I think we're going to have to burn her once we've moved everything over to the *Flyer*. If I had to, I think I could get her back to a sphere with a dry dock…but we're better off moving over to the void ship and completing the mission."

"There's space," she promised. "Thirty decks, each of them twenty yards across. The orientation and structure will take some getting used to, but she's got the space for all of us and all of our stuff."

"Good. Windheart and Paintrock are organizing packing for transfer," Cat told her. "We…"

He sighed and blinked away tears even she wasn't supposed to see.

"We lost too many people," he admitted. "Axfall is in surgery. Seventeen dead, another eleven missing."

"Who?" Brushfire murmured.

"Of your tribe? Springlove, Petal, Loyal, Sanctity, Honor, Blade and Battlestrong," Cat reeled off instantly. "I'm sorry."

She winced at Petal's name. The young gobvar woman had taken to the rigging like she'd been born to it, but she'd been a cook first—and she'd been Fistfall's on-again, off-again partner. Brushfire had been less convinced of their long-term chances than some of her other tribesvar, but she'd agreed with the assessment that Petal would be good for her younger brother.

"We knew there was a risk," she admitted. "We chose this ship, this mission, knowing that following the archmage could lead us into danger."

"It did," Cat said. "We did a good thing, burning out a nest of His Dark Brothers, but the cost was too high."

"It's only the beginning, though, right?" she asked.

"Yeah. We have the ship Armand wanted, and I'll learn to fly her. But this is only the beginning."

From *Star*'s deck they both turned to look at the void strait, a black-and-purple bruise in the aether that drew everything toward it.

"That's the next step," Cat said grimly.

CHAPTER 54

Armand had slept for most of a clock-day by the time he awoke. The *Void Flyer* he woke up in felt like an almost completely different ship from the one he'd gone to sleep aboard—though he admitted, at least to himself, that he'd barely registered the vessel at all before Brushfire had put him gently but firmly to bed.

Curtains had been drawn around the bed he'd slept in, and he pulled them back to discover that the vast majority, if not all, of his things had been moved over from *Star* while he slept. His clock was present—allowing him to confirm how long he'd slept—and even his cooler units appeared to have been tucked into one corner of the rooms Brushfire had selected for him.

Those rooms filled nearly the entirety of one of the *Flyer*'s decks, with a pillar on one side containing ladders up and down the only piece of the deck that wasn't explicitly part of the suite. One side of the space was walled with var-high crystal panes, artifices of divination magic that allowed him to look outside.

While those panes made it hard to tell, the suite was about the same size as his envelope aboard *Star*, which explained how they'd fit most of his stuff into it.

What he *wasn't* sure of was which way he should go to locate his officers. On the other hand, with his things present, he was able to quickly dress and reach out with his senses. Even if he couldn't sense the two focuses he'd built for them, he could sense both Cat's and Brushfire's power at some distance.

Both were up from his suite. At the very tip of the ship, he judged.

It took him most of the time he spent dressing to identify what the thrumming vibration running around him was: the rocket tubes at the bottom of the ship were firing. Armand was, at least, familiar with the concept of action and reaction, and could guess how the ship functioned.

He'd never seen the principle used to propel a vessel, but it made sense in theory. The *engineering* would have been far beyond him, but it hadn't been beyond Bellowforge.

Armand suspected the befuddled and stressed darvar they'd met and rescued might be that rarest of all mages: a true genius. Not an archmage, not a doctor—and the type was often a terrible student, in Armand's experience—but a possessor of the rare ability to put together base concepts and synthesize something entirely new from the knowledge others gave them.

If his officers were at the top of the ship, then Armand guessed that the controls were at the top of the ship.

There was no way, after all, that Cat Greentrees would let the ship be actively maneuvering without being able to watch over Bellowforge's shoulder at least!

Fistfall was waiting for Armand in the ladderway, the big gobvar leaning against the wall and clearly favoring one side.

"Eldest sister asked me to see you to the control room once you were awake," he said simply.

"How's your chest?" Armand asked.

"Pretty sure I saw bone after getting hit," Fistfall grunted. "Smallwolf patched me back up, but it took a lot from her."

"That's why we have mage-doctors, my young friend," Armand told him. "The rest of us *can* heal, but it takes quite a lot of energy." He considered the big gobvar and then smiled gently. "And it *hurts*, if she didn't mention that part. We take away more pain than we take on, but we do feel some of it.

"You impressed that one if she healed you that much."

The blast had been meant for Smallwolf, she'd said, but Armand doubted that she'd been properly trained in *any* kind of healing. That meant she'd healed Fistfall on instinct—and *that* took powerful emotion as well as magic.

That part, though, he'd leave for Fistfall and Smallwolf to sort out on their own.

"Lead on," he instructed. "I want to see just what we've been getting up to while I slept."

It was a long climb. His Dark Brothers might have had teleporters in their own complex, but building them into the *Void Flyer* had clearly been too difficult. Instead, Armand found himself climbing almost sixty yards of mixed ladders and extremely steep stairs.

The *Flyer* was only slightly larger than *Star* overall, but she was arranged *completely* differently. The climb left Armand panting from the exertion by the time they reached the top—and from the way Fistfall was hovering beneath him, the big gobvar hadn't been entirely sure he wasn't going to fall off at some point!

But despite his conscientious companion's concern, Armand made it to the top of the ship without incident and entered the control room.

The control space took up the entire top level of the ship and had more than enough space for everyone in it. It still managed to feel a bit crowded, mostly because it was reasonably obvious that the ship had been designed to be flown by maybe four people.

All five of *Star*'s old officers were in the room, along with her three shipmasters. All eight of them were gathered in a rough semicircle behind Alloy Bellowforge, watching the darvar work.

"Look up," Fistfall said from behind Armand.

The archmage obeyed and inhaled a sharp breath as he took in the ceiling. The crystal panes in his suite had prepared him for the concept, but a set of two-yard-by-one-yard panels was a far cry from a twenty-yard-diameter perfect circle.

The void strait in the center of the crystal diviner didn't hurt, either. Its purple haze seemed to reach out for the *Void Flyer* like it was hungry.

"Archmage," Cat Greentrees greeted him before Armand had recovered. "Welcome."

"Captain." Armand nodded to the elvar and took in the rest. "I see we have everyone here."

Most of them looked at least a bit the worse for wear, but every officer and Master from *Star* had survived. Bellowforge was the only person who looked *better* than the last time Armand had seen him—rescue and freedom suited the darvar well.

"Bellowforge is giving everyone lessons on piloting the *Void Flyer*," Cat told him. "But I wanted him on the controls for the passage."

"It's that time already?" Armand asked.

"We're coming up on the strait fast," Bellowforge confirmed. "I'm cutting the rockets. We'll want to just slide through, nice and easy."

"A journey no other ship could make," Cat observed. "That's why we're here, right?"

"Exactly," Armand said. "Thank you, Master Bellowforge. Your assistance is greatly appreciated."

"You saved me and my family," the darvar replied. "Piloting this ship is the least I can do."

"And you'll be even more use once you have a focus, but that will take me some time," Armand told him. "For now…any concerns about the trip?"

"Plenty," Bellowforge told him. "But none that can be fixed. We only have so much fuel, so if we don't find a source of some kind along our terrifying route, we'll need to take it slow.

"But we won't gain time by going anywhere for more fuel, so…" The darvar shrugged, checking the sextant next to him for the angle.

"Approach is clean," he announced. "We'll enter the strait in about five minutes."

"What about *Star*?" Armand asked Cat.

"We set fuses and some fire charges," the captain said sadly. "She'll burn, a fitting pyre for the crew we lost. I put her on a course for the ember at Brokenwright's heart, too. If any of her survives the fires we've set, Brokenwright's fire will consume it.

"Her pyre, as well as the crew's."

"That wasn't the fate I hoped for her," Armand admitted.

"We always knew we'd leave her behind here," Cat replied. "The *Void Flyer* is our ship for the rest of this journey, Armand. She's the only ship that can take us into the void."

The archmage nodded, studying the purple horror in the rocket ship's path.

"Do you think there's any truth to the Void Seeker's claim that these spheres are hungry?" he murmured.

"I wouldn't trust any word out of her mouth," Brushfire said grimly. "But since we know nothing about what happened to these spheres to *make* them void spheres…I would suggest we assume they are unfriendly at best."

"'Unfriendly,'" Bellowforge echoed, the darvar rolling the word around his tongue. "*Something* destroyed all life and aether and air in the place we're going, Officer Brushfire.

"I'm not sure 'unfriendly' covers it."

"Neither am I," Armand confirmed. "It's just the only way to travel where we must go. Our answers lie beyond these spheres. That void strait is the only way into the territory of the Quadrumvirate that doesn't go through Her Crimson Sisters."

"What happens when we reach the other side?" Streamwater asked.

"I don't know," he told them. "All I know is that there are four spheres of only void between us and the Clan Spheres. I'll worry about the mission and the dragons.

"I need all of you to focus on getting us through the void to the other side."

VOID SPHERES
AETHER SPHERES BOOK 2

COMING TO KICKSTARTER
NOVEMBER 2023

JOIN THE MAILING LIST

Love Glynn Stewart's books? Join the mailing list at: GlynnStewart.com/mailing-list

Be the first to find out when new books are released!

ABOUT THE AUTHOR

Glynn Stewart is the author of Starship's Mage, a bestselling science fiction and fantasy series where faster-than-light travel is possible—but only because of magic. His other works include science fiction series Duchy of Terra, Castle Federation and Exile, as well as the urban fantasy series ONSET and Changeling Blood.

Writing managed to liberate Glynn from a bleak future as an accountant. With his personality and hope for a high-tech future intact, he lives in Southern Ontario with his partner, their cats, and an unstoppable writing habit.

VISIT GLYNNSTEWART.COM FOR
NEW RELEASE UPDATES

CREDITS

The following people were involved in making this book:
COPYEDITOR: Richard Shealy
PROOFREADER: M Parker Editing
COVER ART: Elias Stern
LAYOUT: Janine Milstrey
TYPO HUNTER TEAM
KICKSTARTER BACKERS
FAOLAN'S PEN PUBLISHING TEAM: Jack, Kate, and Robin.

facebook.com/glynnstewartauthor

OTHER BOOKS BY
GLYNN STEWART

For release announcements join the mailing list or visit
GlynnStewart.com

STARSHIP'S MAGE

Starship's Mage
Hand of Mars
Voice of Mars
Alien Arcana
Judgment of Mars
UnArcana Stars
Sword of Mars
Mountain of Mars
The Service of Mars
A Darker Magic
Mage-Commander
Beyond the Eyes of Mars
Nemesis of Mars

STARSHIP'S MAGE: RED FALCON

Interstellar Mage
Mage-Provocateur
Agents of Mars

Pulsar Race: A Starship's Mage Universe Novella

DUCHY OF TERRA

The Terran Privateer
Duchess of Terra
Terra and Imperium
Darkness Beyond
Shield of Terra
Imperium Defiant
Relics of Eternity
Shadows of the Fall
Eyes of Tomorrow

SCATTERED STARS

SCATTERED STARS: CONVICTION

Conviction
Deception
Equilibrium
Fortitude
Huntress
Prodigal *(upcoming)*

SCATTERED STARS: EVASION

Evasion
Discretion
Absolution *(upcoming)*

PEACEKEEPERS OF SOL

Raven's Peace
The Peacekeeper Initiative
Raven's Course
Drifter's Folly
Remnant Faction
Raven's Flag *(upcoming)*

EXILE

Exile
Refuge
Crusade
Ashen Stars: An Exile Novella

CASTLE FEDERATION

Space Carrier Avalon
Stellar Fox
Battle Group Avalon
Q-Ship Chameleon
Rimward Stars
Operation Medusa
A Question of Faith: A Castle Federation Novella

DAKOTAN CONFEDERACY

Admiral's Oath
To Stand Defiant
Unbroken Faith *(upcoming)*

VIGILANTE

(WITH TERRY MIXON)

Heart of Vengeance
Oath of Vengeance

BOUND BY STARS: A VIGILANTE SERIES
(WITH TERRY MIXON)

Bound By Law
Bound by Honor
Bound by Blood

TEER AND KARD
Wardtown
Blood Ward

CHANGELING BLOOD
Changeling's Fealty
Hunter's Oath
Noble's Honor
Fae, Flames & Fedoras: A Changeling Blood Novella

ONSET
ONSET: To Serve and Protect
ONSET: My Enemy's Enemy
ONSET: Blood of the Innocent
ONSET: Stay of Execution
Murder by Magic: An ONSET Novella

STANDALONE NOVELS & NOVELLAS
Children of Prophecy
City in the Sky
Excalibur Lost: A Space Opera Novella
Balefire: A Dark Fantasy Novella
Icebreaker: A Fantasy Naval Thriller

OUR
KICKSTARTER BACKERS

This book was originally released as a hardcover edition thanks to a successful Kickstarter campaign in June 2022. The following is a list of backers who helped make this project possible.

THANK YOU

Edward A ✺ Phil Adkins ✺ Jonathan Amundsen ✺ Raphael Artischewski ✺ Richard Böddeker ✺ Bahr Family ✺ Jeffrey Barnard ✺ Travis Bass ✺ Dave Baughman ✺ Ernest A. Blanchard ✺ Ed Block ✺ Peter Blom ✺ Chad Boyer ✺ David Bradford ✺ Will Brandon ✺ J.P. Brannan ✺ Robert Brown ✺ Max Brown-Bass ✺ Theresa Buch ✺ Nick Burrows ✺ Robert W. Callahan ✺ Sam Campbell ✺ John Casenelli ✺ Chaply ✺ Nicholas A. Charlebois ✺ Jacob Chartrai ✺ Kory Christensen ✺ Nicole Chupka ✺ Valentin Churavy ✺ Nathan Ciaio ✺ Derek Cofer ✺ Brendan Coffey ✺ Caitlin Colbert ✺ Deborah Corte ✺ Corvus_Null ✺ Cameron Craig ✺ Patrick Cussen ✺ Matt D. ✺ Jasmine Davis ✺ Marvin de Bruin ✺ Maxime de Hennin de Boussu-Walcourt ✺ Joshua DeVore ✺ Ivo Dominguez Jr ✺ Josh Donner ✺ Ganesha Duggirala ✺ Scott E. ✺ Klara Edelgard ✺ Matt Edgmon ✺ John P. Edmundson ✺ Gareth Luke Edwards ✺ Larry Edwards ✺ Joe Erickson ✺ Doug Erling ✺ Joshua Ertische ✺ Michael Esparza ✺ Read Fenton ✺ Randall Fickel ✺ Sam Fischbeck ✺ James D. Forrester ✺ Nicholas Kristopher Forrester ✺ Cindy Fortenberry ✺ Niaka G. ✺ Jim Gagliardi ✺ Martin Gayle ✺ Matthew Gerboth ✺ Charles Gillanders ✺ John Gilligan ✺ Glitch Fire ✺ Peter Gold ✺ Jerry Goodnough ✺ Donald Griffith ✺ Drew Griffiths ✺ R. Randall Hall ✺ S. Wayne Hamilton ✺ Mason Harris ✺ Samuel C. Hearld ✺ Cy Henningsen ✺ Jannik Herbst ✺ Josh Hernandez ✺ Rob Hodgkinson ✺ Austin Hoffey ✺

The Hollands ✶ Dan Hollis ✶ David Holzborn ✶ Patrick Hunter ✶ Jeff Huse ✶ Ferdinand Ibel ✶ James Mackenzie Jackson ✶ Aaron S. Jacobs ✶ Ryan Scott James ✶ Andrew Jefftee ✶ Amanda Jennex ✶ Jeffrey M. Johnson ✶ Nicholas Johnson ✶ Jacob H Joseph ✶ David W. Jurgens ✶ Juliet Kavanagh ✶ Kerry aka Trouble ✶ John Koblosky ✶ Dylan Korn ✶ Kyle Krone ✶ Mark Kurta ✶ Cooper Lacasse ✶ Thomas Lambert ✶ Samantha Landström ✶ Rob Lazenby ✶ Patrick Dalziel Lewis ✶ Lex O' ✶ Skye Lowell ✶ Clara Luca ✶ Karen M ✶ Adam Marinovich ✶ Marci M. Matthews ✶ Marshall McGowan ✶ Susan Margaret McKilligan ✶ Chris Meyer & Gary Holm ✶ Howy Modell ✶ Juan Cintron Mojica ✶ Sebastian W.H. Moon ✶ Derek Morgan ✶ Richard Morgan-Ash ✶ Mo Moser ✶ Randy Murphey ✶ Thomas M. Murtola ✶ Joan E. Myers ✶ Kelvin Neely ✶ Adam Nemo ✶ Andrew Nichols ✶ Ben Nichols ✶ Gregory Parsons ✶ Patr ✶ Matthew J. Peloso ✶ Duane Perkins ✶ Arne B. Petersen ✶ Gabby Magat Pettera ✶ Phyxius ✶ Jordan Placer ✶ Jon Poloff ✶ PPreiss ✶ Paul Raulerson ✶ Zachary J.V. Rhodes ✶ Timothy Ripperda ✶ Trevor Rivet ✶ Matthea W. Ross ✶ Dominik Rudolph ✶ Julie Seau ✶ David Seidl ✶ J & G Sessions ✶ Shado ✶ Phil Shepherd ✶ Bruce R Sheppard ✶ Scott W. Shippee ✶ Shultzman ✶ Kip Slayback ✶ Martyn Smedley ✶ A.C. Smingleigh ✶ Dave Smith ✶ Joshua Smith ✶ Michael Smith ✶ Paul Smith ✶ Scott Smith ✶ sonicthe ✶ Anni Sørensen ✶ Ingrid Spera ✶ Frank Springall ✶ SR ✶ Rob Steinberger ✶ Sam Stoliker ✶ Paul Stone ✶ Sara Stonehouse ✶ Devon Stork ✶ Jenni D. Strand ✶ James L. Suhr ✶ Michael Sukovich ✶ Melody Tharen ✶ Nic Thompson ✶ Jeramie Vens ✶ Vespry Family ✶ Eric Vilbert ✶ C. Joshua Villines ✶ Esper Wadih ✶ Phillip Walker ✶ Alishia Wallace ✶ Kimi Wallace ✶ Ray Wang ✶ Daniel Ware ✶ Grant Weaver ✶ Jonathan C. Weaver ✶ Susan Weber ✶ Robyn K. Weimer ✶ Liam West ✶ Joe White ✶ Kyle G Wilkinson ✶ C. Wilson ✶ Wilson ✶ Sarah Woodson ✶ Paul Zagieboylo

Made in United States
Orlando, FL
10 June 2023

33982326R10224